Praise for Beverly Coyle and *In Troubled Waters*

"[A] complex and fascinating novel . . . [Coyle] tries something very daring, and succeeds, in fictional terms, beyond the reader's wildest dreams." —Carolyn See, *Los Angeles Times Book Review*

"Coyle's economical prose can deliver an astringent phrase, an eloquent image, and a witty quip all in one sentence. Her telescopic eye and feeling heart mark her as a novelist of mature talent." —*Publishers Weekly*

"[A] compelling and seamless story of contemporary Florida . . . *In Troubled Waters* is [an] ambitious book . . . Coyle plays to her strengths, relying on her considerable talents at creating true characters and putting real words in their mouths to address the bigger themes of fear and love."
—Craig Dezern, *The Orlando Sentinel*

"Arresting—and heartbreaking . . . [Coyle] reveals her skill in catching the sudden, inexplicable stabs of passion in the troubled voyages of solitary lives."
—*Kirkus Reviews*

"Coyle's depth, artfulness, and wisdom range so wide that finally it is in the sheer multiplicity of its virtues that this novel's magic lies." —Andy Solomon, *St. Petersburg Times*

"A tender and intriguing [novel], Coyle's orchestration of this multitiered drama is tight yet subtle, while her articulation of the disgraceful legacy of racism, the tragedy of Alzheimer's, and the shadow of impending death is both compassionate and frank."
—*Booklist*

PENGUIN BOOKS

IN TROUBLED WATERS

Beverly Jones Coyle was born in Miami and is the great-great-granddaughter of central Florida farmers. Her first book of fiction was *The Kneeling Bus* (Penguin). She is the author of two books on Wallace Stevens, including *Secretaries of the Moon*, of which she was the co-editor. Currently a professor of English on the Mary Augusta Scott chair at Vassar College, she lives with her husband in New York City.

IN
TROUBLED
WATERS

BEVERLY
COYLE

PENGUIN BOOKS

PENGUIN BOOKS
Published by the Penguin Group
Penguin Books USA Inc., 375 Hudson Street, New York, New York 10014, U.S.A.
Penguin Books Ltd, 27 Wrights Lane, London W8 5TZ, England
Penguin Books Australia Ltd, Ringwood, Victoria, Australia
Penguin Books Canada Ltd, 10 Alcorn Avenue, Toronto, Ontario, Canada M4V 3B2
Penguin Books (N.Z.) Ltd, 182–190 Wairau Road, Auckland 10, New Zealand

Penguin Books Ltd, Registered Offices: Harmondsworth, Middlesex, England

First published in the United States of America by Ticknor & Fields,
A Houghton Mifflin Company, 1993
Reprinted by arrangement with Ticknor & Fields
Published in Penguin Books 1994

The author gratefully acknowledges permission to quote from the lyrics of "Tears
on my Pillow." Copyright © 1958 by Gladys Music, Inc., and Vanderbilt Music Corp.
Copyright renewed and assigned to Gladys Music and Sovereign Music. International
copyright secured. All rights reserved. Lyric reprinted by permission
of Gladys Music and Sovereign Music.

PUBLISHER'S NOTE
This is a work of fiction. Names, characters, places, and incidents either are the
product of the author's imagination or are used fictitiously, and any resemblance
to actual persons, living or dead, events, or locales is entirely coincidental.

THE LIBRARY OF CONGRESS HAS CATALOGUED THE HARDCOVER AS FOLLOWS:
Coyle, Beverly.
In troubled waters/Beverly Coyle.
p. cm.
ISBN 0-395-57437-4 (hc.)
ISBN 0 14 02.3301 6 (pbk.)
1. Race relations—Southern States—. I. Title.
PS3553.0945I5 1993
813′54—dc20 92–44152

Printed in the United States of America
Set in Bembo

for
Dorothy Lee Jones

ACKNOWLEDGMENTS

I want to thank Karin Cook, Jane von Mehren, Ralph Sassone, Brett Singer, and my sisters Nancy Ford and Laurie Jones for all their help. A very special thanks to Ann Imbrie, whose careful readings were such gifts; and to Archie Gresham, who allowed this book to enter into his life in a way that touched me deeply. Many thanks are due my editor, John Herman, for reviewing crude structures with a sense of possibility. Thanks to Henry for continuing to provide music and joy around the house.

IN
TROUBLED
WATERS

I

TOM GLOVER was amused at the fact of young boys taking up fishing in front of his house. Then he became something closer to annoyed. He knew boys. When they got bored with the slow biting down there in the lake, they were likely to keep coming out of habit and then bound to look around for what they ought to do *next*. Let one of those kids walk fifty feet in this direction and his snub nose would be pressed against Glover's windows. The old man slept with his face to the wall in a big frame house where he was born, where a huge new refrigerator vibrated against his bed at night. He wouldn't hear the breaking and entering.

Nor would his daughter and son-in-law. They'd moved in with Glover last year to oversee the remodeling and then to stay for good. They were older than he was in many ways — two innocents asleep upstairs, and himself a dried-up deaf old codger with his back turned. None of them would know a thing until morning.

The boys had somehow discovered the deep spot that Glover had dredged out himself over fifty years before. It was the only smart place to fish. But he was an old man nevertheless, with young boys being so close and full of the devil. They wore clothes that lit up at twilight — bright Gap clothes whose colors were too bold, too recent, for the old man's weak heart. He was ninety-one. He owned bank stock worth several million dollars. At first he came out on his front porch every evening to keep an eye out and think how to buy himself some protection until gradually the summer afternoons lengthened enough for him to observe with a little astonishment that one of those boys was black.

Who would have thought the sight of one black kid might ease the conscience of a man living as much in the past as he was? A hundred years ago they all used to swim down there together, blacks and whites, too easy in their bones for people to believe nowadays. They had grown up and gone to work picking stump out of every other burned off field in this Florida county. Seminole County. He used to swim down there by the hour with a boy named Lucky Apple who would stand at the edge of the water with a quarter in his mouth trying to make it look like a silver tooth. This was Point Breeze, Florida. In Glover's day she sat a long way east of Orlando — a whole morning rocked to sleep beside Lucky in a wagon. Now politicians and conservationists called everything Central Florida. Everything had exploded into tract housing. Rangers coaxed the two remaining panthers down into the Everglades last year. They were said to survive down there in high-frequency collars. Point Breeze was a bedroom now, a bedroom for another kind of business boom: land too valuable to farm unless one belonged, heart and soul, to Minute Maid.

That would be some college professor's T-shirted boy down there fishing. These days Florida had a university for every turn in the road. Imported black professors got traded around at high prices, just like ball players.

But they were good news for Lucky in his grave. They gave ballast to the original colored families whose young men didn't want to pick fruit anymore, whose young women got jobs at Disney making change. Very few of them escaped to something better unless they beat a little education out of the system and beat it harder than a rug on a clothesline. A whole lot of them still

went up in a little burst of fireworks, as Lucky had done —
Lucky Apple who had died of his burns right here in this house.

The new boy could pass for Lucky in size and shade. He held
his head a little to the side, a little arrogantly perhaps since his
parents didn't hail from around here. Once, through his binoculars, Glover thought he could see the intelligence in the boy's
face — some northern kid who was easy to pick out after that
with the naked eye. He was always the one in the brightest colors
as he pedaled hard in the lead or in the rear or dead in the center
of that moving flow of bikes. The hard footwork was a speed
race to Glover's side of the lake, all of it sending up a strange
rhythm of bobbing shirts. The boys tended to speed up at the
point they needed to stop. They liked to stand up in the stirrups
and rear up on hind legs just before they made a great show of
skidding the whole length of Glover's frank gaze. Then there
was the loud assembling of their gear and shrieking aloud and
calling back any dogs who'd crossed the narrow ribbon of road
and entered the old man's yard. All this they did for Glover's
benefit, pretending to be more interested in getting their bikes to
stand up in the loose soil than in noting whether he noted them.
He felt free to stare or even lift the binoculars openly. White,
chalky boys, for the most part, with no more or less muscle than
the one black kid, all of them twelve or thirteen years old, he
guessed. Every afternoon the boys seemed to think the world
was quite hilarious, especially with old man Glover in it.

By fall he was coming out on his porch to keep an eye on his
son-in-law, who couldn't be precisely diagnosed. Nor could he
be left alone anymore in the late afternoons when he insisted on
watering the front lawn. According to the literature, Paul Barnes
was due at any time to start wandering off the property. If the
literature was to be believed, Paul was in the middle of the middle stage, and he wouldn't remain there for very long. It hardly
mattered that he had been a college-educated schoolteacher
who'd moved Glover's daughter, Lois, from one high school to
another until their retirement, too liberal for the school boards'

comfort. He had taught history of some kind, although Glover
never bothered in forty-five years to find out what kind. All that
mattered now was that the poor man not end up shoplifting duct
tape in a K mart somewhere. Glover one day told his daughter
they could kill two birds if they kept an eye on Paul and those
Gap Kids at the same time.

Lois Barnes, smiling and grateful to him, had said, "*Who?*"

"Those *boys!* You haven't noticed those boys?"

She made a point of noticing them the next afternoon and said
maybe she ought to go down there with some banana bread.

In the short time they'd lived together, Glover had been trying
not to get in the habit of saying things like "Don't be ridiculous."
Lois was sweet and didn't deserve it from him. She had a smart
daughter over in Daytona who said those things to her on a
regular basis. Glover sometimes flattered himself that he'd spared
her more than a bossy daughter by getting her back to Point
Breeze, where she was born, where her own father could help
out with Paul. Tom Glover concentrated hard on not bossing
Lois around. The discipline was good for his mind.

And babysitting Paul every afternoon allowed for a certain
amount of purpose and responsibility for a man ninety-one.
Lois's arrival had provided him regular meals and meaningful
work. Paul had a disease that made the old man philosophical; he
killed an awful lot of time in his porch rocker musing on how
Paul's mind worked. His son-in-law hadn't been under his roof
for many months before he would look up and admire the sight
of those boys in their colorful clothes. Between one afternoon
and the next, Paul apparently lost touch with the boys just
enough to feel pleasantly alarmed at each new gathering. He
would express a small exclamation of awareness ("They're
back!"), and Glover began to understand. Amazement was the
strongest emotion in this disease. Perhaps the only one. A person
watching could understand and almost envy it. Such pure moments, such renewable joy in a small commotion of bicycles
every day in front of the house. In the returning flash of agony

and insight, the victim also seemed to understand that he had nothing but surprise to look forward to.

Toward fall the afternoon light kept failing again, and that tended to turn those terrible shirts back on. The whole gang became a bright and then a brighter set of luminous forms. One day Glover himself received something of a surprise, after which he slumped in his rocker and forced a nitroglycerin pill under his tongue. Paul accidentally frightened him out of a little dream about Lucky Apple. From deep sleep the old man heard someone shouting that *they were back* and opened his eyes at the wrong moment. He thought he saw the Klan loping toward him from a distance, those boys' shirts looking for all the world like torches bobbing up and down, for all the world like the soaked and flaming rags of the Point Breeze bunch. There was a time when Tom Glover had known all those boys. His father, Virgil Glover, had been a big enough man in Point Breeze for those boys to warn him whenever they were going to set up over there on the other side of the lake. They had held an open-air meeting for the three nights it had taken Lucky to let go. It was not a personal thing. Those boys had sent a few men over to the house to let Virgil Glover know it was not a personal thing.

THIS AFTERNOON it was too early for boys, but he had posted himself in plenty of time, as old men tend to do. At his great age there was no being late, there was only missing the whole she-bang.

Paul stood at the spot in the yard where he most enjoyed pointing the hose and running up sky-high water bills in these long, disorienting months. Sometimes Glover tried to think what other task the man might be put to. All sorts of disaster lurked in otherwise simple-seeming jobs. Weeding, for example, would tend to take a victim from one thing to another — to the far corners of the huge lots on Glover's property and then out of sight. Since sitting here with one eye open was the old man's last assignment on earth, he didn't want to botch it.

Fifty years ago he'd had his first and last emotion for Paul. At the time he was not counting on a schoolteacher to floor him by marrying his only daughter, his only child. Being floored was not a thing that usually happened to him, and he'd railed at his wife that he hadn't sent Lois off to college to meet a schoolteacher. He'd assumed his wife knew that without his having to spell it out.

How Jemmalee had cried over his unhappiness. Jemmalee was a midwestern girl who believed in schoolteachers of any kind. When Paul Barnes, handsome and unsure of himself, had climbed on this porch to be introduced, not even Glover had known he was going to rise out of his chair and tell the man that he'd like to have him shot.

"Sir?" The young teacher laughed, a good-natured boy; he had looked behind him for some other person being addressed. He turned back smiling and holding out a hand, which ended up touching his hair, the awkward gesture that made not only Jemmalee but several middle-aged ladies in Point Breeze fall in love with him, an auto mechanic's son from Ocala. The auto mechanic himself was said to do some preaching as a sideline, and in his wife, Jemmalee's, opinion this might be where Paul got some of his quiet charm. He was a Gainesville student at the time, thin as a reed, and all the wives wanting to fatten him up. When Glover told Jemmalee privately how the man had invited himself into fine homes in order that he might survey the virgins, his wife had looked at him as if she hardly knew him. "Survey the *what*?"

And she'd never understood Glover's panic, never understood how a student on one's porch was exasperating, even frightening. Jemmalee had demanded to know why. He'd not been able to explain. Somehow in Paul's unlined and youthful face he'd seen his daughter's whole uninteresting life flash in front of him.

He must have had in mind some girl in an earlier century, a girl waving permanent good-byes from the back of a mule train; her letters arriving by pony; her photographs showing off some sod house in Nebraska. It was absurd what he had had in mind. Paul had taught out his entire career never leaving Florida, and he had done it with the full advantage of telephones, automobiles, superhighways, vacations, and practical clothes. And whatever else Paul and Lois might have seemed during the next fifty years, they'd never seemed poor. Paul bought solid used cars from his own father; he had a benefit plan, a retirement plan; good families rolled out the red carpet whenever he and Lois and the daughter took trips up north. All over New England affluent people, gone back home for the summer, seemed happy to put up the family. Paul had a three-month vacation every time Glover turned around. What had he been thinking? Well, he'd been thinking of hard times, naturally. Of his father's day, when all the teachers were old maids, when all the preacher boys sold hair tonic to get by, and, much later, burial policies.

Glover turned his head and caught a glimpse of the older Lois pushing open the screen door a crack to check on things. Some time in their eighteen months together, they'd gotten this pecking order straight — Glover watched Paul and Lois watched *him*. He used to eyeball certain sick cows the way she did him — the one or two he'd find deep inside the cabbage hammocks, seeming to lean against scrub pine and low palmetto clumps to elude detection.

"*Dad?*" His daughter couldn't help shouting. She had no talent around hearing aids. "What can I *get* you at *Publix*?" He could see the little cords bulge out on her neck, poor girl, as she strained to be clear. "I'm going *out* now to pick up *candy* for tomorrow *night!*"

He smiled and shook his head to let her know he couldn't hear a damn thing. She rested. She tried brevity. "The *candy*, Dad!"

Tomorrow night was Halloween, which they both knew all too well from a recent blowup they'd had about it. Lois's volume caused Paul to look up from his spot. The sight of someone new on the porch made him appear utterly glad, relieved to see her, confused at the idea of her seeming to go in and out of view all day. Lois smiled and waved at the man to reassure him.

"I'll be *glad* to pick up anything else you *need!*" Lois smiled. "Dad? Did you *hear* me?"

"You can look in the doodads aisle and get me about a dozen dish towels," Glover said, surprising her. "Terry cloth. And I want them striped like this one." He took his right cane and lifted up a yellow-and-brown-striped dish towel that he'd spread out over the railing to dry. His railing was a hundred and ten years old, and there was over thirty feet of it. From way up here, the whole of Mirror Lake was quite a view. The narrow road was only a mile around, shaded almost the whole mile in ancient live oak and Spanish moss, in dense palmetto and cypress, all the close green water foliage to put a collar around the whole thing. If he could just die right here in this chair, he wouldn't ask to be admitted into heaven.

"Striped terry cloth dish towels." Lois wrote it down.

"Make it a dozen."

"All right." An effort to look through bifocals put a jaunty thrust in Lois's small chin. She was a chin-up sort of girl, and Glover often thought how she was not so much a disappointment as she was a daughter. He'd been too much the pure tyrant to find out if she'd ever been any more interesting at an earlier age.

She was getting up there now, but still blessed with a trim figure and hair as unchanging as that of her mother, Jemmalee, who had died without much more gray than Lois had now. So while it seemed possible that the girl was sixty-nine, it was difficult to believe. His own life seemed so long and hers so short. Now she'd brought herself and Paul home and seemed to have little memory of how hard Glover had been on her. He never asked if she remembered his tyrannical parenting. He observed only that she approached her husband's dilemma with a stiff upper lip most days of the week, and he admired the way she looked right now, standing with her Publix grocery list, her car keys in hand, a capable woman not yet starting to feel her age. He told her to sit down and take a load off. He knew that each time she needed to run errands she was reluctant to leave him the burden of Paul.

"Sit down!" he said.

"It's lovely out there, isn't it?" she said. Then she shouted something else he couldn't make out.

"What!" Glover said. He cupped an ear. But one side of him was as dead as the other.

"I said I want to *thank* you, Dad!"

"*Thank* me?"

She stood looking out for a moment or two. There were tears in the girl's eyes. "For *watching* us like you do! *Thank* you!"

"You bet," Glover said, waving her off. He didn't like her sentiments; they tended to choke him up. Paul must have done all right. There was that old saying. Better to be lucky than rich. The daughter, Carol, had sailed through college and graduate schools on scholarships, and, as other sixties families started needing air conditioning and Caribbean cruises, Lois and Paul had always seemed so sensible in Glover's way of thinking, a throwback to himself. Their counterparts spent all their money; the whole country was ruined once credit cards came into use, and the bankers converted everyone over to deficit spending and living beyond his means. Up north, where it all started, every one of those bankers was a smart Jew.

But Lois and Paul never went in the direction of having to have; they were modest people. The most excessive thing Paul ever did, as far as Glover remembered, was to come out here on the porch whenever they visited and read novels.

Lois said she'd better go and get back, if he was sure he didn't mind watching Paul. But she didn't use those words. Paul would hear and look up at the sound of his own name. She was shouting again, trying to tell Glover something in her secret code. He let her shout. He pretended that he got the words.

This chair might even be the very one Paul had used. When they'd come here on visits, he used to like to sit here reading or else stand in the kitchen with Jemmalee and listen to her stories as he helped her set the table. As a young bride from Iowa, Jemmalee had been close to Glover's mother, Alma, and to his father, Virgil Glover, before they both died quickly in the same year, along with Lucky. Jemmalee had her own version of all the deaths, one upon the other that year in 1920, before Lois was born and Jemmalee believed her marriage had ended. It wasn't true, but she said it once to Glover and then waited for years to let Paul become her confessor. Paul Barnes's big fault had been never seeming to want to know Glover's side in these matters, although the latter had done a great deal to put the man at arm's length from that bad beginning on the porch. He regretted it now more than ever. Over the years, whenever Paul accompanied Lois for their visits, he would spend the women's naptime pushing his infant daughter around the lake or rowing her to the dead center in a boat. In the long quiet evenings, he was always grabbing and hugging someone, or smiling at Lois's profile when she was unaware of him, the both of them agreeing with Jemmalee over something amusing that the baby, Carol, had said. It had made Glover jealous. He knew that. Had they all sat watching TV at night, he'd have felt less excluded; alone with Jemmalee there was the wonderful silence of a blue television set between them. But when the kids were home he could sometimes walk into a room and feel unappreciated and quite beyond their self-styled amusements. He'd felt it strongest in the year he was appointed to the bank board in Point Breeze. He had won that place by raising cattle on pastureland made from scratch. Every inch of ground had a drop of his sweat and a drop of his mathematics. He knew money; he knew borrowing and lending; it was obvious to bank boys that a man like Glover could sit on the far side of a table deciding the worth of a man at the other end. A man with his hat on his knee. That kind of thing made the real, real world go around. He'd arrived home in his three-piece suit, and there might sit his visiting son-in-law with his feet up on the railing, deeply engaged in a book big enough to crush a vital organ and giving him only the vaguest of smiles or waves as Glover pulled his Buick to the back of the house.

"I *guess* I'll *go* now!" Lois was saying. She patted his arm. They were both still behaving a little cautiously toward each other due to their recent argument.

"Don't worry about us," Glover said, looking up at Lois. "You go on and run your errands." Glover said softly, "He's not going anywhere with me right here."

"I know, Dad. What would we do without you?"

"You go on. You have to get things done if you're leaving early in the morning. Did you call Carol? Did she bake you a cake?"

Carol couldn't cook. Carol's son, Petey, age nine, was a better cook. For this fact and a further one, involving Carol's having managed to get Petey without so much as a husband, Glover never knew what to think. The boy had come from a sperm bank; he'd been ordered out of a catalogue! Glover's only grand-daughter, yet another teacher gone up to the college notch, per-petually resided in the old man's mind as something between a heroine and a crackpot. She never finished her advanced degree and was always about to lose her job as an adjunct. Carol, at almost fifty now, was famous for either *never* doing something, or else managing to do it only within an inch of her life. That boy, for example.

The old man felt Lois leaning down now to kiss him on the cheek, which he allowed by lifting his face, tears filling his eyes for no reason. Perhaps it was merely her goodness all these years. He hadn't deserved to have her so available for *him* at the last minute. Once in a while he could choke up just looking out a window in a sudden thought of Jemmalee or of his parents, Alma and Virgil, or of Lucky and himself; and even of Lois and Paul, of Carol and Petey, the brevity sweeping over them all so in-stantly, as in some killing tidal wave. He would like to have saved them all from himself at least. It seems a man goes through his whole life without knowing any more than he can know at the time.

He had not known to be amused, for example. Yes, amused. It was so simple now to think of himself breaking out of character and saying to the history student, "Ah, so *you're* it?" He'd have given a whole lot now if he'd just known how to break out of character. He'd hurt them badly. All their lives would have been slightly different if he'd known just enough to say, "Good heavens, what a surprise."

"Thanks, Dad," Lois said.

He felt for her hand and held it a moment. "Hon, let me tell you something."

"Of course. What is it, Dad?"

"You be sure you get back from Publix by five." He felt her lips touch his forehead again in a little kiss. "You're getting too old to be driving around in the dark."

SOLITUDE. It had been difficult for them to arrange. Tomorrow Lois was going to drive Paul the seventy miles over to Daytona Beach for a little visit with Carol and the boy. A few days alone was all the old man could really count on, and while he was used to lowered expectations — he was an old boy on two canes — he wouldn't mind knowing what to call a pleasure so completely pared down to nothing. A weekend alone in his own house. Pure, perhaps. Pure quiet. Life was maybe never so simply defined. Because now that plans were in the bag and it was the eve of the departure, Tom Glover agonized to think what it had cost a man with his assets to get his way.

An invitation had arrived about a Halloween contest at his great-grandson's elementary school. Glover had found he couldn't *order* Lois out of his house to attend. He'd come close several times to giving orders and had seen how Lois was boss now by virtue of Paul's sad slippage and the increased likelihood of her own father's falling down and breaking a hip.

Since she couldn't argue with Paul about leaving her father for a weekend, she had become quite graphic with Glover once they'd really started in on each other — an old man all alone in this big house or out in the spacious side lawns and groves where he kept old chairs here and there in which to plunk down whenever he went for some exercise. What if he couldn't get up? What if he had to sit out in the groves or stay flat on his back until she returned? Of course she would like to go visit Carol and Petey, but she couldn't just call time out on her father being in the feeble state he was in.

He'd done everything by hurtful means for a few weeks in order to get Lois off her high horse. He'd tried first anger and then pouting. Her wounded looks merely encouraged him to get more into his best role — his rude sighs of disappointment in her, his awful daily retreats inside his quarters, his flat refusals to come out at mealtimes. He told her she might as well have put him in jail if she was never going to let him out of her sight.

When she wept, he pressed on. He accused her. She was in violation of some deal they had which dated from the moment they agreed to combine households. Even though it was absolutely untrue, he'd hinted at his deep regrets now in having invited her into his home in the first place. He had used the word "home" the better to underscore what perhaps she owed him. The truth was that he'd told her many times how he'd meant her to have the house long ago, how he'd never intended to live this long.

Lois gave in, but she might not now be able to relax for Petey's school event. She'd been made to feel so confused. He wasn't sure how he was ever going to take back his behavior and contentions. Now that he'd won, he spent time arguing with himself: in inflicting pain, her drawn face notwithstanding, he had made it clear that it was she who needed a vacation from him. And that had to be true. He told himself the very worst that would happen in all this mess was that he might be too tired to enjoy being all to himself. But, in fact, he doubted it. It was going to be quite wonderful.

Mysteriously, the Halloween pumpkin had been an inspired idea of his. It had made Lois start to yield in his favor. In suddenly asking her last week to be sure to get him a pumpkin and some candy, she'd been put on course because she was glad to think of his wanting to have contact with the neighbors. They had no visitors. After fifty years, Lois's year-and-a-half residence in Point Breeze involved the funeral of her high school friend and two more of that same friend's parents. Lois herself had not yet met the neighbors. She never got out of the house.

She was more than glad to carve Glover a pumpkin with the help of Paul, who was still able to work with his hands. Paul kept calling the thing a watermelon, but in their separate ways all three of them had been pleased with the result. Last night Lois put a candle inside and lit up a happy mouth of three significant teeth. Paul had marveled aloud. When Lois smiled, Glover saw that he was already forgiven. "I want to thank you," he said, tears coming into his eyes.

"You're welcome, Dad."

"And I want you to know I'll behave myself while you're gone and not get into any trouble."

"Dad, I'm sorry we fought. I love you so much." She had begun to shout already. "I *hope* you *know* that."

"Know what?"

"That I *love* you."

Glover shook his head and smiled and touched the little wheel on the side of his head. "What did you say, hon?"

"I said, I *love* you!" She was smiling with exasperation. She had two old men. One couldn't talk to her and one couldn't hear her. She resorted to shouting once more at the top of her lungs — I *love* you! — the words going off like small bombs in his head.

Glover looked at her. "Well, I'm tired of you, too! That's been my whole point."

She had laughed and laughed, and he'd been relieved to see the girl capable, finally, of understanding his whole point. Yes, he had said, laughing too; he was tired of the both of them. All they needed was a little vacation.

ROUNDED OFF, he'd lived a century and watched Florida go from swamps to advertising. He remembered everybody as being about equally poor during his childhood. A wonderful growing up at a time when the very weeds down there on Mirror Lake had amounted to spirit and flight, to brushes set among flags, occasional spells of adultery, occasional violent deaths. Never robbery. They had petty thefts of eggs or a chicken, but no robbery. He remembered hymns and baptisms down on this lake; religious conversion and arms reaching up in real belief. The place sang with urgency sometimes. Lucky's mother, Nelly Apple, said she didn't want her boy swimming in that lake, where all those sins were being washed away. But they'd swum and dived deliriously down there anyway, with more than one or two boys, whites and blacks. And at age ten or eleven they were all treading water in that deep swimming hole, stunned one day by the sight of a woman they knew rushing toward them and then down the bank, with her dress going up in flames. It was Nelly Apple. It was Lucky's own flailing mother in the cool of day. She'd looked like a walking scarecrow as she got close. A burning rag, twisting and moving forward to find them at dusk. She'd been using turpentine straight out of a mason jar to light Alma's cookstove, as she always did when the boys failed to leave her a box of stick pine. And somehow she'd been able to run out of the house and make her blind way many feet to the bank, where she fell and saved herself and lived on for several days. Glover had had a complete blackout between the time her body hit the smoking water and the time they buried her.

"Well, is it true or not true?" Glover's young wife had asked not so many years later. She was Jemmalee Ginn, the Iowa girl. When he married her he was only eighteen, and the two of them lived together with Alma and Virgil in this house. Jemmalee was Alma's best listener, but the girl was always coming to him later to see if the old lady's stories were reliable.

Is *what* true? Glover would say.

The boy Lucky! Had he or hadn't he been adopted after Nelly died?

Alma hinted frequently to Jemmalee about all kinds of things. Alma hinted she'd taken on the boy as her own only to have him run away with his feelings hurt. Glover's young wife often asked him if it were true or not, because she knew it would have been a rare thing. She was curious to know more details in and around the fiction and in what facts she could piece together for herself.

At some point Glover decided, for Jemmalee's happiness, that Lucky's adoption by his parents was, for the most part, true. Lucky couldn't have lived alone in his mother's cabin. But the facts of those years were blurred with more of the swimming and hunting and knocking of heads. They'd been inseparable; that was all he could really remember. Lucky may have moved in with them more or less, which was certainly Alma's version to Jemmalee; but damned if Glover could remember whether it was just an image or two he had of Lucky in a bedroll on the porch. Or something much more than that. It was clear to him that the boy had lived on Alma's cooking and been doctored for influenza and other ailments right alongside her youngest and last boy, Tom Glover, sitting here on this porch at ninety-one. Any time either of them killed a hawk in the yard, Alma gave out a box of shells as a reward. That was such a clear memory now. And Lucky had been driven in the family wagon to church, where he was forced to listen to the preacher from just outside the windows. Maybe the picture Glover had of Lucky sitting outside in the wagon during church had happened only once or twice, or else a hundred times. But Glover remembered clearly the boy's being given a piece of ham to eat so he'd have some incentive, and a high-spirited moment on a Sunday's ride home from the service when Virgil Glover had quizzed Lucky to see if he'd paid attention. Even Alma had laughed, though she was not a woman of mirth.

One day someone had come running to the swimming hole yelling about a mad dog up under this house. That day there was a church picnic taking place in the swimming hole, Methodist families and their kids and one or two of the regular blacks like Lucky who never got out of that lake in the summertime. At the news of a mad dog, the men ordered the women and children to stay put near the water. Boys like Glover and Lucky would be tolerated if they followed behind. A steep incline in the bank was always slowing Glover down whenever Lucky was in a hurry, and to this day he remembers Lucky yanking him up the bank, the hot, dark grip of that boy's hand; he remembers his father running to the house to get a rifle in the quick way those things were decided. Supposedly it was some stray dog getting out of the July sun and being spotted by one of the maids going back and forth between his mother's cook house and the picnic. All he remembered now was the excitement he felt when they got up to the house and he heard his father tell them to crouch down and see if they could see anything. They all got right down to look. Glover remembered being blinded by bright squares of day that poured under the house from the other side. The white squares seemed fifty feet away, and in between was a cool dead smell until somebody spotted the dog behind a brick stanchion smack in the center. Someone whistled softly. Eyes adjusted to the explosive light beyond all that blackness. The dog was trying to hide. He wasn't moving. They could hear him wheezing once their eyes began to adjust.

"Get on under there, boy," he'd heard his father say.

Such a point of view — too preposterous now. To his own granddaughter, Glover knew he and his father, their whole constituency, must seem as innocent as heathens. And as inconsequential. One ended up ashamed of all that made those complicated days exactly what they had been. But one didn't enjoy forgiveness from the likes of Carol. She had sat here on this porch not one month ago, and in the brooding silence that opened up between them, he had felt himself revered but discounted in the same instant. And his father, too, Virgil Glover, a wonderfully strong and comprehending sort of man. Right now Tom Glover can still feel his soft boy's hairs rise up on his arm as he hears again his father order Lucky under there after that dog. His groin had moved with the danger in such a thing; his heart had raced. How else were they going to get that dog?

Moments before, Lucky had successfully dunked him in lake water and then laughed until he about choked, the both of them choking on their foolishness over one thing or another. And now Lucky was about to enter some truer domain. Glover, as young as he was, knew that all blacks lived there after a certain age. Lucky was admitted right then and there. Glover himself was still a boy, keeping his eyes on those squares. He heard Lucky say softly in the new tone of a grown man, "Boss, I can't be crawling under there."

Glover was afraid Lucky would not pull it off, would begin to cry and get himself in trouble.

"You go on now." His father's voice had become matter-of-fact and practical; he didn't want any of his time wasted. "We got to get him out before the sun goes down and he starts to cool off. I want you to go on now and get that dog out here where I can shoot him."

Glover had acted like he wasn't there. Everything had faded except for Lucky and his father's rifle and the bright squares of light and that dog. He was a big dog whose heaving and wracked form went in and out of focus. Glover had closed his eyes and seen white squares burned into his lids. He'd heard his father's rifle crack open again. When Virgil Glover snapped it closed, no one looked; eyes dead ahead; they all knew of the privacy between a man and a buck, that long end of a rifle pointing back and forth between Lucky's upturned face and the dark underside of the house. "Go on now." Lucky had better mind. Virgil Glover said that it had to be done quick and Lucky knew it as well as anybody.

They reported later how Lucky went on and did what he was told. But there were no words to describe how the boy's pause made the moment soar right up to a terrible white heat of silence. Then all they could hear after that were the soft sandy scuffles as he crawled on under the house and took care to position himself. Someone may have coached him a bit, made him wrap his shirt around his free arm and then take hold of the loose skin behind the dog's head. Glover couldn't remember who gave advice. No one else could remember much after they heard the high moan of that sick dog being thrown off balance and dragged by the scruff, an unreal sound that made a boy want to run for the water. The dog was hauled out on its side half crazed, its neck in a vise of fear, as Lucky moved straight backward and was probably coached on whether he should move faster or slower as he came from under the house any way he could. He was absolutely covered with dust. "Hold on, now, hold on!" Virgil Glover had an awkward shot that nearly grazed the boy's frozen arm but gave him a chance to let go. He managed to throw himself some distance before the second shot took the dog's head.

As if it were just yesterday — blood splattering in a perfect arch on the side of this house, and suddenly all the women and maids up here on the porch screaming, so that time had started ticking again. No one had seen or heard ladies gather here to watch. Glover had barely a moment to feel his own legs before he was appointed to go with Lucky to show him where to take the dog, as if Lucky didn't know that well enough himself.

But the wind had changed. Virgil Glover was finally mad at somebody. "Tom! You go with that boy and show him where you want the hole!"

Lucky stood there looking at him. *Where did he want the hole?* as if Lucky didn't live right there and know exactly where they buried things. Lucky had looked at Glover like he didn't trust the moon and the stars. Glover had felt hotter than an iron. He'd wanted to bash Lucky for giving him a certain kind of look that would not have been allowed if Glover had been older. "Come on," he had said, and gone and got two shovels. He'd helped

Lucky dig and had hated the way the boy held that quarter in his mouth, crying, his nose flowing shamelessly.

They didn't have pockets for quarters. They barely had britches. It was the first summer of Glover's life that he'd wanted some money. With a father so flagrant, he'd felt it right on the tip of his tongue to tell Lucky either to stop that bellowing or else give that quarter to him. One half hour before it would have been an outrageous request. "This here quarter? You *crazy!*" Lucky would have laughed out loud. He'd always lived as a boy permitted to throw himself on the solid ground laughing any chance he got. Now a twinkling of an eye had twinkled. They were digging a grave now, and Lucky was standing on an inch of shifting ground, the little cusp remaining to him — the last moment between a black boy's being able to laugh at a white boy ("This here quarter? You *crazy!*") and just about having to mind him.

He woke with a start and didn't see Paul anywhere in the yard.

Glover tried not to panic as he brought his rocking chair forward as far as it would go in an effort to survey his property. He was proud of the modest estate his father came into when the Yankees had tried to start up the citrus business and gotten frozen out. Paul was nowhere to be seen in either of the huge lots that had once been Yankee groves. The groves his father had replanted after the '95 Freeze were still at the back of the house and over in Mitchell Hammock and scattered here and there throughout the area. The side yards were filled with live oak now and birdbaths and Jemmalee's efforts at crepe myrtle trellises.

"Paul!"

He got up finally and made it to the west end of the porch to look in that direction. One or two of the original fruit trees, older than he was, hung on in the shade of the big oaks. He always enjoyed the outdated appearance of five ancient concrete benches placed at great distances from one another. Glover had never permitted Jemmalee to replace them with proper lawn furniture despite her observation that those old benches looked like tombstone slabs. He had seen immediately that she was correct and had understood better why he was so drawn to them. "Paul," he called out in a weak voice. He'd regretted the loss of sex far less than the loss of his once deep and frightening tones. They were ten years gone. He feared that now he sounded like a rabbit.

Turning back he felt strangely observed by old ghosts. He supposed he ought to put out a call to Lucky, too, while he was at it. "Lucky? Mama? Jemmalee?" The dead know they'd better keep an eye on you. Only the living can't imagine for a moment that you were ever dangerous. They assume you were just ignorant, both then and now.

"Paul!"

The house was long, and if Paul were in the kitchen he wouldn't be able to hear. Glover waited and then saw the man standing just inside the screen, almost invisible. Glover hated to appear startled, but he saw shadowy wings seem to rise from behind the teacher's quiet shoulders and then disappear. "Oh, there you are," he said. "I was just wondering if you were around."

Paul Barnes often had amazingly quick answers. "I hope so," he said. "It's good to see you. How've you been?"

"Oh, fine. Tip-top." Every half hour or so they behaved as men who'd not seen each other in weeks. When Glover finally grew accustomed to it, some strange logic in the disease had been granted him. "You're looking good yourself, Paul."

The thing about the schoolteacher was that he could be heard. If Lois had to shout in her conscientious efforts, Paul had turned out to be naturally brilliant around hearing aids. No one was sure how he managed it. The relief of getting crystal clear phrases out of another man's mouth was one of the last blessings in Glover's life. Whenever Paul spoke, it was almost like the story of the toothless man able to eat rare steak. Glover loved him for it. And on this particular afternoon he was profoundly relieved that Paul hadn't gotten into trouble. He'd been dozing on the job.

"Listen," he said, "those kids are due any minute, if you care to join me. I'm out here at my usual post waiting for those boys."

"Who?" Paul stepped on through the screen and then looked in the wrong direction.

"Those boys!" Now it was Glover who had to remember not to shout. "Come on out, Paul, and sit down! I'm interested in the Negro, and you said yesterday you'd picked out one of the others for yourself. Let's sit right here and wait for them."

They had this exchange every day. Glover pointed out the one black down there every chance he had in order to see if he could wake up Paul to his old hobby. Evidently, once upon a time the teacher had been a civil rights enthusiast, and now there seemed to be nothing left of the matter. Now everyone's job was to keep this freedom rider from riding out of his own front yard.

Glover would not have known a thing about the affair had not his wife, Jemmalee, let the cat out of the bag in a moment of weakness. Lois had sworn her to secrecy. Back when, Paul had apparently gotten himself shipped out of one of his high schools when the board members found out what he'd been doing over his summer vacation. He'd spent his time either sitting at lunch counters in Tallahassee, or else singing and holding hands on their buses up there, or registering voters, or, in general, making a nuisance of himself. One way or other he'd finally done the right thing and gotten himself arrested. It amused the old man now, all that time going by. Glover liked to reason that if Paul could not distinguish blacks from whites any longer, which seemed to be the case, then True Integration had come to get him with a vengeance. True Integration had built itself into the very structure of the man's brain, where once upon a time it was nothing more than a song and a dance.

When Paul was seated beside Glover on the front porch, he had one of his small seizures of recognition. Rising tall in his chair suddenly, Paul said, "They're back!" as the neighborhood Gap Kids at long last came racing into full view on their bikes. Now

Glover could relax into satisfied old bones. It seemed he'd made it through another day without kicking the bucket.

The boys, as usual, pumped furiously and made their whoops of laughter soar up and down as they prepared to skid into place. Skidding was the contest every day; they never tired of it.

"Look at that!" Paul said.

The sight of color and movement out there in the road seemed fresh once again, even to the old man. But the euphoria in Paul's odd moments of joy could sometimes make Glover's temper rise right along with his pity. "Sit back, Paul." Glover almost growled out the order. "Sit back and relax," he said. Tears had overwhelmed the man. Every day Paul thought the sight of those boys quite beautiful.

"My word," he said.

"You like that? Which do you like? The boys or all those dogs?"

The Gap Kids had brought with them their usual assortment of golden yard dogs, which ran before the flying front wheels, panting and smiling the whole time to keep from looking like chaperons and bodyguards. The dogs had a good amount of dignity for this unrewarded task. A gangling mixed breed of Labradors and mongrel hounds and terriers. Glover completely approved of most of them, of their long, loose legs and intelligent faces. He had two strong emotions left in him for dogs — approval and disapproval — whereas once he'd possessed more subtle feelings for their complex displays of character. There'd been times when he could hear in a few distant cries everything a man should try to express to his own wife.

In an instant the whole gang of flashing boys swept in. They landed on the little grassy strip. Soon they'd be out of sight below the bank, quite beyond old men. But for now the whole explosion was visible and the two men watched a dozen boys jump around, stretching legs and quacking in the humorous, predictable agreement of ducks. Glover squinted to make out the black kid, and Paul flinched at the boys' careless disregard for bicycles, such shiny new equipment flopping down on the grass.

"There they go," Paul said, and he meant the bikes falling down and also the flag-bannered boys and dogs disappearing at the point where a path opened up between elephant ears growing high. The bulrushes. Glover explained to Paul how that deep spot down there was exactly where he'd brought in the dragline, oh mercy, sixty years ago now. He'd been using a dragline down in south pasture and had decided to bring it up here to the house and have the man deepen that fishing spot, the old swimming hole.

"Is that so?" Paul said. "I never knew that."

Almost every day Glover explained the deep hole as he and Paul watched the boys arrive and congregate and then disappear. It was Glover's afternoon picture show, his little matinee before his supper and bedtime. "Yes. And I planted all those cypress trees you see down there, too," Glover said.

"You did?" Paul said. He never tired now of Glover's stories.

"Oh yes," Glover said, closing his eyes, thinking how he would be alone tomorrow, how Lois almost certainly had not yet told Paul he was going to Daytona with her. One didn't tell him of things like that — not even of a doctor's appointment or of a trip to the shoe store — because his newest symptom was one of agitation over places and events he could not imagine. This was a disease of the relentless present tense; one had to keep the man aligned with what was in full view — that lake, those boys, this yard.

But curious, to Glover's mind, was how Paul understood the difference somehow when he was being told about an event that had already occurred. In those instances Paul had in no way forgotten the ordinary politeness of an enthusiastic response. This touched the old man deeply.

"*You* planted those trees? I didn't know that."

"Oh yes."

Glover often marveled at how it was possible for a man to be stripped of everything but impeccable good manners and, more-over, how it was possible that manners went such a long way

when it was all a man had left. Simple civility was the last remaining card up Paul's sleeve.

"Those trees, right there? *You* planted all those beautiful
trees?"

"Yes, every one of them."

Paul had mostly very short phrases left in him, but there was
one long exclamation he could still put together. It went something like the one he managed now. "Those are the prettiest trees
I've ever seen in my life."

It was sheer character in any man to retain that particular
sentiment above all others. If God himself had told Glover he
could pick, in the year or two before his death, a single bit of
complicated syntax, would he have had enough aplomb to pick
that one? So serviceable, so elegant and unsentimental a description of one's own destruction. Because those trees out there were
not the prettiest trees Paul had ever seen in his life. He had no
memory of his life. He did not know who he was, that he'd ever
taught school, or once loved Lois or had a daughter and a grandson. Stoic politeness was required of Paul to keep telling this old
man (whoever *he* was) that these were the prettiest trees he'd
ever seen in his life. Paul remembered nothing except how to put
in his voice the hope that they were, the real belief that surely, for
the old man's sake, they must be.

2

THE NEXT DAY his energy started up as soon as he opened one eye and felt Lois and Paul moving around the house. They were getting ready, at last, to leave him. Glover reached to the floor and heard their low thumps through his hand. Some new promise coursed up into his arm from the boards; he didn't know what it was exactly — the clarity of self, perhaps, his sins the less to be dreaded, the more to be remembered. When the movement stopped and Lois and Paul were on their way, he got up and looked at his newly renovated room. Except for the length of a church service on Sundays, this was the first time he'd been alone in it. He wondered for a moment if this was going to make a difference. Part of Glover's new room took in the old parlor, where his mother had set up a bed for Lucky in his final four days. Lois had had her workmen knock down a wall, and for a week last year unknowing builders and electricians and plumbers had moved back and forth over the old spot as if it were nothing. She had badly wanted to help Glover arrange his furniture when the time came for him to move into his new quarters. The silly look of Glover's own private arrangements had upset her for months — his two oak desks jammed together side by side, and then the file cabinets and Jemmalee's BarcaLounger and several crowded rockers, and then his refrigerator as a final insult. Glover had had the men put the refrigerator up against his headboard. And Lois had long before agreed not to enclose the new bath; a man Glover's age didn't need to be rounding corners for the toilet. She could put up a wall after he was gone. Glover arranged his bed so that he could use the toilet from a near sitting position. That she understood, although the bed next to a toilet didn't look sanitary to her. But the thing that had really gotten her down was the fact that his purring refrigerator tended to move the bed across the new pine floor while he slept.

"Dad, it just looks terrible." And she had to be thinking of the sacrifice she'd made in cutting down the size of her new sitting room just so *his* room would be more spacious. "I don't understand why you want absolutely everything over here under the windows."

"So I can hang on to things as I move around. I'm less likely to have a fall."

He had two canes he frightened everyone with. They made his slow, wooden walk appear unlikely, an insect's bulbous body held up by mere hairs. He called one of his canes Cain and the other Abel, and with all this last-minute equipment he was not planning on stomping across the very spot where Lucky had died. The old man was mildly superstitious. Right now he took milk and cream out of his Frigidaire and blessed that monumental girl rising up in her new bright coils at the head of his bed. She was fine right where she was, close by and intimate. She performed her feminine, hygienic job of self-defrosting every morning while the old man got dressed.

From his two desks he watched the sun come up on one side of Mirror Lake, blanketed in fog. The sun would climb around all day up there and go down tonight on the other side, spectacular in both directions. The bowl of cold cereal waited a long time while he sipped his coffee. He preferred to boil coffee up about as strong as he could stand it whenever he was in no hurry. He sat and watched the fog lift and reveal the colorless lake beneath, as blank as paper this morning. Large cattails swayed under the weight of a few early birds. A few sparrow and wren were already out there stuffing themselves.

He was amazed to experience his old verve this morning, enough to give him something more than just gumption. He typed out a letter he owed a cousin in Texas and then sat in his favorite rocker and turned pages of the *Orlando Sentinel* for its crime, gossip, and coupon bargains. A woman serial killer turned out to hail from his granddaughter, Carol's, neck of the woods. He felt good enough to read and clip an editorial for Carol on the Fed's bailing out a forty-billion-dollar bank in Chicago. It made his hair rise, but he doubted whether the girl ever took his points to heart. In college she had liked his clipping service; now she seemed only amused by it. Not so long ago she was here visiting and he'd tried to tell her about those banks failing; bankers were fad men now, going after first oil and then gas and then farm equipment and then South America. What next? He felt sorry for the old conservative Jews spinning in their graves while today's bunch got way beyond caring in the frantic race to lend more money.

But Carol was the sensitive type. Say the word "Jew" around Carol and she would practically fall out of her chair. He hadn't meant it the way she chose to hear it. He'd meant the money boys in a general way. He had tried to ignore her and go on in an effort to help the girl. The debt system made us much easier to pacify, he had explained; much easier to herd together like kids in a playground. We spend and spend beyond what we have, as the bankers show us how we can't get along without the government bailing them out.

But often in conversation the two would dead-end at this point — the point when Carol was likely to say she heard the phone ringing or her checkbook bouncing or her hangnail hanging.

Why didn't she just say that his days were long gone? He said it himself plenty of times. A man couldn't clear a field these days without waiting for Tallahassee to vote. That was all right. He understood that. Too many of us now; individual gumption had to die out in order for people to survive in the big equal soup we all want. People didn't seem to care that they'd been corraled and sold down the Roosevelt River. Once Glover had told Carol he regretted only not being able to live long enough to see the next mess they were going to get us into. It sure looked like dictatorship to him. Give out a lot of free candy and everybody is happy for a while. No, he wouldn't mind sticking around long enough to see the next mess.

He dozed a bit. At noon he got up and put Lois's pumpkin on the porch and then realized he was starving. Back in her new kitchen he cooked a pound of bacon for his lunch. Today, for some reason having to do with the economy never looking so bad, Glover was a powerhouse and he spent a few hours in his room with his *Wall Street Journal* and a magnifying glass. The *Journal* had grown into a mightier and mightier task in the last three years. On some days he was wrung out to the last drop of whatever else he had left in him. He suspected he was made up of little more than blood and sugar water now. His old heart was rusting away in there. But maybe it was the pure scandal, the daily stupidity in Washington, which elevated his blood pressure and kept him going day after day.

At four o'clock he decided to groom himself for the trick-or-treaters and their parents. He found he had such a steady hand with his safety razor that he was prepared to go all the way. He was fifteen minutes humming a hymn tune as he did his toenails. This was advanced old age, knowing how to pass the time once one's eyes got too dim to read. There was artistry in an ordinary diversion. A man had to know how to make the minutes go slow and the hours quick. His simple ablutions he found to be a slow-breathing, risky pleasure. A bath was always an exciting proposition, for example, and although he had promised Lois faithfully not to go near an open drain until she got back, his word turned out not to be worth a damn.

He took a daredevil shower that afternoon, sitting up in his high chair with the fittings that let him swivel slowly for a whole 360 degrees. Lois had had the workmen put a handhold in his new bathroom at just about any spot Glover might think to grab, and a few more besides. The place looked like a jungle gym.

On his big bed he laid out the new striped dish towels she'd bought him at Publix. He had wanted stripes so he could see better how to fold them into a five-inch diaper. Just last summer he'd noticed that he was starting to leak and wondered how long he'd smelled bad without knowing it. He'd remembered his uncle Fate, telling him how the old boys were the last to know.

By late afternoon Glover was feeling glad not to be worn out for the mild diversion of Halloween. He threw in an ounce of talcum for the occasion, and then suddenly his hairbrush felt heavy in his hand. When he finished buttoning, he had to sit down and take a pill and was not so sure he would make it out there to the front porch with a basket of candy. He reminded himself that he never knew his own limits until five minutes before they shut him right down. Before Lois came to live with him, this was the hour when he'd always gotten down on himself and hoped he'd somehow die in the night.

Over the roar in his head he rested and tried to think how easily he'd once made physical labor into a shape or a target, a prize. At one time he'd known how to work himself and six strong men into the ground. Not just the fencing and roping, the marking and branding, but the real walking hell of an entire day picking up stumps in a burned-off smoldering field. He'd never made money on his cattle. He'd made money clearing land he bought for two bits an acre. Between a bust and a boom was how they'd all learned to live. Florida was always either going under or bobbing to the surface, and a smart man had to be a loose cork.

THE GAP KIDS failed to show up for their fishing that afternoon and their absence made the old man a little excited to deduce that they might be planning to show up after dark for candy. He wouldn't mind having a closer look at those boys. They were a bit too old to be bumping into the little kids. They'd be late. Glover wasn't sure he could wait for them, but the amusing thought of scaring them recharged his batteries; by five-thirty he'd managed to drag his rocker to a spot behind the pumpkin. Then he rested to get his strength back before he went inside to get the basket of candy, which he planned to place on the little table inside the front door so that it would be the last thing he'd have to carry out when the time came. He was organized as hell. He had another twenty minutes to rest, to sit again and watch Mirror Lake take on a few pinks at the far west, these recent sunsets due to some volcano going off in the Philippines — dust refracting light, the kind of science that made him feel his ignorance completely.

There was a time when he'd known enough to work men until they were too demoralized to kick a stump before they reached down for it. Florida rattlers would rear up and bite a man too blind and tired to kick before reaching down. A July working day in any part of this hard interior made cold pump water boil inside a man's mouth. He remembered his body getting as hot as a furnace and his enjoyment in the way paid workers needed to see the man burning alongside them. The more he cooked, the more shame and tears and blood he had been able to get out of the few who'd hung in with him, respecting him, refusing to walk away from a good deal. He was known for paying on the nail, paying for doctor calls, locking a man's money in his own safe when it looked like money that might get away. He himself had had to learn how to keep from drinking. He'd had to learn how to come home dead tired at night and wake up the next morning still worth something.

Glover prepared a light supper of milk and bread before dark, and sure enough that was when the first little child battered at his screen. He lowered the volume inside his right ear and made the few careful steps from his room into the hall. On the other side of the screen stood a ghost-child who was small enough to be a penguin someone had draped in a sheet.

A father, a man about thirty, smiled and called over the ghost's head. "How are you this evening, Mr. Glover? I'm your neighbor, Cooper. Will Cooper. This is Sean. Say hello to Mr. Glover, Sean!"

There was full resistance behind that silent sheet. Glover could see huge brown eyes and a red mouth saying the words "Trick or treat!" *Sean* must have been a boy, he decided. Boys could often be heard while girls tended to sound off in short squawks or hisses.

Glover handed the father the basket of candy from the table by the door. "I wonder if you'd mind taking this for me. I'm going to sit out here for the rest of the festivities."

"Oh sure! Here, let me have that." Cooper jerked his small son out of the old man's way, reached for the large basket, and held the screen wide so Glover could take up both his canes. Two walking sticks used to hurt his pride. In time he'd learned that the more of them he came up with, the more remarkable everyone thought he was.

"Nice and cool tonight," Glover said. "No bugs."

"Yessir, it's about perfect out here," Cooper said, giving himself away with that slow *sir*. It was required of boys below the Mason-Dixon. Glover guessed Georgia.

He lifted the matches out of Lois's carved pumpkin and asked the young man if he wanted to do the honors. Will Cooper sprang at every little task. "Wow, look at that, Sean! Look at Mr. Glover's pumpkin."

"Where you from?" Glover asked.

"Sir?" The young man was smiling. He had both hands resting now on the shoulders of his boy, who clearly wished to get on with the transaction. Glover startled the child by throwing into his little sack two handfuls of large candy bars. They made a mighty crash and it pleased Glover to see a ghost back off in genuine alarm.

"You're not from around here," Glover said.

"Sir, you don't remember me?" The young neighbor helped

Glover ease himself down into his chair. "I'm Bill Cooper's grandson. Doctor Cooper? I believe you knew him well."

"Good heavens," Glover said. "Sit down, sit down!" But his other rocker was several feet away from where he had dragged this one, and young Cooper demurred. He remained standing and grinned all the wider.

If Glover could describe his next sudden feeling it would be of a horrendous welling up of grief. He had gone the whole day feeling first up and then down. Now this sudden drop out of the bottom of the bucket. "You're Doc Cooper's boy?"

"His grandson. My wife and I came around to visit you this summer when your daughter invited us in to see the renovations."

Well, he certainly didn't remember such a thing. No one had come around here to visit him in ages. If the boy was actually here at the house he must have spent the whole time with Lois and her little tour. But Glover smiled and nodded. Young Cooper was a fool not to have come visiting on his own. He could tell him a thing or two about his relatives, although right now there was only this very sudden emotion in Glover's chest. He barely managed to whisper. "Your grandfather was quite a man, quite a man."

"Well, my dad's the one who told me a whole lot about *you*, Mr. Glover. Dad says he grew into a man just from hunting with you a few times."

Glover cleared his throat and looked off over the lake. He blew his nose on a handkerchief. Lakes were mum. They never had any answers about what it meant to come to this. There was a flutter under that cropped sheet, after which the tiny boy named Sean sneezed.

"Bless you," Glover said, and closed his eyes. His body ached to be tucked into bed for the night or for eternity. Doc Cooper's son had become a state supreme judge of some kind. Glover had never let Doc bend his ear about what all had happened to his four boys *after* they'd hunted on Glover's cattle land and then each gone off to reproduce themselves. Old Doc himself was moldering peacefully in the ground just as he should be. All this progeny. Glover hoped they didn't take themselves for granted, but they no doubt did.

"You a lawyer?"

"Yessir." The boy was humble. "Real estate mostly."

"Well, that's fine, that's splendid."

"I've been meaning to get around this side of the lake again and have a chat."

"You boys stay pretty busy, I expect."

"Yessir."

"Your dad still up in Tallahassee?"

"Retired last year."

"And you've decided to settle here," Glover declared. He made a little lift with his right cane. It was as quiet tonight as an empty church, but the boy admired the whole purpling sunset scene before he nodded. "Yessir. It's a great spot, isn't it?"

Young Cooper was probably the only other person on this lake now who knew a little Point Breeze history, but then again he'd never come around to sharpen his wits any. That alone told Glover a lot about the boy. To hell with him.

DOCTOR COOPER and Bill Greene and just about everyone else had slipped off naturally to the grave to give their boys a little room. No sons for him, so he had been allowed to live, perhaps as a kind of punishment. He couldn't *remember* gambling with his son's life in order to get a longer stint for himself on this sorry planet, but maybe he had. In his harebrained youth he may have struck some bargain he could no longer remember, he and Uncle Fate during a drinking spree. Fate used to boast of all the bastards he'd got and hoped never to meet in this life. And how Glover had sat back laughing at the idea. A few years later Glover's own

firstborn son was lost as a baby, and Glover practically right on
the scene when it happened. Tom. They were calling the boy
Tom, still in diapers. Glover's own grief had become so thickly
layered he couldn't release it. He'd felt that way for a long time,
like a stuffed trophy, a stuffed and mounted mule deer head. For
years he hardly breathed, and Jemmalee had been too forgiving
to stand. He would sometimes strike her for some complaint or
other whose content he never could call up later, until one morning almost twenty years down the road he had somehow come
out of it. Losing Jemmalee's love in that time had become the
bigger tragedy. He'd killed that, too.

Lois was eighteen then and off for her first year in college. He
had suddenly woken up realizing that his blurry baby had finally
become quite outrageous. He seemed like the dead boy out of a
folk song about someone's baby falling down a well. Glover was
on the bank board by that time and could remember only having
kicked stump and burned in the sun with his men. When he'd
come home tired and whipped, his wife and daughter would look
up from needlework. That much he remembers. They would try
to guess what his mood would be. He was never reliable — all
right one evening and furious the next — for their whole lives,
until they'd escaped him.

It took only a few years. Were those the fast years in order that
these could become the punishing slow ones? — death eluding
him, giving him time now? It had been a whole other twenty
years since he'd sold his last pieces of land and moved up on this
porch, retired.

Some time in his long life he'd realized that if his son hadn't
died, he might not have amounted to much in the eyes of the
world. He'd been a celery planter without much ambition until
the moment of that heart-stopping search of the side yard and
house for the baby. He'd imagined in his initial bewilderment
that a hawk had lifted the boy and diaper straight into the air. For
years, in order to numb himself, he'd worked in the sun the way
winos sleep in the shade. Completely unconscious, completely
successful. One day he was suddenly respected in town.

"I'll come back to see you some afternoon," young Cooper said. He'd returned from having taken his child into the house to let him get a drink and now had him by the hand while he stood promising Glover something.

Glover looked up and touched one of his plastic wheels. "How's that?"

Cooper had turned full attention to his son, who maneuvered the tall porch steps, one at a time. The boy was holding his own winding sheet to keep from stumbling head over heels.

"Say good-bye to Mr. Glover, Sean. Say thank you."

The steps were too steep. Glover himself had a lot of trouble with them. "Good-bye," he heard himself call. He found he could not say Sean. He was too old for names like that.

Both men watched the boy's feet thunk into place until he had himself on level ground, at which point he tumbled anyway, his bag of candy crushed under his chest. Candy broke the fall, but the child's pride was damaged. Lots of wailing and gnashing of teeth. "Up you go, Sean. You're all right, son. Up you go."

Glover sat almost stricken suddenly at the thought of his own son as a few collapsed bones, if he was anything at all. Now, against his will, he would start to think of Jemmalee, whose stroke had given her a few days too many. She had worried about her first baby being so much further along than she would ever get. Clean out of it, she'd said. Now Glover knew what she'd meant: he'd never catch up with either of them.

And sometimes when he skipped the part about his son, when he was able to go back further and even skip the terrifying images of Lucky and of Lucky's mother going up in flames, he could sometimes sustain a brief glimpse of himself at his youngest point before any of them knew what lay ahead. He'd been a straight-arrow boy with a pair of knobby legs and two smoothly sanded feet, grinning. He remembers his mother, Alma, wealthy enough to have gold teeth toward the end of her life. He remembers as a child loving her intensely, and, in a box of photographs, there was one photo of Glover and Lucky that he liked to examine closely now that he had all the time in the world. The both of them were standing up in a buckboard with Virgil Glover, who seemed to be looking to one side and perhaps far off into town. His father was not grinning in that picture or any other, and town was a very early Orlando, with a shipping trade just starting to pan out. The long drive from Point Breeze to Orlando would rock Glover and Lucky into a trance every time. On one occasion grown men had shaken the little boys and made them both climb down and examine a stalk of bananas lashed to a crossbeam outside a packinghouse. They knew banana flavoring only, in the rare and creamy centers of hard Christmas candy. They'd never guessed at the fruit itself, its shape and color, its capacity to look like food from another hemisphere, another world.

He had watched in amazement when his father negotiated the purchase of the entire contraption of fruit, the only stalk of banana that had made it this far inland. Perhaps the stalk had merely traveled from Cuba, but the thing was longer than Glover was tall and had lain in the back of the wagon like a fresh corpse giving off a kind of cheap cologne. A mile out of town his father stopped the mules and then got out his knife to cut each boy a sample. They'd tried to break open the long skins from the center, and this clumsiness had sent the pulp shooting out and around tough hide like a pudding. And the excitement in the first taste had swept him away. Heavenly. There was never enough sugar in those days, and what a fine deprivation; so that a simple new fruit could seem like an invention, could turn out to be the first real delicacy of his life.

"Trick or treat!"

Someone had given his arm a light touch out of fear and respect. When he opened his eyes he was face to face with a witch and a princess. "Well, look who's here!" he said. There was also an angel. Her wire halo sprang up and down of some secret accord. A designated mother kept her distance in the middle of the old man's front walk ("Love your *pumpkin*, Mr. Glover"). Her brave little girls had come right up to his nose.

Glover said, "And just exactly what *are* you beauties?" He found he could hardly open his eyes.

The beauties had no idea what to tell him.

"This witch here is better looking than my wife," Glover said, and his observation caused the witch to smile and show how she had blackened one tooth.

"No," he said. "I guess my wife's better looking after all."

The child was too young for this little bit of ribbing. Her bottom lip started to droop faster than he could find words to take everything back.

"I'm joking, hon."

He held out the tremendous basket and watched tiny be-jeweled hands reach in to select one candy bar carefully. "No, no," he said. "Take a lot. Take three or four of these things. I want to be popular. I want to get into office!"

The witch, princess, and angel began to stare again.

"Go on!" Glover shouted. "A fool and his money are soon elected."

On silent cue they each chose one extra candy bar, selecting more quickly this time. His offer was too extravagant and they all knew it. They were protecting him from himself, as women will do.

He remembered his own father, grinning, seeing that he had exceeded himself in the children's eye with his bananas, suddenly shouting at them that they should take more. They, too, had sat in disbelief. And Virgil Glover was such a hard sort of good man that neither Tom nor Lucky would dare make a move until he'd taken his knife again and cut Lucky a half dozen bananas that the child, laughing, couldn't hold in his arms. Virgil had cut the same for Glover, who had grabbed up burlap to hold his share of the loot. The altered stalk lay resting on its naked spine for the rest of the journey — a stick of a girl in a hula skirt.

Someone was startling him again with shouts and stomping of feet. For the next half hour, children all the same height seemed to come in groups. The bigger the group the less inclined were the mothers even to bother addressing him. Women stood talking out in the road, arms folded, their big heads together. In self-assured little clans, they did not so much as wave, and for their rudeness Glover began to penalize the children, who stared out at him from behind masks and makeup. He began giving four huge candy bars to every child except for one per group. To that one pirate or Cinderella, the smallest or the dumbest, depending on his mood, Glover took to saying, "None for you. Sorry. None for you this time." And the children were so polite, so stunned to have a clear demonstration of pure meanness, that they waited, patient and wordless, for their candy before hightailing it back to the road, everyone eager to report him. There was always a little confab then, the mothers bending down to get a version of the incident, which the children attempted, unsuccessfully, to explain as an outraged chorus. One uncertain mother usually came up out of the huddle and turned to wave at him to show no hard feelings; the children *must* have misunderstood him.

He enjoyed the confusion out there in the road, the adults finally getting behind their chicks, shooing them, cheering them back into a merry band of optimists. Usually a mother's curious face would turn to have another look at him. There was always that predictable little wave of someone wanting to give him the benefit of the doubt.

"Bye-bye, Mr. Glover. Thanks."

He tried not to kid himself that he was any longer much of a terror. These working parents were in charge of things now, as they should be. Central Florida was not about tough farming or cattle or improved pasture waiting for the sons of Tom Glover to keep improving it. *Improving* it? Environmentalists today fainted dead away at the thought of the Glovers of the past, clearing all those acres without permits, draining all those wetlands, putting down all those wells. It was the end of the world as far as environmentalists were concerned, and maybe they were right.

He used to think the stakes were big, but saw now how humbly small they'd been after the Mormons came in, and then Del Monte and then Minute Maid. You had to have a corporation behind the whole farming affair now. You needed the Minute

Maid boys in Tallahassee behind you. You needed the private jets in Washington. He was the looker-on now with his pinecone past and his mother's gold teeth. Not born yesterday. And he was sure glad of it.

He wondered if he didn't remember young Cooper's wife after all. And, yes, Cooper himself. Lois had shown them both around the house now that he thought of it. But men working behind desks these days — they were such sissies now. They strolled around Mirror Lake holding hands with their pencil-thin wives; they knew how to middle-manage chains and investment firms and real estate conglomerates and they wore T-shirts that said things he couldn't make out from up here. Save the Seals. Make My Day. Play My Song. Coming around the lake holding hands and, in strict observance of the law, walking their dogs on leashes. If they jogged at all, if they weren't afraid of heart attacks, they wore their glasses strapped to their heads. No one touched red meat anymore. Now Glover himself was as female as the next man, keeping an eagle eye on boys.

When he counted how many decades that hole had been fished and swum in by now, it helped him understand his granddaughter's dismissal of him — old cattleman turned sheepherder at the end of the century and with only one lone head of sheep on the lawn now.

Just this afternoon in grooming himself Glover had used a hand mirror to study the deep crosshatches cut into his red neck. At some point his whole head had gotten thrust far out of line. He looked like a slow box turtle now — someone's pet. His big break at ninety-one was in getting to babysit instead of being babysat. And it ought to be enough for a man ninety-one to think what small efforts he was saving Lois, whom the disease had worn down to saintliness. He should be content.

But tonight he would like to have something equivalent to a stalk of bananas to purchase, circa 1910. There was no such purchase to be had. Granted, Publix grocery stores were a miracle in food. Few people had lived, as he had, to see a strawberry go from the tip of a finger to the size of a walnut. Cauliflower heads were as big as grapefruit now, and grapefruit as big as cantaloupe. And was there anyone around who still remembered how those sorry watermelon rinds used to be as thick as your arm to crowd out all the good sweet center? Today a person should cut a watermelon and be amazed at how the smart science boys could push nature's protective rind into the service of watermelon centers exactly *double* their original size. And not many seeds anymore. Even a plant felt it no longer had to work for a living.

He was tired. He would ordinarily blow out the candle and give up the ghost. But when he brought his rocker forward a bit, he saw that the Gap Kids were, at that very moment, loose-goosing it in front of the house, trying to decide if the pumpkin really meant his place was in business. Glover eased back in his chair and played possum. Then he saw that they couldn't see anything but the pumpkin anyway, now that it was pitch-dark. Three lone boys finally started up his walk in a sullen clump, and the rest followed in a bigger clump.

It was just as he had envisioned. The only way to trick-or-treat at their age was to create an atmosphere of mild intimidation. No costumes, no outfits. They carried their candy sacks with the same careless grip a man sometimes used to show off just the neck of a bottle. Illegal booze. From door to door, they were making quite a haul, but it was the disrespectful edge that amused them. They were after whatever hints of delinquency they could suggest by sheer numbers. They were sure to have a ringleader in their midst so that the rest of them didn't have to think too hard.

People had not questioned them, of course. They were easily recognized around the lake. Some might even have young brothers and sisters who'd made this round in the last hour. Still, they knew how obnoxious they were as a group, and Glover could almost see how it half embarrassed, half delighted them. They'd brought one good Labrador with them, around whose neck they'd hung a plastic death's head.

It was the Labrador dog who hung back when she got halfway

up Glover's narrow walk. She turned around and went back to sit in the road. The boys all hesitated at that warning, but the three in the lead came sauntering forward. They hadn't yet seen the old man, who watched carefully, who then had a quick thought that pleased him. Glover reached up in the dark and tipped the basket of candy over the porch railing. It fell without sound into the mulch Lois kept around her azaleas. The large basket brushed a few branches and fell out of sight.

"How you boys tonight?" Glover said.

The three bravest ones stopped. Leadership faltered. The dog whined a bit out in the road.

"We're okay," one boy finally said. Then the three continued forward, climbing the high steps where Glover sat watching. He tapped one of his canes with impatience. The boys took it slow.

"We came to say hello," one of them had the wit to say. They'd assumed it would be the old lady giving out the candy.

"Good," Glover said. "I'm glad you did."

Now they were at the top of the stairs and he could see two boys behaving almost politely, giving him honest smiles to let him know they knew he'd got the drop on them. But their companion, the third boy, was a tall redhead and not mature enough to be quick on his feet. He gave Glover a sullen look. At very best he didn't have much poise. *Man, were they* crazy? *They should have passed this house right by.*

The two friendlier boys stared. The redhead suddenly let out a blasting laugh that was aggressive and mean-spirited.

Glover smiled. The two, at least, were fine boys. Full of the devil. It pleased him more than he'd been pleased in a long time that he obviously had just the slightest edge in the situation. "I've been meaning to come down there and have a talk with you fellas," he said. Glover pointed with his cane at the elephant ears they'd been beating aside every day when they raced down that bank with their big feet. They'd left a permanent hole in the screen of ears. In the darkness of Halloween, the hole looked like an entrance to the tomb.

"My dad says it's public property," the redhead said. He was back to scowling, and Glover sensed that he was frequently several steps behind his two friends. He looked around him for some support and got none.

"Your father's right," Glover said, and this caused the same boy to shrug, to draw more of the wrong kind of attention to himself. Glover had never cared for the redheaded look on men. This one was pale and freckled, and his friends seemed to take in this liability with fresh awareness as they came into better view.

For several minutes now Glover had been aware that one of them was the black kid at last. And he looked like old Lucky all right. Glover did not wish to appear startled. Only his right cane slipped a bit at the side of the chair and made a noise.

He was the shortest of the three, perhaps the youngest and their mascot. Glover saw his face, dense as coal, no white blood, none of the high tones of the day. The boy had even, steady features and large, unblinking round eyes. Glover noted that he sported a late-breaking fancy haircut with a scar shaved in three parallel lines at the front. It was more than all that blackness in him. He had good posture, which went along with some obvious ease and confidence he'd acquired from somewhere. And the other boy, too — a husky blond kid who was shooting up in front of his parents' eyes no doubt.

It was this blond kid who spoke. "What'd you want to talk to us about?"

Somewhat as a reflex, the old man reached into his hip and pulled out his wallet. He took out several twenty-dollar bills and held them up. "I wanted to hire you to do something for me," he said. He was not that much ahead of them; he was barely ahead of himself.

The boys looked at each other. The redhead began laughing and then was unable to straighten himself up. Everything to do with Glover seemed to destroy him now, and this only made his friends the more sober.

"I want you boys to help my son-in-law do a little fishing."

"Your *son*-in law?"

These were boys. They didn't talk to anyone about sons-in-law. They were kids.

"Yes. He can't do certain things without some help. I need to hire someone for him."

The three stared at him from the other side of life. They'd stepped into a dimension they were never given any credit for understanding. In a second or two a man might have these boys eating out of his hand. If he chose. He noted that the dog had left the road and found the candy in the shrubbery. She was starting to whine. Inside Glover's hearing aids, the nearby whining was like a siren.

"Mr. Barnes is the man in question. I'm quite fond of him. And he knows how to fish. He won't cramp your style down there." Again Glover motioned with his cane at the lake, at the spot in front of his house. "I'll pay you good money to let him fish with you. One hour a day. Maybe less."

The old authority rising in his thin voice seemed to send all three boys into a little trance. They'd sauntered up here for kids' candy and come face to face with a businessman. Their fathers were university professors and lawyers and accountants and advertisers who jogged around this lake in support hose. Some of their fathers wore beards. Right now these three boys had hit pay dirt without even knowing the term. They knew they'd hit something, although the redhead couldn't contain himself, and just the way he glanced sidelong at his companions suggested he was something of a bad egg, a weak bully who had expected some other kind of excitement that he really had no imagination for. He saw he was being ignored.

The black kid said, "How much?"

"So it's going to be *you* two?" Glover said. He didn't give them a chance to answer. He took his cane and tapped the foot of the redhead, who stood a moment unable to comprehend that an old man was ordering him off his porch. "Go on," Glover said. "My business is with these two. Not you. Go on down there with the others." He heard his father's voice, Uncle Fate's voice, a few of the men Glover modeled himself after a long time ago. Orders were what you either gave or took. One or the other, but never both.

The black and white kid watched their buddy leave the porch and join the hangers-on who immediately took one of their own back into their circle. These were types with more curiosity than know-how. Some, he could see now, were younger brothers his great-grandson's age. Ten at the most.

"So," Glover said, "sit down. And call off your dog. I don't want her down there in those shrubs."

"Gracey!" the white boy called. "Get out of there!"

This was how it always worked. One gave an order instructing someone else to give an order, and the chain of command was in place as easily as when one closes a hatch. "Gracey!" The dog Gracey came waltzing into view under two nicely hinged hips; she slowly floated to the road and flopped down, obedient but with her pride completely intact. If Glover could have that dog, he would.

The boys clumped in both locations; they all stayed quiet; but the ones out on the walk wouldn't hear Glover's words if he managed to get his pitch low enough to cause these two boys to bend in a little.

"Twenty-five dollars for a while."

It was an outrageous sum, but he felt so wonderful he immediately doubled the offer. "Make it fifty for a week. If you do a good job, I'll consider more or I may up and fire the both of you. It's worth a good deal to me if you're kind and considerate to him. Do you know who I'm talking about?"

Neither one of these boys dared shrug. The black boy finally spoke. "Is he the old guy with the hose?"

"That's right. You come up here next time you see him in the yard, call him by his name, and tell him who you are and that you want to take him fishing. He's gone for a few days now. You come get him the first time you see him out here. I'll pay you up front the first day." Glover lightly tapped his cane, looked off over the yellow lights dancing in the lake. He waited.

"I can't come every day," the blond boy said. It was not an apology. He stated it as a fact.

"You both come every day for the first few times, after that you can split the job between you."

"Same money?"

"I don't know. He has to get to know you, and you have to be smart enough to look him in the eye and give him confidence. You two seem smart. Both of you come for him the first few days. I'll see how you do."

"Okay," the white kid said. "I can do that."

The kids were trying to act casual, but they were still a little dazed. The black one continued to look Glover over, but he was relaxed, more curious than anything. Finally he asked, "What's wrong with him?"

Glover chose to ignore this. "Do you both know who *I* am?"

Silence. Finally the white boy shook his head, no.

"I'm Glover. Tom Glover."

The boys stared. They didn't know what to say.

"Who are *your* parents?" Glover said.

The white kid hesitated, so the black gave out both names. Glover didn't know the families. The white was a Bradley and the black a Johnson. Lord, Glover had worked so many Johnsons he didn't dare ask. It had been too long. He used to know forty families. And then he almost blushed in the dark when he remembered this "Lucky" was imported anyway. None of *his* ancestors ever worked this neck of the woods. His daddy was over at the university.

Suddenly Glover felt his old bones starting to poke through the bottom of his chair. "That's all I wanted," he said. But his dismissal was too abrupt for young boys. He saw they were doubtful now that this had been a serious meeting. Maybe it was the old man who was crazy.

"You can think it over, if you want to," he said. He knew his next move only by a hair. "You go home and talk it over with your parents. In fact, I'd be glad to explain the proposition to them. That might make everybody more comfortable."

This proved the more effective tactic.

"My parents won't mind," the white kid said. The black kid just stared at Glover, and then he actually smiled. "It's okay. We can do it for you." Glover hadn't seen teeth like that since he retired.

"Fine. Then I'll see you back here in a few days when you notice Mr. Barnes in the yard. Probably Monday or Tuesday. He won't know I'm paying you. We don't want to insult the man." Glover looked the boy Johnson straight in the eye. "There's nothing much wrong with Mr. Barnes. But he can't remember his own wife. Doesn't quite know who I am, or you either. He has to fake everything. You boys just act friendly and give him a chance to fake it. He'll pretend he knows you if you're friendly. Allow him his dignity and you've got the job."

The black kid folded his arms and gave the same kind of good look he was being given.

"He doesn't want people alarmed," Glover continued. "That's why I admire him. He doesn't want people worried about him."

He feared he may have blown the deal now, however, because he was suddenly choked up. He was sure they'd heard his voice crack, and darkness was all that saved him. He'd have to push on through it unless he wanted these two boys standing here waiting to see if he'd collapse.

"I admire any man who doesn't have anything left but just how fine a person he is." Steel came back into his heart.

Nobody moved.

Glover looked out over the lake, where a pale disk had come up lopsided. "A full moon missed Halloween by just a few days this year," he said. "You're going to get you a full moon on Tuesday."

They finally took this opportunity to give each other looks.

"Okay. See you boys next week."

Dismissed properly, they sprang into motion and took the steep stairs in a single leap. One of them was able to call out "So long" before they joined their tribe, where, Glover could only guess, there was probably no talking. The clump moved as one glowing group of shirts, first out of his yard and then several dozen feet still in view. Soon the whole bunch was swallowed up in the little road, which made a sharp bend at that eastern point. Glover watched one last boy go out like a firefly.

Profound silence returned and sat with the old man like a hugely enveloping ghost sits on one's lap. Glover felt himself wanting to talk to it. So. That was interesting, he thought. Divide and conquer. That's just about what that was.

But he found he had nothing more to consider on the matter. His move had been only instinctive perhaps. But now he had two boys working for him. They'd take better care of Paul than they would one of their own sisters.

In the middle of the night he woke up and the whole thing struck him funny when he thought how out of step he was for the times, how he'd half expected that Lucky boy to be naturally low on the totem pole, when, in fact, the opposite was true. It was the white boys now, the redheads, who had to jockey for position when the blacks were on the same social standing; this one's educated parents owned a quarter-million-dollar home on this lake. Glover wondered for a moment if, consequently, stakes were no longer very high. In his day, a man's dog didn't whine at the smell of candy; she whined at the smell of sex and blood and sweat.

It was two years before they found out that Lucky was all right, that he hadn't gone very far. Virgil Glover came home one day and announced with some irritation that he was living right in town. In the back of Riley Hanson's livery in town.

Alma was impatient. She wanted to know what *else* about him? She wanted a full report on the boy. Virgil said for one thing he looked a whole lot older than he really was. He said it was amazing how in no time old man Hanson's livery had needed a boy like that. Overnight Riley Hanson had become a cautious braggart. It was Lucky's blind skills that had loosened the old man's tongue: apparently the boy could put hands under a raised hood with startling know-how. He was like Doctor Cooper poking a sore appendix. He could fix any situation, Hanson said, if one could get him the right tools. And Hanson couldn't hold back his praise for Mr. Ford's outfit shipping down tools by the box load. Rural free delivery. Lucky just named what he wanted and Mr. Ford sent it right on down.

"I didn't recognize him," Virgil told Alma.

"Well, what did he look like if you didn't recognize him?"

"Straight up and down. A beanpole. I asked him what he was doing with himself. He hardly answered me."

"Well, they get shy," Alma said.

"Some get mean."

"You don't know that he will."

"No, I don't, and I'm not going to ever know a thing more about that boy if I can help it."

Tom Glover wouldn't achieve any height to speak of until he was seventeen; his boyish nose didn't seem to stop running until he was eighteen. He knew he was still all wet, and he didn't particularly want to see Lucky Apple under unequal circumstances. And so he had to stay clear of the livery, which was a hardship because one couldn't be incurious about the new cars. In a year's time old man Hanson had jumped from servicing one Model T to servicing a half dozen. It was the main show over at the livery — all those new motors breaking down and a few people in real debt. Mr. Hanson was a religious man and not been known to talk much before the car business dazzled him. There was only one way for Glover to explain to his own conscience his wanting to stay away. Here he was dreading a Negro.

One day rumor went around town of oral surgery. Glover and Virgil were in the dry goods store when someone yelled that everybody had better shake a leg if he wanted to see old man Hanson pull a tooth. Riley-boy had himself a customer and somebody better stop by a wagon and pick up some whiskey. The whole thing was going to be over pretty quick unless everybody shook a leg.

"You go on, I'll catch up with you," Virgil had said. They'd already loaded the wagon. Virgil said he'd spend the time getting a haircut. Then he changed his mind. There wasn't going to be anybody at the barbershop. Everybody was going to be over at the tooth-pulling. So the two had started out together, and when they got in the street it had looked like a parade — grown men and boys hurrying in case there was still some standing room. Once upon a time it had been a common event to see Hanson break a jaw, but lately there had rarely been anyone innocent enough to get himself in the old man's clutches. Tom Glover had run down the street toward the livery just like a boy and run right in the path of that Negro he'd been dreading, who even grabbed his arm and leaned into his ear and spoke casually, as if they'd seen each other the previous day.

"Have you come to see the suffering, Mr. Tom?" His "Mr. Tom" was entirely the wrong tone.

Glover couldn't take in the metamorphosis at first — Lucky as tall as verbena bending over him. The voice and the stance had changed, and there was hardly any of the original boyish stamp in his face. Lucky looked grown.

"You better come with me if you want to see anything. Forty men back there already."

The boy was a much more serious thing than Glover had feared in his absence — too friendly, too curious, but not over-weening enough, so that Glover had known what he'd been avoiding. From the picnic until now, Lucky was always and forever going to use the wrong tone with him. He hadn't gotten over that dog, wasn't planning on getting over it.

But in a moment or two he released Glover and shoved his two hands inside his armpits. The gesture made him look cold on a cold afternoon. Lucky should have had on a coat of some kind so he wouldn't look so gaunt and Glover maybe wouldn't have remembered the metallic blood-smell of the dog they'd buried and then remembered his own fear and Lucky's sobbing.

"Come on," he had said then. And he'd turned, motioning Glover to follow him around the back of the livery. The worst part of seeing him was over. There wasn't much else to do. And he was only Lucky. That was all he was.

At the back of the old wooden building, Glover scrambled up

a ladder that led to the quietly pitched roof of Hanson's, and from up there they could see, from one end of the street to the other, Point Breeze's low businesses and the one tiny bank. The wind was bitter, but when they lay down Glover felt the warmth of the sun. Sun had soaked all morning into the flat new tin and it gave back heat as they lay prone and hung their heads over an opening. The raised square in the roof exposed a small hayloft and, below that, old man Hanson's tooth parlor.

"You're staying here now," Glover said.

Once prone, it was easier somehow to speak. They stared down into the heat of those men below. Most had their hats on and Glover watched an assortment of plaid and wool shoulders milling around as the men grouped and regrouped. Their noise made it all the warmer. Lucky, too, stared down into the opening. He permitted Glover to examine his strong profile and very arched brow, to see that the fat in his cheeks had melted. He had big ears. The inevitable. Alma wouldn't find him so lovable now.

More horse and whiskey warmth came right up through the opening. Below, the whole town of Saturday farmers had crowded into a small back room. Glover couldn't see his father anywhere. Virgil would be inside the livery, talking to someone like himself, a sober, proud type dating back to the Freeze. Men like Virgil found each other out and chaperoned all of the town's raucous and religious occasions. They stood with feet on the running boards of the new cars and talked to each other about the war while yokels played in the back rooms, boys in a poker game. You weren't supposed to gamble, but if there were no women and if Virgil Glover was in the next room you could do it with his blessing. And those few other superior men like Virgil were the ones who, unbeknownst to themselves, raised sons for the Depression thirteen years later — sons who would either quietly kill themselves or bury those who killed themselves with a certain smugness practiced by stoic Yanks after that famous three-million-dollar Freeze.

The back room boys were betting on Hanson's time. A bot-

tle went around the circle fast because the idea was to drink
what little painkiller they might have managed to find in someone's wagon. More sporting of the patient if he didn't drink, if
he had a clear head with which to experience the finesse of Hanson's right arm. Hanson was good. What caused excitement
were the variables: size and condition of tooth; age and strength
of the victim. Coming up through that roof opening, hitting
Glover in the face, was the loud din and vibration of men at a
cattle auction. He felt free to complain to Lucky: "I can't see who
it is."

Lucky got his head inside the opening. It was somebody
young, he said. Odds were high on Hanson's time running to be
as much as two to three minutes. The betting crowd had to factor
in how much Hanson had gone downhill that month. He'd had
a bad chest cold. He was still in plaster.

"Who is it?"

"Don't know him."

"This isn't any good, Lucky. I can't see."

"I'm going to get you closer. Mind your coat."

Lucky curled headfirst through that roof opening and then let
himself drop without injury into the hayloft. When he was on his
feet, he stood under Glover and told him to lower down the
other way, legs first, so he could let him touch his shoulders and
then jump.

The hay smelled perfectly sweet this cold time of year. Glover's eyes adjusted to the dark and he saw how this must be
Lucky's hideaway. He had an old wicker chair up there and some
orange crates turned on end. "You smoke up here, Lucky?
You're going to burn the place down."

Lucky smiled. He was not unfriendly; but he was not quite
right either. "I keep an eye out on that."

Old man Hanson's victim was a traveling salesman but no
charmer like that Huey Long. He was some new dewdrop who
had shown up to make his round in the county and had stopped
to rent a mule and had complained of his jaw, which he'd have
been better off not doing. Hanson could make an upstart drum-

mer feel ungrateful if he tried to walk away from a kindness. By now the man was surrounded, and his protestations happily ignored. There was a look of panic in his light-colored eyes. It had just dawned on him that he was in the hands of a mob. Soon the regulars had him caught inside two croaker sacks pulled down over his torso. It made a snug fit. Someone called out this would keep his suit clean, and the drummer saw now that he was a fool. That was when one of the boys gave him a drink out of the bottle. The drummer's head shot back and then forward as the whiskey went down, and then everyone watched the man have to shake himself hard like a dog inside a coatful of water. Everyone applauded him. He, too, attempted to laugh. He was back to not wanting to be unsporting. These were the husbands of his lady customers. Later he didn't want to meet with women who'd heard that it had gone bad with him in town over a tooth.

"Want to place a bet, Mr. Tom?"

Glover looked up at the sound of that mellow voice. Damned if Lucky didn't have money again today and here was Glover still without a nickel.

Then their eyes met and it was not about money. If those wide-spaced eyes had talked aloud, they'd have said Lucky wasn't ever going to be interested in getting along further than he was right now. He was jammed up against something; there was something stuck in his craw.

It was bad to see him that way, angry and shivering a little like a dope fiend. Glover had to act like he didn't notice. A Negro who worked for whites with this look got fired or run off pretty quick.

And the thing was, Lucky had never once been whipped by Virgil's belt. Not once in seven years under their care. Alma said no, she wasn't going to have that with this boy. Virgil had said, okay, but to look out. It would spoil him.

"You got money to bet me?" Glover said. "I don't have a dime."

"Bet me that hat," Lucky said.

It was a knit hat. Alma gave them out to all the kids, to Lucky too, though he wasn't wearing one.

"This hat?"

"My half dollar. Mr. Riley can't get that tooth out of there under five minutes."

"Five minutes! Boy, he never took five minutes."

Lucky may have made note of the easy tone in Glover now. He'd gotten him to this place in almost no time. "I'm saying five minutes," Lucky said.

"You're crazy."

"Uh-huh. Bet me."

"What would you want with this hat for, anyway?"

"Remind me of you," Lucky said. His little smile was audacious but not yet mean because too quickly he changed emphasis. "Remind me of Miss Alma." And that was when Glover should have known to keep clear of him. His original instinct. Lucky was fishing shamelessly. "She doesn't talk about me anymore, does she?" Lucky said. Glover felt embarrassed for him. Alma. It was easier for him to think of Alma than of anyone else. He had thought the woman was going to stand up for him somehow. Even when she hadn't, the boy somehow retained the hope that in different circumstances, in being given another chance, she would.

Glover shrugged. "She'd talk about you if she had something to talk about. She treated you better than me. What'd you go run off for?"

"Don't know. Felt like it, that's all."

Lucky put the money under his nose next. Two bits and two bits. All for a worn-out hat, which Glover took off his head. They put the quarters inside the hat and then Glover lay on top of it to keep it safe during the surgery. He counted himself fifty cents rich right away. It was that old mad dog quarter. With interest added. Riley Hanson wasn't going to take more than three and a half minutes, which was his absolute outside time on his worst day.

It was touchy politics with all catalogue drummers for a few years around that time. Store men said the mail ordering business was driving them to ruin. What no one knew on that particular Saturday was that Montgomery Ward was going to put store owners *and* these skinny drummers out on their ear when the ladies caught on to ordering by mail and didn't need a soul to explain it to them. Still, Hanson might take a little revenge on a drummer wrapped in two croaker sacks who looked like the type who might flirt with the ladies. Maybe that particular day everybody in the room foresaw this fellow was almost defunct. On some occasions men smell blood more easily than on others.

Everybody in the parlor pitched in to get things set up — turning up the gaslights as much as possible and elevating the chair on top of a little wooden platform. Mr. Hanson liked to stand on the platform to keep his feet off damp ground. And he liked to do clean work; he had his standards. He had a supply of white rags, which he tied around his head to keep his hair back and to keep the sweat fully absorbed. Even on a cold day, the old man could break into a sweat if he got beyond a full minute. Usually he was successful in very little time; naturally it had been those rare longer pullings that kept the crowds up and the bets high. But only a purely wild man went out on a limb of four or five minutes.

Glover had realized in his boy's way that Lucky wanted to lose. Lucky had wanted to gain his attention in some way. Glover hadn't liked feeling the old hat bunched like hard bread dough under his chest as he looked down to see the men getting set up. He wanted to take back the bet just to keep from getting entangled. Overnight Lucky had become an oddball Negro. Glover would be sorry to be involved with one like that. His father was right to say two years ago that they were well rid of someone spoiled. Alma had wept and not forgiven herself, which, after a time, her husband took as a wildly cast aspersion upon himself.

By now they had the chair in place. It was a beaten-up choir chair, and Glover saw the silent drummer lose all color as he was shoved down in it and then had his feet tied. "Don't you fret none! We're going to keep you from falling out. Where's Riley?

Somebody go tell that son of a gun we're all set up here and the patient's raring to go. Where'd he get to?"

"Shut up, I'm right here. You boys get out of my light, and I want y'all to pipe down before I throw out each and every one of you on your head."

Mr. Hanson was modest about his skills. He never claimed there was anything more to what he did than to get a good hold the first time in. It was all in the grip and in not letting go that first time no matter how bad he found the situation.

Riley Hanson was a religious man with not only his own livery, but his own church. He told others that he hadn't found a preacher who was right-minded enough for him until he'd left the Methodists. If you close one door another opens. He'd found the man he was looking for in less than a month. The church Hanson founded had a long name with Pentecostal wedged in it somewhere. According to rumor Mr. Hanson's group had not yet allowed women to join, although rumor also had it that this was a point of furious debate, and if Mr. Hanson was known to be a little bit crazy in the area of the Bible, his business reputation balanced him out. He was the kind of man on whom fanaticism wore better than on most people because he wasn't poor. And he brought good business to Point Breeze now with his car repair, and before that he did all right with horses and mule teams for the rich before the Freeze — all those hayrides and weddings and funerals. Now cars had given him a new lease on life. The tool he held in his hand at the moment was a pair of Ford pliers, right out of the box, never used.

"Was anybody good enough to give this man a drink?"

"Oh, he's ready, Riley. He's not going to feel a thing."

"Son, which tooth is it?"

Somehow this made the crowd laugh. The drummer moved around with those wild eyes of his, and when Glover looked at Lucky he could see Lucky's mind was somewhere else. It wasn't on the fun. The boy looked like he was dreaming. "You're going to lose, Lucky," Glover had whispered. "Riley's going to have that tooth out in fifteen seconds."

Lucky didn't answer. He was dreaming; maybe it was the way he would dream for the rest of his short life. Glover should have guessed right then he wouldn't make it.

The stranger was asked to open wide. The whole crowd repeated, "Open wide." And that made Hanson throw a mean look. He could have been a preacher himself. Everything went dead quiet.

The designated timekeeper was a man named Honeywell, who held a large pocket watch and sat perched on someone's shoulders; or else two men were providing him a shoulder each. Except for Glover and Lucky, Honeywell had the best seat in the house. He had to know when the pliers clamped down, so he could start the count. His business lay between his big gold watch and Hanson's right arm.

Hanson took a moment to investigate the mouth. Nobody dared to cough or take another swig. "Get that light in here," Hanson said, and the light monitor did his best, made men on all sides take off their hats. And those betting on a low time saw immediately that they'd lost. From the way Hanson set his elbows it looked as if it might be a wisdom tooth coming in. Hanson appeared to go in deep once he went in for good and established the grip. When he'd established the grip, Mr. Hanson said what he always said: "Okay, boys, I got it now." Which clearly meant one thing: the war was on.

You could yell once he had his grip in. Mr. Hanson encouraged it by acting as if he were riding a skittish bay mare. "Easy now, son. I got you! Easy now." The drummer tried to look straight up to heaven and not think of pain. "Hold him, Charlie," Hanson said, his voice never rising, as the patient began to buck. "Hold him."

"He's starting to faint," somebody called.

"Okay," Hanson said. "Tip him back, now, tip him back." Hanson saw for himself that he was losing the guy. "Tip him!"

A good look at the bottom end of a drummer tended to lower crowd sympathy. It was the worn soles and his cuffs, his bright argyle socks. Those boys betting on a high time began to grow ecstatic as the chair tipped back and then came forward. The drummer had come to consciousness just fine, but Mr. Hanson hadn't gotten his tooth. It was then that Hanson knew to bear down. In a moment of quiet they could hear the unimaginable root start to move a little inside red bone.

There was pandemonium then. Men started doubling their money. In the middle of the third minute, men were certain that Hanson wasn't going to have success before four. He had one knee in the drummer's lap. "Do we tip him back again, doc? He's going out."

"No, let him go," Hanson said, "it's a mercy." The sweat was pouring off old Riley-boy, and someone took one of his clean rags and mopped him. "I don't know what I got here, boys. I think it's a whale."

Bets doubled again. A new bottle floated and bobbed on the surface of the sea. There was every expression, from concern to awe to outrage. The drummer suddenly came awake for a moment, and they all heard a piteous sound in his throat and then a cry for help. "It's almost over, son," Hanson said.

Lucky had rolled on his back while he waited. The boy sucked on a straw and dreamed. And when the tooth came out and the din in the parlor grew to a deafening roar, Lucky motioned Glover to follow him to a jump-down so they could scoot under legs and be out in daylight before anyone else. Four minutes and two seconds. Hanson's worst time ever, and a bad day for him. And looking back it must have been one of his last pulls, Glover thought. He was sure that by the next summer or two, the old man was dead. His son, Junior Hanson, never did fill his father's shoes.

Outside Glover took the fifty cents he'd won but gave Lucky the hat. A fair trade, a peace offering. "You take it. I don't want it."

"Okay, I will."

On his head the knit hat made Lucky taller and his jaw firmer. Glover could still remember, at ninety-one, how a hat tended to push his own squat frame into the ground at that age. It had taken him forever to reach six feet. He managed it through sheer prayer.

"Can you fix a car? We heard you were learning."

Lucky shrugged as Glover knew himself to do; but it was a mockery of shrugging. One knew Lucky felt the opposite of doubt. He'd gotten himself a boyish shrug to work with and he'd gotten it down just about convincingly, but not quite. That would be his downfall. Now that he had the hat on his head, Glover understood his father placing all the blame on Alma. "It was your own damn fault," he'd said.

"She miss me?" Lucky said.

"Why don't you ask her? What are you afraid of? You didn't have to run off."

The boy never answered your questions now. That was certainly one of his new tricks.

"How's her health?"

Glover had felt the forlornness and the freedom of these studied methods. It had made him feel a wave of jealousy, and then he was mad when he saw that Lucky had guided him into the open, where Virgil would be sure to see for himself the look of a short squat Glover shielding the sun out of his eyes as he gazed up at Lucky, now wearing Glover's own hat and waiting to see the old family wagon out of his peripheral vision before he said good-bye. Glover heard his father call his name and about jumped out of his skin. He was given the silent treatment during the wagon ride home. Virgil didn't have to say anything except for one or two sentences.

"I see you finally ran into Lucky. I see you lost your hat."

After that they'd all seen Lucky better than half alive at least once more. He had a turkey he'd killed and for some reason that gave him the courage to come see Alma, whom he felt to be the only one in the family to care what in the world happened to him. The turkey was for her. A kindness heaped up on her head like burning coals. But maybe the meat would stick in everyone's throat for a few minutes at the table. That's what they all dreaded from the boy.

Glover had come home from school and seen the two of them way off in the grove having a private conference, Lucky towering over Alma, but with his shoulders rounded and his head down while she talked. It appeared she was talking him blue in the face, but Glover had felt a kind of shame about everything. This made him wary as he went on about his chores and tried not to let Lucky see him. Lucky would have eyes in the back of his head. Always had. Always knew what Glover was up to from the time they were little and were the same half size and shared the same endless hot days and singing blue nights. A plunk out in the lake, everything good within a simple cast from this house. Pull a fish out of the water and watch the two sets of hands pounce upon its life. And the lightning speed. Hands made up their own minds — which to hold the fish down, which to get the hook out, which to decide a small trout's fate: eat or throw back? The thing was all done between boys who knew the next full event awaiting them. When they tired of the lake, there were Alma's one hundred yard birds and a hawk darting down on baby chicks. The old mother hen would squawk and raise cain, and Alma would clap her hands and flop out her apron and yell her head off. Glover and Lucky would come running next, still wet from the lake, wet from a dunking, from a rainstorm, from sweat, from innocent nonsense.

Alma talked a great deal over that meal of roast turkey. She said she didn't like Lucky's bony thinness. "He said he's getting paid up at the livery and he knows all about cars. I don't know what's wrong with him. He's lost his spirit. It's going right out of him."

Virgil bit into turkey breast and held it up. "He's white meat. What boy ever come here and give you a turkey?"

"*Gave* me a turkey," Alma said.

She looked at Glover, who had looked away. She was far too late if she had wanted to save anybody. Glover could start to fume whenever he thought how she'd done damn-all that day Virgil ordered Lucky under the house. She'd stood up there on the porch with the other ladies and watched.

"He's lonely," she said aloud.

"Well, hell with him," Virgil said. "He could be out picking stump."

"I guess that's true."

"I don't understand a gloomy colored," Virgil said. "And God help one starting out with a wet nurse like you."

Two summers after Hanson's tooth-pulling both Lucky and Glover turned eighteen but missed conscription. Then the war heroes came back home and bumped Lucky out of his place at the livery. Glover was old enough to get his own news by then. He was long planting celery with Virgil. He was married already, and Jemmalee about to have a baby. He'd gotten her pregnant and had had Alma's own shotgun to his head. A good marriage. It was hard to remember those circumstances now. Only Lucky's fate had stayed vivid. Word was that old man Hanson's son, Junior Hanson, up and fired him without much of a fuss. Certain men told Junior Hanson, during a crap game in which Junior was royally fleeced, that his boy Lucky was fixing cars down in niggertown using tools out of Junior's shop.

Junior sure must have hated hearing this. The boys all knew Junior never liked the whole town knowing how Riley had been so sold on Lucky. It embarrassed him. Junior Hanson was famous for not knowing a tailpipe from a stovepipe.

He fired Lucky on a Monday without letting him walk back on the premises. But everyone knew there was not a more stupid man than Junior. He had the brains of a thimble. And soon it was obvious that none of the returning Point Breeze veterans had any machinist work behind them. Junior was out on a limb. He'd been lied to. Pretty soon Lucky's replacement started bungling jobs. A battery blew up and hurt someone's child. Local car owners quietly decamped to Sanford for better service. In a very short time Junior Hanson was an open drunk instead of a private one, and then it seemed hardly any time had passed before everyone laughed at him whenever he said he lost his car business because a nigger had stolen all his tools.

Nobody who ever knew Lucky believed he stole. Not even

Virgil Glover. But there were people who didn't wish that boy a better reputation than he ended up with. A truck would throw a rod, and he'd acted arrogant. He'd never answered men's questions. His attitude had been that he could fix the problem and they sure as hell couldn't. Glover took it upon himself to report such facts to Alma. She didn't have anything to berate herself for, Glover told her. Lucky was surly.

Of course Alma didn't like surly behavior in anyone; most people didn't. But Alma visited Lucky at his shed in the all-black part of town they called the Hollow. It was only across the highway behind Mirror Lake. Alma walked over there to visit from almost the moment she heard Lucky had left Hanson's livery. In the early days Alma had done so much nursing of the coloreds down in the Hollow that she didn't think of it being 1919. She was thrown back to the fresh poverty after the Freeze days. Everyone knew Alma as a nurse who would come in the middle of the night if she were needed. Not a locked door back then. A colored girl might cross the highway in her bare feet and creep right up the stairs to wake Alma up without bothering the whole family by pounding.

But in 1919 she'd pick a sunny day to go over there to see Lucky just to get her youth back. Enough older black women knew exactly who she was and they would all come out to say hey. Virgil confided in Glover about it not two months after Glover married Jemmalee. Virgil told him how relieved he was that Jemmalee was pregnant enough to distract Alma.

"Otherwise she's going to start getting female religion in her old age." Virgil stabbed at the ground. He was still the Sunday school superintendent, but one knew what he meant — a woman's fear of sins she'd never committed.

"Well," Glover had said, "I wouldn't worry." He took his mother's part whenever Virgil fumed behind her back. Left alone with his mother, he often became Virgil and scolded her.

It must have been for the company, the contact, the occasional piece of clothing she made for Lucky. She kept him in those knitted hats and ordered him at least two Montgomery Ward shirts Glover found out about — one a flannel and one a dress. Jemmalee began to tell on her, but not in a malicious way; the two women were confidants, but then so were Jemmalee and Glover at the time. One time Alma ordered Lucky a pair of fine shoes. It was the generosity of those shoes that almost broke Lucky down. Glover found this out only fifteen months later when the boy had himself delivered to the house in the back of a truck like that rare stalk of bananas. But the poor fellow was scorched to the bone by that time and only breathing through a little hole in his throat.

3

BOYS, LIKE TROUBLE, come in threes.

Tom Glover didn't remember this until after lunch the next day, until after he'd spent a second morning of his vacation feeling better than he could say, as if the small arrow of life's involvements had shot out over the house and would fly a long, long way in the high trajectory of his old strength. He was alone with plans.

That morning he stretched his back and sipped black coffee and enjoyed the sudden, urgent peristalsis of a much younger man. It hardly mattered that it took him the entire morning to get to the workroom behind the house in order to put together a light rod and reel for Paul from what was left of his old stock. It was enough to be busy. Too busy, in fact, to take the pumpkin off the porch, which was what he was musing on as he stood out near the road after lunch waiting for the mail and looked up to see Lois and Paul creeping toward him on his narrow ribbon of road.

Glover watched as the blue car made its practiced turn into the drive. His morning's trajectory did a whining rocket nosedive into Mirror Lake. Not only were they back, but there, riding in the catbird seat, was his great-grandson, Petey, who held his pink face to the window and blinked. No mistake about it. It was the boy, all right. His head bobbed like some leftover party balloon Lois had tied to the door handle.

From inside Lois's quiet ride, the child gazed at the edges of the small lake, where he played whenever he visited. His eyes went wide when he saw the figure of Glover standing by the mailbox, his two stick legs behind, his two stick arms and canes in front. Glover was the Spider, whom Petey had almost forgotten until that hair-trigger second when he exchanged a look of deep regret with the old man and then fell with a loud crash to the floor of his grandmother's car.

"Are you hurt?" Lois whirled around to look for him and heard Petey's robot's "no" of last night's affair, before which there had been tears of anguish at his not having his costume turn out the way he'd planned. Right now his "no" rose up in an abysmally droning, colorless tone. This was Petey's imitation of RoboCop, with whom Lois was only recently made familiar. She had taken the new hero on faith and resigned herself to having brought both Petey and his mechanical friend home for the weekend.

GLOVER'S GRIM thought was that his great-grandson wouldn't know enough to stay out of the way of those boys. He'd be down there in the lake at the first opportunity, too young and wide-eyed to be welcome, and that would confuse matters unless Glover found a way to assure everyone that Petey wasn't part of the babysitting job. They could order him out of that hole if they saw him down there. Hell, they could drown him!

He didn't want to have to explain it to Lois, and then have *her* explain it to the boy. He didn't want them knowing his business, now or later. The idea of everyone's knowing his business annoyed Glover far worse than the fact they were home. His mind grew dark in hearing the ring in that old and bitter truth: it is not in large but small ways that people betray us.

Then he thought, It's only that I have no privacy.

Inside the house she didn't take him aside to explain or shout at him in those paragraphs full of static. The girl was so exhausted she wrote out a note while Petey stood at her elbow reading what was meant for the old man: "BEING AWAY TOO CONFUSING FOR PAUL."

Glover read and felt pity for himself, his own flag lowered so soon. As he stared at the telegraphic words, her new bold headlines, somehow everything registered as a little heartless. And so it was almost impossible to say to her what was expected, although he finally managed it.

"I'm sorry," he finally said.

They should have known Paul would enjoy the drive over and back, but that his staying in a strange house would be too abstract. And there was the added chagrin of Glover's having fought hard for the plan. He'd pushed her into it, and now that error in judgment made him mean.

"I got my own food cooking in my room this afternoon. Don't fix me any supper!"

Now instead of fewer relatives in the house, there were more. Nothing crowds out thoughts as much as people do. People distract an active mind the way television does with its laughter, with its loud bursts of families carrying on lively conversation. Glover looked around him and prepared to return to his room at the front of the house until his eye landed on the boy's T-shirt, where a turtle stood on hind legs and brandished a sword.

"When's your mother coming to get you?" It was the best way to nip this in the bud.

The minute he'd asked, Glover realized the child was in the fourth grade, that he would be gathered up on Sunday, that right now he was missing a whole day of school. "When's she going to get you a decent haircut?"

Petey looked away and dropped into one of the dining chairs at Lois's enormous table. Her new sitting room doubled for all their meals together now. The boy knew his grandmother's rooms had become the center of the household activity no matter how much stock the old man set by his own private front quarters. The old stare-down between them was over, but it had felt awfully good to Glover. Like looking down a barrel at the fairground and watching the boy fall behind a row of ducks. Ping. And there were the fortune-teller booths, as well, in which a mannequin in a purple turban would move his hand over a glass globe and close his almond-color eyes: *You will lead men in battle.*

In the next moment Glover heard Lois shout at him about a topic he least expected to hear from her, although it was the only thing on his mind.

"Fishing, Dad!"

Glover could not hear the whole sentence. He slammed one callused finger into his right ear. He searched for the little volume wheel. "What? What about it?"

"I told Petey he might be able to go fishing with those boys while he's here."

"Those boys? I don't want him down there with those boys!"

The statement sobered Lois right away, but today she looked more irritated than hurt. This was good, Glover thought, already an improvement since the last time they got mad at each other.

And in Petey's pale face there sat an expression of someone who hadn't forgotten the old man's efforts to thwart him in the past. The two had started their relationship years ago in moments when the one would come upon the other climbed on a kitchen counter or buried inside a cupboard with his hand already in the cookie jar, his finger in someone else's pie. Glover had taken many opportunities to let the boy know his goose was cooked, his jig was up, his fat was in the fire. He'd always stood just around the next dark corner in a groaning suit of armor, the cigar store Indian at the top of the stairs, until about the time he got too old to do stairs. That's when Petey learned to escape to the upper bedrooms all day long, and from then on, with that endless creeping above all their heads, Glover couldn't forgive the boy his clever way of managing it. Inside his room, with the door closed tight, Glover sat down and rested and thought how if he had really felt younger today instead of just flummoxed, he might attempt a treaty, an effort at public relations. But not today, he thought. He sighed aloud and rested his head, which was already spinning. Not this weekend.

A man knows he's old when one tiny kink in his plan makes him have to sit down.

PETEY HIMSELF was not for peace. This weekend he was deep into a cyborg he'd named Robo Two-Zon-Flexon, and, as he entered a room upstairs, where he always slept whenever he visited, he sat in position to receive his assignment from headquarters. His job was to debug and secure the house before carrying out surveillance and information retrievals of the highest order. As Lois unpacked the car and sent Paul upstairs with his suitcase, Petey checked under all the beds in the four bedrooms. He crawled around the imaginary land mines he'd set last time. His movements came within inches of blowing them all to kingdom come.

They called him PETE at headquarters. He was a Preferred Exponential and Temporary Extender. That was what a Two-Zon-Flexon could do. And his grandfather, Paul, was a One-Zon-Flexon containing PAUL-programming: PAUL was short for Parallel and Autonomous Units of L-700.

In Petey's new game his grandfather was the first model of his type, and when he came upon Petey in the hall and smiled and introduced himself, Petey introduced himself right back. PETE was PAUL's underling; he ought to have saluted with his secret sign of brotherhood. But Lois was right behind, explaining where to put the suitcases.

"Here in your room, Paul."

Paul looked at her in surprise. For security reasons the PAUL model was programmed to act a little nuts at designated times. "Paul Barnes," he said when he came upon the boy moments later in his closet. "It's nice to see you."

One-Zon-Flexon was an early nineties breakthrough. His outer housing alone presented astonishing simulacrum in the relaxed pose of the back and shoulders, the realistic voicings. Both PETE and PAUL models had Flexon skin — true follicles and hair types that came in four varieties for head, face, arms, and legs. But PAUL was not just some garden variety like PETE was. PAUL was *the* security probe in the "Black Widower" purge, after which some of his operational files came up missing. Or else it was only that Parallel and Autonomous Units of L-700 meant difficult retrievals after any good mission, and that ghost files and possible shadow files would only *appear* to have crashed. PETE was supposed to access him, if and when he could.

"It's good to have Petey home with us for a few days, isn't it?" Lois moved in and out of Paul's room as she oversaw some of the unpacking and then disappeared to her own room.

"Where do you keep your socks, Pops?" Petey said.

Paul looked around. He sat on the edge of his bed.

"How 'bout in this top drawer? Hey, look, you got a ton of socks in here."

Paul said it was the most socks he'd ever seen in his life.

PETE's job was to attempt a friendly interface with his prototype. PAUL's craziness was only a fail-safe device to prevent sabotage. However, after his last difficult government mission, his autonomous loop schedule had continued on line much longer than was thought normal. Most agents at headquarters still believed he would be fully operable once his *parallel* systems booted up and stopped the repetition. Grimmer agents were saying it was a case of an entirely lost hard disk. A permanent virus in the system. How nuts could PAUL behave and for how long before he would have to be taken out of the field?

"Let's hang up your shirts and trousers, Pops. Looks like you have a lot of shirts, too."

But in PETE's regular helpful mode, there always lurked the beginnings of Petey's wishing he'd stayed in Daytona. His game did not do much for him once he stood looking into this closet thinking of the times he'd hidden all over this house when he was little and had been found; all the times Paul had pretended he couldn't find him. And now he'd not be pretending. Too old to want to hide at all anymore, Petey still knew that if he closed himself up in here as an experiment his own grandfather wouldn't hold on to the thought of him very long.

Paul came up behind him and gazed over his head and into the closet full of clothes. "Where did I get all those?" Paul said.

The very sound of his voice going bad made Petey wish he were back home. Who was he kidding, his grandfather had a disease. Florida was the Alzheimer's capital of the whole stupid world.

Then Paul said, "Are you crying? Don't cry."

"I've stopped," Petey said. He laughed and cried at the same time and threw his arms around the man he had loved. Bad luck. He felt he probably had the worst luck of anyone he knew. Lately if you hugged Paul like this, you had to say, "Hug me back!" Carol did it to Paul all the time, trying to make herself laugh. Paul was always glad to oblige by hugging back, but not until you asked him.

And yet, what if one day the fail-safe suddenly gave over a crude template of his files and made possible a very small retrieval program well within PETE's ram? That was the whole stupid game. In Petey's head they were each Robo One and Robo Two, the both of them human beings fatally injured in the line of duty long ago and then put back together in cyberspace and cybertime. Petey's favorite part of the game was visiting the one room upstairs which held their past domestic lives, their loving wives and families, the part he'd stolen from the movie. That one room in the house he loved the most. Lois's room. Petey always entered it reverently, slowly, where he'd pretend to find his people grieving for him, not able to see him anymore because his own memory of them was practically lost in the RoboCop's one remaining tiny segment of human brain. Even if his beloved wife could speak to RoboCop, she would no longer recognize the man in all that garb. His face had been restored behind the sleek metal visors, but no wife was able to look at the horribly exposed network of wires and coils. The whole back of his head looked like a piece of gut.

When she came upstairs for her nap later that afternoon, Lois caught Petey spinning himself around in the wheelchair she'd banned from use during his last visit. She thought he understood. He wouldn't mean to do it, but in time he was bound to chip her new moldings with the old foot props or with all the hardware on the sides of this outdated chair. She knew how much he enjoyed wheeling himself up and down the long central hall and into the various large rooms, but she didn't want him to do it.

"Honey, I'm not going to have you ruining my new moldings. Look. Look where you scraped right here."

As if Lois thought him an ordinary mortal, Petey was shown the expensive restorations in the rosette corners all through the upstairs. "Nothing, Petey, nothing is to touch these ever again. Do you understand? You may not use the wheelchair."

"Could I take it outside?"

He saw her think about this request. Petey closed his eyes and tolerated the soft stroke of her hand in his hair.

"Tell you what. Not just now. Paul won't know what to make of you down there playing with it in the drive. He's just got home. He barely knows where he is."

Petey knew she also didn't want to have to explain to the Spider why she'd agreed to let him have any fun. "It's not a toy," Lois thought to say, and Petey felt a little sorry for her. Last night she was so terrific helping him with his costume and being there when he won the contest and reading to him until all hours. Once she had laughed so hard she'd gotten iced tea up her nose. She had handled every single toy he wanted to tell her about, she had gotten down on her hands and knees.

Now she was home. The Spider was creeping around on six legs down there. No more jokes. How did she stand him? He had heard his own mother ask her this question.

But in a half hour Petey had mastered the wheelchair's smooth and noiseless reverse action. He confined practice to his room, the door tightly closed, and within twenty minutes he'd learned to turn in place and rocket-stop himself within a hairsbreadth of ruin. In one hour Lois got up from her nap and went back downstairs; he was free again to ruin her moldings, but he was sure he wouldn't now; he was very skilled. Along his practiced turboroute, the most dangerous passage was the three-foot gap in front of the open stairwell, where he could so easily be seen glinting by. Anyone looking up from below would see him. But what he loved most about this old house was its spacious privacy otherwise, its many upstairs rooms divided evenly along the wide hallway running the length of the house. All rooms fell east and west of dead center. All news traveled the length of the hallway and butted against doors kept closed to prevent drafts. And downstairs the layout was much the same. To keep from traipsing around, the habit of anyone living here was to find a cozy place and stay there until dinnertime. Upstairs alone, Petey could fling open everything and build an interstate highway.

Paul wandered around the house a lot these days. Sometimes he roamed around in the middle of the night; but day or night he was pleasantly surprised by what he saw even if it was his grandson seated in that odd chair. He seemed glad to find Petey rocketing around and killing his enemies. He merely asked the boy who he was.

"I'm Petey, Pops."

"It's good to see you. You're looking good."

"You too, Pops."

"I don't know why I came up here."

"Did you need something? Did you need something out of your room?"

"Which one is my room?"

He was secure. The files were secure at this level. Petey was now supposed to attempt gentle interface at the *next* level. He dreaded it but went ahead with a sigh.

"You remember when I used to hide in your closet and you'd come find me?"

"Oh sure."

"You do!"

"Oh sure."

THE GAP KIDS showed up at twilight in their core group of eight. Glover was pleased when the anointed babysitters, Bradley and Johnson, saw that the situation was already in place: Mr. Barnes out there with his hose, Mr. Barnes obviously home sooner than the old man expected. Their ability to think on their feet impressed the boss. He watched them first hesitate and then approach Paul in a slow, careful greeting, hardly acknowledging the old man as they made their awkward, friendly, four-legged way up to Paul to attempt an invitation. It was only now that Glover realized his little plan didn't have a chance of working unless these first minutes came off exactly right. If he had been thinking half straight he could have gotten Petey in on his plan. His great-grandson could have taken Paul by the hand and helped everyone get the hang of it. The old man strained to see how this first introduction came off. Paul looked surprised and a bit bemused, the reaction of any adult at a proposition from mere boys.

Above Glover's head Petey pushed out his grandmother's screen and eased out the window to a perch on the porch roof. Below he witnessed some of the most interesting activity he'd ever seen at his grandmother's, other than what he made up inside his own head. He was amazed and dumbfounded to see Paul put out his hand, which meant he was giving out his name to these two kids — one black and one white. Petey had never laid eyes on them, had never imagined Spider knowing kids like this.

"Catch me a mess of fish, Paul!" Spider called. "Go on down there with the boys and bring home some supper. I have your tackle right here."

From the porch roof, Petey intuited that Lois had come to the door, having heard the old man uncharacteristically raise his voice in a welcoming way. Petey could not see her, or any of them, but he began to overhear the most extraordinary conversation.

"Hello!" Lois said. To Petey's ear she had that pleasant timbre she used when she had no idea what was going on. With Spider's very weird cheerfulness a moment ago, and right now, anybody could tell the old man had set up something in advance. "You catch us a mess of fish, Paul." The old Spider kept saying this over and over. Petey had never heard him talk this way in his entire life.

Paul said he didn't have any bait.

"We're using worms, Mr. Barnes," the white kid said. "We've got a whole can down there."

"I have to change my shoes," he said. "I have to turn off this hose."

"We'll get the hose," the white kid said, already in a sprint to the side of the house. He looked up at Petey on the porch roof and saw that it was only a little kid. The older boy went blind in a complete lack of interest.

Glover would have given a whole lot if he'd thought to get Paul's work boots and have them ready. But Lois was on the scent now. Everyone saw her stepping back through the screen door to get some shoes, asking, "You want those old high-tops, Paul?" They heard her say, "This is very nice of you boys."

Up in his perch Petey flinched. Lois was mounting the stairs, but miraculously she stopped and called to him. "Petey!" She was stereophonic. Part of her voice came over the rooftop where he sat, the other part sailed from the hall after he got his head back inside the front bedroom window. "Petey, would you look in Pop's closet and bring me those shoes in the back wrapped up in newspaper. Could you get them for me?"

To the waiting assembly out on the porch it seemed as if Lois were back in seconds.

Where had she gotten those? Paul asked.

"Sit right there on the steps, Paul, and change out of what you have on," Glover said. "They'll be here when you get back from doing a little fishing."

"All right," Paul said, and left his companion to do the small talk he could no longer manage. All the stress of life was in the finer points of protocol he seemed to know he wasn't calling up, such as what came after the handshake.

"Have you boys been catching anything down there lately?" Glover said.

"A few bream," Bradley said.

"They like it when the weather turns cooler like this."

"Yessir, they do." Bradley appeared embarrassed by his own manner and looked to Johnson, who did not help him out. They saw Glover already had the fifty he'd promised them folded under the right palm holding his right cane. He couldn't now be seen by Lois, who had climbed down the stairs to give a hand with Paul's boots and was talking to Johnson, learning the boys' first names. Glover revealed the fifty to Bradley, who double-stepped past Paul, bending over one raised knee and tying those perfect bows he could still make.

Glover recognized the two kids in detail from last night, sober of expression, with fairly honest and reassuring, steady eyes. Johnson seemed the more self-assured by just a tiny bit. Right now he was looking straight at Paul, smiling, showing familiarity, which was somehow the trigger for Paul's good manners. It was correct to hire two instead of one, however. Glover did an automatic rundown of advantages despite the youth and inexperience of these boys: They'd have only to bait Paul's hook for him, maybe not even that; treat him kindly and apply their different styles. What one missed about this ailment, the other could deduce. It was wives who got upset. Wives took dementia so personally. For the middle of the middle stage, one needed only time and money, and a couple of boys like these.

He was pleased Lois didn't seem to get it, even as Johnson and Bradley led Paul away. ("Now what made those boys think of doing this? I'm amazed, aren't you?") Glover pretended he hadn't heard. Once headed for the lake Paul didn't even look back, and the old man saw a new benefit to his fishing idea. This would be a well-placed lesson to her in how to use her imagination a bit more. She had her nose too much in the literature.

"Strange!" Lois shouted. "Dad? Don't you think it's strange?"

Suddenly the old man could tell she knew exactly what was up. It was decent of her to pretend she didn't.

He nodded at the lake, where the color faded from pink to gray. A little cloud passed over, and then in a burst of the bright sunlight the afternoon's blue jumped like a big marlin out at sea. Petey saw it, too. Paul was slipping beyond the fallen bicycles and disappearing into that tomb of ears without looking back, leaving one little world and entering another. Glover felt a hard longing to get himself down there again. You could spend years on two canes and not get used to the idea that a small dip down to Mirror Lake would be your utter undoing. If Glover swam in that lake once with Lucky Apple, he swam there a thousand times. An old man, continuously in limbo now, his sins were being burned away in unexpected moments between a fancy haircut and an addled son-in-law and conscientious daughter. A man wanted to say, See Lucky? You won! You're back, and that's me you're leading by the hand to fish; and this is me up here at ninety-one, good for nothing else but to nod in and out a bit longer.

He felt as flammable as old newsprint. Put a strong light at his back and it would shine through his chest and out the front in a rosy tint, passing through thin blood and wafery bones. Fish bones. His mother, Alma, used to like to boil them up for broth. They knew her visits to see Lucky in the Hollow had stopped by the time Jemmalee was due to have that baby — Jemmalee, the big distraction Virgil Glover counted on to keep his wife in her own yard. You don't anticipate what hell can break loose even if you make everyone stay home. Given what Glover knew, he ought not to let Paul Barnes out of his sight.

Inside the house and inside the boundaries of this yard, all was as Virgil had hoped for in a long pregnancy, with Alma's gray head always bent over the layette choices in the catalogues. She ordered something every month for the baby, sending in her handwritten requests the way ladies were encouraged to do by Mr. Montgomery Ward himself. Not everyone wanted to use the cold order forms, and the great man assured them all at the front of his catalogue that his order form was not necessary; they could, if they preferred, write to him directly and make their needs known only to him. A very famous handwritten request of the day was leaked to the press for publicity: "Dear Mr. Ward: Send embalming fluid right away and please inform if we are to pour it down as he leaves us, or soak him over-night. And we thank you. Yrs. truly."

Poor Jemmalee was forced by Alma to remain politely out of public view. In her last months of confinement they might drive her around at dusk for a little airing. Mostly she aired herself on the front porch after dark in a lap rug.

Then suddenly he was in their lives again, and Jemmalee would finally meet the boy whose life she knew of as an adoption after the death of his mother. Jemmalee was often up in the night after the baby was born; she would slip downstairs so the crying wouldn't wake up Virgil and Alma. One night they heard someone pounding at the back of the house — someone who knew enough to come on the screen porch and knock hard on the heavy kitchen door they kept bolted. Glover came downstairs in his bare feet and a pair of overalls pulled on. He had heard the pounding, too, and thought a storm shutter had torn loose. But there was Jemmalee having opened the door to Wilson, a black man Glover had worked for years. Wilson was in charge of the cucumber they were planting in Flat Hammock. He stood there saying he wouldn't have bothered Mr. Tom if it wasn't urgent. He was shaken up pretty bad. He'd come in to tell Mr. Tom there was a thing he'd just heard had happened over in Littletown.

Glover sent Jemmalee upstairs and told her not to bother the old folks about it just yet. She hadn't wanted to go; she had wanted to hear what Wilson had to say. Looking back, that may have been the first fight of their marriage, nothing but harmony up to that point, and stories and secret jokes and anticipation about the day when the whole house would be theirs. "Go on," Glover had suddenly said to his wife.

She didn't at first realize he was talking to her in that tone. He'd pointed at her like she was a little terrier dog he wanted to make behave. That's what she'd claimed later at a time when she thought she could reason with him about his behavior. He had hated hearing her describe himself in such exact terms — the image of himself pointing at her, the arm aimed more or less at her feet, and that swift motion indicating the direction he had in mind. He'd wanted her to go on up those stairs and leave him to talk to Wilson. She had stared in disbelief until it dawned on her that he might begin to take off his belt. But he was in overalls and bare feet. He would have reached for a broom or a piece of kindling.

A real bad thing, Wilson finally said, when they were alone. He'd come right over to let the folks know. Lucky Apple may have got mixed up in something Miss Alma would want to know about it, and Mr. Tom, too.

What was Lucky mixed up in this time?

Well, Wilson had taken it upon himself. He might be unwelcome, but he had taken it upon himself to come on over the first moment he heard.

What had he heard?

It was a bad killing over there.

Lucky killed?

No, Wilson hadn't heard that. He was there to tell Mr. Tom he might want to drive over to Littletown right away.

Why would he want to do that in the middle of the night?

Lot of mens were going over there right now to see how it all turned out.

How *what* turned out?

A bad, bad thing. He wasn't sure hisself what it was.

That didn't mean Glover had to go, did it? Wasn't any of his business.

One of the colored boys who brought the news to Wilson said particular Lucky Apple was asking for Mr. Tom to come get him out of there. One of the colored boys had barely got out of there hisself.

Glover stood in his bare feet looking at shrewd old Wilson, who had known quite well how to put it to him. There was no way for Lucky to exact anything but a favor at this distance and time. They hadn't seen him outright since that turkey. Now he'd merely sent for a white man to come get him out of some scrape. Glover would remember Wilson's strategy for a long time afterward. It was a simple favor Wilson managed to convey. Glover had a wife now. He had a son. He was so tall he had to pull down his head when he went through most doors. What could he dread from a boy at this point?

"Wilson, you go see if I got gas in my truck."

"I already did that, boss. You got a full tank."

"Come in here then and sit in the kitchen where it's warm."

"No sir. I be getting on home."

"You're coming with me, aren't you?"

"No sir. Can't be doing that."

"Hell, Wilson, you step in here now where it's warm and you wait for me."

"No, boss. I heared they got them enough Negroes in Littletown to last 'em. They stopping black folks at the city limits."

"What are you telling me?"

"Nobody go in or out 'less he be white. That's what they saying."

"That's impossible."

Wilson stopped and looked. "No sir. That's possible."

August was the time for ugly events — for mad dogs and black children and white women running off — hot and sticky, even at night, so humid two coins wouldn't clink together for the poor. But this was mid-February, and he felt the cold sinking to his ankles as he left the house alone. He was still without money; he was land-rich by then, but the only cash they ever saw in the house was what Virgil gave Alma for shopping. They were bartering their chickens for the gas they put in this truck. Alma was strong enough to continue wringing the live necks herself. A stunned hen on the end of a whirling, stiff arm was a terrible sight. Alma could appear as a Ferris wheel, gone atilt — all around her a gathering of trusting birds, but then the woman herself, transformed, the still-point in a quick, deadly halo of feathers and feet.

Virgil was old by then, stone-deaf and in bed by seven every night, and this was freedom of a certain kind whether Glover had money or not. The old man didn't hear the motor turn over whenever he took the truck and went drinking with Fate Rollins on empty nights like this. Virgil was losing all watchfulness and passion. Or maybe he didn't want to know, didn't want to think, how she'd had managed to spoil *both* those boys.

This was their first fine Model T truck that hummed through town and on out the two miles of blacktop where Glover picked up the old Alafaya trail to Littletown. Deep dirt ruts all the rest of the way. It would take him almost an hour to get there — two cigars on the way over, two on the way back. He had suddenly wanted a drink. He associated this stolen truck with liquor and how one's father should be dead by now, one's efforts more advanced than that of slipping out from under an old man's warty nose. Glover ought to have had separate quarters, but with Virgil slapping his hand on his heart after every meal, he hadn't yet seen the point in dreamy plans. By day, he did what Virgil ordered, went where he was told to go, saw whom he was told to see. Gin tasted good to a man still under his father's roof. The real joys were in its tasting better once the old man suspected and couldn't do spit about it.

Someone Glover knew waved him down in the road at the edge of town. It was the famous man with a bottle himself, Uncle Fate, who made a cheap bathtub brew and sold it out of his house. Fate Rollins had heard the Littletown news, already old, and if they didn't get a move on they'd miss the whole thing. He yelled all this as Glover slowed down the truck and was handed the bottle through the open window. "I hear it's quite a sight," Uncle Fate said, pulling his huge frame into the high cab, all his knuckles pale under the strain.

At the turn off onto Alafaya, three white men in overalls hailed the truck. Their car was off to the side, heated up and not able to make the trip. They were not drunk. But it was hot scented news, men's news, this thing that had happened in Littletown. Two of these men were foremen for two of the largest muck farmers in Seminole County. The third was a cousin of theirs from Fort Christmas, and they were all eager to get to Littletown since learning about a killing from a man who had come through town an hour before and found them sitting on the steps of the bank. A total stranger and very excited, he'd pulled up to the curb and told them if they had a way to get to Littletown they ought to arrange to go. He had just come from there and seen the aftermath. Half the town's niggers looked to be dead. The other half was rounded up. He would have stayed the night over there if he didn't have a house to inventory before a big sale in Sanford. He was an auctioneer with his own printed card. He had half a mind to drive back just for the look of the thing.

"Well, Tom's a good driver, but he can't do it with you all speculating. Get in."

Glover thought his silent thoughts on Lucky as they made the long drive. The only thing to do was see if this rumor amounted to anything, while all out in front of him the white sandy road to Littletown promised to be almost sweet — plenty of moonlight on that white road, and open sky, and old Fate telling about getting off his horse wrong and getting himself kicked. "Fate" was short for Lafayette, he had suddenly informed his listener, out of nowhere.

As the truck made its way from open field to pine to open field again, the old man quieted down and the men in the back murmured their stories and whooped out their occasional punch lines, Lucky maybe dead by then. How Glover was going to tell Alma and not get her all worked up, he didn't know; and somehow the thought of their old charge made him furious behind the wheel. That boy had held such sway. Too much affection in the boy for a woman like Alma to resist. She was a thoroughgoing Christian, who, in her day, was said to have had the Cure; she had what simple people believe to be the touch. Lucky's affection made him seem something she'd found and nursed with a bottle. At pint size, when they'd wrestled, Glover was able to bury his face in the boy as he might in the belly of a cub. They'd all wanted him near. Everybody drew near to the orphaned innocence of the boy and his great good nature about it, Nelly's natural child. He'd thrived, and in his thriving so well he'd given them back man's simple state before the serpent spoke. He was like a plant with its roots in pure air. One look at him in the knowledge of sudden death, and one got back intensified life, the sweetness before grief and shame and accident and spectacle. There was a radiating heat along one side of the boy as he sat fishing and showing off assurance in the perfect bend of his arm. Some people were as free as the birds. Glover would crawl out after him on the roof at the top of the house and look down on the lake. Nelly's flame made the boy anointed and blessed, even to Glover, and the two of them had remained a little above the world until Lucky left. They were pointed out by an old mammy smoking a pipe while she washed cut celery at the packinghouse one day. They'd gone over to steal ice, and when she got up groaning from her camp stool to chip them two big pieces, she spoke her mind. "I know you children. You children gots to plead the blood now."

Glover had sucked on his ice and asked what she meant.

"Yessir, you gots to go out someday and plead the blood of Jesus."

"Of *Jesus!*"

"Don't you talk big with me. You can't be seeing stuff like you seen 'less you plead the blood when you gets growed."

"Who says?"

"Me. That's what I says. I says you be pleading the blood of Jesus someday. That's exactly what you be doing."

Virgil complained of such things at the table. "Those darkies are bound and determined to have a miracle. I never seen a single miracle, but I *know* they don't look like Nelly."

This kind of irritation grew here and there in strange ways. Virgil hadn't liked the mammy mentality; he didn't like those colored women coming around to throw flowers in the lake where she went in. Off and on one would see them down there washing their arms with the sacred mud. A few were starting to tell the others that the mud cured rheumatism and gout. And if they happened to spot the two boys in the yard, so much better for the healing. Virgil had gone down there personally a few times to chase out the regulars. "You sisters go on home and quit this nonsense. You're upsetting my wife."

"She God's angel, too, Mr. Virgil. We never seed an angel like her."

"No, and I'm not going have you coming down in here to spy on her. You go on home. You wash off that dirt and get on out of there and go home to your husbands." Glover had felt as if he could have flown down off the roof sometimes and picked up those women like a hawk dipping down on chicks. Lucky said a hawk sometimes changed her mind if she got back to the nest and found the stolen chick still alive in her talons. She sometimes changed her mind, raised that chick right along with her own big biddies. "I heard that," Lucky said.

Otherwise the boy took his special status in good style; but the women couldn't leave the matter alone and they were always wanting to pet the boy and say a prayer or tell Alma of some other fresh miracle, since Alma was the keeper of Nelly's celebrity. So how could it not be a relief for Virgil when he almost accidentally managed to scare that boy and send him packing. Virgil claimed he never planned the event.

There were many reasons perhaps for Lucky's disappearance to be a relief, finally, to a man of Virgil's ordinary doubts and heavy responsibilities. Lucky had simply up and gone right after the picnic, which, by the time it happened, made Glover himself understand why his father might be glad to see the spell broken. A few days later he had lurked in the lonely stairwell, eleven years old, listening to Virgil yell at Alma behind the closed door to the sitting room. Alma was sobbing, and Virgil was not moved. He yelled and cursed and Glover finally heard him ask her, what was he supposed to do, take that boy in for good? send that boy to college?

Glover had strained to hear what his mother would say to this. She had provided a long pause, giving Glover time to get to the bottom of the stairs and closer to the sitting room door.

"Smarter than any of *your* boys," Alma had said.

THERE WERE MEN and torches in the road on the outskirts of Littletown. A man with a flag waved them down. He was backed up by a man with a rifle on his arm. Glover slowed to nothing, threw his cigar out, and made Uncle Fate put away the bottle. Glover greeted the border guards cautiously. "We were told we better get over here."

The man with the flag didn't talk to Glover until his helpers had checked out all the passengers and lifted up the empty croaker sacks in the back of the truck. "You can go on in. Just don't transport any niggers on your way out. That's all we ask. You do that and we'll shoot him. Maybe shoot you."

"Can you tell us what happened?"

"It'll be there when you get into town. It'll be there on your right when you get to the schoolhouse. Sure ain't going nowhere."

Glover saw a brace of dogs, then. At least one was a good bloodhound. Littletown was so poor they wouldn't have had very many animals like that one to show off. He was howling from his throat as if someone had brought the world to an end.

Glover stayed in low gear for the crawl into town. Everyone white was milling around in the road, and he had to watch out for children. The people were a little hysterical. These were farmers normally tucked in bed long ago with Bibles and catalogues and letters from relatives, if they could read or write. Littletown was an entirely cracker town of pickers and ditchdiggers, of men putting down the railroad beds. Schoolhouse? Glover would have guessed they'd never bothered over here in Littletown.

But there it was, a small churchly affair in a big field of weeds, the school doors thrown open and the gaslights on. They were using it as headquarters because the main event had occurred in a shack just to the side of the school, where a fire wagon sat now, its two sorry horses straining to munch the low weeds. One might assume the fire brigade had put everything it had into keeping that shack from burning down. But they were an anemic bunch. A few old men poked at the foundations, which sat smoldering around a stout chimney, standing like a woman with her hands on her hips, purely disgusted with them.

A small boy jumped on Glover's running board for a few feet of free ride. The boy was missing front teeth; he had straw blond hair stuffed inside his cap. "They was drunk as coots," he said, delighted to meet strangers who had just arrived and needed a guide. "They went all through town hooting. I heard it. I was in bed. I'm wearing my pajamas right now." He was determined to show Glover the collar of the pajama top he pulled an inch out of his coat neck. "See that?"

"What were they hooting at?"

The small boy looked surprised. "At everything. They was

calling the moon! They was on a tear." He pointed at what was left of the house. "That's where they got burned out, right there."

"Well, who owned the house?"

The boy was dumbfounded at their ignorance. "Ain't nobody lived in that house, mister. God made them run in there so he could get them on the fence. Only God hisself coulda done that." By now the boy was pointing to the high fencing behind the burned house. But he assumed Glover and Fate had already seen the corpses hanging there.

"Mary Margaret," Fate breathed.

It was a heavy double or triple layer of chicken wire fencing, put up for children who recessed every day on the other side in the schoolyard. Right now the fence sagged heavily with more bodies than Glover could count. The motionless figures appeared determined still to make the leap to the playground. But they'd not been successful.

"See, we throwed in the gasoline and when the house blew up, they tried to get away out the back. They run into that fence and got roasted."

One or two Littletown men were in close with torches so that once in a while one of the figures grew bright enough for Glover to see what he'd come to see until the sight dropped into darkness again and left him profoundly uncertain. The brief illuminations were exactly as in some gruesome picture the brain was known to throw up in utter fantasy.

"Them's them. They was *all* of 'em niggers, but they don't look like it now."

No one who was not in some official capacity was to approach within fifty yards. Glover's truck was waved to the opposite side of the road; his young guide told him he could walk over to where there was a buckboard. "When you climb up there, you can see good."

At the buckboard Glover attempted to make the step up and felt a friendly hand reach out and pull him. "Mind yourself now." It was a man holding a baby who sucked its fingers and stared at Glover while someone else, shoulder to shoulder, pointed out to the newcomer how heat from the exploded house had been a hot furnace for a very short time, intense enough to melt some of the fence. But the three layers of chicken wire on sturdy posts had withstood all the weight. The man with the baby pointed out more to Glover. See how the fence leaned hard but kept those men up there? Glover saw for himself that its angle into the schoolyard was precarious, and that the little bit of give in the posts had kept the bodies suspended during the explosion. Like flies in a big old web, another man offered as he kept his eyes straight ahead. Last he heard, only one boy had dropped to the ground and managed to crawl away. He was alive inside the schoolhouse, last he heard.

Glover tried to count and kept losing his place.

"Eleven," the man with the baby said.

Somehow with the right count Glover had a harder time believing any of it was real. Everything was entirely burnt away on the charred backs of those boys, or else hung in stiffened shreds of bloody fabric and skin. All the small buttocks somehow showed and, below that, the small muscled legs and tapering bare feet. West would have been the direction away from the heat of the blast. Glover perceived this fact instantly. Each had run straight out the shack and managed to make one hard leap up the fence, which had sagged with the spring of their jump but had not let them scramble. The blast must have hit solidly all at once and had given them the briefest chance to turn heads only. Eyes right at the proper signal. All the burned bodies looked west in the stiff pose of men, eyes right, on parade.

Glover heard the soft observation of a man behind him. Not a hair left on any of them that *he* could see.

A man with no teeth climbed into the buckboard for his second or third look. Without his teeth, his breath whistled into the back of Glover's neck. The niggers hadn't wanted to give up the fight without they get themselves blasted. They was warned they better, but they was too chicken to come out. It were gasoline, he heard, that got tossed in the front door and ran to an oil burner in there. With the windows all boarded up, that little box went up in a big *wham*.

When he felt himself sicken, Glover jumped off the buckboard and walked around for some air, which restored him. He tried to get inside the school but was told nobody was allowed in there. When he couldn't find Fate, he got in his truck and drove through Littletown to the cow pen down by the railroad track, where they were keeping everybody who'd venture out of the colored section when they'd heard the news. Nobody colored was going to be allowed to move an inch more, much less claim bodies. The county sheriff was due to get here soon. A few black women were crying. Glover had a close look at some of the stoic-looking young men. He took off his hat and called out "Lucky Apple!" The whole area went dead until a white man came up to Glover with a shotgun and asked him what the hell he thought he was doing.

After that he drove back to see if the one they had taken inside the school was still alive. By then he knew it was Lucky, and even now, all these years later, it seemed to him that out of eleven dead and the hundred or so in that cow pen, Lucky was the only one who could have been causing that big stir by hanging on.

"He can't close his eyes," someone was heard to say when Glover finally got admitted in.

"His eyelids done burned off is why."

Glover stood looking at the impossible form they'd stretched out on a long table. It was the only time Lucky had enough sense to get almost the right tone in his voice.

"It's Mr. Tom," Lucky said. The boy's voice cracked with relief because he must have known those crackers were standing there seeing how long he could last, and in speaking up for the first time everyone stopped talking long enough to turn their gaze to the tall stranger with his hat pushed back. "Hello, boss," Lucky said with a little smile. "I see you made it."

Glover had had to wait several hours before he could get the sheriff to help him clear the schoolhouse and then make it through the guarded checkpoint. At first he thought there'd be a riot and the sheriff had to tell those boys who Tom Glover was. In the long wait he'd had to act indifferent and Lucky played dead. After that it took a deputy to threaten those Littletown boys. He told them he didn't want any of their stubbornness; this wasn't one of their niggers and if they didn't get away from this truck he was personally going to shoot somebody.

In the wait Glover found a telephone upon which to call home. Lucky hadn't been able to grip his hand when he got back to his side and told him he got ahold of Alma. Neither of the boy's hands looked human. "When you get me in the truck, you can put me on my face. I can't ride on my back like this." And it was then that Glover realized that Lucky had looked okay because they'd laid him burn-side down. On the hidden side Lucky was going to look pretty much like those boys on the fence and that's when Glover smelled eager death in all that crowd of whiskey and cigar smoke.

He'd gone running out of the schoolhouse then and been sick before he could find that man with the baby and ask him if he couldn't get him several bails of hay and a blanket. Fate had a dollar to give the man and Glover told Fate he'd pay him in the morning.

"I know that," Fate said. "You shut up and drink this."

Fate drove so that Glover could sit in the back and keep Lucky calm. The three other men in the Point Breeze contingent decided to stay to see when and if these people were ever going to take those bodies down. Someone had heard there'd been a decision to cut down the fence and roll them up in it.

"You boys find out all you can," Fate said before climbing behind the wheel. "If I know Lucky he's got a car over here he came in. You see if you can't get that boy's car and drive it on back for him. Don't you be letting Littletown keep this nigger's car. You hear me?"

4

PETEY KEPT WATCH on the fishing hole from the porch roof until Lois suddenly missed him and called him to come downstairs and help her shell some peas. He took the stairs one at a time, a certain lonesome feeling moving into his bones. He pushed open the screen hardly expecting to have to face the old man alone. Lois was not there to buffer him. Right away the old man looked up and then ordered him to his side with one of his quicker canes.

"While you're here I don't want you down in the lake. Not this time or *any* time. Is that clear?"

"Yessir." But Petey felt his anger rise up like bile. He thought he'd secured protection against more insults. "I wasn't going to go down there," he added, and it was a bad mistake.

"Well, I'm just making sure you don't. I've never known you not to need some directions."

"You don't have to give me directions. I don't *live* here." A lame retort but the best Petey could do on short notice.

He turned on one furious heel to go back inside the house, but Lois was shouldering open the screen ("Here we are!"), three bowls nestled together, old newspaper under her arm and the sack of black-eyed peas she'd bought at a roadside stand coming into town this morning. She scooped Petey's allotment into a bowl, handed him a piece of newspaper for his husks, and Petey went off to the big bench swing at the far end of the porch. Oh boy, Lois bet it was certainly dirty over there; she hadn't had a broom over there all this month.

"Tough titties." Petey breathed this out with air through his teeth, hating even her and feeling the tears of homesickness suddenly thickening, his throat hardening into a huge muscle. Why was he here? He'd die if he couldn't get Carol to come for him right away. He'd die, he'd die, his head back against the swing, one pointed toe making contact with the floor to keep the swing moving enough to keep tears from spilling out of him, for fifteen silent minutes or more until they saw the black and the white kid bringing Paul back across the road. Petey sat straight up. The boys were both grinning, Pops was holding up a fish he'd caught. Lois put down her bowl and wiped her hands on her apron like some old pioneer lady in a late-night movie.

"Not bad," Glover said.

Bradley explained. "He wanted to come right back home."

"That's okay," Glover said.

Johnson looked pleased. "He can fish, man."

"Well, tell that to him!"

"Mr. Barnes, you already know how to fish! We thought we were going to teach you."

"Teach?" Paul was politely bemused. "I've fished all my life, boy." Hearing this Lois grew pale, but Johnson didn't seem to mind being called "boy," and Bradley talked right over the faux pas.

"Want us to get you again tomorrow?"

Bradley's sudden question put a worried look back into Paul's face. The word "tomorrow" was more or less a concept.

"We'll come get you, Mr. Barnes," Johnson said, making a statement instead of a question. Johnson was a quick study.

"All right," Paul said.

And as she was helping Paul get into bed that night, Lois thought of how she ought not to have scolded Petey so badly when she found him wheeling around in her new upstairs again. He'd promised her faithfully he'd leave that chair alone. As she was turning out Paul's light, she couldn't help mentioning to Paul that maybe he ought not to call that young black man a boy. "It's not quite polite. His name is Ted."

"Who!"

"Ted. Ted Johnson lives with his parents here on the lake. He's one of the two young men who took you fishing today."

"I don't know any young men," Paul said.

And as he drifted off to sleep that night, Petey mapped out where he'd be tomorrow when they came to get Pops again. He'd get himself down in those weeds to have a better look at the action. Somehow in the easy way he drifted off he began breathing in and out, and may have even felt he was getting back something of himself at last. Perhaps in one of those huge sighs lowering him into healing sleep, he eased that elaborate robot game right out of himself and would not want to play it much more from then on, since from then on he was going to be part of whatever those boys were up to. He was sure they were up to something.

BEFORE SHE PUT herself to bed that night, Lois took out a hot line number printed on a calling card she'd been hiding inside her wallet behind her driver's license. She had wanted to call all day and hadn't found the time from the moment she pulled in from Daytona. Here was her chance with everyone in bed by nine. She was fighting sleep herself. She was exhausted.

In the sitting room sat her father's ancient high-necked telephone dating back before anyone's time. The thing weighed a black ton. In hurricane weather Lois used it to hold down the newspaper, the *table*. Once Carol had hefted it and asked her when in the world was she planning to update? This old thing reminded Carol of a time when people murdered in the home were found truncheoned to death.

Lois dialed the hot line number and then sat listening to an extensive but soothing message from a woman who sounded awfully young. The woman made an apology for missing Lois's call; she explained that the office hours were nine to five and that the caller should please hold on for a list of Orlando-area support group meetings. A list followed that was long and quite wonderful — a movieland of show times — until suddenly a live voice broke in on the recording. "Hello! We're here! Don't hang up," someone called. It was the same young voice on the recorded message. "Hello?"

Lois sat listening. She wasn't sure if she really believed in groups. It was Carol who did and who said she couldn't talk to somebody who wouldn't go out and get herself a little help with this disease.

The young woman called, "Anybody on the line?"

Lois hurried to explain who she was and that she was trying to get some general information. Almost before she'd finished she heard the person on the other end begin to yell at someone else. "Answer the door! I'm taking a call here."

Lois tried again. "Miss?"

"No, ma'am. This is David."

"Oh, I'm sorry," Lois said.

"Hey, it's all right. I have this major woman's voice. Everybody gets confused."

Lois heard a lot of racket next, the clomping of feet and then a body seeming to fall over an empty garbage can. "Shut the mother up!"

"Why don't I call back in the morning."

"No, please, I can help you, Lois. May I call you Lois?"

"Yes, that's quite all right." For a moment she felt vulnerable at the frank intimacy of her name. No one had used it in ages.

"Is everything okay at your house, Lois? I'm supposed to ask you that right away."

"Oh, this isn't an emergency."

"Good."

"I was calling about your groups."

"May I ask you a few questions first?" He sounded like a nice boy. "May I ask if your loved one is a husband, a parent, or a sibling?"

Lois closed her eyes. Her one sigh. "A husband."

"I'm sorry, Lois." The young man let his true regret for her hang on the air and she felt suddenly grateful to him.

"It runs in my whole family," he hurried to assure her. "I guess you know this is the fourth largest killer in the nation."

Lois liked to believe people meant well. "Yes, I think I read that somewhere."

This David shifted suddenly to a formal mode. He seemed to read his next question from a sheet he'd finally located among other papers. "And where, may I ask, do you reside?"

When she told him Point Breeze, the boy said, "Hey, we're neighbors practically!" Then he was annoyed again: "Shuuuh!" Someone was still throwing things in the background. "Hey, you're dead, okay?" Then David was gracefully back: "May I ask if you are under or over fifty? I need to know your age, but just approx."

She'd never objected to surveys on the telephone. She found them soothing. She was basically a person who had preferred to let others feel in charge, and all the literature told her she should never expect to feel this way again.

"How long have you had your husband in the home in his present condition?"

Lois didn't know how long.

Well, could she describe his symptoms?

At first there were the usual things one read about — memory losses of a trivial and nontrivial type. His mind, like a good strong heart, merely began skipping little beats at first. Then a big skip and an entire chapter of their marriage would sail right into the blue. She'd be reminiscing and realize from his friendly demurs that he'd forgotten he had a grandson.

Would he get angry, David wanted to know. Was he angry now?

No, he went in and out of awareness that something was very seriously wrong with him and now he was slipping fast. Two years ago he'd been the most worried about his condition. Once they were spending a week in Ocala closing up his parents' old place. They'd held hands and listened to the faint bumps of the moving van workers above their heads. Paul had suddenly come up with the notion that it would be a good idea if he shot himself, and Lois had said, "With *what*?"

The question had just popped right out of her mouth.

He had laughed at that; she always tried to remember what a good sense of humor he had even as recently as twelve months ago. "Lois," he'd said, laughing, "I don't *know* with what! With *something*! How about a gun?"

"Then what happened?" David said.

If she could only say adequately, she wouldn't need a group.

Their whole life began seeming like a missing persons bureau. Petey and Carol and Lois would be sent into limbo for a little scare. Paul would always return to a state of knowing who they were again, and when that happened they couldn't act much differently from released hostages. "We're back!" Lois would want to say in relief. "Thank God, thank God, we're back home, safe and sound."

This week he had taken a turn, that was clear. ("I'm sorry, Lois. What kind of turn?") At her daughter's house he'd failed to recognize the mailman. He'd gone right to the phone in her daughter's kitchen and dialed the police.

David didn't sound surprised. All business. "Has he done any serious wandering yet?"

"Any what?" Suddenly Lois was guarded, and she couldn't have said why. "No, of course not. There's nothing like that yet." He had tried to walk away from Carol's house a few times, but she didn't count it as serious wandering because he'd never done it in a setting he knew. The idea of a wandering stage frightened her more than some of the more dramatic symptoms. The wanderers wore I.D. bracelets that looked like penicillin alerts and they all had to be registered by number at a central clearinghouse in order to prevent people from trying to contact their families for money.

"Good," David said, "no wandering yet." He paused and then said, "How about violent behavior?"

Lois felt her eyes sting. "No, no." She felt she should hang up. People, she suddenly realized, could be awful. And teenagers. She had forgotten about *them*. Why was she talking to one? "You see, my husband was a teacher before he retired."

David paused. He seemed to want to be tactful. "Guess what, Lois? My dad was a preacher and he got real violent." Then the boy tried to be lighter of heart. "We're Church of God around here. What are you folks?"

"I beg your pardon?"

"Do you go to a church or synagogue of your choice?"

"Oh! Presbyterian. We're Presbyterian. I just didn't quite understand . . ."

"My mother is a deaconess and everything. My sister's a missionary, if you can believe that. Are you able to drive a car?"

"Yes." Lois saw her husband's whole life flashing before her. His was now hers, like it or not, and so many people were out there in her same boat, happy to know her. She was an excellent driver; she would be asked to get a commercial chauffeur's license; she would be asked to drive victims around by the busloads and to brighten the corner where she was. Wasn't this the sub-rosa message in all recent conversations with Carol? The girl sometimes came within an inch of ьhouting, "Mom, get off the dime!"

"Because if you drive . . . hold on, let me just check something. There's a meeting in Altamonte you could go to tomorrow at eleven in the morning."

"In the morning?" She felt finagled. These were Church of God people.

"If you're new at this, Lois, you may not know that morning is the easiest time to leave them on their own."

She sat on the windowsill from which she had a view of tiny Mirror Lake, although she was looking out a side window at the back of the house. Her grandparents were baptized in that lake. There was an almost full moon lighting it up a bit. "I've given you the wrong impression," she said. "I can leave my husband on his own. He's fine."

"I know. But hey! Lois!"

"Yes?"

"Come on, you did the hard part. You called. You should just get in your car and drive yourself over to Altamonte in the morning."

"But . . ." She wasn't sure what she wanted to say. "He doesn't wander yet. My husband doesn't wander."

David was a pro. He chose simply to wait her out a moment. Even his friend in the background became quiet. She recognized this quiet as the same one she heard sometimes in the middle of the night when her heart thumped. She guessed it thumped for its life. Because life as she'd counted on it had already dramatically forked in the woods. Last night in Daytona her heart had thumped with odd excitement when she realized Paul had taken a rake from Carol's garage and hidden it in the closet before he went to bed. All the literature had warned her. Hiding simple objects tended to come at the end of the middle stage. The victims started to see strangers everywhere, indifferent people who came and went and never said who they were. What else could they be but thugs who might break into the house after dark?

"Hey, Lois. You did the hard part. You called."

She was trying to remember without panicking if the Church of God people were the ones who went door-to-door. "Will you be there, David?" Her mind was racing. What did they do in these groups? She dreaded that they did things involving Twelve Steps and prayer chains. Exasperating at the very least was the fact that the victim of this disease couldn't go to his own meetings; the wife had to go.

"No, Lois, I won't be there. You've reached a hot line in Orlando. Remember? Altamonte is the support group nearest you."

The kid in the background had resumed walking into cans or bottles. Throwing them against a brick wall, it sounded like. Lois looked out through the window and saw only her reflection now. She hadn't the heart to tell this David that she had her grandson visiting, that she couldn't attend a group meeting with him here. It sounded like the most ridiculous excuse she could have dreamed up to use. Now David was starting to give her directions to a house on Olive Street behind the Altamonte Shopping Center. "445 Olive Street." He paused and then laughed. "Lois, it says here the house coincidentally has olive trim."

She let the silence linger for so long David laughed again and called out to her, "Hey, Lois! You're welcome."

"I'm sorry. Thank you. Thank you so much."

"Will you call me back and let me know how it went?"

"Of course. Good-bye. Thank you again."

She hung up and wondered a little frantically what Carol would say about her finally finding a group run by the Church of God. Then finally her head began to clear. The group might *not* be that, and so what if it was, and there were some things in the literature that suggested she need not tell Carol things involving her private business. According to the literature Carol herself might be angry at her father and somehow even more angry at Lois. Anger was right up there at the top of people's symptoms. You had to learn two sets of symptoms, first the victim's and then your own. Two to tango, the literature said.

Lois knew her symptoms. At least one of them. In the year and a half she'd read up on the horrors that might happen to Paul before the disease got around to killing him, she had realized there was little way a spouse of fifty years could avoid feelings of stark terror. Terror was starting to be her biggest downfall, driving the memory of Paul right out of her head — his charm, his intelligence, his simple courage. She could leap back to him as quite a young and dashing suitor while not being able to reconstruct in her mind the man she'd lived with most of her life. And thus, of course, she was not able to reconstruct most of her life.

Everyone in the home ends up with the disease in a related form, the literature said.

Wedding anniversaries will be traumatic for you, the literature said.

Unthinking old friends will still send cheery cards. They have little idea how macabre this is, and you must forgive them wishing you many more happy days together.

In the early stages, the literature said, *try putting up simple signs around the house ("Bedroom," "Bathroom") and drawing an arrow. This can save you wear and tear when your loved one keeps getting lost in the house.*

She jumped when the phone began to ring right under her hand, which was resting on the old receiver. She must have been sitting like this for several minutes. It would be Carol on the other end, Carol who sent her home yesterday with an adorable reading light that attached as a paper clip to the pages of a book and then cocked its curious head over material containing short explanations of paranoia, psychosis, and violent behavior.

"Some men walking into a bedroom will suddenly smash a mirror if they mistake themselves for another man in the house. In the middle stages, the caregiver might want to consider removing all domestic mirrors, or else draping them in something attractive."

"Ma? You okay?"

"Oh, yes. We got home in record time. We've had a pretty good day."

"Petey asleep already?"

"He and your dad fell sound asleep in the same bed while I read aloud to them. I had to walk Petey down the hall, but he never seemed to wake up. We're all tired."

"Wait till you see your picture with Petey in the local paper. You're such a genius, Ma."

"Me? It was *his* idea."

"I know. But the roaster tins! Honestly, if you hadn't thought of the roaster tins, I don't think he would have won the contest. The little plastic machine guns strapped to his arms. A work of pure genius."

"How much loot did we win?"

"Five dollars!" Carol had a deep smoker's voice, though she had never smoked. She had the voice of Hermione Gingold —

Ms. Gingold in a faded dashiki and beads. She switched her dress back and forth between American Indian and Chinese worker. In her way she was a sweet person, Lois thought.

"Mother, I really want to thank you for coming, even for the one night. It made a difference to Petey. And me, too!"

Carol was certainly welcome. She'd be glad to know Petey had finally dropped the robotic voicing late tonight. For herself, Lois was quite relieved.

Carol swore it sometimes went on for days and days. What had the old Spider made of it?

When Lois said that old Spider might be losing his ability to be around children, but had done the amazing thing of hiring two boys for Paul, she heard Carol's voice go into another gear. It was how all their arguments began, and Carol right now had missed most of what Lois had explained.

"Did you hear what you just said, Mother?"

Lois thought to herself, Oh Lord, here it comes. "No, hon. What did I just say?"

"You said that he might be losing his ability to be around children, and I'd just like to know what ability you thought he ever had. Was I ever not terrified of him? Didn't he used to tie you to a tree in the front yard? Tie you up, Mother. To a tree!"

Carol always made it sound as if Lois had been gagged and bound, when what had happened, apparently, was that once Glover had tied her up more or less like a puppy for running away. "Honey, it's never bothered me. It's a little moment in time that bothered my mother much more than it did me since I don't even remember it."

"That is so *like* you, Mother."

The tie-up had been a favorite horror story that Jemmalee enjoyed telling to Carol when Carol was beginning to understand tyranny. Lois always hated Carol using the story as a piece of ammunition. Wasn't her ability to forgive and forget a good sign? Lois had argued. This idea had appalled Carol, who, in certain moods, claimed it merely demonstrated that what Lois knew about basic psychology would fit in an acorn.

This was how their arguments escalated, often at the moment Carol pointed out that Lois had said something that was just like her to say. Lois had a whole other set of books helping her figure out how not to touch the tar baby when she was as exhausted as she was right now.

"Hon, I'm pretty tired. I'm going off to bed."

Carol was trying, too. Lois felt the girl begin to back off gently. Sometimes Carol could laugh about the time Spider thought he ought to tie Lois, age five, to a tree to punish her for running away. Once she had called up exasperated with Petey and wanting to know what kind of rope Lois thought Spider had used. Right now Carol backed away from one potential argument and nudged ever so gently toward another one they sometimes had.

"Did you call that number in Orlando yet? Because I have another idea to suggest if you didn't."

"Oh good. Let's hear it."

"I think you should get to know your neighbors on the lake!"

Lois sat listening. When was she supposed to have time for this?

"I think you should let me throw you a little tea party or something. You may not be a support-group sort of person." (Lois knew better than to ask what *that* meant.) "But your neighbors, Ma! What a good resource for you! I bet there are terrific people in Point Breeze with the university so close by now, don't you think?"

Lois smiled. At this stage of her life she'd hoped to amble over to the university and take a poetry course. But she didn't have to read the support-group literature to figure out that caregivers don't normally find time for a poetry course beyond the middle stage.

"Well, a party sounds nice," she said. "You realize they're all quite a bit younger than I am on the lake." It was only her private joke about the Gap Kids, but already Carol's temper was shooting up. One time Carol had told Lois that *her* mother-daughter literature suggested that all daughters have small Scotches before telephoning. "I knew you'd find some excuse," Carol said.

"I'm sorry. I wasn't making an excuse."

"Let's not fight, Mom."

"All right."

"Will you just let me give you a little tea party? I need to get to know the people on the lake as much as you do, right? I might meet a nice married man."

Right now Carol sounded completely kind and throaty in her little joke.

"I think it's a great idea."

Modern poetry had been what she'd had in mind for herself over at the university. She'd always wanted to learn how to read it.

"Thank you, Carol. Thank you for thinking of this."

When they hung up Lois realized she'd forgotten to tell Carol about the rake, which had so startled her last night as she was lying in one of Petey's twin beds, reading. Paul was asleep, and Lois's gaze had traveled across the floor and into the closet where Carol's new green rake leaned against the wall like a young woman with green hair. Home wrecker! Lois had felt so furious she'd walked to the closet and grabbed the thing by the neck; she'd asked it what in the world it thought it was doing there!

Later she'd meant to get it back in the garage; then she'd meant to tell Carol so that Petey wouldn't find it when he got back. Petey would understand immediately. His knowing everything broke her heart, and Carol's heart, too. What did they think his robot game was all about, Carol had once asked.

"Really?"

Oh sure. One time they were watching that old movie about the body snatchers, and he'd just up and said, "That's what's happened to Pops!"

"Oh, hon. I'm sorry."

"Me too, Mom." Carol had cried and cried that time, inconsolable. "I really miss him, Mom. I didn't know how much I was counting on having him around."

"I know."

"Remember how funny he was? Remember when I used to

say things like 'Far out!' and he'd shout back at me, 'Close in!' "

And when they'd pass the Dairy Queen, Paul used to read the BRAZIERS sign and yell out "Brassieres! My favorite fast food."

Did Lois remember that?

She had kept quiet. It had dawned on her that Carol seemed to be remembering Paul better than she did Lois. Lois tried not to feel sad about it. It was just a fact. And that was certainly better than not being able to remember anything, about either of them. Because as for herself, she knew *she* could no longer remember a damn thing.

5

THE NEXT DAY Petey left the house shortly after lunch, hours before the neighborhood boys were due to arrive. He waited until Lois came upstairs for her little afternoon nap. He told her he was going to walk around the whole lake.

"Fine," she said. She stroked his hair, glad again that he'd dropped the robot voice so she could finally talk to him. "Listen, honey, I'm sorry about the wheelchair, and I'm very sorry about the fishing."

"I don't care about fish, Grandma."

"He's trying a little experiment with Paul and he just doesn't want you down there this weekend until he sees if it's going to work. You understand that, don't you?"

"I guess. It doesn't take a genius."

He let himself be kissed for this.

Downstairs in her pantry he found a pair of old binoculars that he slung around his neck; he put cold water in a plastic bottle; he found a small bag in which to put some leftover Halloween candy. Then he went out the back and made a wide circle through the east side yard so that neither Spider nor Paul would see him. Paul might want to drop his hose and go with him; Spider might take one look at all his equipment and read everything there was on Petey's mind.

Once off the property he headed east on Mirror Lake Road in order first to visit the one remaining orange grove on the lake other than the old grove in the back of the house. The last lakefront grove, a short distance around, used to be Spider's. He had sold it years ago, and the grove was finally a set of lots. Petey knew that the red ribbons, in a few of the trees, marked the ones that would be left to stand as ornaments to the front and side of the new houses. Pops had told Petey once that the old man's father planted these trees. "How about that? That would be your great-*great*-grandfather."

"But you aren't related to him, are you, Pops?"

"No."

"I wish *I* wasn't related to him."

"You don't want your Glover genes, Petey? You'll live a long time on a few good genes."

But where had his Glover genes come from if his father was in a sperm bank? Paul had looked surprised to hear the question. "Well, what about your mother and grandmother? They're Glovers. So are you, kiddo."

"But not much, right?"

Paul had thought about this a moment. "You don't need much."

"But I have more of your genes than his, right?"

"A few more, I suppose."

Fully half of Petey's supply had come from someone they would never meet or judge. Carol said the donor's file contained only a few anonymous statistics — the guy's height, weight, color of hair and eyes, educational and family background, date of birth, and hobbies. That was it. And, as if that weren't little enough information to form an opinion, Carol said she could now no longer remember the hobbies. Not one. Petey was floored. Couldn't remember? How was that possible? Well, she said maybe it was because she was such a book person. She realized it was terrible of her to forget the hobbies, and she had surprised him one day last summer by suddenly driving him to the Orlando clinic where she was artificially inseminated. "Let's go learn all of his hobbies," she said. "What are banks for, anyway?"

A dour and skeletal man at the desk had looked at Petey with such an odd expression when they walked in that for a moment Petey was sure it was the donor himself. The sour-looking man worked there; he could donate any time he wanted! Petey had run crying into the bathroom where Carol found him and put him in her lap. Look! she had his father's file! And when she opened it up, hugging Petey to her, telling him what a terrific kid he was, all three file pages slipped out of the smooth folder and sailed under the door of one of the stalls.

Petey had memorized every word. The man was young, only eighteen. He probably needed the forty dollars for school expenses, Carol said. He was in college, his major "undeclared"; they were able to make out from his bad handwriting the declaration that he was "leaning toward a career in computer science."

The guy had brown hair and brown eyes and no distinguishing birthmarks. But Petey's heart had beat wildly when he happened to notice a startling, unexpected fact: The guy put down under "height," six feet two inches. All Petey's anger had fallen away. He was so grateful to Carol that he'd thrown his arms around her neck. "See?" she murmured, kissing his ear. "I'm not so dumb."

He'd never expected his father to be tall. No men he knew were very tall, only strangers at a distance and basketball players on TV. He had searched frantically for the hobby section. The list had been a mile long — football, racquetball, tennis, waterskiing, boating; the guy hoped to get his pilot's license someday; the guy wanted someday to backpack across the country or the USSR. There was another almost illegible sentence about this: "I'm a person who can't sit still." Carol had laughed and then sighed when she saw Petey didn't think anything was so funny.

"I'm sorry, Petey. It's just that he's just so young in every way," she said, sighing again. "But he sounds great, right? I remember it all now. I sat here thinking, well, he's just a kid. All I cared about was his health."

"Not now," Petey said, his father's first defender. "He's twenty-seven now." And Petey had put together a composite drawing in his mind of a tall athletic student-man with backpack and leather jacket, hitching rides on state highways, putting out his big thumb and grinning, holding a cardboard sign to his chest: GRAND CANYON. Sometimes Petey had dreams of riding a rented mule straight down into the Grand Canyon. In his dream, he is smiling the whole time, knowing that when they get to the bottom, which they never quite do, he will be allowed to turn around in the saddle and see his father's face.

HE'D HIDDEN in this last great grove many times before. From here, when he was ready, he could slip down the bank unseen and work his way around to the fishing hole in front of their house. He was not quite able to frame his feelings of fear. It was something of a survivor's fear of older boys. If one didn't know enough to fear older boys, one was a dead duck. Petey knew better than anyone how little kids were unwelcome. Skunk farts were more welcome.

The sack was smart. He hadn't known about the muck on the lake this time of year, and he was forced to take off his shoes and socks. He put them in the sack. When he slid down the bank, he was at twelve o'clock on the lake's round face and had to make it all the way around to six, where the fishing hole was. When he looked he saw that either direction he might pick contained a hazard. There were high snakebite weeds at several points, both clockwise and counter. The binoculars brought the various terrains of the lake bank to his eye, and he spent a long while moving from his point at twelve o'clock to three o'clock, then four, five, and six. At six he saw his own house, right under his nose, and the old man out there in his rocker. Paul was watering. Through the binoculars Paul's head was huge like the pumpkin head. Paul was smiling at the ground as he watered. One would think that he'd seen Petey and was pretending not to notice. Petey went on from there to seven o'clock and then stopped his survey at eight. Now he knew what to do. He had merely to climb the bank and follow the road on around to eight o'clock, well out of view of the house. At that point someone had land-scaped a smooth and fairly grassy slope down to the water before the weeds started up at seven and extended all the way over to the hole and beyond.

The road was narrow and old. He'd walked it all his life, Petey had; or else been pushed around it in a stroller, or dragged around it in the back of a red wagon he remembered well. Paul at the handle, looking back over his shoulder, had asked him if he wanted to go faster. He'd taken a spill out of that wagon some-where on this road. He remembered that, and being carried home by Paul, who heaved him up on the kitchen drain board and put Petey's banged-up legs into the sink and let the water cool the burns while he bent his head to survey the damages. Petey had found a balding spot on his grandfather's head and stopped cry-ing. "Pops, you don't have hair up here!" and Paul had looked so surprised. What! His hands had clapped to the back of his head. "What! You've cried so hard my hair's fallen out?" It was a joke. "I'm bald. Oh no, I've gone bald!" And after that, any-time Petey had wanted to attack Paul in a football tackle, he would tell him anew that he was bald so that the hands would clap to the back of the head and his whole torso would be ex-posed for the full force of Petey body-slamming him like a line-backer. Paul pretended never to catch on and allowed himself to be tackled with great ferocity. "Ooof," he had always been fond of saying. "Now I'm bald *and* on my knees. What next?"

Petey hurried down the slope before he was seen from the fancy house. The grassy taming of this bank ended abruptly in a wall of high growth, elephant ears mainly and thick cattails standing right up out of the water so that the choice was either the deep muck on the bank or the water itself. Once he made the choice he found a narrow trail some kid had made in the elephant ear. But trail or none, he sank in muck up to his midcalf and higher. His foot touched a cypress root from time to time or found a hard spot, which held him as he made slow progress to the fishing hole and then saw right away how easily the boys would spot him in his bright T-shirt through these green stalks. But at seven o'clock he came upon a real miracle. It was someone's worn-out old rowboat turned belly up with a set of huge holes so irreparable that the cattails and elephant ears rose up through those holes, and the lesser vines, more patiently, took over the rest. A slick green oilcloth of mold was rotting the wood beneath. He was sure that the boat would pull apart in his hands when he lifted one side to see if it was possible for him to hide under there. Moccasins crawled into places like this and the short but deadly coral snakes whose mouths were so small they could bite the little bit of webbing between your toes. The boat had rotted lighter than a feather, but it held. Both the board seats fell of their own weight into the muck. But, when he tried it, the second board held him up. He needed a piece of plastic to cover the board so he could lie down in here. One of the giant leaf bags from the workroom. He was sure he had time to go back for supplies and then return ahead of the boys. He would merely retrace to eight o'clock and then run home quickly by the road, where he'd be seen by Paul and Spider, but it would seem only as if he'd just done a once-around on foot. No law against it. He had to wash his feet and legs and put back on his shoes so they wouldn't know he'd been in that hole.

The old man actually gave him a wave when he came up the long drive, keeping his distance and going on to the back, where Lois was already up from her nap. She was out watering a few plants near the garage. By her look he realized she would deny a boy very little who'd been banned from fishing, who'd been banned from using her wheelchair.

"Hi, hon."

In her pantry he found a box of kitchen bags. He took two. She might miss them, but he didn't care. He took a third, and then he found a dark towel in the dirty clothes hamper. He could rinse this out and put it back later. What else would he need if he were going to be flat on his back or stomach? Something to put his head on — another towel, rolled up. If he went out the back again she might ask about her towels. Instead he'd take the route through the sitting room and down the long hall out the front right past the old man, who was not one to ask about towels. He'd sail right past him, down the steps past Paul's watering, down the drive, a left on the road toward eight o'clock. Simple.

WHEN GLOVER FELT the air stir around his ankles, he woke up and turned in his rocker toward the screen opening with Petey coming out wearing those missing binoculars around his neck. He looked like a second-day snoop, the old man mused. He'd already been all over the house with a fine-tooth comb; he'd been in the drawers and closets, the crawl spaces and tax returns, the last wills and testaments. Glover suddenly realized that he linked both this boy *and* Lois with the end of his privacy. This unknown quantity was Lois in the form of a sprite who passed through cracks and under moldings like a mouse flattening all his tiny, unbreakable bones. Where had he found those binoculars?

Petey stopped dead in his tracks at the question. The binoculars had lost all their weight around his neck, and so he had forgotten them completely. He looked down and saw them hanging on him, as obvious as a sign saying, THIEF!

"In the pantry," Petey said. He tried not to blink. "They were in the pantry."

"What do you suppose you're going to do with them?" Glover said.

"Nothing. Look through them." This was their first conversation since yesterday. Petey's bad luck seemed phenomenal to him.

"Someone took those binoculars out of my room over a month ago."

"It wasn't me."

"I don't care who it was." The old man stared. It was the first time Petey had really seen that his eyes were sky blue and that all around the tanned but translucent skin his blue, blue veins were a map of rivers. They flowed into the taut nostrils and along the prominent bones in the cheek. Moles floated like islands on both temples. Old, old men could not smell this perfumed without preening. Now Petey understood the strong colognes. There were oils and creams squirreled away in that stark bedroom he was not allowed to enter. There was a big safe in there that he admired and a set of wooden drawers no bigger than cigar boxes which were marked TOOLS, CHECKS, COINS, PICS, MISC. He was sure the whole room was rigged to explode.

"Here," Petey said. "Here." He put his cache of towels and clean plastic bags on the floor of the porch. He took the binoculars from around his neck and held them out. "Here!"

Old Spider merely squinted and looked away. "Go in there and put them back on my desk where they belong."

He'd gone too far as always.

"I never took them off your desk."

"Go on." Glover waved.

Petey felt himself age several years. He was about to cry, and to keep from doing so he shouted. "I *found* them for you." He shouted again. "You might not have *ever* found them if it wasn't for *me*."

"What are you talking about? Just go put them on my desk and don't touch anything else."

Petey blinked and understood something new: the old man was deaf just to be mean.

But then suddenly the blue eyes had softened. "Son, what did you need with those binoculars?" It was a change of heart but much too late.

"I *didn't* need them." Petey could only shout. He knew he was a bit hysterical. "I *found* them for you. I never *wanted* them."

"Why are you crying? Is that what you do when someone tries to have a conversation with you. You cry?"

It was a dream! It must be. Only in dreams was he ever treated this badly. There, very cruel people would turn out to be full of feathers whenever they broke in two, or else when something spilled out of them, such as grain or white rice, which would climb up his own body until only his head was free.

Blindly he stooped to pick up the towels. Then he merely turned and entered the house. All he knew now was the reason why Glover's room was always heady with smells; but being told he could enter that room gave him no pleasure at the moment. Petey found the first of two ancient desks. He flung down the binoculars, half hoping to break them, and then headed into the hall and to the back of the house. With his grandmother, his tears would protect him now. She wouldn't see the towels he carried or wouldn't mind if she did see them.

"Petey, what's the matter? Why are you crying?"

He could have sobbed and sobbed into her, but instead he stopped and yelled at her. "I'm going away. I'm going off until supper. Please don't call me. I'm not coming back to this stupid house until supper. Don't call me."

"I won't. I promise."

"Good-bye!"

"G'bye." Lois was smiling in sympathy as if she knew it was, again, the old man. "Be safe."

At point eight o'clock on Mirror Lake he stopped crying and congratulated himself. She *would* have called him. It was a brilliant intuition. Just about the time those boys arrived and he was safely settled under the boat to watch them, she would have wondered where on earth he was and aroused the suspicions of the old man, too. Now he wouldn't be expected home until supper. She was not to look for him. And she would keep her promise. He'd been quite brilliant by accident, and he was soon running down the grassy bank and re-entering the jungle, where he saw his old sunken foot holes. This time he managed to avoid them, finding firmer spots, bending down the elephant ear stalks to hold him up for a second or two as he easily moved toward the old boat and felt his wicked motive in doing precisely what the old man had asked him not to do. Yesterday he had been afraid and obedient; now already, in one day, he was brave and recriminatory. In his secret thoughts he believed himself to be a new person, someone with balls.

He didn't want to roll the boat over; it would break down too much of the water foliage and the boys might see that and know someone had moved it. He managed to prop one side of the boat a few degrees, enough to put down first the two sheets of plastic and then the largest towel and then the smaller one for his head and then himself, being careful to take off his T-shirt. One brush with the green slime on the boat, and he would give himself away at the house — a snoop, a brat who wouldn't take simple directions, fooling around down there with those older boys the old man wanted for his own purposes. In fact, Spider was the very topic he heard first from the boys themselves several minutes later as two of them came sliding down the bank quite near him but had no idea he was there. They argued from the moment they slid into view, followed by five smaller boys, kid brothers about Petey's age, going farther off, toward five o'clock, to be by themselves. These two older boys nearest Petey looked fifteen, and the redheaded one started right in on Spider and the fact that the black and the white kid were going to bring down the loony to fish with them again. Paul. His grandfather. The loony.

"I'm going to throw him in the goddamn lake."

"Don't start with that stuff, Fluke. My brother can hear you and he tells my mom about your mouth."

"Your brother's your problem, Ronnie." Fluke called out to five o'clock. "Aren't you, John Boy?"

There was no reply from five o'clock.

"That idiot, he's deaf. Relax."

The one called Fluke was first quiet and then falsetto, incredulous. "That old man is paying Ted and Larry! I *know* he is. What do you think that was the other night? He threw me off his porch. Too white for him. He wanted a black jigaboo." There was a moment of silence in which Petey stopped breathing.

"Fluke, why don't you shut up with that stuff?"

They baited hooks, two boys having stripped off sneakers and squatted barefoot in the muck at the water's edge, two boys washing hooks and baiting them from worms inside a large coffee can. Fluke stayed quiet and Petey was fascinated to see how his lanky legs rose on either side of his head as he squatted, lots of red hair, freckles the size of peanuts and bigger, a cursing boy who was all-out loud and forced, yet real, too; it was very real talk of stuff his dad said about the niggers. His dad said nigger jigaboos were taking over and you had to kiss them if you wanted to stay in business; if you were white, you might as well roll over and play dead. Coons and Cubans. Everywhere you look, man.

"I don't know," Ronnie said. "You're the one who lives next to him."

"What's that supposed to mean?" Fluke suddenly wanted to know.

"Nothing."

"You're a stupid zero brain, Ronnie, I hope you know that."

"Shut up, they're on their way down."

"What do I care?" He suddenly called Ronnie a name Petey had never heard and didn't understand at all. Petey felt his hands sweat.

"Don't call me that, okay? Ted used to be *your* friend, so don't get mad at me."

"He was not. He knew me two seconds when they moved in and then he took up with Bradley."

"Well, I don't care. You act like this is my fault or something."

Fluke was quiet. "I'm telling you, I'm gonna *do* something. You don't like it any better than me."

"What are you going to do? You always talk, Fluke. You never do anything."

Someone among the five younger kids sang out. "You never *do* anything, Flukey-Fluke." The younger boys were not deaf, it turned out. They could hear as well as Petey could. Every word.

The elephant ears were parting. Ronnie said, "You don't have the nerve to do a thing."

It was Pops whom Petey saw first and his heart pounded because Pops was smiling his robot smile, and Petey would have liked to spring out and hide him from the boy Fluke, who had already started to laugh at the sight of that smile.

He thought, *Pops,* but could not move.

Behind his grandfather the path leading up the bank suddenly sprang alive with first the black kid and then the white. Ted was the shortest with a very round face. Bradley looked taller than he did yesterday, if not as tall as the redhead; but he was sober and carried himself as if he were the oldest, as if he were a little proud of something. Petey was sure Spider's boys could take Fluke and certainly Ronnie. Ronnie was what was called a real runt, not much bigger than Petey.

It was Fluke who started laughing right away, the odd squeal of somebody wanting to start up the trouble. When Petey looked he saw that Paul had his hand out to introduce himself. But even Paul could tell when he was being laughed at. Petey saw his grandfather's hand ease up to touch his hair and there was a moment of dead silence.

Without a doubt, Paul had done the exact same thing yesterday. Fluke's laugh soared higher as he turned and dramatically doubled over for the sake of all the younger boys who watched, grinning, at a distance. The loony.

Ted Johnson made his way nearer the boat and stood calling, "It's okay, Mr. Barnes. Let's get you baited up."

"Baited up?"

"Yessir. We got to get the fish's dinner on if we're going to catch him."

"I guess that's about right," Paul said.

They all began to spread out. Paul came to the far left, closest to the boat, and soon Ted started talking to him, holding the hook for him, handing him the worm, looking over his shoulder at Bradley, who had his back to Fluke.

"What's so funny, Fluke?" Bradley said, not facing him but turning to look at the lake while he waited for Paul to put his line out first. "You and Ronnie got a problem again today?"

"Looks like you guys have the problem, not us."

Bradley and Ted ignored this. Paul seemed not to be paying the least attention. He was enjoying the worm. "Good," Ted whispered. "Yesterday you got one. Today you get two." Petey could have reached out and touched Pops's hunting boot.

Then he heard Pops say, "I wonder whose old rowboat this is?" Petey closed his eyes and stopped breathing.

The laughter started up again, soaring very high this time in unison. Ronnie and Fluke thought this was the most hilarious thing they'd heard because obviously Paul had asked the same question yesterday. Perhaps he'd asked it several times. He tended to do that.

"We don't know, Mr. Barnes." Ted spoke softly. "That boat's been here a long time."

"Somebody just went off and left it here?"

There was more laughter from Fluke and Ronnie.

Fluke started whining, "Somebody-just-went-off-and-left-it-here?"

"Hey!"

"Hey yourself, Ted," Fluke said. "Tell your old man to hey. If I have to hear all that garbage about the boat again today, I'm going to throw up!" The smaller boys thought this was funny. Fluke had everybody's attention now.

"You do that," Ted said.

"I will."

"Go ahead."

"It's time to go home," Paul said, as Fluke began to bend over. He was pretending to be sick.

"Not time to go home yet," Ted said quietly. It was soothing.

"You're a good fisherman, Mr. Barnes. Cast her out there and see what you can do."

Even Petey was startled by the cast, although he'd seen his grandfather do some amazingly dexterous things. He could drive a nail home in two perfect blows to the head. The zing went out over the lake and Paul spread his feet as if the whole sport came back to him, now that so much of it was in place. Ted watched and then passed around behind Paul, and in the meantime Bradley had begun talking low to Fluke, who had folded his arms over his chest and drawn himself up as tall as he could. Johnson quickly baited up in the silence.

A second zing sailed out into the water. Petey could sense the pleasure in the mechanism of such small efficient rods. He longed to be holding one in his hands. Both rods were poised at the same angle and seemed short and covetous things, their top ends tapering to thin twigs where the line went out, and then the line itself, in a fine silver thread, caught little hyphens of light that danced up and down. Everything was still until they all heard the hidden word in the picture. It was as if a fish had teased up, shown itself out of water. *Nigger.*

"A nigger every time I turn around."

Petey had never felt the terrible pierce of a word. He wanted to swim madly away and out of danger instead of lying this close to it. There'd always been at least the other side of the street, a distance to this kind of thing.

"Am I supposed to be shocked, Fluke?" Ted had walked over to where the other boy stood waiting.

Fluke just laughed and covered his small teeth with his freckled hand. "You ought to let that old man kiss you up," Fluke said, still laughing as Ted prepared to fight him. "That's what he wants. He wants to kiss up black boys. My dad says you niggers better watch out because — "

Petey could see Fluke standing and being hit. He laughed. He just wanted to talk. "I can say whatever I want." Each time Ted hit, he stepped back with his fists knotted, waiting for a real fight. But Fluke only urged Ted to come on and show him what he could do for the old man's money. "He's got some kind of hard-on for you, Ted, the way you look after his loony like you do."

Paul was no longer frozen. He had blinked out of it about the same time Petey had. Petey watched his grandfather put the rod down in the muck. "You boys," he heard Paul say. Paul said that he thought they ought to go home now. Something like this happened yesterday because Bradley was throwing down his own rod and shaking his head. Bradley came and picked up Paul's line, reeled it in for him, muttered to himself. He took Paul by the arm and carefully headed him back up the path, up the bank. "Bye-bye," Fluke called in his highest falsetto. "Bye-bye!" That touch further amused the younger boys at a distance. Fluke, his two pointy elbows up beside his head to protect himself, was saying bye-bye in an awful descant, and when Paul was gone Ted Johnson threw everything he had on top of him. The two rolled right to the edge of the water, Fluke not laughing now. He ended up on the bottom and tried to get his bare feet out of the mud, to get some kick to his legs. Petey watched his bent knees working to get up under Ted's crotch or belly while Ted took Fluke by the shirt neck and slapped his head and shoulders in the muck. "Hey, cut it out. Damn it, Ted. Cut it out now, stop it."

It must have felt fairly good to pound that head on something soft. Low risk but satisfying. But he didn't get much chance; he was hit from behind with a tremendous crack. Ronnie had come up from behind, his fist inside the empty coffee can. He brought down the bottom edge of the can right on the crown of the head. Ted grabbed the spot with both his hands, but Petey had already felt it, as if he'd cracked his own head on the car door. While you hold it, the welt rises right up under your hands and you have to press to keep back the pain.

Nobody took any more chances with this turn of events. It was over. Ronnie threw down the can the minute it made contact. He didn't look back over his shoulder. He left his rod, his shoes, his gear, and everybody else did just about the same. The smaller boys made off with their own equipment, but they'd blazed a new trail behind them and they were gone. Fluke took a moment to stand up and have a good look at all the blood. "I know how to get you back, Ted. It's so easy to get you, it's not even funny." Then he ran, too. "Bye-bye, you piece of garbage," he called. "I know a piece of garbage when I see it. We're not fooled by what's mounting up around here."

HEAD WOUNDS BLEED. Carol told Petey this once to help him stop crying so she could take a look. It was okay, she'd said. Lot of blood just under that thin bit of scalp, and in the black boy's sculpted, unreal hair the blood looked full, riding like a heavy soup on top of a carpet. He was alone, and he still couldn't take his hand up for the pain. Petey heard him trying to brave it out, rocking back and forth to make the pain subside. Ted whispered a lot of things to himself. They all sounded like curses, too.

A startling sound of feet running back down the smoothly worn path and the parting of fanning branches caused Ted to jump to his feet and whirl around. It was Bradley returning from delivering Paul to the house.

"Whoa," Bradley said seeing the blood. He was a good friend. He stayed quiet and watched Ted strip off his T-shirt and dip it in the water for a compress. "Hold this on it, man," Ted said. "Press down on it, man." It was a strange tableau. Bradley would press hard and then whistle whenever he released the compress to peek under it. "*Fluke* did that?"

"It was Ronnie."

"Ronnie? You kidding me, man?" He dared to laugh.

"Shut up. It was Ronnie."

They both sat, feet in the water, Bradley chewing on a little twig, thinking. "This is my last day, man."

Ted sat up. "Don't be stupid."

"No way, man. They're just going to keep doing this. It's getting the old guy all upset. He knows they're making fun of him. That's why he gives up. They're going to keep it up."

"I know. Shut up. I'm sitting here dying. Can you just shut up?"

Bradley put another small twig in his mouth. "You know, I don't need this. I got my own problems, man."

"Come on! You made a deal, Larry."

"He can pay *you* all the money to do the job. It sure as hell doesn't take two of us. But I'm telling you, they're not going to let up. It just works so perfectly every time they start laughing at him. He knows. I don't blame him for wanting to go back."

"I could kill 'em."

"You're on your own, Ted."

Ted kept whispering and holding the back of his head.

Bradley grinned and spit his twig right in Ted's face with some affection. He got up, extended his hand, and pulled Ted up, and together they began to gather their gear. Bradley looked around at all the other stuff, and his eye even wandered over to the old rowboat where he seemed to gaze straight into Petey's face before he spit again and offered one last opinion. "It's not going to work. They're just going to keep on spooking him." His next idea came out in high mocking tone. "Hey, boy! You better get yourself another *job*."

"Don't. Just don't."

Larry Bradley gave him a fake sock in the arm, then a high five. "Yeah, well, you better watch what you step in. Fluke's just setting you up. All summer he thought you were going to be his friend and the first thing you do is be the new kid at school. He's mad. Sooner or later, he's making plans."

When they were gone, Petey crawled out and looked around. Fluke and Ronnie's gear seemed amazingly exposed, the two last rods lying at different crazy angles. A new tackle box, with its tier of hinged compartments, stood open like a three-dimensional greeting card. Before he left Petey slammed shut the box and hid it with the tackle and gear under the boat as he might do his own mother's pocketbook, stash it under a towel until she got back from a hot dog stand. Petey hurried out of there by his own seven o'clock route to eight, up the grassy bank in front of the fancy house, and back up to the narrow road. As an extra precaution he took the small access road between Mirror Lake and the big highway that ran behind his great-grandfather's house, giving his grandmother enough time alone with Paul to realize that he was in bad shape.

There was no one at the back of the house when Petey entered. He entered through the screen porch, got rid of the towels in the hamper, and washed his hands in the new half bath. The large kitchen was empty and the sitting room ticked loudly from its one huge clock on the mantel. The table was set out in soup bowls for supper.

"Grandma?"

The long hall echoed. Brilliant light streamed through the open front door, where more light hit the lake and threw the outside into a presunset gloom. The crickets had started up; next the fireflies would alight, but not as many as when Petey was small. To the right of the front door, the smaller door to Glover's room remained closed when Petey came up on it. He could hear the old man rummaging in there, completely unaware that things were now somehow turned in the wrong direction.

Petey found Lois standing in an upstairs doorway, watching him climbing but also watching Paul inside his bedroom doing something Petey could not see. He could feel it, almost guess, but not quite. Lois shook her head and whispered for Petey to go back downstairs. Then she changed her mind and motioned to him. He reached her side and felt her bend down. "Paul says he has to go home now," she breathed.

Petey looked up. "He *is* home now."

Lois nodded. "I know. But he's having a little episode. You go in and talk to him for a minute and I'll go downstairs and make a phone call."

Petey peeked around his grandmother's hip and into the bedroom, where a suitcase was up on the bed. Paul had changed to navy slacks, his coat and tie lay beside the tiger yellow suitcase. The smell of mildew was strong in that suitcase, but Paul's bed was as smooth and white as an ironing board. Petey came close and saw that his grandfather was packing all his shoes. He'd already nestled them toe-to-heel in matching pairs. They looked like pets in a shallow grave. There was nothing else he'd decided to take with him but his shoes. All of them.

"Wow, Pops!"

"I'm going home now," Paul said.

Then Petey thought to say, "Aren't you just going to the store?" Paul said, no, he thought he'd go on home. He'd been here a long time and he wanted to get on back now before dark.

In Daytona, Carol and Lois had had to stay up all night with him when he wouldn't go to sleep. He'd wandered through the house, wanting to leave, but Carol had not allowed Lois to drive back in the middle of the night.

The suitcase came down over the shoes and left only the old smell in the air. "That's mildew," Petey explained. "Where'd you get this old suitcase, Pops?" But Paul was concentrating. Petey watched him lift the suitcase off the bed and put it on the round rag rug. Someone had saved all the red for the center of that rug. Paul once told him about the trick. You saved the red rags for the center if you wanted it to look like that. Petey could remember as clear as day Paul telling him this, letting him sit there until Carol came and got him. *Tadpole*. Someone had picked him up off that rug and called him Tadpole.

DOWNSTAIRS LOIS dialed the hot line number in Orlando. David, young as he might be, told her exactly what to do when she explained that just now her husband had decided he wanted to go home.

"I'm sorry, Lois. It's not unusual."

"He's packed up all his shoes in a suitcase."

"Yeah, well, the women pack all their pocketbooks. Fascinating, huh? Where is he at the moment?"

"At the moment?"

"Your husband."

"He's upstairs."

"Well, if he comes down still determined to leave, don't try to talk him out of it. You tell him you think it's a good idea to go home and that you're all set to go, too. Let him put his suitcase in the trunk himself and then you drive him around town for a while. Going out on a highway is actually best."

"What?"

"I know, Lois, I know. But it works! Buy him a milk shake. Take some time. After a while you head back, and when you see your house in full view you call right out, 'We're home! Isn't it good to be home!' "

David let this sink in. "I know how it sounds."

Just when she thought the stage she was in was profoundly sad, she'd arrived at sadder.

"Some people say it's best not to take the suitcase out of your trunk until evening when he's asleep. It's hard to know what's the best strategy. But when you do decide to take the suitcase out of the trunk, it's definitely best to unpack it in their absence and then you should leave the empty suitcase in plain sight for them. Sometimes just seeing the suitcase is, like, reassuring. They might not need to use it for a while."

"But then they will?"

"I have to warn you. Some pack it every day for a week."

"A week?"

"And then they often stop."

"And you think he's been upset by something? My grandson is visiting. I can't believe that's it. He loves Petey."

"Hey, it's no one's fault. Don't try to figure."

She should *never* have taken him to Daytona.

"Now when you come back from your drive, call me. I should be here. Lois?"

"Yes?"

"Take your grandson along. Tell stories, okay? Stories are calming. And call me. I'll be saying a little prayer for you."

"Well, I don't want to bother you."

"My word, Lois. It's no bother. Call me!"

Paul came through the sitting room door with Petey right behind him looking ashen. Lois sat watching them from her chair by the phone, and she let Petey climb into her lap. The boy leaned back on her to wait for her chest to rise and fall like that of an old cat he used to listen to this way.

Lois said, "Paul, I have supper all ready and Petey's hungry. Don't you want to eat first?"

"No, I want to get there before dark." He was as matter-of-fact as he might be about some small difference of opinion. He'd stayed long enough, he said; it was time to go.

The rise and fall of Lois's chest entered through the back of Petey's head. He watched his grandfather looking around the sitting room, looking for his hat and Lois in no particular hurry to help him find it.

"Is that suitcase all you want to take?"

"Yes," Paul said. His hat was on the mantel and he finally located it with a sprightly pounce. "Here it is."

"I'm glad there's plenty of gas," Lois said. "We've got a full tank. We filled up last night, so the car's all ready to go."

"Good." He had his hat in place; he searched around the room again and said he thought they ought to get started before it got dark.

Lois looked at Petey and then tipped him out of her lap. "It'll be good to get back home, won't it?" She kissed Petey on the knuckles. "You'll sit up front with us! Will you do that for me? Will you sit up front and help me drive?"

In an instant she saw how frightened yet excited the boy was. He was searching for a voice with which to say something. "I don't know how to drive, Grandma."

They watched Paul turn around once more in the room and then walk out through the kitchen door and out to the porch and suddenly Lois was whispering. "You take the key and open the trunk for him and help him put the suitcase inside."

"Grandma!"

She paused and looked him over. "Bet you're starving!"

But the old man had come out on the back porch. Old Spider legs. There he was with both canes way out in front. He was breathing hard, trying to decide what was going on. He could see Paul out there with his hat on his head. "You all aren't going to strike out somewhere, are you! It's rush hour out there!"

"Dad, there's soup for you on the stove."

"I don't want you out on these roads." He looked at Petey as if this must be his idea.

Lois called, "We'll be back!" She had placed Petey to stand there covering for her as she left the porch.

The old man was furious. He shook his head and turned around and started back inside by way of the kitchen, his breathing hard, his color bad. He shouted that he didn't know what a boy needed so bad it couldn't wait until morning. But Lois had handed Petey the keys to give him courage and when Petey felt those keys come to life in his hand, he ran off the porch in a sudden rush of happiness that they were going home. They were going home!

"Good," Paul said, when Petey had opened the trunk and then pulled it down again with a slam that would make any boy feel wonderful. "Now let's ride. They'll all be wondering what's happened to me."

6

DEFIED BY LOIS, Glover left the back porch and entered her kitchen, creeping on all sixes, slow legs and arms, slower canes, easing him toward the stove, where he began to smell the good, strong soup before suddenly stopping dead in his tracks. It was not as if he'd never come in off the back porch to find a total stranger standing in his kitchen. At ninety-one it was bound to have happened before. But he didn't like jumping out of his skin like this, his canes clattering to the linoleum, the man stepping quickly to catch him.

"Mr. Glover!" The stranger was slight of frame, if not skeletal. Instantly Glover felt a premonition. His own death perhaps, although that was nothing to fear exactly.

A firm hand entered both his armpits to catch him, and for a moment the only sensation he felt was of his legs going limp. Glover saw the top of a head, a man in Bermuda shorts, supporting him, then bending to pick up one of the canes, a left hand still gripping him with frankness. Tomorrow he was going to feel a stone bruise way up in there around the lymph nodes.

"I couldn't get anyone to answer so I came on back. The door was open."

He had retrieved the second cane by this time, and when Glover snatched it from him, the man stepped back casually as if Glover hadn't just about broken his neck.

"Looks like you haven't had your supper," he said. He appeared to be under forty.

A painful imprint lingered up there in among the glands. Glover felt hung up in the crook of a tree. This wasn't Death. This was some idiot salesman in shorts.

"I'm sorry. Luke Teal." The man put out his hand formally this time, but the two canes were a problem. He abandoned the gesture and explained that he was a neighbor, the father of one of the boys who fished out there in front of the house.

Teal. The name rang a bell, but Glover couldn't place it. On the other hand, this was a little unexpected dividend to a fishing idea. He was pleased to be looking into the face of the new breed on Mirror Lake who ran to the post office in their jogging outfits, thinking nothing of it.

"You *are* Mr. Glover?"

He was still rattled from almost taking that fall. Glover continued to remain silent in the center of his kitchen. A foot scraped for better balance. He stood waiting for the bad news. Or maybe it was good. It was bound to be one or the other.

"Mr. Glover, I live with my wife and son just over in Osprey Landing." Luke Teal pointed over his shoulder to the new development behind the lake where some of the lush homes had partial views. "I've been in Point Breeze about five years. You met my wife a few years ago when she came around to let you know about the Neighborhood Watch program? We're from Pittsburgh originally."

Glover remembered what a hard time he'd given that poor woman. He'd sent her packing.

"I understand you were born around here, Mr. Glover."

An awkward silence would do them both good. It kicked Glover's adrenaline up about as well as coffee did. Anger pumped too much to his heart, but over the years he'd learned that an awkward silence shot him just the right amount. There was a loud clang from the oven's cooling down. He watched the stranger first frown, then decide he had to take charge, open his mouth to come out with it, which was just the right moment to throw him off by interrupting him. "You say the name is Teal?" Glover called.

"That's right."

"Pittsburgh?"

"Yes!"

That was Glover's cue to go silent yet again. His timing may have been off, but he didn't think so. If one was going to be this age, one had to take advantage and keep people waiting. Silence worked like smoke. One had only to throw on a little moss and everything ran out into the open.

"Sir, it's about the boys."

"What boys are those?"

"Our boys here on the lake. I think they've had a little misunderstanding."

These imports were sensitive types. They didn't have much to do these days but get mixed up in their children's affairs. He'd told Mrs. Teal that Neighborhood Watch sure sounded like a social society to him; he didn't want to contribute ten dollars for their little get-togethers. He'd tried to tell her how the Klan used to gather on this lake for their little klatches; they used to parade around the lake once a year and hold all their meetings over on her side. The woman had said she had no idea what he was trying to imply. He hadn't been implying anything. He half thought she'd sit down and ask him solid questions, get some history of the place. Clearly she wasn't the least interested.

All he could do now was suggest to Luke Teal that they go out on the front porch and sit down. On the long walk down the hall Glover picked a crawling pace calculated to paralyze an opponent this young. Way at the front end of the house red light came pouring through the tunnel and showed the lake burnished and menacing. Maybe a storm was about to lower the boom. In the length of time it took Glover to get them on the porch anything could have happened — an eclipse of the sun, a second coming. At long last everyone was seated. "I have my hearing turned on," Glover said.

"I beg your pardon?"

"If you don't shout, I'll get everything. Which is your boy? The redhead?"

The guess was wild but a bull's-eye. Glover had noted Teal's weak mouth back there in the kitchen, but, in the slow stroll, one or two other things had fallen into place: the redhead had reported on him, turned him in. Well, it was going to be either up or down with this man Teal, and Glover didn't care yet which it was. He could use a diversion. Don't cut him any slack, is all.

"Mr. Teal, I ordered your boy off my porch on Halloween. He looked too old to be coming around for candy. Did he tell you how I threw him off this porch?" He smiled hugely to show his perfect teeth, so many of them quite remarkably his own. "I hope I didn't make your boy mad. What's his story?"

Teal thought about this. "We don't know him to tell stories, Mr. Glover. He's our son. I'm not sure what you're getting at."

"I apologize. I'm jumping the gun here. You go on and tell what you wanted to tell."

The man was growing red on the tops of his ears and around that mouth. "There's been a misunderstanding among the boys, and I gather from your attitude toward Luke that you know something about it."

"No. I just met him the one time. Halloween."

"This has nothing to do with Halloween, Mr. Glover. This has to do with yesterday and today down there in front of your house where you sent your son-in-law in the care of a minor."

"A minor?"

"Ted Johnson is thirteen."

"Is that what you call a Negro boy these days? A minor!"

"It's what I call all boys his age, Mr. Glover. It's exactly what he is."

"Well, I hired two minors in that case. Two boys, Mr. Teal." He held up two fingers more or less in front of his face and watched Teal stare at them.

"I only know of Ted Johnson," the man said.

"Well, there's Bradley, too."

"I'm not sure to whom you're referring. I know all the boys on the lake fairly well."

"Well, I admire you keeping an eye on things. I don't much anymore. I just watch out for my son-in-law. I hired *two* boys to take him down there and point him at the water. I picked the smartest boys in your son's group. I never thought anybody would object."

"Well, I happen to object."

"What kind of misunderstanding did your boy get into with my boy?" Glover smiled. He liked the ring of that. "Did you never get in a little misunderstanding yourself, Mr. Teal? At that age?" He smiled widely again but didn't feel it was as effective this time. If he could just get back five years, this would be fun, the stakes this low and a grown man this confused over what to do about a whining boy. The redhead had gone home and reported him to his father. Too bad he had a father like this one. Mr. Teal looked pink and white, like a piece of wedding cake.

"Mr. Glover, I've had a talk with our chief of police to make sure I'm on firm ground when I tell you it's a serious matter putting minors in charge of an adult with a disease characterized by violent behavior."

"You're speaking of Mr. Barnes now?"

"And — " The man closed his eyes to keep Glover from interrupting him, which he would not now dream of doing. "And while I'm prepared to hear you argue that these symptoms are not in evidence in Mr. Barnes, I'm also prepared to argue that he poses a threat to children nevertheless."

Glover let his rocker move a bit. Well, well. He wished he still smoked. He felt like pulling silence out of a good cigar before speaking another word in this life. "Mr. Teal, when those boys came around here the other night, I thought they were too old to be out trick-or-treating. Turns out they were too young. Minors, you call them!" Then he looked at the younger man and gave him an expression of surprise. "The police? Our police chief here in Point Breeze?"

"That's right."

Glover rocked and looked out over the lake. "Well, well." He was trying to think of a police chief having to deal with this sort of thing who had not already hung himself out of boredom.

Teal finally spoke. "There is another point which might be made since some of the other parents and residents on the lake have told me they feel strongly about it."

"On first guess I wouldn't have put you down as a lawyer, Mr. Teal. Are you a lawyer, Mr. Teal?" He felt Teal couldn't decide if, as a Florida cracker, Glover was impressed or disgusted when another man turned out to be a lawyer.

"I'm at the university, Mr. Glover. Financial aid."

AT MIDNIGHT that night Glover extended his feet to the floor and realized Teal's visit had upset him far more than was worthy of the occasion. I've hung on so long I've finally become a real character, he told himself.

With his head returned to the pillow, his thoughts moved around as they'd been doing for several hours and long after the lights of Lois's car let him know she'd gotten back safely — from something, from somewhere. It was none of his business. He was a man without any business. When was he going to learn this? His right armpit ached; a kind of fever of anger welled up like a midnight tide coming in. Reason told him how it was all too trivial; the man's meddling was hardly worth thinking about; he should just give it all a hard turn, shut it down like an annoying tap.

The crazy issues raised, and Glover's part in them, kept sorting out in Teal's favor. Just when the old man thought his own good points were all lined up in a row, they'd begin to break rank and mill around of their own free will. To get them back against the wall, he kept returning to his little idea that fishing would give Paul something to do. He tried to make it stand still long enough for him to go over all its virtues — an amusement for Paul; that was all. And it was a plan to help Lois see how easy it was to think of a few innovative ideas for the middle stage. Of this configuration he was fairly confident.

But then he would remember himself sitting in the dark, waiting to have a look at those boys and the fishing idea merely falling down on him like a wisp of fog coming off the lake and settling on the porch, an inspiration, an interesting blip of a feeling bound up in his getting a close look at Johnson's obvious intelligence and happening not to like the cut of the redhead's jib.

Tonight he lost sleep and wondered at Teal's power to push an old man's feelings dangerously high. Was it that he'd had his feelings hurt by him? Why kid himself? Damned if he hadn't gone and let his feelings get hurt. It had something to do with Teal's skill with words and groupings of words, especially "violence" and "minors," which had a circus tent chemistry to them. As long as that chemistry worked, the man would keep using the combination to send up little explosions of logic and law. The police chief. The neighborhood. People could be fooled because these types were very clever strategists, especially when they became bored. Very dangerous, in fact. They were men who knew that in some arenas of life, having nothing to do with anything they could act on, they'd been pricked. They were the kind who never seemed to think they got what they really deserved. Here was an intelligent man who sat like a cat on cactus, an articulate man who had more or less lost his mind in the experience of being surpassed, unaccountably, by others. Glover had seen it happen before but had not observed the phenomenon in quite a while — completely established men, free, white, and twenty-one, who woke up one day full of vague disappointment and unease. They woke up galled about something they couldn't put a finger on. Gall was a feeling like none other Glover knew.

Even he himself had had to beat it into the ground once or twice as one did a snake. Certain men ruined themselves by letting it grow. Gall worked very much like a poison that doesn't kill. Protective poison, an acquired taste. An uneducated and ignorant man would usually find the Klan right there to take him in and give him a group. Your educated boys went at it a little more privately and gracefully, but sometimes destroyed more people in the long run.

Interesting. Men like that might come the closest to guessing Glover's part in a thing like Halloween night. The children weren't old enough to relate to their parents how the old man had sat up there in the dark calling the shots. He'd done it merely to get back the sensation of catching them off guard and seeing them hang back like that. Quick thinking. A quick cane easing the candy over the railing.

But Teal had a disappointing son, and the disappointment had sharpened his wits. He might have your number, Glover thought. *Seems* to have it, the way you've gone and got your feelings hurt.

He remembered now how the redhead had wanted to be included with the two smarter boys, the more exciting boys, who'd come on the porch to speak to him, get a look at him. They were tolerating that redhead well enough in spite of his sullen bad manners. Glover had thought him immature. Whatever he was, Teal's son hadn't made the cut with the old man any better than he had with his peers. That was a small part of the father's being galled anew. It was Glover who had kicked the son out of the ring, drawn attention to what the father already knew: Johnson and Bradley were putting up with his boy, just barely. They knew they were smarter; it was that simple.

As young as he was, maybe Teal's son already saw for himself how he shared a weak mouth with his father and the same pointy teeth and the same futility in all efforts at leadership and power. Perhaps father looks at son and hates seeing himself reflected — another idiot, a look-alike who keeps digging in the ground and hitting water mains and lead pipes.

Before he left Glover's porch, the father had made one last speech, again to draw attention away from his real purpose. Or else to show Glover how an old man's action would appear to other people, how Teal himself need never fear from other people the least possibility of detection. Teal had started something just to keep himself active, but no one would suspect him of it.

"Mr. Glover, I just don't understand people like you. We have a nice community here. It's obvious everyone gets along fine if you basically leave people alone to make their own way. Things rise and sink according to their personal value and worth. I would have thought if anybody around here knew something as simple as that it would have been you."

It was not that Glover understood the precise drift in this speech until sometime later. But what came next was clear enough.

"I wouldn't have thought you'd want to single out for hire a child whose ethnic background places him in a minority and makes him somewhat vulnerable to be taken advantage of by a man like you. Or seeming so to others."

Glover hadn't quite seen this coming, because while he recognized the cheap chemistry of the words "ethnic background," "taken advantage of," he'd experienced that trick only in newspaper editorials. A kind of racism hiding behind a lot of today's jargon. His first reaction was to feel respect for Teal's mastery of it.

"Let me make sure I understand you," Glover had said. "You're telling me people around here think I'm treating that boy like a nigger?"

"Believe me, Mr. Glover, it's crossed more than just my mind, yes."

"And you told this to the police."

"I told him about your son-in-law down there with mere boys. Your ethical behavior is your own concern, Mr. Glover."

"I see."

Of course. A man like this would *not* tell the police about Johnson's being black; if he did he might risk having his own resentment show through. Educated men hid their jealousy awfully well. Insinuation was their best defense, their best offense. Teal had told the police only that there was a potential liability in the placement of an adult among minors. But to the parents around here, Teal would insinuate things — the idea that Glover had, perhaps through sheer ignorance, demeaned a minority child. Young Cooper would hear of this, for example. At the worst Cooper would find the news of Glover's hiring a black babysitter a little distasteful. Before Luke Teal left the front porch, he gave Glover a full opportunity to hear just how ignorant he could make an old man sound to the parents on this lake.

"Ted Johnson is fully integrated into this community, Mr. Glover, and perhaps not quite old enough to realize how you've made him appear to his friends."

This gave Glover a small opening at the time. "I guess Johnson's too dumb to decide for himself whether I've mistreated him or not. And your boy tried to explain it to him? Your boy have a hard time getting it across? Since Johnson's so dumb and that boy of yours such a whip."

But this Teal was some piece of work. He merely smiled in reply. He was in the early to middle stages of being galled and was shrewder than he would be later when his illness started to eat more holes in him. Right now Teal was understated and still capable of playing things close to the vest. He obviously enjoyed it; he enjoyed imagining how all he *didn't* say to Glover would be worked out in the middle of the night in the old man's own imagination and hurt pride, all those other families on Mirror Lake shaking their heads over this little business, over *him*. There would be sighs of disappointment at suppertime, and a chorus of polite regrets. That old man over there had singled out a black child in this day and age! Singled him out and created a *situation* in an otherwise fairly workable arrangement.

Because it suddenly occurred to Glover in the early hours of Sunday morning how proud everyone must be around here of Ted Johnson. Whether they liked him or not, Johnson was an awfully good reflection on *them*. He was a measure of real progress, of a white community able to move into a black and white century. Point Breeze was going to enter the future gracefully if it killed these people. Hopes rode on boys like Johnson — mannerly, polite, straightforward, at ease. Affluent black parents surely didn't hurt his reputation. Now this. *What a shame. We shouldn't let this turn into something ugly.* Young Will Cooper, the real estate lawyer, thinking, *It was just our boys fishing. What a shame.*

"Mr. Teal, you never told me what the misunderstanding was. Was it just mostly to do with your boy? I hope he appreciates you coming over here to help him. A boy doesn't always know how far a father will put himself out."

"Mr. Glover, what happens next is all that really concerns me."

"I see that," Glover said.

He was strong and young enough to play it close. However, as Uncle Fate used to say, a spleen will eventually go out on a man just like a bad heart will. It would be a while before this man's bitterness caught up with him and started inevitably to tell on him just as badly as wrinkles, as age spots on an old socialite.

But Mr. Teal had finally left the porch with a great deal of poise. Having said good-bye, he had paused as if in an afterthought. One of the reasons he'd come over tonight was to pick up his son's rod and tackle box down there. "Evidently it's already been stolen. It wasn't very smart of my son to have put his wallet in the tackle box."

"Quite a bit of money, was it?"

"Yes. It's too bad. He should have known better than to carry that kind of money anywhere. But, sadly, it does go to show what kind of thing can get started when men don't exercise a little foresight, Mr. Glover. I'm not sure how I'm going to convince my son that Ted Johnson isn't a thief." The man took a well-timed opportunity to smile broadly, a smile that said everything if one knew how to read. The man was enjoying himself.

"I guess you wouldn't consider bringing your boy over here and letting me talk to him."

"Oh, thanks, but no. It's hardly necessary, Mr. Glover. I'll be talking with him, of course."

Talking with him? Glover sensed the man might have been torturing his boy with that same superior smile. *Son, I suppose you expect me to go put the old man in his place? Is that what you're asking me to do for you this time?* Such confrontations were the best moments in the man's day. Teal didn't mind at all if Glover saw right through him now; in fact, he was counting on it.

And for a moment Glover had felt a wave of fear for the boys. They *were* minors, after all. How did one protect minors from this? From a man who had given up on his own son, or else begun to use him and others for whatever small dramatic parts he could still land for himself?

Glover let himself wonder. It must make quite a few men a little crazy. They can't go off and join the Klan and raise hell with a burning cross anymore. Not these university fellows. They were too High Church for that. They know they're jealous. Low-class people don't quite know that about themselves. They put on a bed sheet and ride around trying to get something out of their systems. A good part of the time they just need to whoop it up. Whereas educated men like Teal have to have more finesse: the sheep's clothing, the highbrow manners, the right opportunity, the clever timing.

Glover had sat briefly on the porch watching the financial aid man head into the narrow road and make his left turn for the walk back around to Osprey Landing. It was gorgeous in that direction, the sun having finally overcome the know-nothing clouds and broken through at bottom to show a fairly spectacular disk of orange and fuchsia. To the far edges Glover noted the rarer clashes of reds and the cheaper dime-store pinks. People came outdoors for this kind of flashy sunset, and it was into one of those affairs that Mr. Teal strolled off, a Neighborhood Watchman. Glover had had time before it got dark to think about his little trajectory of yesterday looping back on him and accidentally snagging this piece of tissue paper, this mysteriously galled Mr. Teal. No one would suspect him of it. In this day and age, he wouldn't have to go after a boy like Johnson with a rope. All he had had to do was go tell on him. How convenient that he'd been able to tell on a white man, too, so that it all looked sociological. By now everyone knew the situation — that old man Glover had hired, of *all* boys, the *black* boy. Didn't he know how confused blacks were? How fragile their identities? And now there was missing money. Meddlesome old man. At the very best thoughtless. How thoughtless of him! They had all heard such good things about him, too. But, then again, maybe he just didn't know any better, the old coot.

Glover sat up in bed at dawn and felt the wetness of his pajama top. He'd broken into a cold sweat. He looked up and thought with a certain kind of alarm, It's because I've gone and had my feelings hurt! And, among other things, Teal was smart. He knew just how to do it to me.

7

ON SUNDAY MORNING Glover slept late and then had trouble getting himself up and dressed before his daughter found him out. It was no dream that someone had come here in her absence and made threats about the police.

"Understand you were born around here, Mr. Glover."

He knew he'd gone downhill in the night but hoped that perhaps the meltdown of another inch was not as obvious as he flattered himself it once was. If she noticed, she might stay home from church on his account. Such things used to be among his biggest dreads when she first moved in — that he would have to battle her concern for his appetite or how he'd slept; he'd dreaded that he smelled bad from time to time. Now his new worries felt too much beyond his energy and scope as he turned and found her looking at him from a crack she always made in his door. She had to do this because he was never able to hear her knocking.

"Dad?"

He called back harshly that she should come on in! He tried to be his normal put-out self so she wouldn't notice the real story. He'd gone downhill in simply trying to figure out how to break a little bad news to her. The latter stages of Paul's mental state had loomed out in front of her for all these months. It would be her husband who would begin the spiral downward and her father who would finish it.

She was fully armed with her pad and pencil this morning so she could, if need be, write out her tabloid headlines — yesterday's little invention.

This was bad. Pad and pencil were more than Glover could take after a long night under the weight of his thought. He felt anger spring up like some old curse of his. "Just talk slow. I'll get it if you keep it all one tone."

She was suddenly successful at this. Consequently Glover heard news as bad as his own. "You say he packed a suitcase on you?"

Lois closed her eyes. "It was a little episode. We have to expect them from time to time."

Glover looked down at his lap where his legs used to take root. From time to time, but why right now? He would bet money on Paul's episode having something to do with that man over in Osprey Landing. Sheer luck gets on the side of these people.

"Maybe we have to reconsider the fishing," he said. "I'm not so sure the fishing was a good idea."

"You're wrong," Lois said. She smiled. "Dad, I wish *I'd* thought of arranging this activity for him." She patted his arm. "I didn't get a chance to thank you because you're hard to thank. There was all the excitement of having to try to take him home last night." He saw tears in her eyes. "He just wanted to go home. The little trip to Daytona could have triggered it."

"That was my idea, too," Glover said.

"Let's not be blaming ourselves. I won't if you won't. The literature says there's no end of reasons for an episode." She smiled. She kissed his head.

Glover nodded. He looked at her standing beside him in her blue suit and white beads. She was ready for church. She took Paul every Sunday because what he couldn't get out of the sermon he managed to get out of the hymns. According to Lois he could sing a hymn all the way through when a congregation was there to jump-start him. She had told Glover this once with tears in her eyes, perhaps not knowing that he'd found it distasteful to imagine her loss; a daughter's loss is not something a father can dwell on easily. All imagined intimacy is a little revolting when one is a father. Chin up. As a child she'd never been allowed to do otherwise. Chin up or get out. That was how he'd done it as a way of handling grief. Later she'd thank him for it.

He offered to check on her roast while she was gone.

"That would be a big help. All you have to do is go in there at eleven-thirty and turn it off."

"I won't forget," he said. And once she was out of the room he realized that he really didn't want to be alone for an hour. It was too exhausting to have this much on his mind.

After church and the big noon meal, Glover stayed at the table while she cleared away dishes and food. She was forced to note him, lingering in her company, a thing he never did. Petey saw, too, and scooted upstairs to watch for his mother. Severe homesickness had by now shown up in the boy's face, and even Glover was starting to feel sorry for him. "You didn't finish your pie," the old man called, but Petey was out of there, and Glover remembered barking at him over those missing binoculars. He'd yelled at him again later in the afternoon, not knowing that the boy had been made to watch Paul pack his shoes and demand to go home. Hell, the boy had even helped Lois pull off the job. The two of them had driven around in just enough circles to trick Paul. In the whole of the emergency all he had managed to do was yell at Lois, his anger a liability from moment to moment.

For most of the Sunday meal Paul had seemed his old self, smiling over the roast, the best roast he'd ever had in his life, taking polite pleasure in the company of these familiar strangers and then disappearing somewhere into the large and quiet house. This was often the time of day in which Paul might sit with a novel in his lap. He had retained some abiding memory of something hefty in his hands, and Lois had scattered all the rooms with big books for him to find and pick up on his own, although he could no longer read. It must be the familiar weight in his hands that gave comfort. Some kinds of heft are for keeps.

"I need to talk to you," Glover finally said.

He watched his daughter stop to take this in. She gave him back a friendly stare, and he was overcome with the thought that he was about to change a habit, and to change a habit had the smell of death.

"I need you to give me some advice," he said, as if her advice was required frequently instead of never.

She stood with the table crumbs cupped in one hand. She had an expression he had not seen lately; it was like that of her mother — cautious but willing to be on uncertain ground with him. In rare moments such as this, the cautious, friendly smile suggested a host of women willing to hold out for some kind of break-through with men who never gave them any reason to hope for one.

"I think I may have gotten us in a little fix with the neighbors."

"The neighbors?"

"The parents. Some of them — I don't have any idea if it's one or ten. They seem to think we put Paul down there in that fishing hole to break up their kids' fun and cramp their style. They're mad about it."

"When did you hear this?"

"I have no way of knowing how many there are. I'm hoping if the parents just stay out of it, the boys will start up fishing again and it will all blow over."

"You mean they've stopped? When?"

"We'll have to see. Maybe they'll be back this afternoon. But they want us to keep Paul out of there." He couldn't bear to take the thing back to several nights ago when he'd thrown a redhead off the porch. Nor could he bear last night's Mr. Teal. Right now, with the roast gravy congealing on the table, it all seemed a dream, that candy falling in slow motion, that yellow dog whining in the road, and an old cane tapping that redhead on the foot.

"I'm paying those two oldest boys, of course." He looked to see if this was somehow wrong of him in her view.

"Well, of course you're paying them. Maybe when the parents realize you have an arrangement, it'll all be fine." She stopped and reflected on what she'd been meaning to tell him. "You did this for Paul, I realize that."

"No. I didn't. I did it on a whim."

He saw she didn't believe him. Lois didn't believe he *had* whims. She touched his hand again. "You did this for me and I want to thank you."

"Don't thank me. I wasn't thinking of anybody. It was just some selfishness. I should have minded my own business."

But truth is the greatest lie. There was not a thing in Lois's face but gratitude. Or else sympathy. The living always forgave an old codger, and for a moment he dared credit Mr. Teal for having the wit to see it otherwise. His women never did.

"The question is what do you want to do now? Is it going to be more upsetting to Paul that he can't go back down there with those guys, or less upsetting? You're the expert in this thing."

Well, she doubted that.

"I hate him being banned from my own fishing hole, but we can't have anyone upsetting him. I don't want those parents coming around."

"Dad, I can't imagine them coming around! Don't be silly. If you paid those boys and they agreed, then we'll have to explain it to them. Paul's not going to cramp anyone's style. And he has a perfect right to be down there."

"I know that."

He was getting nowhere. Tell her about the police having already been consulted, and she's going to know the neighbors are jumping on the violent behavior symptom. Once upon a time she had wanted to talk to Glover about it and he'd bitten off her head, accused her of just feeling sorry for herself, handed down the famous Glover decree: "I'm surprised at you. I don't want to hear another word." Boss your men and shame your women; that was a rule of thumb with him. Odd how shame found its rightful place in life. Misused, it certainly made you want to kill someone.

Already the exhaustion he felt, sitting upright at this old dinner table, was a lot like being punched in the chest. He'd been sitting here since he was a boy; he'd been sitting right here, in one posture or another, for ninety-one years. Many a bad moment had arisen without any of them being the ones to have prepared him for this one. "I should have minded my own business."

"Dad, I don't want you worrying about this," Lois said.

Glover couldn't easily take this in. He had reached out his hand to try to pat her on the arm and noticed how erratic his own movements were. He saw his own speckled hand taking pathetic little slaps. He was so old he couldn't give a pat anymore, and she was too nice to guess what was up. His own little Halloween scheming, just to have a little of his old boss days back, had turned up this Teal. Out of nowhere.

Upstairs, Petey wasn't feeling well. He was sitting in the new, renovated bathroom with the unmistakable premonition that now he was going to be sick. At church this morning he'd taken peeks at Paul and decided that he didn't have to tell about the fight he'd witnessed if his grandfather had completely forgotten it. But Petey was right under that boat and had seen what Pops had seen. In their long drive to trick Paul, Lois had said, "I wonder what's upset us all?" But she had not expected Petey to know the answer. She had taken them all to a Dairy Queen for Blizzards and on the way home had asked Petey if he knew any stories. Stories were calming, she said.

He hadn't told her anything — or that she ought not to let Pops go down there with that guy Fluke. If he warned her now, she'd have to tell Spider about it and then Spider would know he'd gone down there with those boys just exactly the way he'd predicted. *"I've never known you not to need some directions."*

Downstairs, Lois was still learning not to shout, to reach out to the older of her charges, the one who thought his little plans had upset the neighbors. "Dad, honestly, the fishing was a good idea. I don't want you worrying about what anybody thinks." She looked him over. "You're not feeling well, are you?"

He was in a choke of emotion. He couldn't help noticing that he was being spoken to as if he were Petey ("Dad, what's the matter?"), which he well deserved. He would like to tell her how tired he was and how he couldn't understand why he'd insisted on staying alive just long enough to get her into something like this. Had it been that black kid? All these months out there, teasing him with his own boyhood and then coming up on the porch finally, just close enough to make Glover start acting like a fool? Hiring boys. What was he thinking? The one hand he'd extended for her to hold had ended up over his eyes, and he could only say he had no idea where these emotions came from, although secretly he was starting to guess. They came from some murky place to which he'd been tossing all such feelings all his days. His shames. Now they were bloated bodies rising to the surface just in time to give the serial killer away.

Upstairs, Petey blew his nose and sipped water after finally giving up his dinner and feeling like he could walk again. He sipped at water and then thought he heard (oh joy) Carol's car pulling up in the drive. Downstairs, Glover's voice ventured out until it finally found that hard edge of the pure business at hand. "My worry is how Paul's going to react when he sees those boys down there fishing this afternoon without him."

"Then the boys haven't stopped?"

"I don't know. He won't remember that he ever went fishing, will he?" Glover was able to take her hand then. Lois sat amazed at this display, tried to lean her body toward him to comfort him.

"Dad, he can go down there to fish if we want him to and he wants to go. I'd like to know who these parents are!" And she couldn't quite let her father get away with a miracle. "It's your bad hearing, Dad. You've missed out on most of that part. When he gets hung up he can remember to ask me when he's going fishing about forty times a day. I've counted."

"No." Her father opened those big blue eyes of his. This was news to him.

Lois opened her own blue eyes and stared right back at him. She stared him down, because she suddenly felt so angry. The literature warned you that others wouldn't know what kind of boat you're in, wouldn't really want to know. The one most needing to hear someone say the right thing was the one least likely to hear anyone ever say it. *"Forty times? Lois, I had no idea! It must be driving you crazy."*

Oh, she'd actually dreamed of someone saying that just once, bringing her home from a long dinner conversation, touching her cheek, and saying, *"Lois, I had no idea!"* Or else he would make love to her and then prop himself on one manly elbow and say it to her afterward. And it would be as with a tremendous weight lifted off her shoulders to hear anything at all that was said in an intimate moment. It was not just the loss of her husband's hand; it was the change of that hand into something quite high-tech. A robot's hand replaces the husband. RoboCop. Dead but quite alive — a strange humanoid wandering about her house, his mind in a perfect groove, his voice like a needle jumping back into that same groove if the floor shook. Sometimes she would hide in the house somewhere. If nothing moved, then the needle might not jump into the little groove of the day. *Are they back? Is it time for me to go fishing?*

"Paul, do you know who I am?" she had asked him once.

"Of course."

"Then tell me!" It had been a mean moment that she had not be able to avoid. A very mean moment. She had wanted to know. "Who am I? Tell me!"

"I know who you are!"

"Then tell me. Go on! Tell me."

He had looked frightened. "You're one of the girls."

While Lois sat holding her father's hand, she stared out the bright window of her sitting room admiring the countless blossoms on the old shrimp plant this year. The hummingbirds seemed to be interested only in those flowers and in keeping her and Paul amused for long mysterious moments in which she couldn't be sure she had not become more lost than he was. A big part of her life was over. Once she accepted that, she had felt less raw for a time. It was over. She accepted it and let herself imagine that he had merely died like so many husbands do at seventy — a heart attack, a stroke, cancer. He had simply died and now all she had to do was wait awhile until this humanoid in her house wore out and she could take it to the junk heap.

Everything was completely quiet, and it was a time in which she might have told her father a few more of her revolting ideas about this little situation. Few would believe it; but her father was a tough old bird. He would believe it. Full-time watch from morning until night made the wife think of murder. She'd noticed with Carol that as soon as she expressed the least sorts of painful thoughts, Carol wanted to figure out something by way of an answer. Oh, there were things the wife of a victim could do in her new situation; there were groups, there was study, there was the getting of a life the way parents manage when a child turns out to have Down syndrome. Think of it that way!

She had tried to think of it that way. Some days she was good at it and other days she wasn't. Some days she was very Zen and other days she went to the workroom to stab at pieces of wood with a screwdriver. Some days she went to her room to look at old photo albums and pretend that she was an old lady; it was just a matter of time and all this would be over. She was not without her quiet pleasures. Some days she took a hot bath and let hot water fall out of a saturated washcloth. She would hold up the cloth and let the water fall over her breasts. No two days were alike. Only Paul remained the same, that steady machine, while she on the other hand was like a recovering whatever, the recovering wife who gets through it all a day at a time, through each event with grace, with guts, with any means at her disposal. One day she is a trooper and the next day a terror. One day she is gentle and the next day violent. *"Who am I? Tell me!"*

"You're one of the girls."

"Oh listen! There's Carol," Lois said. She wiped her eyes. "I think I hear Carol's car."

Petey ran out into the lawn and jumped into his mother's tight arms.

"Oh-*ho*," Carol said. "Somebody missed me!"

"Take me home!" Petey moaned. He whispered so that Lois

wouldn't hear. But Lois didn't have to hear to know he was feeling homesick, exactly the feeling the wife wishes she could describe to the imaginary friend who will listen and not panic. One is home all the time, but feeling homesick. A woman had written a statement to this effect in one of the caregiver magazines: "I wake up in the night and I think I see the door to my own house. I pound and pound and suddenly it's my husband standing there smiling. 'Well, where have *you* been, Angel?' And he throws open his arms and sweeps me into the house quite dramatically and promises never to let me go; he missed me so much he thought he was going to die. Then I wake up and I'm really in my own house, only the same feeling of sickness has returned because then I hear him bumping around in the next room. He is trying to hide something in the closet."

GLOVER COULDN'T have been more grateful for the arrival of Carol and all the great commotion she caused in her shouts of hello and what a nice drive over she'd had and here were some tomatoes she'd brought him and did Petey have a good time and was there any roast left because she'd forgotten to eat and she was hungry — all of it was breathless and loud and done in a way that enabled an old man to slip into his room and be out of the way. Women were finally so sobering, weren't they, with their shouting and hugging and loud excitement over nothing more than sheer arrivals and departures. Their nonsense was liberating.

Inside his room he was amazed to think how close he'd come to breaking down. This was merely old age. Perhaps the longest week of his life had merely come to rattle him about a few things at the last possible moment. Old Man Scrooge. It was natural to have a bad conscience at this age. A man ninety-one who didn't have a bad conscience wouldn't be worth knowing.

But he was in a weakened condition with a smart man like

Teal. A galled man can rattle bones and make an old one feel like an idiot and keep him from sleeping, from being fit for anything but further nonsense. Teal was not, after all, a serious contender. He was not the sworn enemy of Lucky Apple dying flat on his belly just on the other side of this room while the Point Breeze Klan paid a polite call to the house to warn Virgil that they had no choice but to have one of their regular meetings on the other side of the lake.

"How regular?" Virgil had come to the door pulling on his britches by the long belts of his loose suspenders. "What kind of regular meeting? What are you trying to tell me, Carter? Don't stand there in the yard. Come on this porch and tell me what it is you're trying to say."

The local Klan boys were a lame bunch, but they had known better than to start something without warning the old man, who dated back. This was Virgil Glover's house and lake, and they didn't want him to take it too personally. Carter Davis had shown up himself to make sure Virgil didn't misunderstand them. And it wasn't as if Virgil had never been at a meeting or two back when.

"It's not personal," Carter said. He'd tried to yell it from where he stood in the yard.

"What are you doing standing out there? I can't hear a damn word you're saying."

But Carter Davis had clearly not wanted to get any closer. "We're gathering!" Carter finally cupped both hands. "For a meeting! I'm here to let you know."

"Know what?"

Carter had looked around him before climbing the high steps. He shouted into the old man's face. "It was pure back talk over in Littletown last night and we got to take their point of view into account."

"What point of view is that?"

"Back talk. Some of their niggers tried it with two white men and a woman. Nobody knows what they thought they were doing."

"Carter, I don't care about those Littletown people. This is my boy I got set up in here, and if you fellas are going to start some trouble I'm going to be ready for you."

"We're not going to start any trouble. We're going to keep trouble from happening. That's why I'm here. You got that boy in your house, and you got the Littletown bunch thinking you're trying to throw something in their faces."

When Virgil had finally gotten the gist of the thing, it had sobered him. "You don't have to shout, Carter." Finally he'd kicked one of the porch rockers. "Sit down and tell me what's going on."

Well, it was simple. Lucky had been in that mess over there and now the Littletown Klan thought it a pretty poor example Point Breeze was setting for its own niggers. They came over here only to find out that the one survivor was being looked after by a prominent white man.

Virgil was eighty-three at the time. This was nothing he'd expected, but it all made sense once Carter could get him to hear. They were just going to be over there on the other side of the lake, some of the fellas. The Littletown boys could even join them and it would calm everyone down. Nobody was throwing anything in their faces. Those boys were pretty worked up. From what Carter had heard there wasn't a Negro left in Little-town. Some of them were staying over here. The boys over there got it in their heads that Point Breeze was taking in their niggers. They didn't like it.

"You're not going to be right here in front of my own house, are you, Carter?"

Carter was hurt. They were going to set up all the way over there on the other side of the lake, where they always met. Just one of the regular meetings.

Virgil took Carter's arm and made him help him down the steps so the boy could point out to him just where he meant exactly. Virgil went to Lucky's bed in the parlor later and had a talk with him about it. They were going to have one of their regular type meetings and it would help them show those Littletown boys that they knew damn well what Virgil Glover had under his own roof. Alma could put a blanket over the window if he wanted.

Lucky didn't answer. He stared out with that persimmon eye of his.

And Virgil was true to his word. No one got any closer to the house than that — a mere reflection of light in Lucky's one eye. Nobody was going to start any trouble. Lucky was going to be allowed his peace. This was Virgil Glover's house.

But Virgil was a man who couldn't resist trying to find out a few details.

"Boy, what were you doing over there with that bunch of monkeys?"

CAROL SHOWED Lois and Petey the newspaper photograph of Petey in his winning costume. There were several other winners in the photo — the Little Mermaid, the Can Opener, the Cowardly Lion. Lois and Carol and Petey reminisced about the best moment of two nights ago when it had come time for the award ceremony, and the school principal had mistaken Petey for the Tin Man. Someone in the audience, another kid, had stood in his seat and yelled that Petey was supposed to be RoboCop, was he blind? Everyone applauded at having this matter cleared up. The principal gave a public apology and said that *if he'd only had a brain* he'd not have made such a mistake. The crowd went a little wild. Everyone wanted the smallest winner, Petey Barnes, to feel the good will in their applause, and he had accidentally rewarded them by intoning his best robotic "thank you" into the microphone.

"You were terrific," Carol said. She winked at Lois across the room. "So Petey, what are you going to do with the prize money? Don't you think you should split it with Grandma? Fifty-fifty?"

Carol liked to tease. Petey smiled and squirmed in her lap. "It was Grandma's roaster tins that beat out the others, right?"

"I guess."

"So go over there and give her your fifty-fifty hug. We got to get rolling back to Daytona."

"Thanks," Petey said when he reached her chair and felt mysterious vibes in the room — Lois not yet having told Carol how Pops had packed his shoes, how they'd had to get him in the car, how she had wondered aloud what might have upset him. Now he felt Lois hug him warmly and then heard her whisper, "What a good sport you've been." It was clear she wasn't going to tell Carol a thing.

Carol stood and stretched her back. "Petey, I never asked you what you did these past two days. Did you hook up with the boys and do some fishing?"

"No," Lois said, "no fishing this time. Maybe next time. It was very quiet around here. We were all a little bored." And then she winked at him. He loved it when she winked at times that Carol couldn't see her. He knew she knew he loved it. Still.

Carol sighed. "Hate to go. You should maybe run and get your duffel bag from upstairs, kiddo." She looked at Lois when they were alone. Carol reached out to touch her mother's arm. It was the famous family pat. "So, Mom! It's been quiet around here? Dad more or less back to normal?"

Lois started to speak and was politely interrupted.

"I found the rake in the closet," Carol said. She shook her head. "Mom, I know you might not be the group type, but there's no getting around a few facts. You're going to need support. You need it right now."

"Guess what," Lois said. "I finally called them."

"No kidding? Mom, that's great! See? It was easy, right?"

"Oh yes, it was no trouble. They have a group in Altamonte."

"That close!"

"It's very convenient."

Suddenly Carol was throwing her arms around Lois. "Mom, think of it as a present," she said. "It's a present to yourself. You have no idea how much this is going to help you."

"It's helped me already."

"Really?"

"A very nice man on the phone gave me a few pointers."

"See?"

Out on the porch Carol woke up the old man to thank him for the new folder of clippings he'd put out for her on the side-board — a whole month of clippings about the economy. He'd put her name on the folder in big letters, and Carol waved the whole collection in thanks at him as she left for her car. "Is it the end of the world yet?" She was worse than her mother in her tendency to shout. Carol tended to look straight at one's hairline. "Can I take a guess what's in here and how it all comes out?"

With one eye cracked open, Glover watched her junk heap of a car jerk out of his drive and into the road. He was never so settled in his mind that he'd done the right thing to set Petey up with a trust fund instead of leaving money to that girl. He'd kept it all a secret. He didn't wish to hurt her feelings. She was a kind but hopeless soul at forty-five wearing those same tired beads and teaching part-time with that hair still down around her waist. Turning gray! If she was counting on the boy's genius to get him through school on scholarships, she might hit the jackpot. Apparently his IQ was already off the charts. But his mother had jumped on the mother bandwagon with no way to pay for his very likely need to have his head examined later. He'd been handed over (artificially) to a very nice, not young, woman who taught grammar at a community college and who had no interest in either money or a husband. Money or a man seemed a bottom-line requirement. But not to have arranged for either one — what were these women thinking?

He'd always liked Carol. He'd never known how in the world to tell her he liked her, the two of them oil and water since she left home and took up the Girl movement. She was like her father. Two missionaries. They'd both have been better off in the Congo, where it was clear that some people were born needing sulphur pills and others were born needing to hand them out.

But missionaries had gone out of style for Carol's generation. Instead she'd found work volunteering at a halfway house of some kind over at the beach. For boys, she'd once tried to explain; it was for boys who couldn't survive at home. The idea had reminded the old man of those last two panthers in electronic collars. But how could a person not admire Carol when all the rest of the world went crazy on credit cards. Carol was a steady eccentric. Harmless enough; likely to do a bit of good in the world if only by accident. The girl could be a bit off-putting, but she certainly never sat around feeling sorry for herself.

They'd had an odd conversation not long ago when she'd been over for a visit and had seemed in a good frame of mind. They were both watching Paul water the lawn, and Glover, feeling himself start to choke up all of a sudden, had asked her a rather innocent question, which came out sounding all wrong.

"What kind of history did he teach?" Glover had mused aloud.

But Carol snapped back at him like a snake. "Why didn't you ever ask him when you had the chance?"

The answer cut him to the quick. He hadn't seen it coming. "I was too ignorant to ask," he finally said. He watched with relief as the girl nodded that at least this was true and she was glad he knew it. Finally she sighed. "Well, as a matter of fact, Dad never taught history at all."

"He didn't?"

"It was a family joke you thinking it was history. One time you introduced him to someone early on as a history teacher, so he and Lois decided not to set you straight."

Glover was so floored he'd had to take shallow breaths and curl his hands quietly around the arms of his rocker.

"The truth is, Dad taught Latin."

Glover was sure he hadn't heard her. "What did you say?"

"Latin, Granddad, Latin! My father was a *Latin* teacher."

"Well, you don't have to blast me out of the water."

"I'm sorry."

The two of them were alone. He'd sat thinking how Jemmalee would have known all those years.

Lois must have sent Carol out to the porch that day to visit with him, Lois always sensitive to the fact that they might seem to be leaving him out of their socializing. She was always sending Carol, at every stage of her life, to the porch to have a chat. Or maybe that day Carol had come to sit with him entirely of her own accord. Carol never felt that they left him out of anything, and she had never cared to slink around his house feeling guilty. For this he'd been grateful; and for some of her blunt ways, too. They had reminded him of himself.

"You always let people know it was hard on you that Dad taught school. They were sure Latin would make it harder. So they never set you straight. And in forty years, you never bothered asking."

Glover finally said, "They were right. I was afraid they were going to starve, that's all. I didn't know any better at the time. Don't you realize how ridiculous I can be?"

Carol had actually smiled at this. If you admit you're ridiculous only once in ninety-one years, the effect is quite splendid.

"Well, he was a Latin teacher. Do you want to ask any other questions while you're at it?"

"I'd like to know about that time he got himself arrested. Your grandmother hinted at that, but I never got the story straight."

"It's not much of a story, really. He went to Tallahassee to help with voter registration, and there were a few bad riots up there that year. Mom made him come right home. I don't think he came home until he'd spent a night or two in jail."

"Your father's a fine man," Glover had suddenly said.

"I never thought you believed that."

"They don't get any better than Paul."

"I wish I'd known you felt this way when I was younger. It might have helped my mother, too. We never felt we got your approval."

"You didn't."

He liked having the last word, and with Carol he often got it if he talked himself down a little. It reassured her. Women her age liked self-deprecation in old tyrants. Went a long way, and for the old man it cost nothing like what it would have cost him when he was young. When he was young he'd found he could never get off his high horse. He had sat around thinking about this fact for ten years after Jemmalee was gone and had realized that his last-word business had more or less ruined what otherwise would have been a pretty good marriage.

BY FOUR O'CLOCK, no Gap Kids had come to fish, or disturb the long afternoon. Glover decided to keep watch for them anyway, so he could explain to the hired ones that the deal was off. He wasn't going to have his son-in-law shaken up by the sight of parents or cops; *you boys can understand that, it's not part of the deal.* And, in his own mind, he decided that if Paul asked to go down there when he saw the boys, they'd have to talk him out of it, they'd have to cross that bridge when they came to it.

Meanwhile there were no boys at all this evening. Maybe each and every one of them had vanished into thin air. Without the sight of them in front of his nose, Paul had no awareness they existed. He stood watering a whole lawn, which itself must have ceased to exist in the long interim since yesterday.

Then Glover remembered Sundays were days when not very many boys ever showed. On Sundays the Mirror Lake parents spent time taking them to one or the other of the tourist traps in the area. Relatives were down visiting from the north and they couldn't all sit home. In Florida the young professionals were always entertaining their parents. Or, if it was the retiree parents who'd move down, then it was they who entertained the professional children from up north. Nobody got together on this thing. Which was good for the tourist traps. Your people needed a place to go once they deplaned and reunited with you and then realized how damned hot it was.

Sunday was when the Gap Kids got paid allowances and went shopping for Reeboks in refrigerated malls after church. Quicker than Paul Barnes himself, any Gap Kid on this lake could fill a suitcase with nothing but his Reeboks, and on this feeble joke Glover drifted off for a third snooze. He was as far off his guard as possible by the time Ted Johnson came up on the porch and talked right in his ear.

"I'm here to get him, Mr. Glover," the boy said. "Is he ready?"

Apparently Glover's mouth had stood open a long time in sleep. When he tried to close, his entire jaw caught.

A small mail order catalogue Carol had brought the old man this afternoon had, at some point, traveled to the floor. It looked bright and slippery in the free hand of this youth, who offered it with a certain awkward frankness. "Here," he said. He'd shaped the thin pages into a long tube. "Where's Mr. Barnes?"

The boy was hardly thirteen, if he was that. He thumped the catalogue a few times on the porch railing and this caused Glover's brain to go blank. He was bone-dry from snoring, from opening up wide enough for a nest of screech owls. He might not have come up with a thing to say had he not spotted the bandage on the back of the kid's head.

"What happened to you?"

"Nothing."

"Somebody get you from behind?" The round bandage on the boy's crown looked like a Jew's skullcap. Glover couldn't ever remember the name for it. He finally had to grab the catalogue away from Johnson to stop that dull thumping sound.

The boy made a small shrug only having to do with getting hit from behind. His too huge gaze took in the back wall of the porch and on up to the high ceiling, where an old dirt dauber worked on an elaborate hive. Glover had been watching the very same dauber when he was bored and wanted to think of the slow, painstaking insect business — all that architecture of rooms and passages pre-existing in the cells of eggs not yet stored there.

"Where's your friend? They get him, too?"

Johnson's reply was simple. "Bradley split."

"Too hot down there for him?"

The boy suddenly smiled. "Yeah."

"But not for you, eh?"

This time he grinned. "I *like* my job. Mr. Barnes is okay."

Glover didn't much care for natural charm like this unless it was his own. The challenge sharpened him up. "Mr. Barnes doesn't seem to be getting much fishing done."

The boy stretched one arm above his head, perhaps weighing his next words. "It's the others. They kind of shake him up. That's what Bradley thinks."

"Ah, now that I hadn't thought of," Glover said, almost to himself. "I hadn't thought of that." He slapped the tube in his hand, feeling himself flummoxed. He slapped himself with meaning while part of his own boyhood rushed at him like the back draft from a fire — an image of himself at thirteen or fourteen being cruel and taunting someone, pulling the trigger of an unloaded gun jammed at the base of a cousin's head. Just to scare him. And worse things. Here he'd gone a century later and turned Paul over to boys! Minors! What could he have been thinking? His own cousin had been retarded. Whenever any adult had his back turned, the village idiot got strung up by his shorts.

"Did they hurt him?" he said, eyes watering. He hadn't the stomach for this, not at this point. He slapped the magazine across one leg. He felt like getting his gun and shooting someone. How many last days was he going to be reminded of his own slippage, forgetting the garden-variety cruelty of boys. It was a virtual law of nature. How stupid could he be? Teal's own boy had been down there poking Paul with a stick!

"They just said things," Johnson said.

Dear Christ, Glover had yet another blip of himself at thirteen — some boys in a boat; someone in the water crying, trying to get in the boat.

"I can take care of people saying things," Johnson said. It was an out-and-out boast. "You get into that by the time you're about this big." He measured out an inch with his fingers.

"What'd they call him?"

"They talk to *me* about him! You know. They use him to get at me. I don't think he hears. Nothing's happened to him."

"His mind won't take it," Glover said.

At first he thought Johnson wouldn't reply, but it turned out that he'd been expecting something like a white man's scruple, and he weighed his words again. "I can take care of him, man."

"No, you can't, and I'm not blaming anybody. I didn't see the whole picture. It's nobody's fault."

The boy seemed to spit a little piece of thread out of his mouth, something invisible he'd been chewing on to keep his wits about him. "I'm sort of *in* this now."

Glover didn't grasp the point at first.

"You know? I'm *in* it, man. I can't let them think they've run me out of that hole." Johnson rushed forward: "Or him either. Mr. Barnes either. It's public property down there."

Glover could only stare at him.

"I tell myself it all depends," Johnson said.

"On what?"

"They're saying I stole Fluke's wallet. I didn't, but it's gone, man. It's gone if they say it is, and if I quit coming it'd look like I was scared to return to the scene." The boy turned and looked off over the lake.

"Who's Fluke?"

"Fluke Teal."

But Johnson, who'd been explaining his personal situation from a half-sitting position on Glover's porch railing, had turned back again and was now easing to his feet. "Hey, Mr. Barnes."

"Paul Barnes." The man who'd pushed open the new screen was already putting out a steady hand.

"Yeah, so I was just telling Mr. Glover that the fish are biting down there this afternoon. Looks like we have it all to ourselves."

And then it was Lois at the door, glad to see Ted, bubbling over at him. Whatever gauntlet was thrown at the old man's feet was taken up by her in her innocence. "I'll get his shoes!" She was gone again and back again, and the movements of the screen flying open and then shut seemed to set the whole world into motion. Glover could only sit and watch. Too many people talked at once; his hearing aids popped like corn in a pan of oil. From then on, and throughout the time it took Paul to put on his shoes and Lois to bring out a brownie for Johnson, Glover stared at the lake because it was clear that for the rest of the evening no one was going to pay him the least attention.

Without any of the taunting down there the two fishermen did just fine. No cops showed up and Johnson had the right touch in the work of keeping Paul's mind on his task. For an hour the fish seemed to be in on the new arrangement. Something took a bite at their lines every time they winged them out there, which Glover once or twice almost thought he heard. And again in the middle of the night when he woke up, icy, he was sure he heard that old sound. History never repeats itself, it just rhymes. The eerie zing of Lucky's fishing line, and of his own, hour upon hour so many long lost years ago. Lucky had died saying he could hear that sound.

And so finally *I'm* dying now, he thought. That's all this is; I'm dying and my life is flashing before me as in a slow leap off Niagara.

8

ON MONDAY MORNING he wandered into the sitting room and felt he was in the middle of someone else's household. Paul was about to sit down to a plate of fried fish for his breakfast, looking enlivened and more focused than he'd seemed in a long time. Paul's clear and unstrained voice moved into Glover's head for the rest of the day. "These are the prettiest fish I've ever seen in my life," he said. "Where'd we get these beautiful fish?"

Lois and Glover dodged around each other that morning, keeping private reservations to themselves. Lois wouldn't have minded having a look at parents who said her husband was cramping their style. Glover ruminated silently in a different direction. He was going to have to take action if Teal had already reported Paul being down in that hole again yesterday with a minor.

After the noon meal he sat on a stool helping Lois dry dishes. He sat thinking how he was stuck with her, how there was no privacy in this house for emergency situations. One moment he doubted Teal had called the police, and the next moment he was sure he had. The cork going up and down made him dizzy and blank.

"Dad!" Lois shouted. "I'm thinking of joining a support group!"

"A what?"

"A support group!" Her hands in the soapy water moved against a lone fork she'd missed. "They have *groups* now! For people like me! I'm thinking about *joining* one!"

"What? Today?"

She turned to look at him. She was tired of this. "As a matter of fact I could!"

The relief Glover felt was so profound he was afraid she'd see it in his face and become suspicious. If something would take her away this afternoon, it would be an answer to prayer. He imagined dispatching the whole sticky situation in a single afternoon if he were on his own and could think straight.

"You do that, Lois. You talk to those people. You find out everything you're going to need to know."

He dared not meet her eye. He polished, front and back, an old saucer and examined its familiar fine cracks before finally hearing his daughter concede that, well, if he really felt so strong about it she'd only have to make a telephone call.

"I wish you would, I really do. You go in there right now and find out." He waved his towel at her. He felt old impatience in his veins. What was holding her up? "Go on and call those people!" And in his imagination he saw himself standing tall on the front porch this afternoon. He saw himself shooting from the hip.

TOM GLOVER couldn't say for sure what might come, in the very next breeze, to rattle his confidence — Lois's accidentally shouting too loud again before driving off, or another leak in his lower plumbing, or a son-in-law left alone for five minutes while his back was barely turned. Glover went to his room to change his diaper sling, and in the time it took him to achieve snugness Paul sat at the table pasting first-class stamps on a batch of letters. He evidently thought Lois's newest sheets of bright stamps were tuberculosis seals; he evidently thought it was Christmas.

"What are you doing?" Glover said.

Paul said he was getting these letters ready to go out in the mail.

Glover could only stare in disbelief at all those clean white surfaces overappointed — so many new stamps all set to ride on the backs of Lois's electric and phone bills, on the backs of her bank deposit and monthly car payment. A single stamp cost what a grown man once earned in a morning's pay, and Glover knew he should try to enjoy the free adrenaline he got in being this completely stunned several days in a row. The excitement would kill him.

He wondered vaguely if he had strength to steam off stamps at this late point in his life. He thought of the heavy stool he would have to drag to the stove and the two boiling teapots he would need. He would also need solitude. His lack of solitude made him furious enough to yell at Paul, who had no idea what the old man was angry about. To soften the blow in being yelled at, Paul tried to change the subject.

"Where did she *go*?" he asked. He looked out the window and was trying, heroically, to calm himself. When Glover saw that he'd made the poor boy's eyes water, he wished he were dead.

"She'll be right back," Glover said. He'd tried to make his voice steady and cool.

Paul grew quiet and then he mused aloud as if it were all so curious, this new life he experienced every day, all that disappeared into thin air. "She always finds somewhere to go."

"And she always returns!" Glover said.

Paul seemed to hear a little joke in this observation. "Yes indeed," he said, "she always returns."

It was Johnson who returned to cheer the Latin teacher up. At four o'clock Paul waved at the boy pedaling around the bend on his bike and then said, "He's back!"

"Hey, Mr. Barnes, how you doing?"

Glover was sure now. Paul absolutely no longer knew black from white. Glover watched the handshake ritual and heard Paul introduce himself. To remember the difference between black and white, one surely had to remember the whole shebang in which the mess belonged — history, time, accident, and sin. Even Latin.

Otherwise all cats are gray.

This afternoon Johnson seemed to smile at the whole house. He seemed to have no fear that in arriving alone like this he could pass, new red jacket or not, for Glover's lawn boy.

Glover was confident that he must need the money he was getting a whole lot less than he needed his federation of friends. But the Gap Kids were phenomenally absent again today. Absent for good. Nothing around the lake moved a hair. This was an out-and-out boycott. But the boy shoved hands in his jacket and looked around him while Paul changed his shoes. Every now and then he looked at the old man and nodded, as if he approved of the house and Glover's good setup.

Old cypress trees rose up in silent sentry this afternoon, and the entrance to the tomb looked shut. When Paul had his boots on, Johnson broke the silence. "Let's see what's biting down there today, Mr. Barnes." Glover attempted to call out after them, "Enjoy yourselves!" but felt a knot of anger in his throat, swollen hard. He was going to have to fire this kid. He couldn't have the police coming around here, upsetting Paul, ordering Paul out of a hole Glover had dug himself with his own dragline.

But who was it, after all, who was most upset at the moment? Glover himself, that was who. Himself, and not Paul, and certainly not that kid out there. And he found the realization somewhat amusing, now that he was alone again. He put a shaky hand inside his breast pocket, where he kept his pepper pills. Under his flat tongue, the Nitrostat started to fizz and bring him to life. Glover felt like a frayed old electrical cord that someone had just shoved into a wall socket.

He eased forward enough to see the elephant ears divide and

let the pair slip away to that famous hole. The steep slope in the bank at this point and the consortium of high green weeds finally hid Paul and Johnson from Glover's vantage point. But around the clock face of the lake people would see those two easily enough this afternoon — white man and black boy in a kind of throwback, something out of history. Maybe Johnson brought along that red jacket to make himself easy to spot, to help make Luke Teal's point for him: our black kid has lost face; this is what happens when an old man tampers with the natural law of integration.

The fall lawn raking, too, was a throwback, a Central Florida agreement that all should take part in an old myth. Once upon a time the world was deciduous and now it was not. Now the world was temperate. No bothersome leaves fell here. Mirror Lake residents came out in early November to rake as part of the remembrance of imperfection. There was nothing urgent to be gathered up, or burned, or carted off; no winter ground to prepare. They had the leisure to lean on rakes and note Johnson's new red jacket flashing out at them from inside the bright green weeds this afternoon, where once there'd been a heartening show of boys. Someone had poisoned the ground over at the hole in front of the Glover place. They kept their children home.

Of course, in a life as long as this, an old man is bound to have seen a boycott before. Lucky had lain flat on his stomach on the other side of Glover's new room, smiling at it — a kind of boycott flickering with light in his eyes, although they wouldn't have known to call it that. No one came or left the house in the three days, except for Doctor Cooper, who first went around to talk to those boys about it. He was a family friend. Nobody was going to keep him from crossing the picket line.

Getting him home hadn't been a problem. Uncle Fate and Tom Glover got out of Littletown at dawn and had left everyone with the dead bodies to keep them occupied. Alma was standing ramrod in the yard when the truck pulled up with Lucky on a bed of straw. Several Negro women waited with her, and Wilson was there to help unload him. Uncle Fate tried to make Alma take a drink before she looked to see what kind of condition the boy was in, but Fate only infuriated the woman. In her mind his smelly overalls and unshaven face had something to do with what she was about to see. White men on a rampage. When Glover folded back the blanket her expression hardened, her face became the fixed eyes and mouth of a hawk. She began giving out orders and taking charge of the difficult transport from the truck to the house. She'd already determined that she was going to have to keep him out of drafts, and her parlor was where the oil heater was. She saw he could tolerate only lying flat on his stomach with only the unburned right side of his face in any shape to stand the softest bedding. It was the position in which the blast had caught him. She said "Wait!" when the men had put him down the wrong way. "He can't turn his head! I don't want him staring at the wall, I want him to look out into the room!" But he couldn't be lifted again, and so she'd had the men turn the whole bed around with him in it.

His right arm and leg were the most damaged. They had to bring the bed somewhat out from the wall in order to put his right arm on a kitchen chair with a flat pillow under the arm. The bed wasn't wide enough otherwise. But Lucky lay looking out into the room the way she wanted him to. If he could have stared at that arm he wouldn't have been in any doubt that there was little way to survive. He wouldn't have been in any doubt if he could have stared at his charred back, his exposed buttocks and legs. There was no flesh on his back or his right arm or leg, although no one glancing at him could see that for sure. There was a lot of blood lying on the surface of what might have been flesh to an untrained eye. By noon the first day the pain kept him talking and asking them if they were sure he wasn't still on fire. Doctor Cooper took Virgil and Glover out for a private chat in the hall. Lucky was like a piece of meat that finishes up on the top of the stove. "He's going to keep cooking. The heat is trapped in there." Doctor Cooper had put it to Virgil in just those terms:

in a burn as bad as this, one might think of the victim continuing to smolder.

By sunset Lucky was wide awake when the Point Breeze Klan started up their first regular meeting on the other side of the lake. Nothing personal. Part of his strength was in never losing consciousness for the whole affair, his good eye seeming never to close. When anyone went in to put a little broth in a spoon, or give him a piece of soft soaked bread, he was always staring out and keeping his wits about him.

"Are they coming in here to get me?"

There was no explaining to him that the lights he saw were for show — one group of boys out there letting another group know that the situation was in hand.

Anyone allowed to enter the parlor could study his body from head to toe without Lucky's having to know he was observed. He had no view of the visitor first entering, forced to stand and see what could happen to human flesh after another twenty-four hours. His long body was still intact even as they noticed a dramatic loss of shape. During the first night the fluids raised the under-skin everywhere and by morning turned the boy into an old log in brackish waters. Once he asked what day it was. When he tried to speak his eye fluttered shut and then sprang open again, that bright red persimmon clouding over. He was far-gone but still brilliant. He put fear in everyone, especially in Virgil, who came in to pray. Later, in his first delirium, he had asked Glover when they were all going to Littletown to pick up that car. Then his head had cleared again, and Glover had gotten down close and thought he'd heard him say that he never understood anything.

"Did *you*?" Lucky whispered a few times.

"Did I what?"

Wilson risked his life that night and came in through the back. He had a version of what had happened. Lucky had been over in Littletown to get a car he was supposed to tow home for a new motor job he'd agreed to do. Trouble had already started at the edge of town. He had stepped out of his truck when some boys came running at him, young boys, flagging him down but then not stopping. He must have been caught by the horses coming out of the darkness in front of him, and then everybody rushing past him because he and his truck were too late to help them. He wouldn't have had time to turn the truck around. And he'd probably panicked right along with them. His truck had been found sitting where he left it when he started running.

On the third day he turned thick white, and Alma posted herself round the clock to fan him lightly because he said it felt necessary. On his right arm and right leg they began to see down into places where some of the flesh tried to crust and pull open the bone. Soon his skull came through the back of his head precisely as he'd caught the blast, Glover understanding all over again how the fence sagging under the weight provided an angle for the heat to sear up and down the right side. His entire back was bursting with fluids at the end of that day. Doctor Cooper said he would die of gangrene. It would go right to his heart.

Alma kept opened bottles of violet water near his bed. And she burned bay leaves and put wintergreen around. He began to run a higher fever that final day, but he couldn't be covered and at times the tremors of cold in his frame shook the bed. Alma made them string clothesline around so she could stretch blanketing over him and down to the floor without its touching him. He said blankets worked to keep down the drafts, which he felt once the fever set in again. And no one argued with any crazy thing she wanted to do for him. Doctor Cooper was there again to look him over and to tell Alma she was going to kill herself. And she had said, well now, that was surely an exaggeration.

Lucky never did get back the right tone in the few times he spoke from that bed. First he said, Mr. Tom, he didn't want the colored ladies from the Hollow at his bedside practicing their voodoo. And he didn't want any of them worrying about him. He'd be all right, he said.

The slow hours seemed to tick by one tick at a time in the night. Toward the end Lucky started to whisper so that Glover had to bend in low to hear him. Once or twice he smiled. He said he understood everything now.

"What?" Glover said.

"Don't ask that, boss, if you don't already know."

OVER IN ALTAMONTE, women sat on either side of Lois in a living room so small they had to put the family Bible under the aquarium stand. While they waited for the meeting to begin, one woman leaned in and whispered in Lois's ear that she had an Alzheimer's husband at home who couldn't be left alone anymore now that he kept trying to cook. What stage was Lois in? the woman was polite to ask.

Lois turned to look at her — another caregiver in her same boat; the room was full of them. The husband kept trying to fry things, the woman breathed. He once tried to fry a lid off a saucepan. One time he put an aerosol can inside a hot oven. Naturally she was worried. Her sister was over at her house right now looking after him.

"You all!" A younger woman's earnest voice rose up from the other side of the room, interrupting the flow of whispers all around Lois. Everyone was confiding an episode in whispers. Lois hadn't realized it would be like this, like lying in bed listening to the anecdotes in her literature recorded on a live cassette of whispers. For a moment she surprised herself in the thought of bolting for the door. She was not the type to do something dramatic.

"You all! Let's come to order now so we can get started."

Someone named Georgiana was in charge of a devotional opening, a small passage she read from an inspirational book and a brief prayer on patience. During the prayer the woman next to Lois whispered on. She thought Lois ought to know that every time, right after the devotional, there was a young girl here who dominated the group meetings. She bet Lois a dollar that right after the prayer that girl over there in the short skirt would take over the meeting. Her name was Charleen, the woman said. She'd be the first one to tell what happened at *her* house that week. She always wanted to go first.

When the devotional speaker said amen, Lois was amazed when Charleen started right in. Lois felt the woman next to her nudge her hard in the ribs.

"We had something real strange happen Friday," Charleen said. "Y'all listen to this if y'all want to hear something strange."

Charleen told everyone that on Saturday her father said out of the blue that people were coming into the house and replacing everything with something counterfeit. "It's like he is thinking of the government," Charleen said. "He told us they had come in and made our whole house into a duplicate house. It was an exact copy of the house he built twelve years ago down to every last thing in all the rooms. And then he said that Mama was a duplicate."

One woman opposite Lois in the circle folded and unfolded quiet hands in her lap. Lois was afraid she heard crying.

"All this weekend whenever we were over helping Mama, he would point at one of us and say, 'I want you to tell me who she is.' He said it was because of Mama that he figured out the whole thing."

Charleen was interrupted. "Darling, you mean he didn't recognize your mama?"

"Well, he did, but he just didn't think she was the real thing. Everything in the house would have fooled him completely, but he said his wife didn't fool him. With her it was easy to see she was a counterfeit. Last night he took me over to a picture hanging on the wall to show me all the trouble they went to to fool him. Then he said, 'Except for her,' and he pointed at Mama. He said with her they didn't try very hard. With her they didn't seem to go to no trouble."

·   ·   ·

IN HIS LIFE Tom Glover had never prayed, unless one counted those spontaneous wonderments any man might utter. *Dear God in heaven!*

Teal's chief of police was no bluff. Glover opened his eyes and saw a white and blue squad car easing around the north bend on Mirror Lake Road. Five? maybe ten miles an hour? Glover watched the thing pull off the road and shove its nose against Johnson's fallen bicycle. The motor went down in a flutter of post-ignitions and desperate gasps while the chief, or perhaps only his deputy, sat unmoved for several pumped-up moments in which Glover listened to his own heart. Incredibly he let himself imagine Johnson grabbing Paul by the sleeve and leading him out of that hole by an escape route they should have discussed.

The police chief (if that's what he was) didn't like the sound of his engine; dirt in his carburetor. He spent some time listening to the trouble. When he finally opened his door, he stood up and stretched; at his highest point he was not as high as the light on his roof. The man appeared relaxed. His broad back was to the water, which today was the pure blue of berries or cornflowers. But the chief's first interest evidently was in eyeing Glover, who nodded at him and then recalled how men used to give each other nods like that whenever blacks were anywhere in the vicinity.

Glover wished he could take it back, but the chief wasn't going to let him do that; he touched his hat to show he appreciated it. Then he turned and walked to the slope, where the boys' path opened up. A very broad back and just that hat became the last slow things to disappear. All Glover could think to do was get up off that porch so he wouldn't be called on to nod a second time. Inside the house he felt dizzy.

In Altamonte Lois felt much the same sensation as she stared at her hostess's family Bible under the aquarium, whose motor, apparently, had gone bad; a loud whine overwhelmed the soothing bubble effect. Lois stared down at the coffee table, which already had a creamer and sugar bowl and napkins set out. There would be refreshments later, she guessed. Fresh coffee and cookies, punch with ginger ale and lime sherbet floating in it. This had been her life; it had all come back to her — PTA, Girl Scouts, book clubs, and circle meetings in a succession of several decades blending together.

Someone gave a tremendous sob, and Lois was floored to realize that it was she herself. In the middle of a group member's account of a daycare center, Lois suddenly stood up in the room.

The hostess smiled. "Honey, it's just down the hall and on your left. I've got a light on in there."

At the end of a short hall, Lois found a bath and two bedrooms. She found a pink princess telephone on a blond nightstand in one of the bedrooms. She found tissues in her pocketbook, and then she dug out the Orlando hot line number and called David.

"Hi, Lois," David said. "Is Paul okay?" He listened to her sobs and then said he'd never received an emergency call from anyone while they were actually attending a support group meeting. Was it really that bad? he asked. Personally, he'd always enjoyed them.

Within moments Lois was no longer out of control but found she could only sit with her head in her hands. She wanted to leave, but she didn't want to go home.

"Lois, I think you're having an episode. It happens to caregivers all the time."

"But I can't afford an episode. I have my father to think about, as well as Paul. Now it's the neighbors."

"I want you to tell me all about it," David said. "I really do. But right now you should politely get yourself out of the meeting and get to another phone to call me. It says here you're near a big shopping center over there."

"Yes, it has a Publix," Lois said. "I need to pick up a few items."

"Fine. Do your shopping and then call me from the shopping center. I don't want you going home right away. Promise me."

"Well," Lois said. "All right."

·   ·   ·

TOM GLOVER hadn't used the phone since Jemmalee died. After she died he had answered the phone a few times to discover all the calls were from salesmen and advertisers wanting the lady of the house. Glover took to shouting, "Hold on while I get her," and then he'd let the receiver dangle by its cord for an hour, for the rest of the day. It was his favorite prank before he stopped answering the phone for good. *"Hold on while I get her."*

But right now who would he call, what would he say? That the police chief was parked out front? He closed the front door behind him and thought of trying to dial Lois at that number she'd left. The fragrance from her noon ham was still in the air. He stood in the long dark hall of his house, refusing to go into his own room. He would *not* go near a window, where he might be seen peeking. He determined to walk slowly to the back, where he could kill time in Lois's kitchen, hunting down a brown bag in which to hide those letters from her until he knew what he wanted to do about the stamps. He could spare her knowing about those stamps. He sat and rested on his stool once he got back there. He sat staring at the letters loaded up with enough credit for trips around the world and to the moon. He wouldn't mind going.

Then he retraced the long hall and arrived at his own room, where he just had strength enough to pull all his shades and sit down. If he could just figure out how to do it, he'd gladly let other folks try to figure it out. Lois and Johnson and Teal and the chief. But he was just like all the other troublemaking old boys he used to observe in his youth. Hangers-on. These days they hung on for their hundred-year-old birthday greetings from the White House. Some people didn't know enough to drop dead.

Ten minutes later Glover felt sure it would be all right if he looked to see if the chief was gone. He was. And apparently he hadn't yanked the fishermen out of that hole. Neither had he come knocking. Glover felt oddly demoralized. A chief today wouldn't think enough of him, at ninety-one, to walk to the house to talk over the situation. He was back in his rocker on the porch by the time Johnson brought Paul home. The boy seemed surprised to be questioned.

"I didn't talk to anybody."

"I saw a policeman go down there," Glover said. "I need to know what he said."

"Nothing, man," Johnson said. "I'm not kidding. He just looked at us. He just had himself a good look."

"He didn't say a word to you?"

"He said hello. That was it."

Glover opened his mouth and then closed it. Today the sound of Johnson's lilting syllables with all their nuances of nonchalance and friendliness only reminded one how the boy wasn't white; how they were both in over their heads. It would be wrong to have him come again for Paul. He must order him to stop coming right now. Right this minute. Hell, tell him not ever to come back!

Johnson sat down on the steps and watched Paul take off his boots. "You can sure fish, man." The twilight slipped down on them a fast notch or two, a jump into darkness that all November skies attempted this time of year. Johnson continued to sit. Glover watched light drain out of both him and Paul as if someone had flipped a switch. In the change of setting he tried out something else: "Where do you live? You never said."

He may have heard the boy laugh. He wasn't sure. "I don't live far from here."

There was the bike; how far could he live?

"Where are your folks from?"

"Right here! Where'd you think?"

"I mean originally."

"Who knows, man. Nobody knows where we're from originally."

A smart aleck. Son of university people. But if Glover could get used to the slight irreverence in Johnson's retorts, he might get somewhere with the boy, assuming he knew more or less where he wanted to get. There was that lilt of utter confidence in the boy's voice that he just couldn't quite trust as real. How could he interpret such a thing, floundering upstream in the great distance that age and inactivity had carried him away from a boy like this one.

"Do your folks know you're doing this?"

Another shrug. "Sure," Johnson finally said.

Glover knew nothing. He was too far-gone. One was inevitably too much behind or too much ahead to know what to ask a boy whose outer edge barely touched his. One's knowledge and life were utterly nonnegotiable; nontransferable. Write a check on your knowledge and watch it bounce!

He saw the boy's ease and certainty rise and fall in the small, silhouetted shoulders. They heard Paul excuse himself to go into the house. Something in Paul's innocence caused the boy to smile. Darkness dropped down another visible notch, and he turned to face Glover and give him a more lively shrug; perhaps it was the sight of just the two of them, a return of mild amusement. What a hoot, he might be thinking. Glover didn't know the local expressions, white or black — *what a gas, what a hoot, what a scene.*

"Something funny?" Glover said. The boy was standing on the steps.

"Naw, man," Johnson said. "I gotta get on home." He looked embarrassed, or else just awkward, barely a teenager but with huge puppy hands and feet.

"Sit down," Glover said. He motioned Johnson to stop that thumping and to sit down in the other rocker. "Sit down. I want to show you something."

"Okay, but I gotta go soon," Johnson said.

He was limber. He could spring from standing to sitting in one snap when he wanted to. He was like a movie run backward.

Glover pulled out the brown bag he'd shoved inside his large sweater pocket. "Listen, I'm half blind and I've gone and put these good stamps on the backs of my letters. I thought they were TB seals. I've gone and put over thirty dollars' worth of first-class stamps on these letters."

Johnson leaned forward to investigate. Then he shook his head at the mess. "Man, I don't know what to tell you, Mr. Glover."

Glover lowered his voice. "You take these on home and see if your mother can steam them off and use them."

Did he *have* a mother — an aunt, a sister?

Johnson laughed. "You sure you want me to do that?"

"I don't want her bothering with this kind of thing. She's high-strung."

Glover surprised himself, giving this out on Lois. But he dreaded her coming back, finding out all he still had not yet told her of Mr. Teal's campaign. He couldn't put off telling her about the police. Right now all he could do was hold out her letters. "You take these and mail them for me when you get the extra stamps off. Somebody over at your place can go on and use them."

Johnson sounded doubtful (*"Man! . . ."*). In the one syllable he could jump from incredulity to joy and back again. He let the batch of mail pass into his jacket, and Glover thought he heard him say, "Don't worry about it." He gave no knowing exchange of glance to show he'd caught on that it was Mr. Barnes who'd done this. Johnson wasn't going to expose that fact if the old man himself didn't choose to, and it crossed Glover's mind that this was why men preferred each other's style over that of women.

"Don't worry about it, man."

Johnson's hand came back out of his jacket. This time the boy held a clipping someone had cut from a newspaper. To unfold it, he shook it roughly, almost in the way he thumped everything else, half in pleasure, half in indifference. "I almost forgot to give you this."

"What is it?"

"It's *you*, man." He said this as if Glover ought to be as embarrassed as he was. "When I saw it I couldn't believe it was *you*."

Glover took what was being offered into his own hands. Even in the semidark he could see it was only an old photograph of him they reprinted once in a while to advertise the local history museum. *Thomas M. Glover of Point Breeze shown here with hand-operated crop sprayer of early farming era.*

In the photo Glover was as stooped as ever, a trained bear on hind legs. He was shown holding the handles of a contraption that looked like someone's ancient ice cream churn affixed to the top of a tiny plow. Indeed. An ice cream churn on a plow was more or less all that a crop sprayer was in its earlier inception. One man pushed while another walked alongside and turned the crank. Slow work if you could get it.

Glover put out a bent finger and tapped. "I'll tell you something. The poison we put inside this gadget was strong enough to burn a hole in your shoe. Strong enough to curl the hair on a conservationist."

"I couldn't believe it was you, man."

"We knew what we were doing. Where did you get this?"

"My mom cut it out and gave it to me. She wanted you to have it."

Ah. So he had a mother. And where, exactly, did that get them?

"Man!" Johnson said again. He still thought the photograph was either amazing or ridiculous and shook his head a few times. "I couldn't believe it."

"It's me all right. They took that picture about ten years ago."

An awkward gap opened up in the otherwise little bit of rhythm just starting to flow between them. It suddenly hit Glover that the big difference between the two of them was in how much more experience any kid had in the larger world than he did. Johnson had been growing up just about the same length of time Glover had been in retirement. In the natural scheme of things, Glover should have expired on the day Johnson was born. They were not meant to have ever had a thing to do with each other.

Johnson finally said, "You want this for your scrapbook?"

"My scrapbook? Now that's an idea."

The retort made the boy fold up his clipping pretty quick. Had Glover inadvertently made fun of his mother's thoughtfulness? Dear God. Glover thought he saw eyes flash out the clear message that he could stick this clipping up his wazoo.

But Glover had read him wrong. The boy smiled and got up to go.

"They took that picture the day I cleaned out my warehouse. I took them over to my warehouse and they made off with a truckload of antiques." He felt talkative suddenly and wouldn't mind saying how perhaps the whole history of man could be seen in a crop sprayer. Routine and drudgery, he wanted to brag to the boy; that's how they did it, an inch at a time; history was just a snail moving in a line; the past was nothing but one contraption replacing another.

"Hey, man, I wanted to ask you something."

Glover felt his heart move. "All right. Ask away."

But the boy hesitated. Evidently he had a problem with the idea of invading Glover's privacy. Or else he was pretending some hesitancy if the question proved delicate. Or else he was just being charming. Johnson cocked his head, and there was strategy in that delay. He made Glover beg him.

"Ask!" Glover said.

"Is it true what somebody told me? A lady told me you were *born* in this house."

"That's right."

Johnson couldn't sit still. He preferred to get up from the rocker, to pace, and then to ease himself onto the porch railing as if he were going to have to stay awhile now. Glover let him know he couldn't stand that thumping.

"Sorry, man."

In the silence Johnson looked around at the porch for any details he may have forgotten. There was the old dirt dauber nest of yesterday. Johnson gave the nest a little squint. He seemed to have no more questions.

"Who was the lady who told you I was born in this house?"

Johnson smiled to let Glover know it had only been a friendly little trap. "My grandmother," he said.

"Your grandmother! You're not from around here."

"My grandmother is. And her mother, too."

Ah. So that was it. The boy was as old as *he* was.

9

DAVID'S LINE WAS BUSY when Lois tried the pay phone inside Publix at the shopping center. She hung up and watched a young woman in a tailored suit come in from the parking lot pushing a cart. The woman's crying baby sat in its jump seat looking so obviously not the child of a businessperson that Lois wondered if she was seeing a kidnapping. She got a Doppler effect of sound as the cart sailed passed her. The baby's loud wail became a thin trail of unacknowledged grief.

At bottom Lois wanted to give in to whatever that baby had given in to in being pushed backward, unable to turn around in the direction things were headed, bare feet, like two hard red potatoes, kicking. She didn't want to be here either; she didn't want to be at this stage of life.

She dialed a second time and was put on hold because David was taking another call. This was a busy time of day for the hot line people. In the late afternoon all caregivers had a higher rate of incidents. For one thing there was "sundowner's syndrome" in the late afternoon. Everything about everyone's situation seemed worse as darkness fell. Everyone took turns not knowing where they were.

Lois hung up and got a cart. She headed to her father's favorite aisle — the doodads — where one could always find, in every Publix, the athletic socks on one end and paperback books on the other. Kitchen accessories met midway. The plastic eggs of panty hose sat next to the refrigerator magnets, and, after the magnets, one entered a section where it made some mysterious shopping sense that quilted toaster covers were next to the shelf paper and a selection of outdoor barbecue aprons with printed messages just for men. Lois thought, I'm having an episode.

Someone almost crashed into her cart. A young man let her know in exasperated grunts of breath that she was in his way. He picked out something from the shelves and made a clattering U-turn. She had time to call "Oh, I'm sorry" before he had disappeared in the direction he came from. A smell of nice cologne moved in the spaces he no longer filled, as if the man had stepped right from his toilet of intimate bottles and bracers without bothering to dress, while Lois continued to feel all the less visible. Perfumes and colognes had never taken on her, an odd quirk in her chemical makeup. She sometimes felt she was without great presence in the world, or that she had gone out of style. When she looked up she glimpsed the woman in the business suit passing the opening at the end of Aisle 9 and pushing forward in her assertive way to something more serious — a career in marketing, Lois guessed. How crafty of some women now to own those oxblood briefcases costing more than round-trip tickets to places other women had never been. Lois thought again about the poetry course over at the university she had hoped to enjoy in her latter years. One time Carol had taken her through a very difficult modern poem and had been surprised at how much her mother could decipher on her own. "You've wasted a good mind here, Ma!"

"Well, it's absolutely not true," David said. "You're one of the most intelligent callers I get. Go back up to the part about your father hiring the boys."

"You said I was having an episode?" Lois said.

"Most of the time we feel there's no action we can take. Paralysis is our biggest symptom. Right now you have to get out there and tell people exactly who you are. If the neighbors are really saying Paul shouldn't be allowed to fish, they can at least say it to you."

She knew he was right. Right now the last thing she wanted was to have them say it to her. Not far from the entrance to Mirror Lake, Lois pulled off Highway 419 and parked her car at the old Texaco station. The owner, Kenneth Winton, still had his paper skeleton and black streamers hanging in the window of his tiny office lined with motor oil. She knew he wouldn't mind her parking at his station for a while; she had decided to walk around the lake instead of using her car, which she would have to keep pulling in and out of people's driveways. She would be less noticeable on foot.

She found Kenneth Winton with his nose inside a battered truck. He was a shy boy with no girlfriend, and whenever he gave Lois a tune-up she tried to spend some time with him. "How are you, Kenny?" she said, as he eased his head up to keep from bumping himself.

He'd been better, Kenny said.

It was not a good sign. She could get stuck here a long time with him if she wasn't careful. In their conversations Kenny would bring her up-to-date on his grandparents, whom she'd known as a girl, but after that she'd learned to expect vague complaints from the boy about one thing or other — his back, his teeth, his feet, his left hip. Kenny was only twenty-seven and a real health liability. He was perhaps what abject loneliness produced in this town.

"Kenny, I'm going to leave my car parked over there for an hour. You don't mind?"

"No, I don't mind." But his hopeful look started to fade.

When she left his station and crossed the highway, she entered the sunken lake area by a small right-of-way ending at Mirror Lake Road. Once this was a mere trail, and now it was one of two entrances to the lake. Odd to feel the hint of childhood available in one's simply having gotten out of the car. The scenery slowed down to a walking speed. She used to use this road every afternoon on her way to and from school, walking with three or four other children in deep wheel ruts passing through the center of an orange grove her grandfather had planted. The old homes still had their dirt yards at that time, some with chickens in coops or chickens running loose or stout women taking in the afternoon laundry, turning to call out greetings as children split off and separated, something flashing in the sun which must have been all the empty lunch pails. The newer homes now still retained their broad frontages. They were the mixed-brick houses of the late sixties, all with their big picture windows and globe table lamps.

Lois decided to brave the first house she came to. It had a lone boy's bicycle she thought she recognized under the wide portico. The bike stood beside a spectacularly large, uncarved pumpkin, the kind shipped down here from New England. Someone looking through the picture window spotted Lois before she got more than halfway up the front walk. A door flew open and a woman in a shiny exercise suit waved at her, then hesitated politely. "Hello." But Lois was not the person expected. She slammed her front door firmly behind her to indicate she was on her way out in case this was a volunteer from the Heart Fund. She swung a tote bag, snug with tennis rackets and all the other youthful accouterments to make a woman start to lose her nerve. Lois braved it out anyway. "I'm your neighbor, Lois Barnes," she called. "I wanted to introduce myself."

"Of course!" the woman said. "How are you. I'm Joyce Knight."

It was not until Lois said that hers was the Glover house that the woman said "Of course!" once more. She was eager to tell Lois that she was the woman who'd heard Lois's father calling from his bathtub several years ago.

"I beg your pardon?"

"He didn't tell you? He got stuck in his tub one morning! I guess it was before you and your husband moved in. I think he got turned around with his bad arm on the wall side and couldn't pull himself up. I heard him yelling clear out in the road!" Joyce

Knight lowered her voice in sudden inexplicable secrecy: "Those were my jogging days." The woman laughed and her volume went way up again. "Not a jogger anymore, am I? Right now it's tennis, tennis, tennis." And then the tones were top secret: "We're such beginners, we just bat the ball."

Meanwhile Joyce batted the air. She was waving at someone pulling up in a white sedan who confirmed everything Joyce was breathless to explain. This was her ride over to her club. Tennis and then a girls' night out. "My husband and kids are on their own. Margaret! This is Lois Barnes, who's over in the Big House now." Joyce again dropped to her low pitch in what Lois finally determined was her imitation of a stand-up comedienne: "Did you know we called it the Big House, Lois?"

Lois tried to picture this woman once hoisting her father out of the claw-foot tub he used to use in his old bathroom off the kitchen, but Joyce was hurrying on to her next topic. "You're our Tara, did you know that, Lois?" She could walk backward; she walked backward while calling over her shoulder, "Margaret, haven't you and I admired the potential over at the Big House? You have such a prize. If you ever want to put a little money in landscaping, we know architects."

They had come to the end of the walk together and arrived at the white sedan. "Hi," Margaret said. She was a slightly prettier version of Joyce, her features a bit smaller and more classically composed. "We're late!" she said, but her concern was affable enough. She smiled sweetly at Lois.

And then Joyce suddenly took real pity on their older neighbor, whom they both knew all about, apparently. "Margaret and I want you to know that we aren't very involved in this thing because our kids are girls." She searched for words. "We all sympathized with your situation over there, but we could see Luke Teal's point of view, too."

Margaret nodded at Lois from the car. Her smile was a show of agreement, but with a heavier dose of real understanding. She said Lois's situation was the saddest thing. And then to Joyce: "Did you see that *Nova* program they did where they talked about Rita Hayworth having Alzheimer's? My father loved Rita Hayworth. Did you see that program, Lois?"

Lois knew she wouldn't be given much time with these girls and their tight schedule. Margaret's car idled but never shut down. Lois asked who Luke Teal was.

"Luke? Luke organized our Neighborhood Watch. He's an enormously informed person, isn't he, Margaret? Oh gee, what all *has* he done in the last five years?"

"He got us the historic marker," Margaret said.

"And who is he?" Lois asked.

"He had a long talk with your father," Joyce said. "He said your father's amazing. How old is he now? A hundred?"

"Ninety-one." Lois felt dizzy. "Mr. Teal lives nearby? I've never met him."

"Osprey Landing. It's the first house on the left."

"The right," Margaret corrected.

"I'm always backward," Joyce said. "The right! He's an organizer kind of person. You ought to meet him. Nice family man." Joyce looked up and down Mirror Lake Road before she said, "His son, Luke, is kind of a problem."

Margaret disagreed. "He's a big bully is what he is."

"Well," Joyce started to explain. Then she just said, "You know."

Margaret hooted. "A juvenile delinquent."

"Oh he is not, you crazy person!"

The two women began to laugh, and Joyce confided in Lois that her friend Margaret was just the *worst*. Then she hefted her tote bag. Lois knew she'd better be fast and clever. "I'm trying to find out something that is a little embarrassing for me to come right out and ask."

"Oh, go ahead, go ahead, my goodness."

"I have this only secondhand. Are the parents on the lake against my husband fishing with their boys?"

Her directness took Joyce aback. "Oh, gulp!" she said. She performed a pantomime of having swallowed an insect. She looked at Margaret. "We were told you'd agreed not to let him

fish anymore during the boys' hour because of the danger factor."

"What danger factor is that?"

If Joyce seemed mortified now, Lois suspected it was drama.
The girl was quite as much up to direct confrontation as anyone
was: "The violence thing." She took a step forward. A lovely
white hand, spangled and professionally looked after, gripped
Lois's arm for an intimate squeeze. She touched another spectacular hand to her neck.

"My husband is not the least bit violent."

"Well, Luke's *other* point was how it didn't seem fair that the
boys had to look after him . . . you know . . . in their playtime
and all."

"My father must have forgotten to tell Mr. Teal that he's
paying some of the boys."

"Well, yes. The Johnson boy."

"You know him?"

Margaret was not altogether delighted. "Oh, we know Ted
Johnson. Don't worry about that."

"We're not exactly fans of his," Joyce explained. "Ted is a
little troublemaker."

"How?"

"God, it's so complicated." Joyce stared. She glazed over as if
she would go into a little stupor from the effort to express adequately how complicated the matter was.

Margaret looked at her watch. "Yikes, Joyce!"

"What? Oh God, look at the time!" She sprang into the road
and hurried around to the passenger side. "Lois! Good to meet
you finally!" Her head disappeared and then reappeared beside
Margaret's. "I hope you'll say hello to your dad for me. I just
think he's amazing." The women were so completely coiffed,
they looked good enough to photograph — two pink faces in the
plush interior of Margaret's new car.

"Would you mind if I gave you a phone call?" Lois said.

"Oh sure!"

Both of them said the word on the same downbeat, which

made them burst into laughter at how hilarious they sounded. They were careful to repeat their individual good-byes for Lois, but quickly so as to get them all said before Margaret's electric window whined closed and covered them up.

SHE STOPPED next at Will Cooper's house. Lois felt badly that she was just now coming around to pay them a call. They were the only neighbors who had ever acknowledged the fact of her moving here. Phyllis Cooper had brought Lois a casserole.

But the Cooper doorbell chimed in four loud chimes like a clock. Nothing else responded from any part of the house. Lois could see through the hall and all the way back, where blinding light bounced off the patio.

No one answered the door at the next three houses where she looked for more boys' bicycles and dogs, one or the other of which was consistently visible. But the parents and kids were not at home. At the next house two boys passed a football back and forth and looked at Lois. They were used to joggers. Lois was a mild novelty walking slowly toward them in her low dress shoes.

"Hello," Lois called.

"Hi," the smallest boy said.

"I'm just doing a little survey," Lois said. "I guess you know what a survey is."

"Yeah," the older boy said. He gripped the football to his chest, both sets of fingers flexing and reflexing. He waited for Lois to come into the yard.

"I notice some of you boys do some fishing down at the old hole, and I was just wondering if you pick certain days and avoid other days. I live up in the Big House."

"It's public property," the older boy said. He put the football on his hip and thrust the hip out. She'd seen this boy's pose in Carol's high school annuals.

"That's right. Why aren't you over there right now?"

"We're not allowed to fish down there now."

"Not allowed!" She wanted to sound amazed at the injustice of this.

The smaller boy was eager to confirm just how unjust it was. "Our parents won't let us." He came running up fairly close to Lois. "There's a crazy man who fishes there now." He was excited to let her know this, and his older brother threw the ball at his back as if he were trying to topple him. The little boy was outraged and confused. He knew he'd been silenced and his feelings were hurt; big brown eyes had teared up by the time he'd turned back around to face Lois, with whom he was clearly in love.

"That's my husband," Lois said. "He has a disease that causes him to lose his memory. But he's not crazy."

She would have to prove it. Neither boy was the least interested in finding out her husband *wasn't* crazy.

"Are your parents at home?"

The older boy squinted and said no, they weren't. His little brother looked at him in obvious respect; such glib lying.

"Well," Lois said, "another time. Maybe you'll tell them that the wife of the man who fishes down there stopped by to talk over the situation. I think there's been a misunderstanding."

"Yeah, okay."

"I will, too," the little boy said, excited again. "I'll go tell them right now!" And off he went at a run, heels kicking up. He was apparently still so enamored of Lois, he showed off for her that rear view of running kicks.

"My brother's the one who's crazy." The older boy smirked.

"It's not a good thing to say as a joke."

She had forgotten the way boys just a little older than Petey could stare back at adults with such unnerving expressions. The boy fixed on her mouth until she felt herself bite her lip. "My husband's not the least bit dangerous, by the way. He can't remember things. He can't remember his children, for example, which I find quite sad."

The boy was not moved by this information. "Why can't Ted take him somewhere else? Why does he have to bring him down where *we* like to go?" For a moment the boy was so intent, Lois thought tears would spring to his eyes. He didn't let her answer. He had his own answer. "Ted Johnson ruins everything."

It was hyperbole so long used and reused that the boy did not recognize it as such. He merely used it again. "His family ruined our whole school and everything."

"They did? How?"

The boy could only glare at her as a reply. She saw he had no way to tell her what had gone wrong. "Ruined" was all he'd been told, or all he'd overheard, or all that he could take in at his age. He believed people *could* ruin a whole school, the way they might ruin a good linen suit.

"I have to go," Lois said. "Will you tell your parents I stopped by?"

"Don't worry, my stupid brother already told them."

Lois laughed. "You didn't want me to know they were here. Why not?"

"They're in the back trying to get the pool cleaned. Go on back, if you want to."

Lois wanted to like this boy, but it was difficult, seeing how easily he framed everything into a kind of dare. He knew this was a woman who didn't belong to his parents' set, a woman whose very age put her low on the scale of people worth knowing. Lois's own insecurity and niceness showed, and the boy had no mercy. He was glad to practice his skill at making someone like her uncomfortable on an otherwise dull afternoon.

"What's your name?"

"Ronnie."

"Nice to meet you, Ronnie." The last name was on the mailbox. "Ronnie Newell. That has a nice sound. I'm Lois Barnes."

Then the boy blushed, as boys will. She wanted to believe that there was hope for him in that blush, but very quickly Ronnie recovered his advantage over her. "If Ted is down at the hole again today, Fluke Teal's dad is going to call the police." In controversies of this type, boys naturally hoped for the worst. Ronnie was counting on Ted not to disappoint him.

"Fluke Teal? Is Fluke a nickname?"

Ronnie shrugged. He told the truth. "Yeah." He was tired of her now. Lois watched him turn and run through his yard at a slow lope, football curled in one hand, his shoulders drawn up in great imaginary padded affairs. He aimed his ball at the portico and managed to hit the pumpkin with it. She sensed that in hitting the target, Ronnie had reinforced his daily lesson of entitlement. Perhaps these parents wanted their Ronnies to feel confident that they deserved their lives; people who weren't in the parents' circle deserved not to be. All Ronnie was supposed to do was to hit everything he aimed at because he deserved this expansive house, that hidden pool out back, those Reebok shoes, a set of friends who wouldn't ruin the fishing with a crazy man.

When Will Cooper's car pulled up beside her in the road, Lois was relieved to see someone she could ask a few things and clear the air. What had gone wrong at the school?

Will said he didn't have the whole story; he'd heard the Johnsons didn't think much of the curriculum over there. "Not enough African American history, Mrs. Barnes." Will shrugged. "I heard that the boy won't go to his history class. He's making his own little statement every day by sitting out history in the principal's office. They say the rest of the black kids are thoroughly confused." Will smiled. "These people are intellectuals, Mrs. Barnes. University people. They've come down here to show us how behind we are." He turned to gaze at the lake and then shook his head in a knowing way. "The rich Northerners lord it over us, too, Mrs. Barnes." He lowered his voice. "I can't tell who's worse — the Johnsons or the rest of these people. I don't have much to do with any of them. Me and Phyllis found a country church in Walker. Between that and work and the baby, we don't get too involved with these people on Mirror Lake." Cooper shook his head. "I wouldn't be surprised at a thing you told me."

IN THE NEXT ten minutes Lois made her way north where Mirror Lake Road continued in a little loop and then intersected with a small road branching off into Osprey Landing. The Teal house sat at the entrance on the right, a two-story colonial, its American flag flapping at a lovely angle on one of the wide columns. Another open portico ran the entire front of the house. Another bicycle, another freak pumpkin, this one weighing perhaps more than Lois. A black maid in a starched uniform came to the door and behind her the aromas of hot food wafted from an otherwise empty and quiet house. Girls' night out? The maid said that Mrs. Teal was at home; she was resting.

"But I don't think she'll mind. Come inside. I'll get her."

She closed the front door behind Lois and motioned for her to sit down in one of the foyer chairs. The woman may have been older than Lois, and when she walked slowly out of the foyer her arms lightly touched what furniture and doorframes made themselves available until she disappeared into a hall behind the stairwell.

The stairwell was a spacious open affair with two glass and crystal chandeliers lighting the way to a wide set of windows on the first landing. A small trunk sat in the landing draped in an antique quilt and appointed with dolls, a porcelain washbowl. Off the foyer Lois could see into two rooms, a living room to her left and a den to her right. More quilts were nicely displayed on wooden frames and there seemed to be wonderful brass lamps everywhere. Lois liked the way the early American style accommodated itself to lots of crowded plaids and florals. Below the green Victorian wallpaper decorating the small den were wood paneling and shelving loaded down with books and videotapes. It was a lush household of things.

Mrs. Teal came into the foyer from some sunny tea room, Lois guessed; or else a patio or rear family quarters. She was dressed in white cotton everything; red wool sweater arms came over her shoulders, and she had her head cocked in anticipation. A lot of big, gorgeous intimidating auburn hair one found in magazines. She did not appear from her expression as uncaring of this interruption as the maid would have led Lois to believe. When she saw she didn't know Lois at all, she let her skill with Heart Fund volunteers take the form of one syllable. "Yes?" Lois felt suddenly defeated. It was a youthful but gaunt face from which a yes meant no. Such thinness in the body. According to the literature that look in women meant as much anger as discipline.

"I'm Lois Barnes, your neighbor. Am I disturbing your dinner preparations? I should have telephoned."

"Then this is quite a coincidence! My husband just called to tell me the police already have a verdict. They were fast, weren't they?"

Lois let herself be shown into the den, wherein Mrs. Teal kept moving away until she came to a smaller service door at the back of the room. "Please! Sit down." She excused herself for a moment and then returned with a glass dish of brownies. "Annie made these. She'll bring us some tea in a moment." Mrs. Teal sat down finally. "The police completely take your part in this affair, Mrs. Barnes. Did you come to say, 'I win'?" She sighed and looked over her shoulder as Annie came in with a tray of two teacups and a pot. "Let it steep, Miz T."

When Annie left, Mrs. Teal smiled and put her hands in her lap as a show of good faith that she wouldn't pour tea until it had steeped. "I'm glad you're here. I've wanted to tell you myself how upsetting this has been for my son and his friends." The woman couldn't wait. She reached out quickly and lifted up the pot in order to fill the cups. "Someone said you couldn't possibly know who you were hiring when you chose our neighborhood model child." She handed Lois a cup and saucer. "He and his parents are right out of a magazine, aren't they? I tell you, I've learned my lesson about some things being just too good to be true."

"I haven't met the Johnsons," Lois said.

"Oh, well then, you're in for a treat. Forrest and Christine." Mrs. Teal sat back and pondered the names. "Christine and Forrest. We're all neighbors." Mrs. Teal looked at Lois and said, my, she'd like to be a fly on the wall when Lois met the Johnsons. "You'll have seen everything."

"Mrs. Teal, I was told you were upset by my husband."

The woman again put her hands in her lap. "Your husband is a liability, Mrs. Barnes; the Johnson boy is dangerous. Together the whole thing is a mess."

Annie was back to tell her she had a phone call, but Mrs. Teal shook her head and waited until they were alone. She lowered her voice for Annie's sake. "I don't know how many times the Johnson boy can be allowed to pick a fight with my son. His opportunities are unlimited, apparently. We haven't been able to get a teacher, much less a law official, to do anything about it." She handed Lois a small napkin. "We're fed up with the boy's taking everything over the way he does. I'm sick to death of everyone's falling all over himself and *herself* for Ted Johnson. Tired of it. Sick to death." There were apparently a few absurdities in the whole situation which eluded Lois and caused Mrs. Teal to enjoy feeling privately amused: this case was complicated, apparently, but oh so simple. "Every minority group, Mrs. Barnes, has its explanation for every concession they think must be made for them. You are interested, for example, in the rights of mental patients. It's amazing to me. One can't raise an eyebrow in protest anymore. I'm surprised we're not under arrest over here for complaining."

While she took a short break from her soliloquy, Mrs. Teal stood up and moved to another part of the room to investigate one of her quilts. Lois saw her take a small scissors and snip a thread. "I hope at least we don't give in too easily. Right now my son has no interest in going back there to be beaten up and robbed by everyone's favorite person of color. So I suppose we are capitulating. My son is sick of these things too, Mrs. Barnes."

"I'm sad to hear all this."

"Are you? Well, let's talk about you then. Do you see our boys as babysitters, Mrs. Barnes? They *all* have to be exposed to your husband, whether you pay Ted Johnson or someone else to be down there with him."

"Mrs. Teal — "

The woman raised a hand to stop Lois from bothering. "The police agree with you, Mrs. Barnes! Not to worry. I don't know why my husband bothered checking up on *our* rights. Our rights are completely outdated now, I gather. If Ted weren't black, no law official would hesitate to correct a situation in which a mental patient is being put in the way of our children."

For a moment Lois was shaken. Perhaps she was right.

Mrs. Teal looked around the paneled room. She spoke to her walls and furniture with a kind of sadness in her voice. She said she was really tired of this sort of thing and that she felt rather at her wits' end. She had resigned herself to the outcome, but also she had taken just about enough abuse from people who felt they themselves were abused.

And that was when Mrs. Teal rose from where she was sitting and walked to that second door through which the activity of tea serving had gone on. She begged Lois to excuse her, and Lois actually jumped when Mrs. Teal suddenly called out in a loud voice for her maid, who came into the room looking alarmed. Mrs. Teal merely wished that Annie show Lois to the door.

Lois couldn't quite tell how long Annie might have worked for these people, but one thing was clear: Annie still hadn't gotten used to being called from the kitchen to show people to the door. The house wasn't quite grand enough for this measure, but Annie did the best she could to make her accompaniment of Lois into the foyer the right gesture. Lois wanted to remark to her about the inconvenience. But that would not have done; and so as she approached the front door she said to Annie that it had been an awfully pretty day.

"The paper said it's going get cool tonight," Annie said, opening the heavy door and looking. "I'm covering up my crotons tonight."

"Surely not in the first of November," Lois said.

Annie laughed and motioned over her shoulder as Lois stood on the portico outside. "It just dropped down in here about forty degrees." She shook her head at Lois before she closed the door. "Don't you be too worried about it, you hear?"

10

PAUL WENT OUT to get the paper on Tuesday morning and then told the first person he could find that those boys were back.

"Who?" Glover said.

"It's those boys," Paul said. He had the worried look. He'd seen something outside. "They're back."

Glover checked the big clock on the wall. It was seven-thirty. Early-morning fog would still be covering the lake, so he hadn't yet raised his front shades. "Well, let's go see about it, Paul."

On his canes he moved into the hall and to the open front door, where he thought he saw snow in the yard. Snow patches clumped here and there on the ground and enough of it hung from the oak trees to make an old man think he must have died in his sleep.

Paul moved in front of him to open the screen. When Glover got himself to the extreme edge of the porch he began to comprehend from several nearby plastic utility bags that his front lawn was strewn with garbage. Much of it was still in heaps from being quietly dumped out of those bags; and beyond the slowly loosening mounds, bits of everything in the world had scattered a hundred feet west thanks to a good wind this morning. Glover could see ragged paper in both the side yards, but especially due west, where most of it had stopped at Jemmalee's line of verbena. Long strings of paper looped from limb to limb in the giant trees over there. Paper dangled from the lowest branches of Glover's two biggest magnolia and from his one squat sour orange from which she used to concoct her marmalades. Suddenly he missed her terribly.

"Wait," Lois said, having come to the door herself. She didn't want Glover putting a foot down on those steps until she'd had a chance to check them for honey or gravel or pieces of rolling rice.

A young jogger, one of the regulars, had stopped in the road. He yelled at his dog, who was entering the yard and going a little crazy in the smells scattered everywhere. Many a neighborhood pet or bold raccoon had already done some investigating. The jogger's dog was a high breed of Dalmatian, who appeared ungraceful bounding here and there in an excited hunt for chicken and soup bones. Its owner was first amazed at the mess and then annoyed.

"Rachel! Come here!"

Glover stayed back with Paul and let Lois negotiate the steps. She was taking a broom and carefully sweeping a path, but Glover cautioned her anyway. If the girl took a fall, they'd all be in the drink.

"Where's she going?" Paul asked.

"She'll be right back," Glover said. His next thought was they were going to need a bulldozer.

Lois approached the jogger, who met her halfway, stepping through paper and real food to get his animal on a leash. "Look out now," he said, automatically taking Lois's arm and leading her out to the road so she wouldn't slip on anything.

She and the young man had never met, but for eighteen months they'd been waving, "Hi, how are you," and now the man's sheer wonder came out as easily as any of his regular niceties. "My God, I thought Halloween was *last* week!"

Lois turned to look at her yard and house from this perspective. The azalea bushes were draped in green and black bags. Her father and husband made a sweet mute pair on the porch as they gazed at her with a kind of brand-new innocence. Countless distant white specks decorated the large side yards as far as she could see, but between her and the porch were big frightening mounds. Lois half expected to see buzzards.

The kids had had no trouble collecting an impressive amount of material for this mean prank. Tuesday's regular pickup was more or less here, and Lois stood thinking how she'd earlier observed with interest that her neighbors liked to secure their Tuesday pickup under lids that clamped down like quaint canning jars. Some owned festive carts equipped with handles and huge aluminum wheels.

The young man had a loud kind of humor with which to protect himself: "I haven't seen anyone get papered in a long, long time."

Lois didn't know the concept.

"Oh sure. You got several dozen rolls invested here. I didn't know anyone still bothered." He was clearly feeling nostalgic as he stooped to rub his dog behind the ears. "What about that, girl?"

Rachel closed heavy eyes. She was full of bliss. She panted and turned her head in the direction of two more joggers who were rounding Mirror Lake Road, one just twenty feet in front of the other, neither of them noticing a problem yet.

Lois was tempted to ask the young man if he thought she had undergone an initiation rite. Was she merely being taken into the community? Her head was getting dizzy. Perhaps she need only get with the program, as Carol sometimes explained. Getting with the program helped one overcome the stress of the times one lived in. She imagined Carol nudging her hard in the ribs. *This is certainly a good way to meet the neighbors!*

"I'm Lois Barnes," Lois said, turning to the young jogger.

"Jay Jones," he said, standing up quickly and then pushing back his cap. "Look, Mrs. Barnes, this is terrible. I'll make sure we get the parents and the boys over here this afternoon after school. I can't believe this."

"Is this about the fishing?" Lois said. She was starting to spin.

"I doubt if the boys realized they were making this big a mess when they did this. They must have gotten hold of some beer. This is outrageous."

A tall bald jogger was behind the other but gaining. He advertised the University of Pennsylvania on his T-shirt this morning, and the smaller man in the foreground, whose fine features and dark skin hinted that he might be Indian or Arab, was taking off his headphones and stopping to see what had happened. He whistled and told Lois right away that he and his wife had wondered where their garbage was this morning; the truck hadn't come around yet. "Do you have anybody contracted for yard work? Maybe they could send over a crew." But just then U of P had come to a halt in the road. Had he noticed Lois standing there, he perhaps would not have pulled the plugs out of his ears and said the first thing that came to mind.

"Holy smoke! Did the husband do that?"

The question alarmed the younger Jay Jones, who didn't know whom he would embarrass most by saying aloud that this was the wife herself. Jay Jones finally didn't say anything; instead he gave Lois a painful smile. Perhaps he even saw how his neighbor's stray remark had gone straight as a shot into Lois's pride and out the other side where it hit the mute Latin teacher on the porch.

She would surely have spoken up for herself had she not been somewhat transfixed at the clear path of a wounding arrow piercing her husband's life of simple deeds. Up on the porch he didn't seem to feel a thing, but for herself she might as well have been taken back in time to the summer that same man on the porch boarded a Trailways bus and went off against her will to register voters in Tallahassee. Her bad behavior of so long ago lay exposed again for her to see. She might have been a red apple split by that arrow — "Holy smoke! Did the husband do that?" — as a much younger woman still alive in Lois stood crying with the receiver to her ear. *Please, come home before you get yourself killed.*

"I'm Lois Barnes," she suddenly said, looking up at the gathering of men around her. This time it really was an episode, her words sounding delayed and enlarged as if she were talking quietly into a public address system to men at a great distance from her — men standing in the sunny world of birds chirping and schedules to meet. The men introduced themselves — Owen Newell, who was the bald man, and Hinter Ratag, the Indian or Arab. They told their names and smiled at her. Jay Jones rubbed Rachel's ears and waved suddenly at Tom Glover on the porch. "Hello, sir!" he called. "How you making out this morning?" All three men waved in a hardy, neighborly way. Ninety or a hundred, it was the amazing old man up there. "Hello!"

"Excuse me," Lois said. Owen Newell turned to look at her. "I met your son Ronnie yesterday, Mr. Newell." She felt inside a well. Her voice slapped against high wet walls. "I met both your boys. Ronnie and the younger one."

"Allen."

"Yes. Did he tell you I stopped by to introduce myself?"

"I'm sorry. I had no idea it was you." Owen Newell smiled again because surely he was forgiven his terrible faux pas just now. "Allen tried to tell us somebody was out there. I'm sorry we missed you."

"Allen thinks my husband is crazy."

The man gave her a disappointed look. He saw she hadn't quite forgiven him.

"I see you do, too, Mr. Newell," Lois went on to say.

His head didn't move this time. His smile froze as he gave an eye to the two men. Then his expression changed completely. There was nothing for him to do with a woman like this but hold his ground and speak in a gentle tone. "Well, I don't especially like your husband fishing with my boys, if that's what you're referring to."

The two other men pumped lively feet in place, eased off, called their good-byes to everyone. Big grins of *so long*. Jay Jones even called out to Lois that he'd be in touch about that matter on which he'd already spoken. But Owen Newell didn't appreciate this act of desertion. Mr. Newell raised his voice to make sure his buddies heard that he had more guts than they did. "It's Alzheimer's, isn't it?" he said.

"Yes it is!" Lois said. She, too, called out to the backs of the two cowards quietly decamping. When she turned to Mr. Newell again, she realized she was not angry. It was only that she'd not been paying attention to the world very closely. She saw that this was not the time to broach the subject of neighborhood boys "acting out," as Carol would call it, in her front yard. The man was too irritated at Lois right now. Polite hackles were up.

Besides which, Lois was having an episode. At the center of it, her husband suddenly stepped right out of the lost past, and the garbage was completely unimportant to her. "Mr. Newell, you have no idea what an interesting disease this is."

He wanted to give her the smiling benefit of the doubt. "I've not heard it described quite like that."

"Well, you see, it affects everyone around the victim as well." She gestured at her yard, hoping that he might be a subtle kind of person, a man able to come off his high horse with a simple apology for his thoughtless remark, or able to offer help, or suggest that they try to talk all this over. What an enormous opportunity, Lois suddenly realized. She was prepared to die for Paul at this moment. It was a discovery about herself for which she almost wanted to thank someone. Why not this man! Maybe Mr. Newell was prepared to die for his children; they were all in the same tiny boat, the same spinning bit of interesting planet.

"Mr. Newell!" she exclaimed, feeling inspired and uplifted by her little episode. "Would you like to meet my husband? He's a wonderful man."

But she saw he couldn't budge now — the idea that on a Tuesday morning she believed he had time for her and her husband. "Mrs. Barnes, let me just put to you very simply what has been our only point in this matter. There are twenty-four hours in every day. None of us understands why Mr. Barnes has to be down there in the one or two hours after school the boys like to fish. The way it was explained to us, you folks seem to *want* him down there with the boys."

Lois could think only that while no one ever lived in pure goodness, somehow a man had once shone brightly enough to bless her existence. And this neighbor's existence too, although he couldn't possibly realize. "Mr. Newell, it actually helps people to be with my husband."

The man cast his gaze all about him in an effort not to appear too exasperated with her. "Mrs. Barnes." He softened his voice again because, well, if she was really going to be so beyond reasonableness, he could afford for a while longer to take it easy on her. "We don't see it that way."

"We were sure you would!" Lois said. In feeling so oddly unwound, she understood something. Two days ago these people could have come and asked her not to expose their children to her husband and she would have been embarrassed enough to oblige them. Embarrassed! For some reason, they were too late now. She was not in the least embarrassed and felt something of an opposite sensation, which had no name. The opposite of embarrassment was not pride exactly. It was more like freedom.

"Mrs. Barnes — "

Lois pointed to her yard. "Please. You have to meet my husband. All of you do!" She turned then, as inspired as she'd ever felt in her life. "Paul! Come down here and meet Mr. Newell!" Why had it never occurred to her to introduce him before?

But when she turned back she saw that the man had lost not just patience but composure, which she had not expected and yet saw right away was not uncommon for him. It happened to him a great deal, perhaps — so often, perhaps, that he now rarely felt the need to explain why he was ending a conversation without another word, his body already turning, his feet starting to rise and fall.

The man's head was lowered, if not exactly ducked. He was a tall man who took care, no doubt, to relax long neck muscles while he jogged. But still, lowered or ducked, he managed at this moment to appear as if he'd been made to feel exactly where the taproot of all his doubt began.

"Don't be afraid, Mr. Newell. Please." Lois had to call loudly because he was headed home at more than a jog. "Mr. Newell!

I'm sorry," she called. "I'm sorry you can't stop for a minute!" She uncupped hands from her mouth when he finally did stop. For a moment she felt afraid and had to close her eyes and pray and then open them again.

He was less large in the road at this distance. She took a few steps in his direction. She thought she heard all the whimpers in the body's hiding places. She knew all their tricks, their method of sprinting from one closet to another, doors opening and slamming as they ran out of the hippocampus and into the thyroid, out of the spleen and into the liver. She could catch one between doors if she were quick about it. "Don't worry quite so much, Mr. Newell." She came closer. What she was trying to say might not sound crazy to him later. Later, and without fear, he might observe all on his own the arrogant stance Ronnie had developed and that slouch of presumption which was starting to make the boy uninteresting. This prank of garbage, it was uninteresting! "Mr. Newell. You and I — " She started again. "Until this thing happened to me I was about to miss out on a lot."

But some men's fears were greater than any she'd had to suffer. She ought not to have said "you and I" to anyone who showered after a jog and then put on a suit and drove to an office somewhere. The man's eyes remained stony, he would be pleased to know; and his hands on his hips did their quiet imitation of someone only a little baffled by the wife's turning out to be nuttier than the husband. What he could not know or hear was what his many fearful selves were singing aloud as they ran around inside a well-toned body, searching for the life jackets. "You and I" made all his hiding places open wide in the road. Right now, almost unbeknownst to him, Owen Newell's fears were flailing their arms on the decks of separate sinking ships. Lois heard the old emergency phrases for right before the panic sets in: "Run for your lives. Every man for himself." Too bad. A waste of an episode big enough for the whole neighborhood to enjoy.

·　　·　　·

IN THE HOUSE the phone was ringing off the hook. Lois got to it and sat down, her mind going in one clear groove from which she did not intend to be distracted. When she heard her own daughter's whining voice call through the wires, "Ma! It's me," she did not feel her usual strange sinking feeling.

"Hello, darling."

"Mom, is everything all right?"

"Everything's fine. How are you, hon?"

"Well, I'm just calling because I can't figure out what's wrong with Petey. He's been upset about something since I brought him home."

"Why don't you put him on. I'll talk to him." She could say the right thing to anyone at the moment.

"Ma, it's eight. He's on his way to school."

"Oh. Oh, that's right. I'll have to call him there. What's the number?"

"Mom! You can't call Petey at school."

"Don't worry. I can reach him."

"Mom, you can't, he's in the fourth grade."

"I'll call you back later, hon."

"Ma, wait! Are you hanging up?"

"Yes, honey. Good-bye!"

"Ma, don't hang up!"

Lois was surprised when the secretary at Petey's elementary school office in Daytona gave her a hard time. She then remembered to tell the woman that it was her grandson who had won the Halloween contest last week. She insisted that her grandson be allowed to call her right away.

"What's your number, ma'am, I'll have Mr. Staley, the principal, call you."

"Thank you! He can call collect."

And it was only ten minutes or so before she heard Petey's voice, although, sadly, he sounded scared.

"There's no emergency, Petey. I'm calling because I thought we could have a more private talk than we could if you were at home."

"Grandma? Is that you?"

"Darling, it's me. Don't cry."

There was a long pause. "Okay."

"I just called to tell you I'm sorry I left you to tell Carol about Pops's packing up on Saturday."

Next she heard Petey attempt to talk through hysterical sobbing. "I *didn't* tell her," Petey yelled, "and I didn't tell *you*."

"Honey, don't cry. I realize now I left you in quite a spot. You've been keeping my secret all this time, haven't you?"

She heard breathing, then she heard a howling "No!"

"Petey, I'll tell Carol what happened. It's no secret. I sometimes don't tell her things when I haven't yet figured out for myself what's going on."

"Please don't tell her."

She waited for him to blow his nose. "Okay, I won't if you don't want me to. I thought it would help."

"You and Mom don't get along too good," Petey sobbed.

Lois laughed. "Carol likes to boss me around a little. She sometimes thinks she knows what's best for me."

"But she doesn't, does she?"

"You and I have to talk about that. I'm really sorry I acted like nothing happened when she was here Sunday. This afternoon I'll call her and I'll tell her and then you won't have to feel burdened."

"No! It won't help."

"Sure it will!"

"But I *did* something."

"No, darling, you didn't do anything. It's never anyone's fault. I don't know why Pops had an episode. He's supposed to have them. Guess what? We're all supposed to have them."

"But you don't know everything, Grandma."

"Oh, I'm sure that's right."

"I need to tell you something."

"Do you want me to call you at home tonight when Carol is at group?"

"No." He was sobbing again.

"Why not?"

"Because the babysitter always listens in."

"Oh darling, don't cry. You can tell me whenever you want! Whenever you need to."

"I need to *now*! Can't I tell you something right now?"

IT WAS QUITE a lot her grandson needed to get off his chest, after which Lois was able to calm him down and tell him, guess what, she could probably get Carol to let him come back to Point Breeze on the next bus out of Daytona.

"This afternoon, you mean?"

"Sure. It's nothing to arrange."

Petey seemed relieved to hear she had a plan. A boy needed to hear once in a while that his grandmother could come up with something good right off the top of her head, and by the time the two of them said good-bye, they were both excited at what they'd set up. Nothing to arrange, but everything to look forward to when two people are in the middle of an episode. Lois was riding the crest of it.

Paul stood beside the phone waiting for her to hang up. She gave him the receiver because he sometimes liked to put it on the hook for her. It amused him, and in its quiet way the act explained how he didn't care for her talking on the phone when he couldn't imagine the person on the other end. She rose and asked him if he had time to hug her right now.

"Right now?"

"Yes, Paul. Put your arms around me and hug me because I'm forgetting what it's like for you to hug me."

"You are?"

"Yes."

They hugged. Paul's hands somehow ended up near her face. She reached to enfold his long fingers, which were so fragrant from the soaps he still used, and overused. In the middle stage the victims were likely to take a shower every time they wandered into the bathroom because the bathroom reminded them of showering, while the disease let them forget they'd showered or bathed an hour ago, ten minutes ago. In the middle stage they got dressed over and over. They came downstairs dressed for work, for tennis, for church, for a ball.

Lois wondered now why she ever let these things bother her. She stood with Paul for a while enjoying the invisible reality of perfume. Once upon a time she used to breathe in the top of his head, a musky, psychic odor that had been quite heavenly. She felt this blessing now and kissed his temple, and then a corner of one salty eye. She had been so afraid of his condition when it came down to a matter of intimacy. In the middle stage the victims made love and then asked you who you were and where was his wife.

So what if he asks? I'll be happy to tell him.

She was able to see for a moment the old lover's lines in his face — the relaxed lines of his former self, the delineation of his wholeness. Surely he had forgiven her things when it was still possible.

"Did you forgive me back then when you could?"

Paul thought about this. "I think so."

"You probably did, knowing you."

"Knowing me?"

"Yes, knowing you."

The phone rang again, and it was Jay Jones wanting to apologize. He had called around the neighborhood and knew some people who might get the kids together this afternoon and do some teamwork. Lois thanked him. She waited for him to say more, but there was a loud click and Jay Jones explained that he had another call coming in. So again Lois handed Paul the phone and let him disconnect.

She said, well, they surely had better get out there and start picking up all that garbage. Paul followed her to the front porch again where she paused to speak to and reassure the old man, who was still standing and was clearly hurt by all that had been lifted from her. "It's okay, Dad," she said. She led Paul down the steps, and on the place where the front walk used to be Paul retrieved a magazine in and among the soup cans and newspaper, the glass peanut butter jars and Styrofoam packings. There was the occasional shoe and Kotex box and paper toweling tube. But much of it was Kitty Litter and vegetable peel and cantaloupe halves and eggshells and coffee filters. Paul handed Lois a fairly undamaged *Mademoiselle*.

"Thank you," she said. The wet, curling address label marked G. RATAG, 13 MIRROR LAKE ROAD came off in her hand, and after that she more or less snapped out of it, in her need for immediate action. She was top sergeant, and Paul responded with ease as she showed him first how to get the bags off her azaleas and then see if they couldn't be used to put some of the garbage back inside. Did he think that would work if she got him gloves and a rake and shovel? Maybe they should get the big shovel out of the workroom. Did he have his key to the workroom?

Paul was pretty sure he did. The man's last hopes in life were for luck that he might grab at his hat or wallet or pen and get the thing to which she referred. It kept him sad one moment and joyful the next to be pulling out wrong objects but immediately given more opportunities.

"That's right," Lois said. "Those are your keys."

Keys and workroom and shovel were all managed in time, and her father resigned to sitting finally. He'd become quite ashen at the amount of activity that must now proceed without him. She felt sorry, but what else could she do? This was her house now, her business. When she had Paul organized and he'd caught on to where she wanted him to put all that trash, Lois paused once more at her father's chair. Already the old man was refusing to look up at her. Sometimes he pouted like this when he didn't know what to do next, his head tilted back, his eyes staring out at the lake. That was the baby in all men like her father. They got mad at women when things slipped beyond their control. Lois looked out at her yard and smiled and had a very funny thought that she'd never had before and that was not quite like her. She hoped that Jay Jones had trouble getting organized today. She was in no hurry to meet the neighbors — the large irrepressible packs of the Joyce Knights and their Margaret friends. She imagined the cheerful smiles as they did her a good turn and harbored a few unspoken thoughts about how Lois may have, in a way, had this coming to her. Whatever they secretly felt, there would be a bit of pity thrown in — pity for her rather than outrage about their children. She could imagine Owen Newell's punch line in relating this morning's close encounter.

"Never mind the husband, it's *her* you're not going to believe."

WELL, she had gone back in the house finally, and Glover closed weary eyes and tried to get back the sequence of events leading up to this. Hadn't he tried to warn her? Quite a bit of revenge out there in the yard. Never seen it take quite this form.

He sat in his rocker, a little less shocked finally at the meanness of boys. Right now one could stare at their act as one did a corpse for which no feeling seems possible after a certain point. In his lap lay the morning's newspaper, news of yesterday's disaster. Someone had retrieved the paper for him from the edge of the road, but its bold headlines telling of a second Ohio bank going bust failed to stir him.

Right now he would give hard cash to be taken around to Teal's neck of the woods. What he wouldn't give to be right now about to poke the sharp end of a cane in that man's foot, that piece of tissue paper. Glover sat without moving and was able to fix a galled man with his eye and deeply explain: if his son so much as glanced in the direction of this house again he'd shoot him; by God, he'd nail Luke Junior between those close-set eyes of his if he so much as put a pigeon toe in the yard. "And one more thing," he would say, "don't forget I'm older than old. Blowing that boy's brains out could turn out to be the first and last good idea I've ever had in my life, is that clear? Here, let me have my cane."

Glover would have pulled a long point out of Teal's foot and come on back home.

It felt pleasant to imagine it, even if it was not now the method of the times. They sent their kids over to your yard with a load of garbage these days and there was not a whole lot you could do about it but call the police, who have already just about had enough of hearing about you making your neighbors mad.

In Virgil's day a man took the bull by the horns, got himself put in the cab of a pickup, and was driven, ninety-one or otherwise, to the other side of the lake to douse a burning cross single-handedly. One forgets a lot about one's father, but not his authority. *"You boys have been here for four days. I want you all to put that damn thing out now and go on home and mind your own business. If I have to come around here again, you'll be real sorry."*

"Dad?"

Glover looked up. She was back. Good for her, she was no pouter. He tried to smile. "Take a load off," he finally said. "Let's be friends. We have enough enemies." He pointed at the yard. "Look what I've caused out there."

Lois sat and suggested maybe there were things he wasn't telling her. She hadn't known about the Teals and the police until yesterday. She was finding things out the hard way.

"I meant to do it Sunday."

"But you didn't. Who are these people?"

"You don't recognize them? He and the son have a whole lot sticking in their craw. It didn't take a whole lot to cause this." He looked at her. "I have to tell you something else."

"All right."

"I'm going downhill. My plumbing is finally shot and I'm losing weight and my breathing is first good and then not. This neighbor business is the kind of thing to speed it all up. That's how I want it." He sighed; he'd had this speech in mind for a while. "I don't want you calling the 911 people. Is that clear? If you ever find me gasping, I don't want you calling them." He looked out into the yard. "You call those people and they'll bring in a helicopter from Orlando. Did you know that?"

"No. Is that something new?"

"Sure is. They've been trying it out for six months and reviving a lot of people against their will. It's the Disney traffic. They can't get an ambulance in here in less than a half hour, so now helicopters are the new toy on heart attack calls. The bill runs you about two thousand dollars and the emergency team all have a bang-up time tearing up the yard." He paused and then pointed with his cane; it suddenly felt good to make a small joke. "Of course, they'd have a hard time landing today, wouldn't they? They'd have to land out there in the water."

She observed her father with a mix of pain and pleasure she didn't expect to feel. He was in an amazing stage of life, and clearly she had not given it enough of her thought.

"I don't want you dying on me right now."

"Okay. But I'm here to tell you I'm worried about the next thing that might happen. I can't anticipate like I used to. I don't see the next thing coming until it's right on top of me."

TED JOHNSON arrived at noon.

Glover came on the porch to call Paul in for lunch and found the boy helping in the yard. He'd worn his red jacket again today but had removed it and put it with a satchel of books beside Glover's chair. Glover was glad to see him, but all he could think to do was shout at him. "Why aren't you in school?"

Johnson glanced around him at the mess. "I heard about this," he said. "They made sure I heard about this in homeroom." He slowly turned 360 degrees. It was worse than he had imagined perhaps. By now the cleanup job was easier for Paul, who had gotten the hang of things once Glover thought to get him a couple of stiff cardboard pieces to use as scoops. A shovel had been too slow and cumbersome. There was a good pace Paul had finally found in his straightforwardness and faith.

Out of the blue sky, a simple act of courtesy fell on old man Glover. Out of nowhere, out of the extenuating circumstances, he guessed later, when he would remember how easy it had been for him to shout, "Did you have your lunch?"

Johnson froze for a moment. "No sir."

"Paul, how about you? Are you going to knock off and have some hot stew? It's dinnertime."

Glover expected to feel an odd sensation and he was not disappointed as he held the screen and motioned to Johnson to pick up that coat and satchel. He ordered him to step into the room there on the left and wash up. "Paul, you go in there and wash up, too. Food's getting cold." If he was going to break his rule about not letting *anybody* in his room to use his new private bath, he figured he better go on and really break it all to hell. Bad luck otherwise.

Glover waited for them, unable to hear the tap water falling. But soon he was following Paul and Johnson down the hall to the sitting room. He was aware of every food aroma and he felt every knock in the otherwise inaudible shuffles of men walking together on the carpet runner, men coming in after a hard morning picking stump. The women used to start cooking at sunup, here at the house or down at camp. His stomach moved with hunger, thinking of those huge noon spreads. That was "dinner," not "lunch" — the absolute rightness of food and hard work. Tom Glover suddenly felt like he was going to live forever.

Lois was not surprised to see her father coming in on the heels of a black child he'd invited to sit down to a meal with him. She knew she would not be surprised by anything for a long time. But, of course, at sixty-nine years old, what else comes rushing back to mind than the troop of black people who had stood and waited at her father's back door her whole childhood — a community of knocks and requests to see Mr. Glover about one thing or another. Their coming in the front door like this and sitting down at Glover's table would have set the world on its head.

And it still did! Lois stood looking at the boy and at her father and decided that, yes, the world was on its head. Good. She was going to enjoy it.

She showed him where the extra chair was over by the telephone. He should grab that chair and sit right here by Mr. Glover so he could hear. Mr. Glover had trouble hearing.

"Okay," Johnson said. He took a peek at her kitchen.

"You like beef stew?"

"I guess," Johnson said.

Then the doorbell went off and Lois excused herself to go talk to whoever *that* was. It was the driver of the garbage truck, a tall white man who wanted to know what had happened out there in the yard.

"We were papered, I understand," Lois said.

He was not amused. "Jay Jones called me. I got some men out there. Just wanted to let you know we're here."

"To do what?"

"Pick up that mess out there!"

She suddenly felt a small defeat of some kind. It was hard to describe. Beyond the driver's shoulder she saw three black men sitting on the wide fender of the truck. She suddenly waved at them and then wished she could say what was in her automatic gesture, if not everything. Everything people like herself wished were true — the world on its feet and the simple appreciation one hoped and expected from people who were less fortunate. She felt ashamed as she lowered her arm out of that terrible wave.

"How long will it take you?"

The man pushed back his head and looked. "An hour, less than an hour."

She'd waved all her life because these people were always off at a great distance, dotting the fields, walking along the sides of endless highways, sitting on fenders of trucks with their feet dangling. She counted it a great good benefit that these men hadn't waved back this time. She had felt her own hand come down out of a greeting so wrong, so full of fear she'd never acknowledged. That's what blacks saw in her empty wave — the white flag of someone white standing in high grass, letting them know she was here and not to come much closer. She may appear to be alone, but she was never too far from help and her wave was always frantically happy: Hey! It's just me over here. How you folks doing over there? I can't help waving to let you know.

Lois spoke up firmly. "It's a racial thing, you realize," she said.

The man turned and pushed back his hat another notch. "Good lord, did they come over here from the Hollow and do that?"

"No. White boys did that. From right around here."

The driver gave her a curious look then. He clearly did not approve of her having set him up like that.

"Ma'am, you go on in there and have your lunch. Jay Jones already paid me. You have your lunch and we'll get all this up for you." He smiled.

"All right," she finally said.

As she was about to start back to the sitting room, it hit her how odd to think that for the first time in her life there was someone about to have a meal at her table who wasn't white. The phone rang as she made her way down the hall. She remembered then that she'd never returned Carol's call. She picked up the extension in Glover's room and heard the old whine of general exasperation. It was already directed toward Lois in a back-handed kind of way. "Mom, I can't believe you got Petey at his school! They're so rigid over there."

"He called me back collect."

"That's amazing."

"No. It really isn't. Other things are much more amazing. Carol, I want you to write down some departure times. And if you don't call me back I'll assume you've put Petey on the three-ten bus. Trailways. He and I already talked about it."

"Mom, that's what we need to discuss. You and Petey know

what this is all about, but you've failed to tell *me*." Carol paused. "Hello?"

"I know, hon. Right now can't it just be about Petey getting on a Trailways and coming on over here tonight after school? He needs to be debriefed."

"Debriefed! What kind of language is that?"

"I think it's military. Isn't it military?"

"Yes! Why are you using it?"

She listened to her daughter's whines on the other end and was amazed that they now flew up like dandelion seed, weightless and fleeting. She could have weaned herself of her daughter long ago if she'd known what she knew now on an ordinary Tuesday: We're all wasting time. Life is very urgent. For old ladies living with old men on quiet lakes, this is not easy to see right away.

"Ma, you still there? Can you give me just a hint?"

Carol was feeling left out; Lois would now have to cheer her up along with everything else she had to do. "Petey's dying to ride a bus all by himself, hon," Lois said. She put a little coo in her voice. "Carol, how old were you that time?"

The silence was long. "Nine."

"Ah, nine. You were so adorable. Seems like yesterday."

There was another silence. Carol was not completely obtuse. "I take it all you're going to tell me is that there's a three-ten Trailways?"

"Yes, hon. If you can get him on that one, he'll be here before dark and Dad won't be as worried about me out on the road."

"Ma?" There was another pause. "You're being very plucky. What's this plucky business all of a sudden?"

"I'm not really sure at the moment," Lois said. She was proud now of her old skills of politeness, newly applied. "Petey and I and Pops are having episodes. Right now I've got company or otherwise I'd try to explain it all. You should be prepared, because you're due to have one, too. It's in the literature."

"You're not hanging up again, are you?"

"Yes, hon. I don't mean to be rude."

In the sitting room, Ted Johnson was trying to give the old

man something squirreled away in his satchel. Yesterday it had been a photo clipping of an ancient crop sprayer, and Glover didn't really like the idea that now the boy seemed to have something else. When Johnson put three sheets of bright paper beside Glover's soup bowl, there was confusion and the old man's eyes clouded over. He didn't like the presumption. "What's this?" he said.

"Your stamps, man. They took your damaged ones at the post office and gave me these. This is the Hubble series." The boy put a long black finger down under Glover's nose. "That's the Hubble telescope. It's out there taking pictures of the black holes in space."

"You went to the post office for these?"

"They mailed your letters for you and traded me for the ones I steamed off."

Glover tried not to stare at him. It was only that one moment boys were dumping garbage in his yard and the next moment they were saving him from himself. He felt sapped of life's know-how.

"Listen, put those away. My secrets are getting me into trouble."

The boy considered this a moment. "I guess she knows, huh? With that crap out there."

"Seems to know as much as we do."

"She's going to tell me to quit coming?" The boy stared at the stamps a moment longer before he shoved them into his schoolbooks.

"It'd be better if you quit."

Now they both saw Lois at the doorway leading from the dark hall. She was eavesdropping and Glover was glad of it. "What do *you* say? I say we have to think of Paul."

"Think of *who*?" Paul said. They'd forgotten him. He was standing over by the windows watching hummingbird in the shrimp plant.

Lois surveyed the scene. If she happened to feel like leaning in any direction, old men and boys were there to catch her; they had an amazing way of proliferating every time she left the room.

"We can't decide what to do this minute. We have to eat and get Ted back to school." Lois brought her hands together. She clasped them and tried to think on her feet. There was a time when she'd been a spoiled young bride who was allowed to run to her room and throw herself across a bed when things were out of kilter. "Let's get the stew served up."

When she disappeared into the kitchen, Glover closed his eyes and then yelled after her; did she remember to buy crackers? She didn't have any on hand last week. He felt he was showing off for the guest or maybe only trying to help him feel more at home. Or both. "I can't take stew without crackers," he explained.

But it was while he crumbled crackers over his bowl that he wondered aloud why those kids hadn't dumped garbage in the Johnsons' yard last night instead of his.

"Sir?"

Glover had put his foot in it somehow. He could make it worse if he wasn't careful.

"In my day they would put up a cross in *your* yard. Not mine. Might have burned you out altogether. What were they doing over here?"

The boy took this in with a rather philosophical nod of his head after a moment. Then he spoke. "Earl Warren had a cross burned in his yard. Lots of people did." Glover saw the boy attempting to stay in step with his host as he crumbled crackers over his stew and then watched them fly out in all directions and into his lap.

Glover meanwhile had not expected to see the day he'd be compared to Earl Warren. His first spoonful of hot stew scalded the roof of his mouth.

"Besides, no one's home at my house," Johnson offered. "Everyone around the lake knows my parents are out of town."

Lois was surprised at this fact. "Then where are you staying?"

"At my grandmother's."

"Your grandmother's? Here in Point Breeze!"

"Yes, ma'am."

Glover saw right away that she minded his knowing about a grandmother and her not knowing. He saw her shake her head at him and he wanted to shout, well, hell, he couldn't keep track of what all he hadn't told her; things were moving too fast for him, and for her, too.

He said nothing in front of the boy. Lois broke her own crackers and kept quiet. It was difficult for her father to hear when more than one person entered a conversation, so she let him and the boy take turns without her, the latter very suddenly full of explanations. He said Fluke wouldn't want to waste a good idea on an empty house. "He's done a lot of stuff at our place recently. We're next-door neighbors. His favorite thing is to pick fights with me and then leave brown lunch bags on our doorstep. We don't open the bags anymore. And now we're not home anymore. Hardly."

Glover tried to take this in; Lois did too. "When will your folks be home?" she asked.

"Monday."

Lois came very close to saying, "Oh, that's nice," but listened instead to the cleaner silence in being able to stop herself. Stopping herself pleased her very much. She was left to think on what might, if she were fortunate, be allowed to fill the wide wheelbarrow in which she normally carried all her little habits of speech.

"In three weeks they're taking off again," Ted said. "Zoom." He made one hand into an airplane lifting off a runway beside his plate, and Lois heard a familiar adolescent sigh of self-pity and judgment. "My parents are never home for long anymore." The airplane hand made a crash dive into the tablecloth. "We should all divorce each other." He looked at Lois to see if he'd gotten a rise out of her. She smiled in sympathy. What else could she do?

"Who's minding the store?" the old man asked.

"Sir?"

"While your house is empty. Who's looking out for things over there?"

"We have an alarm system."

"An alarm system!"

"Yeah, *I* can't even go over there without setting it off."

Glover shook his head. "Lord God Almighty."

Lois closed her eyes. When she opened them, Ted was looking right at her, smiling. "We're like everybody else," Ted said. This time he seemed to wink.

"Where do your folks go when they run off?" Glover said.

"Washington."

"D.C.?"

"Yessir."

"Lobbyists!"

"No sir."

Ted was having a great time. He was happy to talk to and flabbergast the old man instead of eating his stew. He said his mother was doing her dissertation at American University in D.C. He was glad to have been born up there and not down here, he said. His mother had a job down here now, he said; but not for long if she didn't get finished. They were going to fire her. So she was always flying up there to get her research finished, and his father went along because Washington was where *his* parents lived. He had to close up his parents' house since they had both croaked at the same time, practically.

"I'm sorry," Lois said.

Ted said they were both pushing ninety and seemed to have no idea of his host's great age. She noted the way Ted poked at his crackers with his spoon. His mood had suddenly changed; he wanted her to know he didn't think much better of his parents' absences than old man Glover did. His mother's dissertation clearly irked him. "She's totally blocked," he finally said into his bowl. He moved his spoon around. "She's been blocked for around a thousand years. Forget it."

Glover hesitated and then refrained from adjusting his hearing aid. When the volume dropped in conversation, he'd learned he could get himself blasted a moment later. In Lois's long months living with him, there had been much to say about her failure to be consistent.

They were all quiet. Lois asked what the grandmother's name was, the grandmother here in town, but the old man was becoming quite tired of the small talk. "Listen," he said, interrupting suddenly, "we have a situation out there and we need a plan."

Everyone went silent again.

"I say no more fishing for now." He looked back and forth between Ted and Lois, but in partly hearing that there should be no more fishing, Paul came back into the picture. "Fishing?" he asked.

No one offered to come to Glover's aid.

"Paul," Glover called, "eat your stew. Everything's fine."

"It's the best stew I've ever had in my life."

The old man tried speaking in Lois's code next. It worked well, inasmuch as code seemed to allow Paul some peace.

"I say we get all of that stuff up out of the yard in the next few days. Then we lay low for a while. I'll pay what I pay for the other job."

"That would mean we're quitters," Johnson said.

"What?"

"You think we should give up."

"I'm not going to have any more incidents. Certain people have a right to be kept free of incident and upset."

"Does this include you?" The boy's eyes flashed. "You don't know what's going around at my school."

"What are you talking about?"

Lois interrupted. "By the way, the person most upset by an earlier incident turns out to be a young man we know in Daytona. He's nine. His mother's letting him come over on the bus this afternoon so I can help him sort out a few things."

She suddenly understood the rest of her life.

The old man was floored. "This afternoon!"

"Yes, I spoke to him on the phone this morning."

"Why on earth?"

"As I say, *he* is as upset as anyone we can name in this room."

"Oh, for heaven's sakes, we sure don't need him around here."

Lois studied Paul, who was for the moment untouched. She

felt it important to continue to get as much in the open as she could. "This young man was a witness." She said this to Ted. "He was there when you were hit on the head." But she forgot to encode and heard Paul say, "On the *head*?"

Her father was furious. "Who are you talking about?"

"My Daytona contact." She looked at Paul and proceeded more carefully. "My Daytona man is upset at having seen that situation." She knocked herself lightly on the head. "And he should be upset, of course. He thinks he made his friend worse by not keeping him from seeing it. I guess you didn't know another boy was down there during the incident."

Ted was wary. He glanced in Paul's direction. "I didn't notice him."

Glover groaned. "Oh, for heaven's sake, he was down there all right. You just didn't see that little snoop."

"I saw him," Paul said. "He was hiding from me."

Lois was used to these rattling moments of lucidity; one thinks one's husband is dead and then he twitches in ways that make one think he's coming around. One had to ignore the false alarms.

"And by the way," Lois continued, "I think it's interesting that the Neighborhood Watch is having the garbage picked up."

"When?" Glover said.

"Garbage?" Paul asked.

"Right now," Lois said. "They sent over a crew."

Johnson seemed to take this rather philosophically. "More time to fish."

"Fish?" Paul said.

"No!" Glover said. "Not today. I'm not having any of you out there fishing today."

LOIS DROVE Ted Johnson back to the junior high school in her car because it turned out the boy didn't have his bike. He'd walked. He'd come on foot by the same sleepy route from school that Lois herself used to take, down that hot mile of highway from town and through the access road to Mirror Lake in an age when it was a more normal thing to walk for forty-five minutes. He explained that leaving the school grounds on his bike would have attracted attention to himself. He hadn't wanted to do that because he was more or less campused until after Thanksgiving.

Lois held on to the steering wheel. "Campused?"

"I can't leave the grounds during lunch. To go to McDonald's and stuff like that."

Here she'd been thinking him perfect. The fact that he was suddenly not perfect made her pause over the salad of prejudices she was starting to admit to. If he didn't turn out to be perfect, then when, if not right this moment, would her lady doubts kick in again? Maybe never.

"Why are you campused?" she asked.

GLOVER WAS WATCHING Paul start to climb stairs. Paul never took naps, and Glover didn't like the way he climbed those stairs. Just now he had stood at the open front door, confused at the sight of a yard full of men. He was sure he was at the wrong house.

Glover stood leaden in the hall and waited until Paul came down again, looking a little better set in his mind. He had his hat on his head, his yellow suitcase filled with something logical he'd found to pack. He told Glover when he got to the landing that he wanted to go home now.

"Hell, I know how you feel, son."

"They'll be wondering where I've been."

"Why don't you sit here on the front porch with me and wait for her to get back."

Paul said he didn't think he should wait any longer. He didn't want them worried about him. All of them would be wondering what had happened to him.

"Oh, I expect they know you're all right."

"They have no idea where I am."

"We could give them a call on the telephone, let them know you're here. You don't want to be striking out on foot."

No, Paul wasn't going to have him telephone. He had to go right now. And so Glover asked him if he'd mind helping him down those steps so he could walk out to the mailbox. Paul said, well, that would be fine. The next moments on the stairs were long and drawn out. The men had finished their job by now, the driver waving as he got back in the cab of the garbage truck, his men attaching themselves to various running boards and fenders as the whole gang pulled slowly away. Lois had by then gotten to the edge of the school grounds, where she stopped her car and turned to look at Ted Johnson in the seat beside her. She had to know why he was campused; if she confronted Mirror Lake parents today about their children dumping that garbage, then she needed to know anything he might have done.

Ted Johnson thought about this. "Disclosure, you mean." He smiled. "My dad's a lawyer. Don't worry, Mrs. Barnes, I didn't do anything serious. It was nothing."

She let herself breathe. "What about the Teals' son, Fluke? He's a problem child of some kind?"

"Who knows." Ted Johnson laughed because something had struck him funny. "Like a lot of people around here say, he has these very confused white people as parents. They liked us at first because they thought we would like be falling down glad to have them as neighbors. We didn't make a big deal over it, and when we didn't, we found out that they were, like, this far from hating us." Ted shrugged. He fiddled with the dials on her silent radio, which in the life of the car had never been turned on. "Then when school started Fluke came out of the closet, man. He like really found out it was okay to warn the world about blacks taking over the country. It's the backlash stuff. My dad is into the backlash effect. People watch us progress, but then it's like the Martians have landed. We're getting their jobs and stuff. Everybody gets paranoid. It's catching."

"How do you mean?"

"Fluke found out how cool it suddenly is to not like blacks again. I mean, like, it went out of style to be racists, but now it's back in. People don't mind anymore if you want to start saying scary things about blacks being in this plot to take over. Hate stuff is really in now at the school. I mean, what happens is with these Nazi kids if they find out half the school hates them, that's cool, because the other half suddenly likes them. Before, they were sort of these bored kids with six sections of study hall, and now they attend class so they can heckle blacks and homos. It passes the time and whips up the energy on the playground. You can be an all-star this way, where before you were just a nobody jerk. Fluke used to be a jerk and now he's a goddamn celebrity."

Ted apologized to Lois immediately. "My mouth is permanently a mess. My parents are used to it, my grandmother's having heart attacks."

Lois didn't want to seem shocked. But she also wanted to be herself, and so far the boy seemed to believe that was what she was being. He made her believe it too.

"The other night Mr. Glover saw right away what a dweeb he was and, man, that's something that really got to Fluke. He's like this maniac now. He's got his father all worked up with a lot of crap. Sorry. His father sort of knows the real story about him, but he seriously believes black kids came and dumped that garbage in your yard."

"How awful. I won't have this."

"Yeah, well his whole thing started with my mother."

Lois made a right turn at the post office and headed for the school.

"My mother's like having this nervous breakdown about her dissertation and one time she turned down an invitation to a party Mrs. Teal was giving. Mr. Teal decided to take it all wrong, man. My parents can look pretty stuck-up to people."

Lois suggested that he might be mistaken about that.

"Trust me, they're weird." He shrugged. "They're pushy at PTA and stuff. I'm like this sitting duck for Fluke."

He thought about this awhile. "If people only knew, man. Everybody thinks my parents are, like, these radicals. It's a joke. My parents are practically Republicans." He suddenly snapped on the radio and snapped it off. "They're not Republicans," he said, "but you know what I mean. They have an alarm system, man."

Lois remembered Carol coming home crying from college and accusing her of being a Republican.

Ted suddenly said, "Is she divorced or something?"

"Who?"

"Your daughter, the one with the kid."

Lois thought about this. "Well, no. No, she's not divorced. But she's not married either."

"Oh." He looked out the passenger window and back again. "Is your grandson, like, this total mess and everything?"

"I certainly hope not."

"It's too early to tell, right?" Ted said. "All kids are a mess, believe me."

"He wants to meet you. Is that a good sign?"

Ted Johnson sighed again. "I don't know. Everybody wants to meet me at first."

PAUL HAD the old man firmly on the left side. He held the canes and he let Glover grab on to the iron railing with his right hand. The high step took them so long that the one old man believed he'd managed to distract the other completely and was therefore incensed when they were on level ground and Paul turned back to see his yellow suitcase on the porch. Quick as a wink Paul remembered he was leaving and announced this plan once more.

Glover felt hot under the collar; it would seem that all manner of deranged people were managing to outsmart him. But here stood such a gentle soul, one had to be kind. "Well, before you go, Paul, let's see if there's any mail for you in the box. They may have written to you."

And that was how he delayed things for a short while longer, asking Paul for his arm again, making him walk on to the box so that when they got there Glover would be able to flag down the first car crawling by in the narrow road. He needed help.

They stood together for quite a little while, Glover starting to wheeze and then become suddenly aware that no one was taking the route around the lake in front of their house this afternoon. The boycott had always begun and ended with the adults, Teal's magic having worked far better than even Glover could have predicted.

Finally he saw a small red compact of some kind creeping toward him at the bend in the road. The person driving was forced to stop when Glover walked himself and Paul almost into the oncoming car. A middle-aged woman managed to stop in plenty of time, but she was upset when she stuck her head out the window. "My goodness, Mr. Glover! Is something wrong?"

Glover's temper at this point was rising dangerously to the top of his head. He continued to hang on to Paul on his left side and yet he had managed to get back the power of his cane with his right. Together they walked to the woman's window. "We're just out here stopping cars," Glover said. He wanted to punch the woman in the nose.

She smiled weakly as Paul introduced himself. She introduced herself back, but Glover couldn't hear very well and he interrupted the exchange by shouting, "We're out here taking a poll!"

She smiled. "A poll, Mr. Glover?"

"Yes. We'd like to find out how many of you think my son here is dangerous to your kids. What's your opinion on the matter?" He was suddenly very pointedly mad at her and no one else at the moment. Here she was pretending not to know or remember that their whole yard had been trashed. He turned and pointed it out to her with his right cane. "We appreciate your kindness to us."

The woman wasted no more time after that. "We have an organization, Mr. Glover. I think people let you know about it a couple of years ago. You're welcome!"

Glover gave this a moment. Suddenly it occurred to him that she was a fine distraction for Paul, who had forgotten his plans for going home. And for himself, the woman was not a bad substitute for Luke Teal in letting one get one's anger out. The woman had very little hair. In fact, it seemed to have been recently mowed. Glover sensed that Paul, standing connected to his left side, didn't know if this particular neighbor was of the female or male persuasion. Except for her bright clothing, she was decked out like someone about to be sent to a boot camp.

She took a frank look at the sprawling, excess lot of trees and groves. "We understand it was some of Ted Johnson's friends. We heard you had a falling out with that young man. I was really sorry to hear it."

The woman was suddenly full of information about how things had been pretty explosive over at the school all fall. They all knew he didn't have any way of knowing that, she said.

"You listen to me," Glover finally said. "You better call together that Neighbor Watch you people cooked up. And you better let the rest of them know that if I see *any* boy in my yard again I'm not going to look very close to see what color he is before I kill him."

At first the woman merely blinked in wonder. Glover prayed to be spared a heart attack just long enough to say something else. He wasn't sure what else. She was a woman who had shaved her own head!

Glover saw her look at Paul as if Paul might be able to help her out with this crazy old-timer.

"I'm very, very sorry you're so upset with us about all this."

"No, I'm upset with *you*." That's when Glover took his cane and bashed the top of her car to make sure she understood just how much it had to do with her right at this moment. "You tell them if it's a war they want around here, then that's what they'll get. I've had bigger crosses burned in my yard than this. I can handle crosses and I can handle your boys."

"Mr. Glover!" She raised her eyes above her head in an effort to imagine what he may have done to the top of her car. There was not much else for Glover to do about her but hit the car a second time in exactly the same spot as the first. It felt wonderful. The woman sat so stunned for a moment that he honestly thought he was going to get to tell her the part again about shooting one of their boys between the eyes. But then she was gone, leaving him to squint at the retreating view of a bright bumper and a set of silently spinning wheels. He stood by his mailbox for a time, holding on to Paul and thinking a few thoughts about violent behavior and how all of Lois's literature had warned that Paul's disease might lead eventually to it.

"IF YOU'RE IN ANY trouble, I wish you'd tell me," Lois said. She had reached the junior high faculty parking lot and pulled in behind a large van so Ted wouldn't be seen disembarking. "Fluke's mother is claiming you beat up Fluke, and the neighbors say you're a troublemaker."

"I am."

Lois smiled at him.

"That's not all they're saying, Mrs. Barnes. You better know the worst."

That was when Lois learned that the rumor had already circled around to its being Fluke's house that was trashed, and kids believed it because of things Fluke had been saying aloud at school about Ted. "Half of them are glad because they think he deserved it. Half of them are glad because it proves he was right that we're all a bunch of niggers after all."

Lois was floored. She was prepared right then to go in and talk with the principal.

"He hasn't even heard about it yet." The boy took a deep breath.

"But you said you were campused."

He smiled at her again. "Three weekends ago five of us brothers sort of went to the gym and used the trampoline without supervision."

"You broke in?"

He shrugged. "A guy unlocked a window during school."

"Ted!"

"We were bad dudes."

"I would say so."

"Normally I'm, like, a dweeb person. I have to do something once in a while with the brothers so they won't *kill* me." He put his head back on the seat and closed his eyes. "If my mama gets fired, we get to go back to D.C. I say every night down on my knees, please let her get fired. She was supposed to be done by now, so I just say, fire her, man, I can't stand this place."

"You don't really mean that. Your poor mother. She has a career."

"I mean it. Who ever heard of a hole like this, man?" But he had started to show some emotion and he was quickly out of her car in a sudden lunge that made her jump. Immediately he was off in a slow lope without having closed the passenger door. There were too many parked cars for Lois to follow him with her eye for long, and she only hoped he made a turn toward the low-lying buildings instead of into the far stand of pine and scrub beyond the school. Lois noticed the school's new gym rising up several hundred feet to the south. Some of its top windows flashed her a bit of reflected sun. The kid was homesick.

Well, so was she.

She missed her life. Her misty gaze wandered off into the stand of trees and for a moment she remembered all the shoppers at Publix yesterday being asked to have a Cheese Brittle by a pretty black woman in her twenties standing at the entrance to Aisle 9. It was a free sample, an octagonal square of something so salty Lois had felt the glands under her ears harden. She had met the eye of that woman, who had then looked at the tray so that Lois was free to view a face at sudden close range. One quick look and she'd felt all the years of racial improvement and setback, the two steps forward and three steps backward, more contact and closer proximity amounting to very little in the daily exchange in which blacks and whites in Point Breeze still fumbled around each other. Separate free-floating spheres. No one knew anyone in the other bubble. Employer and employee. They glimpsed each other across grocery counters and in the forced intimacy of domestic service now gone out of style. There was more politeness and anger than ever before. Lois had blamed both sides, which was Lois's way, Carol said, of blaming no one. "It's your whole problem!" Carol had once screamed this as an adolescent: "You throw up your hands and say you don't understand the world! You want us all home for hot meals! You worry about the major food groups!"

Those were the bad old mother-daughter days; now life continued in ongoing days of bossiness and love. Lois could tell a few stories of the earlier screaming matches whose topics would become so unclear. One spiteful moment. A teenage Carol — bad skin, teeth in braces — would be furiously launched into everything. Her father hadn't wanted to come home that summer he set off on his own.

Lois was never able to explain why she hadn't been willing to pack up herself and Carol to be with him. They could have been together, Carol had argued in whispers whenever she brought it up — frequently, it sometimes had seemed to Lois. "We could have *all* gone, Ma."

"But you were only thirteen."

"Was that so young?"

"Two people were killed in Tallahassee that summer."

"It would have changed our lives. You were an uptight person all my life. All his life."

The fight would have usually begun in a friendly way, with a discussion of when Carol expected to be back with the car. One time a fight had started when Carol happened to open a bottom dresser drawer of Lois's and found three old evening bags from her mother's college days. Carol had jumped back from that drawer as if she'd found a nest of rats. Then she'd stood and pointed. "Now there's your whole problem, Mama! Come look at this. Right there is your whole problem."

Lois had not felt ashamed when, smiling broadly, she had met Paul's bus from Tallahassee. But for several years after, she was to feel very hurt by him. He'd seen men with vision, she supposed, but he had never wanted to discuss it. *Never mind. I have you. I have a daughter to support.* He had never wanted to admit he'd seen people with vision, people who knew what it meant to follow Christ, to make a joyful noise, to let the dead bury the dead. She had cried and begged him to tell her so that she could feel closer to him and not be left out. *How am I supposed to explain, Lois? It felt urgent and a little mad, I think. Otherwise I can't explain it. I don't have to.*

You do *have to.*

In the middle of Point Breeze Lois stopped at a red light and shouted at it. "You *do* have to!" All these events had taken place thirty years ago and felt suddenly as if no time had passed. "You do too have to tell me!"

Someone honked at her and Lois drove on.

When her house was barely coming into view, Lois saw them standing in the driveway, Paul with his yellow suitcase.

Ah, she thought. Giddy. Don't get giddy. She rolled down her window to talk to Paul. "Could we wait until I've made a few calls, Paul? I need to make some phone calls."

No, he wanted to get home now, if it was all the same to her.

She would have laughed were it not for her father who was right there, too. Glover had risked the high steps to come stand with Paul until she got back. Glover was afraid Paul was going to strike out on his own with that suitcase, with that hat on his head. The old man's deepest agitation was showing in his face. Suddenly Lois surely did not want Glover to know what she knew — a ridiculous and vicious rumor to distort the truth. But how easy to imagine it! How easy to see how a white kid could set this in motion with hardly any effort. And she had met Mrs. Teal.

Lois didn't turn off the motor. She stepped on the emergency brake and got out to help Paul get his suitcase in the trunk. The old man took it hard. He shook his head.

"It's all right, Dad," she said into his hearing aid. She touched his arm and through his jacket she could feel the taut and frightened bones. "We'll buy us some shoes and meet Petey's bus. Kill two birds. You be careful not to fall getting back in the house."

"I'm not going to fall!"

Paul was feeling for his hat. Lois turned to him. "It'll be good to get back home, won't it?"

"We better get started," Paul said. "It's getting late."

"I'm ready!" Lois said. Actually it felt nice to be giddy. This was the feeling that would save her. What were her problems compared to others? She turned back to her father and gave him a kiss. "We'll meet you there, Dad."

"*Meet* me?" The poor man grew pale.

"Sure!"

This was her second experience with Paul's newest symptom, his wanting to go home. She felt something of the funny rightness and logic of it, now. He was homesick as well and had every right to the feeling. Shoot, from now on she'd take Paul home anytime he wanted. And when he got there, she'd try to take him in.

I I

TED JOHNSON rode over on his bike after school later that afternoon to find the old man alone in his big yard looking half dead.

"You again," Glover said.

To take his mind off his troubles and off that woman whose lawyer would almost certainly be retained by nightfall, Glover had stumped around his grounds stabbing a nail into paper the wind had lifted that morning and scattered off to the west and trapped against the distant fence line. He'd been forty-five minutes in his workroom taking the head off a penny nail and pounding it backward into the end of a hickory stick. Just enough sharp pointer to do the job. Somehow between the hours of two and four he had moved from one scrap to another and then not been able to stop himself, a rare bird on the trail of boys' crumbs.

Ted was frightened to find him anywhere but on his porch. "What are you doing way out here, man?"

Glover had plunked down in an old chair he kept for emergency sit-downs on his exercise walks. "I'm in big trouble," he finally said. "Some woman was just here saying you dumped that garbage. I think I may have dented her car."

"Big mistake, man."

"Listen, don't think I don't have the strength to thrash somebody," Glover said. He was feeling pretty sorry for himself. "Do you suppose you could help me inside the house?"

The boy got him through the back, where the steps were low. Glover used the bathroom off Lois's kitchen. But then the long walk to his room at the front of the house was a test of everything left in him. Finally he was seated on the side of his bed and better able to look at the boy. "We have to talk," he said. "We have to settle something."

"Okay," Ted said.

He was as dark as a negative once you got him out of the sunlight. He chose to stand and gaze around Glover's room with all its furniture crowded into one half, the Lucky corner standing dead empty. Apparently the odd arrangement was uninteresting to a teenager. That empty corner was not something a kid was likely to take much notice of.

"I have to know more about Luke Teal's boy," Glover said.
"You mean Fluke?"
"Him and his daddy have everyone fooled around here?"
There was a long pause. "I hate to tell you this, Mr. Glover."
"Tell me what?"
"Fluke thinks you're a member of the Klan."
The news was a short blade that somehow didn't cut or injure because Ted hadn't been guarded in the telling. It was a fact coming out of his mouth as easily as between two trusting people knowing exactly who the common enemy is. Glover sat on the edge of his bed not wanting to show any surprise, which is what he felt along with a kind of unaccountable relief. Something felt near at hand and a comfort, although the boy himself grew ever so slightly embarrassed. "I never believed it was true or anything."

"You never did?"
"No! Never."
Ah. *Never.* That could only mean the boys had been speculating down there all summer as they fished and watched the old cracker watching them through his binoculars.

"But you were curious, is that it? Is that why you boys came up on my porch, just to get a look at me?"

The boy's eyes narrowed. "I guess."

"He bet you, didn't he?" Glover said. It was purely obvious now, now that Glover had a toehold on idle fishing conversations that he hadn't for the moment imagined until now. Funny how one toehold brings back the way of boys almost entirely — a gang down there pretending not to care about him. And himself on the porch thinking how out of their sphere he was — a stooped but snowy diety, looking down on boys from a puffy cloud. You're sure you can see the whole picture from your high perch.

The boy sighed and waited him out. His black skin glowed from the heat of a blush — from a bet he'd made! With the same boy who'd dumped garbage five days later. Glover thought how a lesser kid than Ted Johnson would have already bolted from the room by now.

"Did he pay up the bet?"

"No."

Ted finally flopped down into Jemmalee's old BarcaLounger, embarrassed, relieved, wishing he were dead. "He said since me and Bradley hit the jackpot on his idea, he didn't have to pay up."

It was easy to see that the boy was kicking himself. He wished he could take it back about the Klan, as if the Klan was the worst thing an old guy could be accused of.

"You tried to beat the money out of him later, is that it?"

"No! I didn't want his money." The boy sat up. "That's the truth."

"So *I* ended up paying you back that bet?"

The boy thought it over. "Me and Bradley wanted to do a good job for you."

Glover felt tired and beat and yet the nearness moved closer to him. Maybe he was relieved to find out that gossip was only what he deserved from the boys — the only ones who finally don't let you get away with much.

"Are they coming back?"

"Who?"

"Whoever dumped that garbage out there. I can't decide if this thing is about me or you."

Johnson nodded. "I don't know, man." There were tears in the boy's eyes. "I'm not too popular."

Glover nodded.

"I asked about the Klan on my first day on the lake. That's how I got to know Fluke so well. We got along at first. He knew a lot of stuff."

"Did he, now?"

"At least he wanted to talk about it and stuff. He said the Klan was real. He said he knew someone who was a member. I got interested. That's before I knew he was nuts. The next thing I know he's following me around all summer and when he saw I couldn't stand him he started this whole thing how I wouldn't have enough nerve to put a foot on your porch. I never really believed him."

"Why shouldn't you have believed him?"

The boy looked away.

"Was it a big bet?"

"No."

"How much?"

"Five dollars. I never even asked him to pay up. He's an idiot."

"So then what happened?"

"You hired me and Bradley. That's what happened. That's all that happened."

The room was spinning and Glover felt himself shutting down like an old pump. "Listen," he said, "it'd be worth some money to me right now if you could get my shoes off. I've got to lie down before I fall down."

"I don't want your money," Johnson said. Glover felt how the entire lower half of himself was beginning to go numb. He watched the boy stoop to untie his thin laces and then pull his shoes by the heel in a rather expert way. "You always talking about paying people," he said as he knelt.

Glover talked into the top of that sculpted head: "I mentioned money because I was reminded of how we had a boy living here once we never paid a red cent. Lucky Apple."

He waited to see the boy's face turn up in recognition, but this didn't happen. Grandmother or great-grandmother, the boy didn't seem to recognize anything in the name. He never so much as twitched. Slowly he began to stand. He was holding Glover's two big shoes at his side in one hand, finger tucked in the heels the way one holds a bowling ball. "You look pretty bad, man."

"You came up here to see me on a bet," Glover said. "Serves you right. You better be careful who you make your bets with from now on."

"You look like a ghost, Mr. Glover. You better lay down."

"Lie down!" Glover shouted.

"Lie down," the boy whispered.

Glover's pillow felt like a stone. When he was finally down, he found he couldn't move his legs; then he felt the boy lift him the rest of the way into the bed. "Don't leave just yet," Glover said. "I want you to go over to that empty space and turn around in it a few times. If you think I look like a ghost, you better go over there and see a real one. Go over to him and introduce yourself and then maybe he'll let me alone."

Ted grinned. "You kidding me?"

Glover felt as if he'd been knocked out. When he cracked open one eye he found Ted looking down at him until something made him turn and do what he was told. He walked to the empty side of the big room and stood for a time in a little void of light while Glover tried to relax into the new order of things. "Just stand there for a while. You owe me."

Glover stared at the ceiling and waited for the boy to come back to the bed. But Ted was lingering. He was standing in the old spot and turning around. "Died in this house," Glover called, "and he caused a real ruckus." The old man closed his eyes and heard how his own words slurred in the moments of near sleep. "I keep thinking I'm going to walk on him." He heaved for a bit

of air before he dropped off into a kind of fainting loss of consciousness, the basket falling over the railing, those three boys
sauntering up the high steps on a bet. They sure had a hell of a
nerve.

TED WAS picking up some of the scattered paper when Lois
pulled in at dusk. Petey had spent the ride over from the bus
station preparing to answer to Spider for having been down in
that fishing hole when he'd been told expressly not to go near it.
So there was no warning at all that the first person he'd see in the
yard would be that black kid, whom he'd let get beat up on
Saturday.

"He's back!" Paul said. Lois said, "Oh good!" And she was
surprised to hear Petey fling himself to the floor of her car with
a mighty crash.

"Honey! Are you hurt?"

He was a wimp, a coward, a sneak, a boy who'd stayed under
a boat the whole time! Why had he let himself get talked into
coming here?

"Let me introduce you two boys," Lois said, too cheerful to
bear.

Ted Johnson was holding one of Spider's canes. A long nail
came out the end, which the older boy was cleaning on the sleeve
of his jacket, and without looking him in the eye, Petey knew his
grandmother's new friend was Starman, bodyguard, hero, genius, brain surgeon.

"Ted Johnson, this is Petey Barnes. Petey, this is Ted."

The boys exchanged weak syllables.

"Hi."

"Hi."

Petey wanted to die when Ted Johnson looked away, bored,

proprietary. "He's taking a rest," the boy finally told them. "He wasn't feeling good so I stayed around."

Lois went to check on her father, and that left Petey in a grip of silence until she got back. While the two waited, the crickets down on the lake went crazy and filled the air with unbelievable screaming. The black kid sat on the front steps and stared out into space. Petey stood at fifty paces and pushed a leaf with his foot. If the old man was dead, then this kid would be sent home, and soon Carol would arrive and he would get to spend time ruining his grandmother's moldings. He wished he were upstairs alone right now, he felt like such a jerk.

Lois was back and asking the boy to stay for supper. "Could you stay and have a sandwich? Could you call your grandmother and tell her I'll bring you home in the car later? I'd like Petey to have a chance to see that you're fine."

Petey yelled, "I know he's fine! I can *see,* I'm not blind."

Lois paused and considered this. "You two could have a chance to get to know each other a little if Ted didn't have to leave right away."

The kid spoke with a gigantic shrug in his voice. "That's cool," he said as if he'd been trapped and was too polite to say no.

Petey did his *next* most stupid thing by running into his grandmother's house and up the stairs. Once at the top, he had no idea what to do with himself. Soon she would be calling him back down. He had made himself look seriously screwed up in the head.

He entered the room where the wheelchair stood folded at the back of the tiny cedar closet. It sat folded precisely the way he had left it to convince her that it had not been touched since her last indictment. He couldn't for the life of him remember what charms that wheelchair ever held for him. There it stood, with its lifeless leather seat hanging down under the weight of absolutely nothing. He knew of antimatter in the universe like this — holes of pure nothing pulling people into oblivion forever and forever.

Earlier in the day he'd heard his grandmother's voice over the phone and had burst into glad tears. The bus ride seemed so complicated, full of planning and activity on the part of his teachers and of Carol, who had to cancel a class to whisk him to the station. She had bought him extra clothes at a K mart; she had given him money and sweet admonishments and two granola bars to eat on the way. He didn't have to tell her the whole story, she kept saying. She knew it was something between him and his grandmother. He might tell her some day when it was appropriate. For now Lois needed him. That's what Carol had said. "Sounds like she just needs you, kiddo."

"I know," he had said. He'd never felt a thing was more true. He loved to be called "kiddo" when Carol said it in a way that meant he was as grown-up as anyone she knew. Kiddo. Pops used to say it to her, Carol had explained; Paul used to pretend he didn't know he had the quotation from the movie slightly wrong: "Here's looking at you, kiddo."

And for the afternoon he'd been a celebrity. He boarded an afternoon Trailways, where a ticket agent alerted the driver that this young person was traveling alone. The driver, a hip guy, had only winked and let Petey know he didn't believe he'd have to keep much of an eye on such an obviously independent person. And then when he arrived he'd helped Lois, who was having trouble with Pops. She was having trouble calming him down and Petey had never felt so completely grown for the time in which the two of them put their heads together and thought up ways to bring Paul down so they could drive him home. He'd heard Carol say it a number of times, so finally Petey said it, too. "You got your hands full, Grandma."

But here was Starman at his grandmother's oilcloth table being asked to eat tuna salad on wheat bread. No one had a thing to say except for Lois, who kept repeating how good it was to be home, and Petey understanding that he was supposed to keep saying it, too. He felt sick to be caught in the middle of his grandmother's old-lady enthusiasms. He wouldn't help her out this time. He hated Pops's blank stares. Lois never had the right food to serve kids, never thought of things like soda. And all the while that Ted guy stared out in front of him. He *had* to be wishing he were home watching a video.

Lois broke into the silence again and was speaking carefully to keep Pops from being aware she was talking about boys who'd not been kind to him. She wasn't referring to the fight about which Petey had finally spilled his guts. She was talking about something new that he didn't know a thing about.

"They must have come in the middle of the night to dump it," she said.

Ted chewed his sandwich and said that probably wasn't the end of it. "They might try other things," the boy said.

"Oh, surely not," Lois said. "Surely they've done enough."

"I wouldn't be so sure," Ted said. "Fluke's into stuff." He looked at Pops and was careful. "He's a new skinhead," he said in a low voice. "It's the big thing in hatemongering. You get to let it all hang out again."

Lois sighed. Here was Petey hearing about something so impossible that she could only think, well, if he was old enough to understand skinhead, maybe he wasn't old enough to grasp the concept.

But if he wasn't told about hatemongering, then the worst period of her own lifetime was in danger of being forgotten. When did you tell young boys about the Nazis and the death camps? What was the recommended age?

She wasn't sure she herself had ever reached the right age to grasp it. She looked at Petey, who had the heaviest curls she'd ever seen on a child and the black eyes of some anonymous father Carol had picked out. This was already the next century; children already had to know a great deal more than Lois would ever be old enough to understand.

She decided to start only at level one. "The boy named Fluke is disturbed, Petey. It's why he was so ugly to Ted the other day, and to Pops."

Paul said, "Are you talking about me?"

Petey couldn't speak for thinking how she had let him come

to her house in the midst of something big. His mind was on the utterly surprising detail: boys had come in the night to his grandmother's house.

Ted looked at Petey and spoke to him for the first time. "He's crazy, in other words. Like a fox."

Lois said, "Why don't you boys take the rest of your sandwich and go out on the porch and have a talk?"

Petey nodded. His grandmother was letting him in on something big. He would never criticize her again.

"Come on," Ted said. He was already scooping up his sandwich and pushing back from his seat.

"Where?" Paul said.

"Not you, Paul. You stay and help me put the dishes away," Lois said.

"What dishes are those?"

"These!"

"Oh! Where shall we put them?"

When the boys passed the old man's room, the kid looked at the closed door. "I give him a week," he said. But they both kept moving, Ted pushing open the screen and holding it for Petey, who came slowly through with half a sandwich in each hand.

"Wanna feed the fish?" the boy said.

"Okay," Petey said.

"I guess it's mean, feeding fish to fish."

Petey watched and then gave a leap from the top step to the ground because Ted had done it, and the act had looked effortless. Petey had not given it a second thought, not until he hit the ground and felt the bones in his legs take the shock. He had the wet sandwich halves in his hands. Somehow he had landed on his backside and then had felt his tailbone knock the earth harder than was safe. He couldn't move. Maybe he would never walk again. When he looked at his hands he saw there was nothing left but two crusts. Tuna had entered the sleeves of his jacket.

"You okay?" A strong hand came into view and pulled Petey up off the ground. Nothing broken, so the kid turned and walked away. He called over his shoulder, "Your grandmother's a nice lady. You known her all your life?"

THE LAKE WAS a blank. Fog hung over it in a kind of low hollow of steam until they drew close to the water's edge and saw the fog seem to move farther out at the very sound of boys approaching. And the insects, too. They sung nearby, but no one could ever get at them. You could step in the direction of their singing and it would all seem to come from behind, those frogs and crickets in the cattails, rubbing hind legs together, getting ready to have sex. But never so you could see them.

Petey had once seen grasshoppers have sex. He found a pair, two by two, stacked on top of each other, one on top of the other finger. Sometimes he would stack his fingers that way and pretend it was fingers having sex, and he could do it right out in the open. Nobody understood what it meant. He had a lot of things representing other things that no one but he knew the meaning of.

Ted broke some of his sandwich up and threw it in the water and said they should walk around to where the ducks stayed in front of some other house. "The fish aren't going to eat this stuff at night." But then they saw the small circles of fury in the edge of the water, where scores of minnows were behaving like sharks. "Your mother's divorced, right?" Ted said this as he threw his last crust and brushed unreal white palms together.

"No."

"I thought your old man had split and everything."

"No."

"What happened to him?"

"I don't know."

Petey heard a long sigh from Ted, who finally said, "What was he, *murdered?*"

"No."

The boy studied him and then said, "Hey, it doesn't matter. It's okay." He sat down on his haunches and seemed to try to see under the fog. "Your grandmother says you saw the whole fight down here and didn't have enough nerve to do anything about it. You should have come out and helped me, man."

Petey suddenly felt like making a run for it.

"Were you scared?" The boy turned on those haunches to look at him. "*Were* you?"

"No."

"So next time you should come out." Then he laughed, and Petey felt it was worse that Ted had laughed, because afterward he seemed bummed out. He was still doubled up and he had his head in his hands. He gave a long sigh, finally, and said he hated everything around here. Petey could hear the brief sound of a lump in the boy's throat that he had to get rid of. Older boys could do that — cry for half a second and then be just like stone again. He wasn't sure how they did it. When he looked down he felt as if his own feet were stuck in the soft muck like two poles. He couldn't move.

"The whole world's messed up," Ted said. "Don't you think it's really stupid?"

"I don't know," Petey said. "Sometimes."

"Well, it is. People are cowards." The boy looked at him. "I don't mean you. I mean everybody." He threw something in the water.

Petey finally said, "I saw that guy Ronnie come up behind you."

"Oh yeah, tell me about it. Did you see what he hit me with?"

"A can."

"It felt like a sledgehammer, man."

"It was a coffee can."

"That stupid kid. Everything's so stupid."

Ted got up and stretched his legs. He looked around him. "I don't see how you could have hidden from us anywhere down here. We would have seen you."

Petey pointed to the boat, and Ted said, man, nobody could pay him to get under *that* thing. Petey had some guts after all, he said. And that was when Petey walked over to the old rotting hull and found, when he raised it up to show off his bravery, that Fluke and Ronnie had never come back for their stuff. He hadn't counted on this and was glad to haul out the tackle box and poles to show Ted. It was proof he was under there, just as he'd said.

"Oh, man. Why'd you do that?"

"Someone might come steal it."

"Yeah, they thought I stole it. You know what they did? My parents aren't in town so they went to the principal of the school. They called the police, man. They had me *questioned*."

"Why?"

"I'm, like, this black kid. Have you noticed?"

Petey didn't know what to say. "Yeah, I guess."

"You *guess?* You *guess* you noticed I'm black? Most people notice it right away around here. This is the worst place I ever lived in my life."

Petey felt the cement hardening around his feet.

"Oh well, what the hell," Ted finally said. He turned his back and examined the lake.

Petey talked to the kid's left arm. "I'll tell them you didn't steal it."

Ted looked at him. "Okay, you do that."

"I will!" Petey said.

"Do you want to hear what the catch is?"

"I guess."

"Don't keep saying 'I guess,' man! Say 'Yo' or something like that."

"Okay."

"Okay what?"

He couldn't say "Yo." The expression made him feel stupider than he already was. But the kid was just being nice. He'd fall down laughing if Petey ever said "Yo."

"The catch is this. You tell them that you were the one that hid all the stuff and it'll look like you're kissing up to me. You know what that means?"

"I guess."

"When the old man hired me to watch your dad we got us some mad dudes around here, man."

"He's not my dad, he's my grandfather."

"Right. I forgot. Your daddy split or something."

"No. I just don't know what happened to him."

"Uh-huh. What I'm trying to tell you is that people around here are seriously out of shape over Mr. Glover and me being friends. He's your granddad too, right?"

"He's my great-granddad."

"Whatever. You're lucky, you know that?"

His hair was so flat on top, Petey wanted to put a penny on it. The guy would never feel a thing. Petey suddenly spoke again. "Honest, I don't know what happened to my father." And that made the kid turn around again and give Petey a half-friendly, half-cynical smirk.

"Too bad. We could use him."

TOGETHER THEY prepared to carry the tackle box and two rods up to the bank, at which point Ted became sullen again. He raised the boat and made Petey put it all back. "Forget it," he said. "Let them find this later, man. If I so much as touch this stuff, I'm completely screwed. Do me a favor. Look in there and see if there's a wallet."

Petey saw nothing by way of a wallet. Just the jewel box of hooks and lures and line.

"Figures," Ted said. He was about to drop the boat hull over the goods. "You didn't take that wallet, did you?"

Petey hadn't known until now what such an accusation felt like.

"No."

The boy nodded. "Come on. Let's get out of here."

They trudged up the steep bank and then Ted discussed walking around to a place where he knew the ducks hung out after dark. "They all sleep in the reeds around at the low point in front of Ronnie's house." Petey was strangely blessed. He was sure the kid had gotten mad at him by now and would go on home. But once on the road again, Ted stopped and pointed to one of the oaks in the old man's yard. "See that tree? I bet I know something about that tree you don't know. That's the tree the old guy tied Mrs. Barnes to when she was just a kid."

Petey stared.

Ted nodded and pointed to the house. "Mrs. Barnes! She's your grandmother, right?"

"Yeah."

"My grandmother used to live in back of the highway and saw her tied up. She told my mama. Every black person in this whole town used to know which tree it was, man. It's pretty famous. My mom's writing about stuff like that. She's writing about this whole town, man. Except she's blocked."

Petey looked at all the trees to the far right, where the boy had pointed; he looked back at Ted, who finally shrugged. "I don't know, man. He seems okay to me. I've been checking him out. Bradley and me used to slip up here and look at him through the windows. Man, I thought I was going to see some stuff. But now I like him good enough. He cracks me up." Ted Johnson sighed and kicked at the ground. "One time my parents drove my grandmother and me over here in the car. We just eased past the house slow one time so my grandmother could point out which tree it was."

Petey looked at his house, at the big side yard, where Ted was pointing.

Ted said, "I don't know, man. Don't look at me. I'm just telling you it's like oral history, man. My mother's doing like this black oral history. It's why we're living down here, man." He gave a bigger sigh. He pointed in a different direction next, more or less to the front of the house this time: "That's where they dumped all the garbage."

Petey blinked and tried to take it all in. The question just popped right out of Petey's mouth: "The black people?"

Ted looked at him and then did this realistic slow-motion fall right on the grassy expanse to the side of the road. He rolled around, groaning until Petey thought he was having a fit. "The black people, man? Are you out of your mind? Did you really ask me if it was the black people? I don't believe you, man." Then he started laughing and wiped one eye with the back of his hand before he propped up on one elbow and looked at Petey. "Look, I like that old man for knowing it wasn't no black kids up to something like that, man. Some lady was here today trying to tell him it was the black kids, and you know what he did?"

Petey stared and shook his head.

"He took a swing at her." Ted took his own swing next with an invisible bat and then lay back against the grass and grew quiet. "I don't care if he was ever in the Klan or crap like that. Right now he's the only good thing in this whole honky town."

Maybe this kid was just one big liar. Petey didn't know what to say as he stood looking at the prone body on the grass. Ted wove his hands together and made a pillow for his head and looked up at the stars. Finally, his voice took on a low trust-worthy tone, for which Petey was not exactly prepared.

"So what happened to your dad? Don't tell me he died, man. If he actually died, I swear to God you're the only kid in the universe whose father didn't split and everyone's going to think you're chicken not to say what happened to him." Ted Johnson got throaty, friendly. "Come on, man, what happened to him?"

"I don't know. She used a sperm bank."

He was sure the kid would start to laugh, but Petey heard a long whistle instead.

"I've seen it," Petey said. "She took me there once."

"You kidding? You mean you saw stuff?"

"It's not a real bank. It's a clinic."

"Well, I know it's not a real bank. I'm not stupid. I mean, did you get to see the sperm?"

"I don't know. The guy at the desk showed me a room. They have a tour they give kids, and a movie."

"A movie?"

"You don't get his name or anything. You get to read his hobbies. It said he could skydive."

The boy sat straight up. "You mean, she goes in there and picks a guy because he likes to skydive?"

"I guess." Petey was lying. There wasn't a word about that sport. The sports the donor had listed were all safe. But Petey pushed on and got back on track before he gave himself away. "He has to put down any hereditary diseases in his family."

Ted Johnson wanted to take some time to think about this. He nodded slowly. "AIDS," he finally said. "They'd have to be checked for that right away."

"Guys do it because they need the money."

"Just think, they go in there and donate and then they never find out if they have kids from it or not."

"I *know*."

Ted raised up on his elbow. "No, you don't. You've never donated. You're too young to donate." He lay back down and looked overhead. He sighed. "I guess I could do it. I'd just go in there and do it. It'd be nothing if you needed the money. I wonder how much they get paid."

"Forty dollars."

"That's all?"

Petey felt like an idiot again. Why did he have to go and open his big mouth? Carol had told him a thousand kids a year came from sperm banks in the early eighties. Now it was ten thousand a year. He bet they could all keep their mouths shut but him.

"I've never met one of you donor guys before. I didn't think you guys would be this normal."

Petey finally sat down on the bank and faced the lake hugging his knees. He wasn't normal. He was too short. He had feared he would end up a dwarf.

"It's amazing," Ted mused. He talked at the stars for a while. "A woman can just go in there and get herself planted. Like a field, man. She wouldn't have much of an idea what she'd get. I mean, I guess she knew you'd be white. Like, they're not going to get the black guys mixed up with the white guys, right?"

Petey thought about this before he spoke up. "We're in this club and there's this one black donor girl. It's a support group."

"But her mom is black, right?"

Here was a point upon which Petey was fairly unclear, how everyone came out the right color for the parents they ended up with. He just knew whenever he told a nondonor kid, he usually was sorry, although for some reason he had told quite a few just this year in fourth grade. His teacher had recently taken him aside and advised him against telling, and Carol had blown up about it. "Well, you have to tell kids, Petey, when they ask you. Don't tell them he's dead. Don't tell them I was married and got divorced. You're ahead of your time. Soon a big group of you guys will be as common as anything." She had kissed him. "But not for me. Your being here is a miracle. Just a miracle."

Petey believed he was a total accident.

"Everyone's a total accident, man!" Ted Johnson said. "Shoot, I have these two parents, but, like, if one of them had had a bad cold on that night, I wouldn't be here, man. It's an accident that that guy happened to go to the clinic and donate you on the day he got paid the forty dollars. But" — the boy made a gesture and pointed at Petey's nose — "there you were for all time inside a bank, and the only other accident you had to hope for was out of ten billion sperm, you'd swim the fastest. You know? You know how that works?"

"No," Petey said.

"They swim, man."

"Who does?"

"The sperm! Who did you think I meant, the parents?" That cracked the kid up, but then he got serious again. "Probably about ten billion sperm in one go. Without some bank saving the stuff it's way less likely that regular kids get born than you getting born, because at least you got frozen or whatever until your mother came along. See?"

"I guess."

"I'm trying to tell you, man, most sperm goes right down the toilet. If a guy's hot, he wastes a whole lot of that stuff all by himself in the shower."

"Oh."

"Believe me!" Ted said. "Soon you'll know what I'm talking about. But see, your mom goes in and you were just sitting there waiting for her. Geez, I wonder how long you were waiting? You could be older than me." Johnson took a deep breath and gestured like a teacher; he slowed way down. "You had to swim for your life once they unfroze you. It's like a contest, man. First one that makes it to the egg is the winner. You, man! You got there first! You deserved it, man. Congratulations."

In the silence of those screaming insects, Petey finally said, "You probably deserved it, too. Didn't you have to swim, too?"

"Sure, but see most guys are such jerk-offs, man, most people don't have a prayer of swimming anywhere but straight down the drain."

Then he couldn't stop laughing. He thought this was pretty hilarious.

"You don't like yours?" Petey ventured.

"My what?"

"Your father. Don't you like him?"

"Sure, he's okay, man. He's into making tons of money, but he's a good dude. At least he's no jerk-off." Then Ted Johnson laughed again and said, man, he'd really cracked himself up.

TOM GLOVER found he didn't want to sleep through a full moon coming up, the one those kids should have had last Thursday for Halloween.

He got out of bed around seven that evening, and Lois was surprised to see him up just as she and Paul were finishing the supper dishes. She heated up more of the stew for his strength. She brought a tray out to him on the porch so he wouldn't miss the moonrise.

"Did the boy get here on the bus?"

"You mean Petey? He's with Ted. They're down in the fishing hole. I'll call them."

Glover stared at the lake. The black boy was down there telling Petey all his old secrets.

Soon they came striding up the darkened front walk.

Paul said, "Did you catch anything?"

Glover figured he'd better make it up to Petey now that the boy was actually here. He'd better keep his mouth shut about orders being disobeyed. It suddenly occurred to him that no nine-year-old worth his salt would have obeyed that order he'd given the other day. "Welcome back," Glover called out. "Long time, no see."

"Hi," Petey said.

Glover told both boys they'd better sit right there on the steps and watch the full moon come up. According to the paper it was due in less than three minutes. He had reason to think it was going to be especially good, as moonrises went. Fall was the best time for them.

Well, what else was there left to talk about, to claim, to forget, to assume was dead, to lord it over, to strike the fear of God in? Just boys. Soon they'd be old men, too.

He watched how they both plunked down together with collective sullenness, which was the nature of boys if there were two or more around to get in cahoots against you. You could count on it happening almost right away. Ted rested a head in both hands as if whatever moon there was had better show up right away or he was leaving and taking Petey with him.

Glover said, "If you stare out like that you'll make him shy. There he is now."

A silver rim pushed up over the edge of someone's roof on the far east side of Mirror Lake. In Glover's youth, there'd been an unobstructed view from over here. A moon like this would come right out of the water for Lucky and him. They would sit out there waiting for it, each one seeing how far they could piss into the lake. Now a person had to get to the St. John's River, out in cow country, to see a full moon lift right out of the water; or else all the way over to the Atlantic Ocean. Petey saw moonrises regularly, according to Carol, who liked to brag about the spectacular ones over in Daytona. Retired people formed clubs because of the event. Moonrise clubs with refreshments, with much oohing and aahing, apparently, before everyone ended up at someone's house to play bridge. When he thought of this kind of thing, Glover would sometimes blame Disney and the northern money boys. They had turned this whole state into a playground and an old folks home. It should never have happened. After the Freeze of '95, the Yankees who had tried citrus had all gone home. That was where Virgil and Alma had gotten all their pride, dirt poor and yet able to move into this house overnight. Alma said she had found china and crumbs on the table. A famous freeze had driven out the opportunists so fast the women hadn't been given any time to pack up. In his crankiest moments, having nothing to do with reality, Tom Glover could sometimes wish the blacks and poor whites had kept them all out for good.

Bridge clubs.

In a few moments Lois was seated in the rocker on the other side of her father and looking at the moon. "It's so lovely," she said. Then she merely whispered to herself. *It's so lovely.*

The full moon floated just an inch above someone's rooftop and now it was doubled in the water. "I've always wondered why it looks so big when it first comes up," Lois mused aloud. "Carol says it's because everything is magnified in the earth's denser layers of dust. It isn't magnified overhead, because there're layers to make it look so huge."

Glover kept quiet. His half-formed thought for almost a hundred years had been that a rising full moon was large because as a moon climbed it simply got farther away; that was what climbing meant. Carol's theory made him feel newly thickheaded.

A boy's voice from the steps said the daughter was wrong. "She is?" Lois said. "Are you sure?"

"It's not magnified at all. If you measure it with your fingers right now you'll see that it's not even very big." Ted got up from where he was seated and went to Lois's chair.

"Here," he said.

He showed her how to make a circle with her thumb and finger so she could measure the moon. Lois made a monocle and stared through its center. The monocle caused the moon to shrink in size by blocking out the rooftop on the horizon. She expressed great surprise at this revelation.

"Yeah," Ted said with a sigh. "A big moon is only an optical illusion because of all the houses close by." Ted returned to his place beside Petey. "It looks as big as a house because it's sitting right on top of one. It'll be exactly the same size later. You can measure it with your fingers."

In the dark Petey and Glover performed the experiment and watched how, in shutting out the human world, the huge moon shrank down to the size of a pea, exactly the size it would be overhead two hours from now. When Glover took his hand away, when he let it all bounce free above his cypress trees, the moon ballooned to its bigger size. Fool's gold. He thought he saw the familiar face up there give him back a dirty look.

"Gee," Petey whispered. He practiced closing and opening his shutter. An optical illusion. Everyone grew very quiet again, and Lois said she could hear the timpani section starting up in the frog orchestra. She wanted them all to listen for the descant of a few violins and oboes. "It's a swimming kind of sound," she said. "It can make me dizzy."

"Swimming?" Ted said, poking Petey in the ribs. She was pleased to see the two boys collapse on the steps in a laughing fit, in some private joke of theirs. They had made friends; their laughter tended to calm her down about the neighbors.

"Yes, a swimming sound," she said.

She was too much for them. They rolled in the grass at the repetition of her punch line. They couldn't stand it. She apparently could not have said a funnier thing if she'd tried.

"What about swimming?" the old man barked. "I better not catch you boys swimming down there."

And that was when Petey and Ted had to run into the house laughing and letting the screen door slam behind them.

LATER SHE drove slowly behind Ted on his bicycle and watched his rear flasher swaying steadily as he seemed to pump to a rhythm of some fast tune in his head. She followed him a short distance down Highway 419 before he made a signal and turned onto Fallen Road. This was an all-black development, which had gone up sometime in the sixties. She guessed that his grandmother had to have grown up in the old Hollow long before this area of FHA homes became available. The long day had begun with a mean dumping, but it had almost no end of possibilities, she mused. Apparently certain days in one's life held all the weight of entire months that came before or after, because here she was crawling slowly behind a young man on a bicycle, whom she knew there was no ordinary way of meeting. He had been hired to take Paul fishing. Paul would have wanted to know this boy, had risked his life once in the hopes of it becoming a natural thing. More votes, better schools, the boy's parents changing the curriculum and living next door and taking office. Much of it had happened, but not with any social interchange. Almost none at all. It seemed incredible. On paper everything was supposed to be working.

"Shall I say hello to your grandmother when we get to her house?" she had asked as they prepared to make the little caravan from Mirror Lake to Fallen Road.

"She'd want to know you were coming," he said.

"Then I'll meet her another day. Give me her name and number and I'll give her a call."

He had thought about this. The woman's name was Wade, he said. Alberta Wade. Then he paused again.

"What's the matter?" Lois said.

The boy shook his head. "It's nothing," he said.

The Fallen Road development used to be a thick pine woods with small scrub oak and dense thickets of cabbage palm. For Lois it was still a little shock to see houses already thirty years old and her still missing those woods of her childhood. She'd been taken to Fallen Road to learn to drive a car when she was twelve or thirteen. It was a desolately quiet and bright stretch of hard-packed white sand in those days. Deer crossed early or late on that white road and rattlesnakes came out in full daylight. Farmers wanting a shortcut to Highway 430 took that stretch back then. Fallen Road got its name from a sinkhole that no one ever saw off in the old woods. For decades the road remained a quiet spot for armadillo, quail, and gopher. They had seen a panther once in a while in there, and then, overnight, the cinder block houses sprang up with lawns and matching driveways and open breezeways, as they were called. A family had a choice between parking a car in the breezeway or screening it in for a porch. Ted's mother's mother. And before that a great-grandmother would have lived and died in the Hollow, which was exactly where it had always been, just behind Kenny's Texaco station on the highway separating Mirror Lake from abject poverty. Lois had never thought it abject exactly. That was Carol's constant usage. But for all her days, Lois had passed the old Hollow and been able to see one or two unpainted cottages with their tin roofs. Beyond those one or two in sight, scores of similar dwellings sat in the dense growth of lush tree fronds below the highway. In her day the sunken, cool, "colored" section was a fascination as the car sped by. One glimpsed the fresh-fruit stands and small grocery store dotting the edge of a small world never available. She remembered a lonely childhood and how one sometimes saw men and women waiting at the edge of the Hollow to catch truck rides to the packing plants or out to the groves. Her father's cattle hands, a few of them, used to wait on the edge of the highway for his pickup.

In front of her was the hope of generations. Ted signaled with his right hand that he was about to turn onto a street marked Myrtle. And then he pedaled faster until he signaled again that he was turning into the drive of the third house. Lois's heart raced in time to the music of those excited legs going up and down and then coming to a stop. The boy, home safe, waved at her, and Lois drove back to the highway on a host of promises and good intentions, and soon she had returned herself to the small access road to Mirror Lake Road and then she found herself making the forked turn at Osprey Landing because now she knew which was the Teal house and which was Ted Johnson's. A set of garages and thick hedges separated the two big homes.

Someone inside the Teals' house had put on the outdoor spotlight. The yard was as bright as a carnival. Individual blades of grass threw long shadows on the leafless driveway. It was a driveway that narrowed at the road, then widened as gracefully as stemware. It was a tuliping expanse of concrete ending up under a basketball hoop.

Three of the most dramatically overarching and coveted live oaks on Mirror Lake belonged to the Teals. Some people took trucks into wooded areas these days and brought back Spanish moss by force to achieve the early-Florida look the Teals had managed. This red brick colonial style was popular forty years ago when all of Mirror Lake's old Freeze houses came down and new ones sprang up in brick. Paul had always said red brick was an odd idea, perhaps a ballast to the state's reputation of quick money and transience, its reputation for airiness and beach life out on the watery rim of irresponsibility. Solid citizens lived in the interior. In their efforts to keep the entire peninsula from floating away, from levitating, many hit upon brick, and quite a few went Victorian in their furnishings, took trips and shipped home antiques from everywhere. Unconscious need for weight, Paul had said. They all chose the heavy wrought-iron lawn furniture painted blinding white. No one sat in it. Lawns were not about lounging or being seen in public. Perhaps an Easter egg hunt in the fifties. Otherwise the residents remained invisible. Uniformed small armies of men from landscape companies did the mowing, and whenever Lois and Paul took Carol for walks around Mirror Lake, and later Petey in his stroller, they had never once met a soul. In these latter days of exercise and fitness, the joggers all waved in the appearance of neighborly affection.

Over the years, Lois had come for countless Point Breeze visits after college and her marriage but never found occasion to get beyond the porch and Jemmalee's needs as the latter progressed painfully from fifty to sixty to seventy. Lois, returning, would bring out all her mother's self-pity and that would be the whole of each visit except for her stories, which she'd preferred to tell Paul in private. Paul was her confessor, she'd once said. She'd told him things Lois was sure she did not know herself, some troubling incidents of marriage and adjustment which had happened before Lois was born. All lost now. In the quiet intervals of decades, Point Breeze evolved beyond Lois's understanding and perhaps beyond her interest. It frightened her to think that she'd not been much involved elsewhere; no communities had interested her. She was that woman or man in some poem who measured everything in coffee spoons. In her less angry moods, Carol herself had suggested that maybe some people were not meant for involvement. Maybe Lois was supposed to have been an artist, Carol had said, and Lois had assumed she was joking. No, Carol said. Women, Carol said. They nurtured by law before getting the vote and then they nurtured by sheer habit and by all that had turned them away from science and industry and money and power. Carol had seemed kind in that moment, telling Lois that she was basically a product of her culture. It was odd how in letting her mother off one hook Carol tended to snag Lois on yet another one. If she were clever enough to write a book about daughters, Lois would have a chapter on their ability to praise and insult you in the same breath.

Lois eased her car to a stop in front of the Johnsons' place. It too had its imposing front lawn and luxurious emptiness. Automatic lights had come on in various parts of the house. She couldn't say what Point Breeze was now, or what, for that matter, most things were in the world. She felt her ignorance and fear sweep down on her head. Who had let her off the hook that she could come this far with less understanding than most people of how reality fit together, how the world ran, how politics ruled, how one must take into oneself the needful cynicism, the economic and psychological explanations for everything? Even as she sat with her Ford humming, a light snapped on in a bedroom window of Ted's parents' house; another snapped off in the kitchen area as if two people were moving about in there.

Clever timing. Could have fooled *her*.

TONIGHT OLD MAN Glover had to squint to make up a convincing face on the surface of the moon. The man-in-the-moon face had always heretofore been tilted a little downward with an expression of compassion. Tonight it took a man's bitter squinting to get the moon to smile on him.

He hoped the moon could find it in its heart to overlook his sins as it climbed the heavens. He had certainly never bothered to dwell much before on what the moon saw as it climbed. Lucky had run away from them on a pitch-black night in August. *Hell, how else were they going to get that dog out from under there?*

He never put it to Lucky, boy to boy, how else were they going to get that dog out from under there. Between the two of them, it was only a moment to find out quick who could and who could not roll around laughing together for the rest of their lives. Neither of them had thought about it one way or the other until it was all over. Lucky had better mind him. "*It's got to be done quick, Lucky. You know that as well as anybody.*"

Alma had wrung her hands for a week — for a week until Virgil had had enough of her insinuations and decided to take her up on a few things. What had she been thinking? Was Virgil supposed to send that boy to college? Huh? Is that what she thought? That he was supposed to raise him up to manhood and send him to college?

Smarter than any of your *boys,* Alma had answered, just when Glover, scared at age ten to hear them fighting, got his ear to the door of the sitting room.

Glover, at ninety-one, felt his heart beat steadily as he looked in the direction of Osprey Landing and wondered in a half-dreaming way if that's what had been going on over there on the other side of the lake — Teal telling his wife almost offhandedly that if the kid next door thought he could boss his son around then he had another thought coming, and his wife snapping right back at him. *Smarter than any of* his *boys.*

Teal. He couldn't be taking the bull by the horns in this day and age, pointing a shotgun and getting the kid next door crouched on his hands and knees where he belonged. Had to play it by ear, bide his time, wait until a few more people had had too much of the new boy's intelligent face, wait until they were all feeling that they didn't like how the white boys on Mirror Lake had started to pale. He had badly coached his son in the meantime, making him mean and sullen and a placer of cheap bets.

If one has never had a son, never seen a boy of his own do poorly in a cockfight, it's still not difficult to imagine the chagrin. What if that's what it was, all those years ago? — Virgil Glover himself seeing Tom Glover doing rather badly, shining like a brass tack next to a silver dollar. It must have galled his father to keep getting up in the mornings and feeling a bit older every time and then knocking into bright-eyed Lucky again right after breakfast, still hanging around the property, picking up Alma's grammar lessons as if they were no more difficult than falling off a log. Lucky used to fix up Tom's verbs when Alma's back was turned. He was a quick study. He had had more to say than was good for him; too quick off the mark, too bushier of tail, too faster on the draw, and Virgil's own boy Tom with his mouth slightly open as if he'd just heard news that the world wasn't flat. Virgil must have hated to keep finding a bell ringer hanging around all the time, hitting his own son on the head just hard enough for him to hear Tom thunk the way a green melon thunks on the Fourth of July. Must have galled him.

12

AT BREAKFAST the next day, Petey asked Lois a few serious questions: Would she let him rent a video for later, could they buy a metal detector so he and Pops could find valuable things in the front yard, was she ever tied up to some *tree* when she was little, did she know Spider had smashed up some woman's car?

He talked and talked and pumped his legs under his chair until the phone rang and he had a little chat with his mother.

"I'm fine," Lois heard him say. "Yes," he said. "No," he said. "Okay." He held out the receiver. Lois whispered that she couldn't talk to Carol right now. "Tell her I'll call her later."

Petey relayed this information and then put his hand over the mouthpiece. "She wants to know what time?" he whispered back.

"I don't know," Lois said.

Petey nodded slowly and then thought for a while before he spoke into the open line. "Mom? She'll call you at midnight."

Collusion had been what the boy needed. He could become so unaccountably miserable that a small amount of collusion sometimes did him a world of good. When he heard Glover bumping against the furniture on the other side of the sitting room, Petey froze. He begged Lois not to make him go in and tell about being under the boat.

Lois said she didn't think that was necessary. She headed to her kitchen to turn down the teapot. "If he smashed a car," she called, "then he's in bigger trouble than you are."

"But he did! He really did."

Lois came back to lean against the doorjamb. "Hon, what are you talking about?"

SHE FOUND her father dressed but looking pale from a bad night lying dead awake. Seeing her peek at him from the hall caused him to fork over the truth right away and then suffer some of her surprise and anger at the fact that he would keep something like this from her when she needed to know everything now.

Well, he hadn't had a good opportunity. He wasn't sure if it was really true; it had all happened too quick. "Are we being sued?" he said. "Have you heard from the woman's lawyer?"

"Dad, for heaven's sake, what did this person do to make you so mad?"

The old man said this was his own business — the last straw for Lois, who stomped out of his room. She slammed the door behind her but not before telling him the position he'd put her in. Here she'd been claiming all this time she had no dangerous men at her house and now it turned out she *did*.

"They're saying the black kids dumped the garbage," Glover called out.

Lois opened the door again. "When did you hear that?"

"This is all Teal's doing. Have you run into him yet? If you don't do anything else for me, I want you to get me around there in the car."

It would turn out not to be necessary; they would all meet in a much more dramatic fashion than anything Glover could dream of. After breakfast the mailbox flag was found standing up. Lois went out on the porch and told Paul that while he was getting the morning paper he'd better check to see what was in the box. "Wait," she called, "I'll come with you," remembering that there might be something upsetting in there, something deposited by a boy who had gotten himself in the habit.

What she found was a typed invitation from the board members of the Neighborhood Watch. Eight o'clock at the home of Joyce Knight, the invitation said; the board hoped Lois would come help sort out the recent misunderstandings. In bright pink ink Joyce Knight had added a personal note. "Hi, Lois! We want you to meet everybody! Love, Joyce."

Neighborhood Watch had raised her flag.

Inside the house the old man put on spectacles and read the invitation carefully. He finally looked at her and shook his head: "Good," he said. He was breathing hard in his chair now. He had gone downhill.

"Dad, I'm sorry we fought."

"You can't go to this meeting by yourself," the old man said. He looked at her and saw she didn't know any better than he what they would do or say if they really got themselves to such an event. "You've never seen self-righteousness like you're going to see at this thing." He had his glasses in his lap now. His hands looked like dead leaves someone had brought him from the yard, but he smiled to let her know he wasn't going to die. Slowly he pointed at the windows; he'd like her to raise those shades for him. "It's a culmination of something," he finally said. Several bright squares of light fell into the room.

"How do you mean?"

"This whole thing I started. You don't remember the Thorn house on the lake. It wasn't so awfully long ago they held their meetings over there where the Thorn house used to be."

Joyce Knight sounded glad that Lois had telephoned. "Oh yes," she said, "yes, we've had the Watch program for three years. We all know who's home when. And the kids have a buddy system they can count on. Latchkey kids." Joyce thought this last remark was humorous. She had a class in ten minutes so she was forced to hurry on: Lois was not to worry about that little incident yesterday. Mary Hilliard had told the board only because it was the first she realized the old man didn't know who'd vandalized him.

"Mary Hilliard? Is that the woman with the car?"

Joyce rushed on to say how shocked they all were about those boys and then Lois heard something else very odd in and around the generally odd things Joyce believed to be true.

"Excuse me," Lois said, interrupting. "Did you say this Mary Hilliard thinks my *husband* struck her car?"

"Well, Mary said she got home yesterday and got to thinking that it *must* have been Mr. Barnes." Joyce paused and then listened for a reply. "Lois?" she finally called out. "Really, there was almost no damage. She wouldn't want you upset about that. You've had enough to worry about."

When Lois felt herself about to fall apart she was able to stop. She was learning how these people managed to fix you at arm's length. "My husband would never strike a car or anything else," she said. "This is very important for me to explain."

Joyce gave a small gasp. "It doesn't matter! Honestly! Mary said she couldn't find a scratch anywhere. There was nothing to it."

When Joyce hung up, Lois sat for several minutes until Paul walked into the room and tried to ask her something. She saw him open his mouth and lose the thread, while in her mind she was still listening to that calculated innocence, that tone of pure wonder at why it would make any possible difference to Lois *which* of her men had struck a car.

"Paul, come here and let me give you something."

"An award?" Paul asked.

She laughed. She didn't know what to say. Finally she stood and said, yes, it was indeed an award she wanted to give him — a good citizenship award and very long overdue.

Paul stopped in his tracks. "I don't know what you're talking about," he said, turning to leave the room. He was in a little huff. He could get quite huffy at all her complicated ways.

Dear God, Lois prayed.

Petey read her horoscope from the "Style" section of the paper. "Proceed with caution and good cheer, all Libras. Social or business opportunities will be an option. Keep an open mind."

"I used to have a mind," Lois said.

Petey looked at her. He had his heart set on a metal detector. "Mom thinks you're a genius."

GLOVER LAY low that morning, resting in his BarcaLounger, which he never used except when he was sick. Getting into bed as he had yesterday would be the end, the very end. Whenever he felt this bad, he used his BarcaLounger as a compromise between wanting to stay upright and wanting to give up. The cheater chair. Its tight lever took him all the way back and raised his bone legs above the horizon.

Today he would drink strong bouillon and extra coffee as boosters. Coffee and bouillon were part of his last-resort emergency kit. If his hand was absolutely forced, he'd go all out and take a Bufferin and get Lois to fix him boiled tongue. She'd come in to try to tell him that the blame for the car incident had fallen on Paul. When she broke down and had to leave him, he could only lie in his chair thinking how every move he made gave Teal another advantage. One lost one's touch. One reached out to push open the new screen door and had no idea whether it was going to weigh a ton or feel as light as a feather. Teal was something either important or ridiculous; he could not call it this morning. But he knew he wasn't quite ready to meet up somewhere on a more metaphysical plane and have it explained to him what that boy Lucky had understood. He still had at least one more fight left in him. Before this thing happened, he'd dreaded that all his last fights were going to be only with Lois.

When he opened his eyes he found she had left a wrapped plate to heat up later. There was a note on his desk telling him that everyone would be out of the house so he could rest. She was going to pick up a few things at the store. And later she was going to try to get herself to that meeting with an open mind.

Women, Glover thought. Give them a meeting and you give them hope.

AT K MART she and her two charges wandered from section to section looking for someone who could tell them if anywhere in the huge, echoing store there was a metal detector to be had. She was quite surprised to learn the gadgets were on sale that week at $49.95, batteries not included. She imagined how she would credit her grandson with the idea when she wrote it up for the caregiver literature: "Consider the purchase of an inexpensive metal detector because it may prove a very good thing for the middle of the middle stage." She would post this winning idea in the next mail.

"Petey!" She was sounding unexpectedly urgent as they approached the empty checkout counter. The boy hung back. He heard the fear in her voice. "Petey, I can't find any of my stamps at home. Did I tell you? Several days ago I bought four sheets. When we get back you have to help me find them."

Petey looked at her in amazement. "With this?" He was holding the metal detector. Lois thought he was making a joke and for a moment she couldn't stop laughing. But the next thing she knew she was crying. The checkout lady gave her a worried look and Petey felt terrible to see her so upset. "We'll find them, Grandma," he promised. "Don't cry. You probably put them someplace really weird."

Lois was trying to think straight. "This morning you wanted to know about Spider tying me to a tree. When did Carol tell you about that?"

"She didn't." Petey was watching her fish for her wallet; he was trying to figure out how to tell her. For him there was a time warp in which things from different eras overlapped. He took it slow.

"Ted's grandmother told his mother," Petey began. "Then his mother told him. And then he told me. It's moral history."

Lois's heart began to beat in time. "Petey, I've got to meet her! I've got to meet all my neighbors, and she's not going to be there at that meeting tonight!"

"What meeting?"

Perhaps some episodes were shared. Not one but two or more could discover how they might be given a chance to be different people in the world — a little chance here and a little chance there.

"Petey, what if we drove over to the woman's house and took her something? What if we stop and buy a pound of shelled pecans for her?"

"Pecans?"

"For Ted's grandmother."

His bad reaction was immediate. "She'll think it's a bribe." Lois could see from the expression on his face that the grandmother was yet another adult who knew he'd been self-protecting while another boy got beaten up.

"I doubt if RoboCop would be afraid of her," Lois said. But she knew Petey was too old for dishonest leaps between the movies and real life. The movies had nothing on real life for giving one the zaps of true terror, the abyss into which one looks and sees only personal weaknesses and shortcomings.

"I'm a little afraid myself," she said. "But if his grandmother knows me — "

"I didn't say she really really knows you. She only drove by the house that time. She showed them which tree he tied you to and everything."

"Petey!" Lois felt her inspiration rising up again as it had yesterday. "We've got to go meet her. Just think what a mess we've gotten Ted into."

"*I* didn't," Petey said.

On the outskirts of town, Lois herself experienced something more than simple fear as she pulled her car under the big shade trees at the fruit and vegetable stand. In a moment or two she was hefting a two-pound bag of shelled pecans and trying to think what Jemmalee used to call these. And then she heard. *Pure gold.* The hard labor in shelled pecans had always made her mother call them pure gold. She paid for the bag and headed back to her car, feeling her motives bob like corks in water: Someone out there remembered her. She imagined herself being spied on from the reeds by a child who had run home to tell her family that she'd seen the girl over at the Big House, tied to a tree.

"Are those for me?" Paul asked.

And Petey had a question, as well. Apparently as he waited, he'd been planning how to recover some of his earlier advantage. "Why did Spider do that, tie you up that time?"

At his age he was bound to be picturing her with chains across her chest and shackled at the neck. "Honey, it was only a dog leash tied around my waist. I think I was four or five. It was to embarrass me about running away from home."

"Oh." Petey seemed genuinely disappointed.

"He lost a son one time. You'd have a great-uncle were it not for a bad accident."

The idea was enlivening. "What happened to him?"

"He had a fall."

"Off a cliff?"

She looked at Petey hanging over the front seat, refusing to stay buckled up, refusing to let this go until he found out something worth finding out. "Your friend doesn't know, does he?" Petey was speaking in the new code. She saw in the rearview mirror that his head had turned to stare at the man whom he had loved to call Pops. "He doesn't know he's your husband anymore, does he?"

"I think he knows that I love him," she said.

The boy was not an idiot. She mustn't simplify things too quickly to Love. She tried again. "Of course, it's just a hope I have." In her rearview mirror she saw she had his attention. Even for the very young the act of observing this disease sharpened the intelligence: Petey had the ability to see that memory was a matter of life and death — that his own personal history was lost in the sticky plaques and folds of Pops's brain.

Lois was sometimes ashamed to think how her own quiet end, her own odd extermination, had brought home the unbelievable newsreels of the fifties — the stripped bodies tumbling from the top of a screen like so many bulldozed trunks and limbs of leafless trees. This was a secret she harbored, that she should dare compare her situation to something so horrible. But she did. She couldn't help it. Paul's disease had wiped out her entire family, and sometimes she felt she was on the trail of a profound analogy.

MYRTLE STREET'S bright quiet that afternoon was welcoming of strangers. Its darkened, empty breezeways and motionless shrubs suggested effortless entry at this time of day — Lois arriving in her cautious carload of unlikely passengers. Surely if it were after school or after work, the neighborhood would be filled with tired men not at all eager to see them. And teenagers. One saw on TV how they felt about white intrusions. More and more, television reinforced the fearful dread — teenagers in bold colors, all of them talking at once, or else not at all, sullen on stoops as they watched strange cars with suspicion from behind Ray-Bans. Now it had become exactly how she looked back at them.

Myrtle Street was empty. Lois spied only one young woman in her yard, and she had the sudden presence of mind not to wave her automatic friendly flag of guilt and nonsense. It was a mother coaxing a baby girl taking wobbly first steps in the grass. "She's home," the woman called, when Lois was out of her car and about to approach the house. There was an exchange of smiles. "You'll have to knock loud," the woman said.

Lois was about to knock when a woman appeared from around the side of the house, her posture a bit stiff as if she might have an injury, except that Lois recognized the nature of the stiffness after a moment or two. Here was a throwback to women who "dressed" in the morning. The woman was wearing a corset!

"Alberta Wade," she said in very firm tones, difficult to read.

Lois introduced herself and her husband. "My grandson," she explained. She wanted to say that she and Petey were in the middle of an episode, but instead she said how sorry she was about Ted; she should have come sooner. "Yesterday I saw how upset he was," she told the woman. "He put on a good front for my sake, I think, but this has hurt him badly."

The woman nodded a time or two, though not in real agreement. It was a nod of recognition. "I've not wanted him over in that part of town while he was staying with me."

"But he lives over there," Lois said. She found herself blushing next. "He's a neighbor of ours."

Mrs. Wade took this in with a great deal of patience. "He's been a fine novelty," she said after a long pause. "Now he's worn off, from what I hear tell."

Petey stood waving the white page of instructions at the woman. Could he please try out his metal detector in her yard? They'd just bought it at the store.

Lois noted how crafty he was, all his nine-year-old powers of sweetness at work to distract the woman.

"You go on," Mrs. Wade said. "There's a world of shrapnel out there."

And after Petey ran off a few paces, Mrs. Wade sighed deeply. "It's all I do — work in this yard."

Lois wanted to say that yards were a problem this time of year, but the woman was right there to stop her. "Has my grandson been telling all my stories over there at the house? It's a bad habit of his." The woman looked Lois square in the face and then began to nod her head. "You know, when my daughter was coming along, you were her favorite story."

Lois waited.

"I bet that's what Ted told you. Because when he was coming along he was always getting me to tell him the story about you. One time you got yourself across the highway and ended up in my yard. You were maybe three or four. I was so glad to see you that I didn't go in and tell my mama. We played for an hour before Mama found you and grabbed you up and ran over there with you. She was hoping they weren't frantic."

Suddenly Lois had hold of a detail she had not been searching for at all. "We made mud pies!" she said. "We sat on a long board in front of your house and made mud pies!" Mrs. Wade nodded and looked away. Lois reached out to touch something and then paused with her hand in midair as she began to see the place where she'd sat bouncing. It was a board stretched out over two supports of some kind, two low barrels filled with sand, the board low to the ground with plenty of spring to it. Suddenly the whole event was there: they had made that board spring up and down.

"I must have known what a novelty you were. But my mother's fear, that's what stuck with me over the years. Just the sight of you! And then Mama rushing to get you home quick. Your folks had that leash around you before she could get me back out of there." Mrs. Wade's voice changed to something quite intimate for a moment: "Do you know, seeing you like that? That left a strong impression on me."

Lois tried to swallow down a tightness in her throat. She had the calm but irrational thought that if she could remember this woman from that time, then she would get back some less fearful moment in her life when she'd dared to cross that highway.

"It's not as if I didn't grow up and figure out your folks were frightened. They were about to drag the lake. But at the time I assumed — " Mrs. Wade shook her head.

"You assumed I was punished because of you."

"Left quite an impression." The woman paused, as if she were no longer sure what her listener was prepared to hear. "Anything happening at the Glover house was connected to Littletown. When my daughter was grown up and ready, she finally wanted to know more about the Littletown thing than about you."

"I've heard such confusing stories about Littletown," Lois said.

"Is that right?" Mrs. Wade nodded and then looked away. "Well, that was the time one Klan saved us from another Klan." The woman paused. "My daughter's writing a history of it. It's why Ted hasn't let you people alone over there."

"I see," Lois said. The boy's motives had never dawned on her, and to cover her feelings of surprise Lois murmured a bit of praise: Mrs. Wade must be awfully proud of her daughter and grandson.

The woman seemed startled by this. "Proud? Of course I am!"

Lois saw in the face a lifetime of pride she knew nothing about. So that even if she wished to ask the most innocent of questions — *And how is your daughter, by the way, how is her work coming along?* — she could not now do it in good faith. Ted had confided in her, but that was hardly to the point of the present moment in which such trust was yet unearned and unexpected. She saw herself as the other woman must be seeing her — someone whose habit of thinking did not readily include that the Klan in one town protected people from the Klan in another town. She wished she could tell the woman how wrong she was.

"Oh, I'm proud all right," Mrs. Wade said, no doubt quite willing to forgive Lois's helpless waves of a lifetime. She was far above taking much offense, Lois realized. It was Mrs. Wade's turn to smile back, which the woman did with some play of sadness in that mouth, its two long corners drawn down. The woman folded her arms and became silent in a way that swept Lois with feelings of admiration.

Together they watched Petey in the center of the yard, reading the instructions to Paul, who seemed to stand listening to the terrible moment fill up with nothing but Petey's innocence as the boy's light drone traveled up and out into an empty sky.

"I'm glad to see one of those things," Mrs. Wade finally said. "I always wondered if they worked."

Lois said she had wondered as well.

Petey was too short to keep the probe its requisite three inches off the ground. They watched how he was forced to let Paul manage the navigation as he stood close by. Apparently a needle would jump inside a small dial between Paul's hands. In seconds Petey had found a nail in the grass. One would have thought it was a doubloon from his triumphant whoops, which attracted the attention of the toddler. She began to make her delicate way across the drive and into Mrs. Wade's yard. The child's mother came up from behind to supervise as Petey's shouts continued to soar. This was no longer a yard now; it was a gold mine.

"He's going to need a sack," Mrs. Wade said.

Before Lois could stop her, the woman was moving toward the house. "It isn't necessary," Lois called, hearing herself as from a great distance.

When Mrs. Wade returned with a sack for Petey, she stood beside Lois in silence and then pointed. That was the cow and the cowbird out there in her yard, she mused. It was exactly the right description of Lois's husband grazing and of Petey snapping at insects the cow stirred up.

"Yes," Lois said.

"Was there something else you wanted?" Mrs. Wade asked. Lois saw then that she was a bit exhausted.

"I'm sorry, I must go," Lois said, and when she climbed behind the wheel, Myrtle Street closed down just beyond the car door, and there was only a powdery fragrance of the other woman, the sun hitting her two hard ceramic earrings as she bent down to look at Lois through a style of kindly spectacles one didn't see anymore. Small octagonal cuts of glass gave off their separate, intelligent glints of the sun.

No hands were patted in farewell. Someone said good-bye. Mrs. Wade stood up and smiled. She even waved and stepped back from the car as Lois put the car in gear. And then that was that.

LATER, WHEN the old man came on to the porch, he didn't know what he saw.

He squinted to make out what Petey was up to in the yard. But he didn't wait for Lois to explain the contraption. He was still in a huff that she was planning to take Petey along to the meeting that night. Moments before they'd stood in the hallway and had an argument about it. Petey was an eyewitness to the fight down there, Lois had reasoned. She had to think of everyone's benefiting from these experiences. "He's all bottled up inside over this thing. So am I."

"All bottled up?"

"Yes."

"Well, by all means, let's go get ourselves unbottled."

"If you get a chance I wish you'd let him know he's forgiven about being under that boat."

"I forgive him," Glover finally said.

"He doesn't know that."

"I can't help it if he doesn't know that."

Lois reached up to remove a bit of shaving cream on his right temple. He was tired. At some secret slow pace of the very old, he'd been grooming himself to a point of collapse. The new shirt he wore was a flannel one Carol had given him over a year ago. Lois assumed he hadn't intended ever to honor Carol by putting it on. They'd heard him complain that flannel hotted him up like a woman.

"That boy didn't come this afternoon," Glover said. "I guess he's quit us finally."

"I talked to his grandmother today."

The old man didn't want to seem startled. "You going to bring *her* to this meeting?"

"No," Lois said.

"Well, I guess that's something to be grateful for."

THEY ALL ARRIVED exactly at eight, and when Joyce Knight greeted them at the door she said goodness gracious she wasn't expecting the whole family, come in, come in, come in. Lois introduced her husband and father and grandson to the woman and then watched Joyce work their arms like pump handles. "We've met," she said when she took the old man's hand and squeezed it hard. She assumed Petey would want to watch TV with her girls? But Petey said, no, he was an eyewitness, and this news caused the woman's happy face to expand into a wide, impossible brightness. Goodness, she had no idea.

Paul, on the other hand, was a very good candidate for watching television with the girls, Lois explained. If that would be all right.

Oh, of course! They'd love having him! Joyce explained to Paul in a very loud voice that her den was this way. *This way, Mr. Barnes, this way! Follow my voice.* And it was a strange feeling for Lois when she saw Paul do just that and never look back.

Joyce's friend Margaret was there to lead Lois and her small entourage into the Florida room at the back of the house. In that rather large expanse of turquoise and shell furniture, four people rose from their seats as in a standing ovation, with everyone appearing somewhat pained. Of the three men, one was Luke Teal and the other Jay Jones, whom Glover and Lois recognized respectively. But everyone else was in a big to-do about where the old man should sit.

"I'll take *that* chair," Glover announced. He knew how

stooped over he could look standing up in a crowd. Margaret and
a few others seemed relieved to get him down, his canes clattering and his body folding in half. The women's smiles made his
temperature shoot up in his head. He hadn't been in mixed company for so long he'd forgotten the urge to kill.

Two or three people asked Lois all at once what she would like
in the way of a refreshment. Someone pounced on Petey to make
him comfortable. During these kind ministrations, Glover felt
himself to be the old stump on the lake. The women wore Bermuda shorts and long sweater arms tied in creamy knots. Luke
Teal had on a pressed T-shirt the brightest salmon color Glover
had ever seen. The light from the shirt almost blinded him.

When she was seated Lois leaned in close to Petey and squeezed
his hand. She wanted him to smile at her and not be nervous.
"Carol didn't really call me a genius, did she?"

But he was in no mood to be jollied out of his feelings of fear.
"Once," he said. He kept his gaze in his lap.

Lois felt bad for him. Earlier he'd been thrilled at the idea of
giving these parents his account of the fight. "Was Carol being
sarcastic?" she asked softly.

"I guess," Petey said. He would not look at her now.

Light chatter floated up and down in the air. Everyone seemed
quite at ease as they remained standing and casting large shadows
on Lois and her group. They seemed to be talking about the
recent cold snap. The old man craned his head to catch a drift of
the conversation. It was he who finally called up from where he
was sitting deep down in a ditch. "It's late!" he shouted. "It's past
my bedtime!"

No one had ever been in a room with him before. People
grinned and found seats by lightly bumping into each other and
murmured soft apologies.

For the second time in three days, Lois found herself in a
support group circle and going a little blank at the idea that here
were people in your same boat. She heard the whispering. *My
husband keeps trying to fry things. He once tried to fry a lid off a
saucepan.*

A man Lois's age opened the meeting by explaining that he was Roland Darby, the president of Neighborhood Watch. He introduced everyone to Lois, who again introduced her family members. Everyone seemed fascinated by the old man's huge, planted feet and by the two long canes between his thin legs and the placement of those ancient, noble hands. But he'd forgotten to take off his hat. She hadn't wanted to be in charge of his hat for fear of making him appear more decrepit than he was. At home he was still rather graceful in his own way, sometimes even imposing. Now he looked like a toad in hat and tails.

But the old man was shouting in the abrupt way the deaf often manage. "Which one of you girls stopped by my house yesterday?"

The whole room darkened in a way that made Lois realize that this was going to be the old man's show if he wanted it that way. Roland Darby looked at Luke Teal, who gazed up at the ceiling. It had certainly not been *his* idea to invite these people.

"I don't usually get mad," Glover continued. Everyone saw him turn to Margaret, the one of their group unfortunate enough to be seated right beside him. "Yesterday," Glover shouted, "one of you girls told me the colored kids dumped that garbage in my yard. It made me mad." He dropped to a conspiratorial stage whisper with Margaret: "Where is she anyway? Point her out to me."

There were a few light coughs. Crossed legs changed their minds and recrossed in the other direction until Margaret spoke up. "She's not here, Mr. Glover. This is the *board* meeting. Mary Hilliard isn't on the board." Glover came right back at her. "Well, that's too bad." The expression on his face was one of someone whose time had been wasted.

"I have to go," Petey said to Lois. "I'll be right back."

But as he hurried out of the room Petey ran into a low coffee table and knocked a large conch shell onto the hard terrazzo flooring. Lois heard the polished flutes shatter like glass.

"No problem," Joyce sang as she scooped up the pieces and went off into the kitchen with them while Roland Darby attempted once more to start up the proceeding. He began by explaining that the board had wanted to help sort out the problems they were having this week.

"Sort out the *what?*"

Mr. Darby was a nervous man whose eyes kept taking in the old man's attempt to hear without taking in the old man himself, who was simply too formidable. Glover noted this, although he had no idea if Mr. Darby had spoken, or if someone else had spoken, or if no one had spoken at all. His best recourse was Margaret. "Don't think I didn't smack that woman's car," he shouted. Then he smiled at her. Margaret was his type — a plump platinum blonde. "Don't go saying my son-in-law did it." He patted her on her knee. "You all are the official lookouts around here, but I do a pretty good job of it on my own, don't you think?"

"Oh, I'm sure that's quite true, Mr. Glover." Margaret grinned at the group.

When he finally caught Teal's eye, Glover tipped his hat. To Margaret he continued to shout in an earnest, friendly way, "Would you like me to tell you something the old-timers used to say around here?"

"Yes!" Margaret said. Her nervousness made her flirtatious as she leaned in to give full attention, clearly relieved to be off the topic of Mary Hilliard and Mary Hilliard's car.

"My uncle Fate used to say that a handsaw is a good thing, but not to shave with." Glover winked.

"That's so true!" Margaret said. She was sure she was his favorite now, and she patted him back.

"Did you ever make one of those instant cakes that come in a box?" Glover said.

"You mean a cake mix?" ·

"I mean the kind you dump in a bowl. The directions tell you to spit on it."

Well, several people in the room thought that was very funny. There was chuckling here and there.

"It's what this whole thing reminds me of — you people all

puffed up. I'm hoping someone will tell me how I managed it so quick."

He didn't give Margaret an opportunity to regroup or appeal for help. "First it was my son-in-law you didn't want down there fishing and then it was the coloreds you didn't want down there fishing, then you send me those heartless boys of yours and then you send me that *woman*."

"Mr. Glover — "

"I don't have any proof who dumped that garbage, but I know which of those boys I didn't like."

Margaret couldn't stop herself. She was on the end of his line. "Which one?"

Teal leaned into the circle to ask Roland Darby if he couldn't get the floor back. Glover raised his volume. "You know, I never was much of a progressive until you people came along and made me look like one. I ought to thank you. I would have died the biggest bigot on this lake if it weren't for you folks."

He felt he had the tiniest of footholds in the room if he could just keep moving. He looked at Margaret. "Don't think I *didn't* smack her car," he said again. Margaret could only stare back at him in some wonderment until, almost in spite of herself, she was saying that she never said he didn't.

"Then it's all these others?" He circled his cane at everyone while Margaret tried to think. "Are they the ones who think my son-in-law committed an act of violence?"

Margaret wasn't sure.

"See, it's that kind of thing that makes me mad." He tapped one of his canes in front of her again, and finally it was Teal who stood up in the room — a move Glover had been waiting for. He wasn't sure what had taken the man so long.

"Sir, if I may. You've been looking at this whole thing from a very narrow perspective."

"Oh, I know that, son. I know that. How are you, by the way? It's good to see you again."

Teal smiled at the group and at Margaret, who appeared uncertain. Teal's smile was to assure Margaret that she could relax now that he was taking charge. He sat back down and began to speak in clear, loud tones. "Sir, we're glad you could make it over tonight."

"Wouldn't have missed our little showdown," Glover said.

Teal took his time. "Sir, that's not quite fair."

"I have a narrow perspective," Glover said. "The way I look at it, this is something you and I started a few days ago."

Teal continued to smile, to glance here and there at the others, at Lois, who might have guessed that her father would upstage everyone. She was glad for him. All week he'd been feeling so helpless to act.

"Let's say I started it," Glover said. "I was rude to your boy and then you were rude to me."

"Rude to you?"

"I'm here to find out what more I have to do. I want that boy of yours to stay out of my yard."

For the next few moments Teal's lingering smile was that of a younger man indulging an older one.

"Your boy has upset our applecart," Glover said. "Since that garbage was dumped none of us have been quite right over at the house. Paul Barnes has been repeating the same request for two days. He keeps saying he wants to get back home."

"I'm very sorry to hear this, but — "

"Got to have a memory to keep from repeating yourself," Glover continued. He paused and looked at Margaret.

"That's very true," Margaret said.

Glover turned to the group as a whole. "History repeats itself because people do. People lose their memory. Nobody here remembers the *last* time we tried to keep the coloreds out of our hair. Looks brand new to us, doesn't it?"

"Sir," Teal interrupted. "That is most unfair."

"My daughter and I don't have this thing as bad as the son-in-law does," Glover went on, ignoring the man. Glover smiled at Margaret. "We're more like *you* people; we forget this sort of thing has been going on for generations."

Now Margaret was certain she had caught the drift at last. "I think it's just so sad," she said, appealing to the group. "Don't you all think it's the saddest disease? Did you all see that program?"

The others could not look at her. Some looked at their laps. General group spirit flagged terribly; this was not the direction in which Roland Darby had planned to head them. "Maybe if we could come back to order," he said.

"Yes," Joyce said, looking around for someone who knew what type of order might now be attempted. This group was used to planning the next cleanup day on the lake. "I think it'd be good if we could just let bygones be bygones."

Lois heard the expression for the first time. She sat listening to its flowering of dark nonsense, its miracle of circularity. When she heard a noise she looked up to see Petey standing in the doorway listening intently, and she was glad to see he'd come back. Somehow all of this moment had a lot to do with the old man and with Petey. She felt such a rise of pride for the both of them.

"Teal and I owe you an apology," Glover said. "We had our little war and it kind of reeled everyone in. We're sorry about it. Aren't we, son?"

Teal lowered his voice. "We're not insensitive to what happened at your place, Mrs. Barnes. We're all glad Jay got that crew over as soon as he could." Apparently the man had paused in order to give Lois a chance to say thank you. There was something sickly in his smile — something in his pleasure that she hadn't been considerate in thanking them upon her arrival. "We were glad to help out," he said. "Miss Hilliard's experience was the first any of us knew that you suspected our boys here on the lake of that prank."

Glover, who had only caught the word "boys," began saying that he was never going to understand why they hadn't dragged them over there to clean up the mess they'd made in his yard! Luke Teal's son couldn't have done it all by himself.

Teal would have stood up again had not Jay Jones quietly urged him to just take it easy. "Relax," Jay murmured, just at the moment he was interrupted by the old man saying he'd better not see *any* of their boys put a foot on his property after this. Minors were dangerous to have around anyone not strong enough to reach out and wring their necks.

Teal told Darby he was not going to tolerate this, and his anger caused Jones to lower his voice as he addressed Lois. "Mrs. Barnes, we don't expect you and your father to have the whole picture here."

"What!" Glover shouted.

"Ted Johnson has been doing things both at school and here on the lake to threaten our boys."

Margaret sighed her deep sigh of just how sad it all was.

"He's as much as said, 'Treat me badly and I'll bring my friends in here.' That sort of thing." Jay Jones was pained to be the one to tell her. How could she be expected to know? The boys had threatened to swamp the lake with his buddies from the school.

"Swamp the lake?" Lois said. "How do you mean?"

The young jogger had found his footing at last: "Well, you know. Bring in everyone." He paused and thought about this. "One or two black kids in here is a fine thing, and we'd welcome it. But a big group of them is not something you'd want any more than we would. Not a big group of them."

"This may seem out of nowhere to you," Joyce added, "but these things tend to happen fast."

"And we were thinking about you," the other woman said. "The fishing hole is right in front of your house."

It was Petey who interrupted, who came forward to make his small announcement in a trembling voice. The tackle box he was carrying belonged to Fluke. "This is Fluke's," Petey said. Lois was afraid he was going to break the large glass coffee table if he tried to lift the thing off the floor. Joyce breathed, "Oh my God," and rushed to help him.

"Lois!" Glover shouted. He saw only that the boy had returned with muddy feet. The tackle box made no sense at all.

"Fluke left this after Ronnie hit Ted over the head — "

"Oh my God."

"Ronnie hit Ted on the head with a coffee can. They didn't want Pops fishing with them because he was asking about the boat a lot, and Fluke called Ted — "

"Oh my God."

"I stayed under the boat. Fluke and Ronnie were trying to scare Pops, and they knew they could scare him by laughing."

And then Petey told them once again how Ronnie had hit Ted on the head with his hand in the coffee can and explained how he hadn't come out from under the boat to help Pops or anybody. Petey's moment proved to be an honest testimony of his cowardly past. And of how he wasn't supposed to be down there.

"Fluke said — "

"I will *not* have my son called Fluke or anything else." Teal's explosion made the whole room jump.

"What!" Glover shouted, and this caused Margaret to give out a short laugh. Poor Margaret. Her face reddened and she gave the group a look that said she could just cut her throat for laughing.

"He made Pops have an episode," Petey said. "My teacher at school? She said she didn't want anyone to hear it. But I already heard 'nigger.' I heard it lots of times."

The forbidden word seemed to give everyone in the room nerves of steel.

"But not Pops," Petey explained. " 'Nigger' gave Pops an episode. Fluke said — "

Teal was on his feet. For a time in the silence he moved coins in his pockets and then said in a low voice that this was hardly a forum in which boys could be named while they were home doing their homework.

"Fluke said he'd get Ted back."

"That is quite enough!"

"He said it was easy to get him back. He called Ted garbage, too. That's what else he calls people. That's why they dumped garbage. Him and Ronnie didn't like Ted bringing Pops down there to fish."

When Petey took a seat, Teal walked briskly across the few

paces between himself and the tackle box whose lid he flipped up
with a bang. "A wallet has been stolen out of here, of course,"
he began.

Anyone could have told him it was the wrong attitude for him
to adopt, that a certain gracefulness would have been more sporting of him, more considerate of him.

"There wasn't ever any wallet," Petey said. "I hid it under the
boat so it would be safe."

"Hid what? The wallet?"

"No, that." Petey pointed. "That's all there was."

"So *you* stole the wallet?"

It was Jay Jones who couldn't stand it. "For heaven's sake,
Luke, will you stop this?"

"You believe this kid?"

"Of course."

Lois watched the man stare at Petey as if trying to understand
how credibility had suddenly seemed to attach itself in one place.
The ring in Petey's account had so little to do with the hard
evidence of a tackle box and more to do with what people must
have already known. That was in Jay Jones's voice — both the
knowledge of what the other boys called his son and the fact that
no neighbor had found a way to tell him. So that betrayal was a
matter of hidden information.

Lois was seated quite close to where he stood now; she could
see him from a side angle as he stared down and fingered the lead
sinkers in the yawning tray. Finally something made him ask if
anyone had anything more to say.

No one did.

Joyce cleared her throat and looked at everyone with wide,
twinkling eyes. The man was hopeless; why didn't he just take
the box and leave?

That was the long moment Lois was not to forget for a
while — herself poised between the one man feeling thoroughly
tricked and the rest suddenly embarrassed by him. In that moment several had tried to give him sympathetic smiles and seen
that he somehow knew that they themselves were not surprised

to see things take this sudden turn. Lois sat measuring the feeling in the room as that of people who knew now that they'd long thought themselves more fortunate than he. Always had. The instantaneous realization of it is the commonest way people have of judging one of their own with dispatch, sending away a less worthy member of their group. His undetected lump has become malignant before he's felt a thing.

Lois spoke out to the man standing near her, refusing to look at her. "It is very odd," Lois said softly. Everyone heard her.

But as soon as she had said it, she saw the costs were too great. Her words caused the man to snap out of his reverie with a little jerk.

"Well, I don't think we're at the bottom of this matter," he suddenly said, half to her and half to the group.

His high tone was too familiar, and the sounds of them caused a quick freeze in the room. He had better not push any further. He was expected to leave; people did not wish to see him backed into any more corners — far worse for him, of course, than for them.

He lifted up the tackle box and headed toward the door, whereupon he turned and called out, "I believe Mrs. Barnes can see that our point is well taken. Don't you think so, Jay? Your information about Ted's friends, for example?"

Jay stood up to play host, to play some normalizing part in escorting Teal to the front door. "Listen, Luke, I'll be giving you a call soon."

There was a pause. Teal accepted this as enough for the moment. "Good," they heard him say. He called over Jay's shoulder, "Well, good night, everyone."

The group called back in cheerful tones. "Good night, Luke!" Far worse than a son being a hopeless idiot was a father not knowing how to save a little face, for heaven's sake.

Lois sat with the group, all of them listening to the murmured exchanges between the two men as they walked out of hearing and down the hall. She tried with some success to take herself back to yesterday morning, to the moment right before she'd had her episode. Yes, she remembered now which of the men it was who had looked at her yard and known precisely what boys were involved. Even his panting, sweet-faced Dalmatian had known.

EVERYONE WAITED to hear the front door close. After that there was a moment's hesitation as they listened to footsteps coming closer and then they all looked up as Jay re-entered the room alone. Everyone but Margaret. Margaret had her head in her hands, remembering only that she'd laughed when it came out that Teal didn't know those boys called his son "Fluke."

"God help us," Joyce breathed. Then she looked at Lois. "You're so right, Lois. It's the oddest thing, that whole family."

"It's not what I meant," Lois said, but again the old man began to upstage her. There was a sudden loud clatter of sticks.

"I'll be out in the car, Lois! It's going to take me ten minutes to get there."

The whole room jumped to its feet for the sake of the old man, who finally had to be pulled up gently, two women on each side, lots of encouragements poured over Glover's bent head still topped in that hat. He was amazing, really, at his age. The conversation started up, and then there was the general and overwhelming swell of people all starting to talk at once.

Simply amazing.

Wouldn't they have liked to have been a fly on the wall when he and Teal went at it?

One or two people saw Glover start to turn in the wrong direction, as if to head off toward the swimming pool lit up just beyond the clear glass doors whose butterfly decals were much too far above his line of vision. People saw that Joyce was there to rescue him, but not before a few winced at the thought of him sailing through all that glass.

It was a relief to make jokes, now that Mrs. Barnes was bending down to speak to the grandson and the two of them were leaving, too, right behind the old man, who followed Joyce's voice into the hall.

Good-bye, someone called. And then the whole lot of them: They were so glad she could come!

Mrs. Barnes didn't answer and there was some suggestion that she was a little deaf, too.

Good-bye, Mrs. Barnes! Thanks!

The woman didn't answer. She was back there collecting her husband in the TV room.

The husband?

Oh, he's been here the whole time.

There is a pause, before a little joke floats up from one corner of the room: she sure knows how to get babysitters for him, doesn't she?

Laughter. Relief. What a week! Can anyone remember a worse week?

The men say yes to beers. The women ask if Joyce needs any help. No one smokes.

Well, I *liked* her. I thought she was sweet.

Jay says he talked to the daughter from Daytona one time when they met up jogging on the road.

What was *she* like?

Kind of wide in the beam.

They all laugh. Jay was terrible! Wasn't he terrible?

There is a bit more ribbing of poor Jay for being so terrible.

But seriously, who was going to tell the Newells about Ronnie?

Well, don't look at me.

They must know already.

I never thought it was the black kids.

Oh ho.

Well, I can't help it. I like to think everything is changing for the better.

Hey, Jay, how much did that truck set us back?

Seventy-five.

That's outrageous!

I never saw the garbage. Rick said it was all of it. Was it really *all* of it?

Owen and I saw it.

But seventy-five *dollars?*

Listen, sue me.

No, Jay! You did the right thing.

Yeah, good buddy. What else could you do?

Jay thinks about this, and then he has bad news. He hates to have to tell them, but right now there's shit left in the kitty.

13

𝕊 𝕊

THE BOY WAS BRUSHED and dressed for bed. He sat in his pajamas ready to pounce on her when she came to tuck him in. "He hates me," Petey said. "He really, really hates me."

It was all about Spider, who hadn't been able to hear him rise up bravely at the meeting. In the short drive home the old man had behaved as if he were mad at the lot of them, garnering mean strength for those steps at the back of the house. But this was difficult to explain to a boy who was tired of all her excuses. The old idea of deafness made Petey more belligerent about being wronged. "I'm *glad* he couldn't hear me."

But just as suddenly his fury fell away. "Look what I found," he said, holding up an ancient lipstick. Its dispenser was the kind operated by a thumb lift he'd never seen. He was eager to show Lois how one had to push the lipstick at the base of the casing, a superior design over the contraptions of his own era. This one was cracked and hard but still fragrant. His metal detector had turned it up in the back of Pops's closet.

"Petey, do you know this smells exactly like my mother? This is a whiff of my own mother!"

How the woman used to grin behind Spider's back, Lois explained. Jemmalee used to grin and shrug her shoulders at his tyrannical ways and roll her eyes until she could get Lois to laugh, the both of them female and able to make their way around the evil spirits that had blown in him but not in them, so much easier to be a girl in Glover's path than to be a boy.

"Tomorrow you go in and talk to him." She was not completely certain she meant what she said.

"Why?"

"If you go into his room tomorrow you'll be granting him a favor. You'll have to apologize first, of course, to get the ball rolling. Then I think he'll tell you he's sorry he's been so hard."

"That means he's dying," Petey said, but it was without sarcasm, which he had not yet mastered in matters of dying.

ALMOST AS SOON as her head hit the pillow Lois had a bad dream, and when she woke up she was sure she had screamed or made a loud cry. She could feel the strain she'd been making in which probably nothing more came out than a small heroic peep.

But the nightmares you can't remember leave you wide awake at midnight. She stared at the ceiling for a time, hearing Paul's loud snore in the next room. Someone had told her something recently about loud snoring — an anthropological speculation that it once served to frighten away wild animals and predators from the original cave.

Then she remembered. She had sat listening to Petey tell about it just tonight before she got him to sleep. He had gleaned his information from a television program and perhaps had gone from there to an image of his own father protecting children whom Petey would never meet. Out of nowhere he had said, "I think my dad is married now."

This was that time of night and rumination when her Alzheimer's heresy tended to settle down on her soul like a weightless fog: we are replaced and then forgotten; the personal life can't possibly matter; how quickly one's own mother begins to slip away like a fragrance.

Often such ideas would begin to make Lois feel uncanny among the lake's old chorus of sounds, the swimming sounds of the ancient frogs and crickets. They were an awful kind of nature which never seemed to run out of steam as they sang and strained hard against oblivion, and from their sounds alone she had sometimes felt herself spiral downward, her heresy expanding to diminish further the human part of creation. It was no more than an embarrassing entanglement of religious and superstitious forgettings stretching back to a murky beginning.

Mankind is a forgetting machine.

One or two black kids in here is a fine thing . . . but a big group of them. . . . Not a big group of them.

Tonight she would lie wondering what part she had played in such thinking. Paul had come back to her on the bus that summer, too moved to talk about what he had seen. If he could, he would no doubt tell her now how his own spinning brain was hardly the tragedy. It was so easy to see now on the old film footage what had been lost, what a rare and less raw time it had been that summer when she'd stayed home fearful, when a door had stood open a crack and a new joy had rung out on the other side — the promise of a whole other way. Easy to hear it now — how the belief had shone so brightly in those songs and rallies — whereas at the time the upturned black and white faces on the evening news, all that joining of hands and animal swaying, had made her feel a little ill.

She stopped breathing when she thought she heard Paul call out from the next room. Lois turned off the light and lay still. Perhaps he would go back to sleep and not disturb her just now.

"Honey, what is it?"

He had wandered in, drawn there perhaps by the moonlight streaming in off the lake. Dressed in his pajamas, he approached to shake her hand and introduce himself. Due probably to the lateness of the hour, the deadness of the night, this moment was a real first — his utter failure to recognize her even as she got out of bed and turned on the light.

He said he hadn't quite caught her name.

"My name?"

She thought about this and then began to hum it, the popular song that had come into her head right at that minute. "You don't re-mem-ber me," Lois sang, "but I re-mem-ber you . . ."

Paul closed his eyes and sang just behind her dim memory of the words. "Tears on my pil-low . . . Pain in my heart . . ."

"Caused by you . . . Caused by you-oo-oo . . ."

There was a long quiet in which Lois continued to hum and do a little close dancing with the man, a little faked bit of two-step with him, her mouth close to his huge ear.

Paul looked at her finally.

"I'm Lois," she said.

He saw it was something of a quiet joke that he couldn't quite get. He was suddenly very quick. "Well, I'think you're a lot of fun," he said.

IN THE DARK Tom Glover lay still and did some calculations in his head to help him fall asleep. Of course, he knew that Ted Johnson's grandmother wouldn't be old enough to be one of the women who dressed Lucky's body here at the house when the time came. But he counted it out anyway, and then he guessed that the mother of that woman would be the right age, or else *her* mother.

Those women were naturally frightened when they were finally summoned. He could remember how solemn and loyal they were, smuggled in after nightfall on the third day when the tension at Thorns had begun to be felt. They had sent out the word that they didn't want any comings and goings. However, there wasn't a whole lot they could do if Virgil Glover brought in a few darkies to help out, and the boys all knew how to look the other way.

They didn't set up at Thorns until the second day. At dusk

Jemmalee had seen the distant gathering from her own windows upstairs — first the Model Ts, which had not frightened her, but then the torches, which caused her to let out such a cry that Glover had felt murderous toward her as he mounted the stairs. He found her sobbing at the spectacle of those torches. "Don't tell me there's no such thing where *you* came from." He had hissed. "You stop this noise. I don't want to hear another sound from up here."

She had not been permitted to come down and see Lucky the first day when the truck pulled up at about dawn. Alma had asked her to stay out of the way until they could get set up and see what the situation was; and there was the baby to look after. Alma's girl was assigned the job of running up and down the stairs to take Jemmalee whatever she needed while they got Lucky set up in the parlor. Now she was frightened to see that gathering from her windows and she wanted to come down.

Glover had not planned to forbid this but had found himself doing so now that he'd been made so hot under the collar by her yelling out as if she were too innocent for such matters. Now he simply said no. Under no circumstances was she to go downstairs while Lucky was in the house. This was not her business, not her affair.

The girl was stunned. "But I live here."

"No, you're my mother's guest. You're not to gape at something you don't know anything about."

She said she had no idea why he said such a thing to her. She wanted to help Alma.

"No. You're to stay up here. If you disobey, I will make you very sorry about it."

There were to be many laws to lay down after that. But later she would date that night, and the night before, when Wilson arrived with men's news, as the beginning of something lost for the both of them, perhaps a certain spirit of adventure or a playful spirit killed. They had secretly romped around this house and been united as a force against the dear old couple. Jemmalee was the newlywed, the pampered young mother and very much the happy center of her mother-in-law's concerns. She had worked hard to be popular with the three of them, but she would never have guessed that her first falling out would be with her own husband.

"Why can't I see him? You're treating me like a child. I'm a grown woman. I helped Alma pick out those shoes for him."

"What shoes?"

Her slip made her braver. "I bet he was wearing them."

He would not give her an inch for her bravery. "Hell, it doesn't matter now."

Glover had wanted to swear some ultimate oath. And perhaps he had. He could never remember later. Only that he had felt like his father. *Damn the women.* But he remembered making Jemmalee sit down and then searching for hard words.

"You're a morbid girl. I'm not going to have you going down there and seeing him. He's as naked as Noah. He's not a fit sight."

Long after that night, it would seem as if she would never have seen this side if it hadn't been for Lucky. Apart form the loss of the baby a month later, which changed them irrevocably, it was the four days with Lucky in the house that must have seemed the beginning of what it really meant to be married to Tom Glover. For a time she had tried to argue with him. She probably didn't mean what she said: "You're the one who's morbid. You want him all to yourself."

It was a spirited pouting; she didn't perhaps know or mean what she was saying. Later he was sure of it. But at the moment her willfulness had caused him to hit her with the back of his hand. Even then she would not be quiet right away.

"You're the one," she continued, getting up from his bed again and putting on a little housecoat he could still remember. "You're fascinated. You always have been. It's the thing about Lucky; he has you all fascinated. He's all I've known any of you to think about. Now he's going to make sure you never think of anything else." Later that night when he had come up to bed, her question had been very sincere. "You're afraid of him, aren't you?" She hadn't meant at all to be mean; she really wanted to help him.

But he learned something about refusing to forgive her for her remarks. It was a strong weapon for the next and third day. She asked him in the morning to forgive her. That was when he discovered that in keeping her at arm's length he was a stronger person downstairs. In delaying forgiveness for a time, he felt less pain as he sat spooning Lucky some coffee milk. Shaming his new wife for another day, holding her off, was dulling to the senses. It was better than liquor. This was something Virgil must have known about, and why he had contempt for his son's drinking: the better man knew the better secret. And after that their sadness over their own son was a huge blur and her girlish spirit went out of her permanently; they both lost the touch for getting it back. At first Glover had relished the evolution in himself; he felt he had matured. Even in the last days that Lucky lived he'd felt a substantial change in himself for the better.

TOWARD EVENING of the third day none of Lucky's features were recognizable on the burn side, which always lay up. That side of his face was as black as pitch by the next morning and his skin smelled like scorched and rotting food.

His "Mr. Tom" was what had broken down Alma, finally. She'd never heard him call her own son Mr. Tom, and she heard how ironically he said it. It made her sick to know how the boy felt. She didn't want him dying with that anger on his head, not toward her. But she couldn't escape the general implication. And she saw he didn't care and would throw away this chance to be home, where she thought he'd wanted to come, where he had precisely asked to be taken so that she could take care of him.

Alma was right there when Lucky suddenly started talking a

blue streak. Hadn't Mr. Tom realized how cold and tired he'd been that day at the livery? He'd thought Mr. Tom would have given him his coat before they parted that day. Mr. Tom ought to have given him his coat that day.

"My *coat?*" Glover had stared at his mother.

"I knew you had another coat, Mr. Tom. If a man has two coats, he should give one away."

Glover couldn't believe it.

But later, Alma had fallen apart. Nothing else had touched her as this had — the anger in that "Mr. Tom," his bitterness over some coat.

"Mama, he was pulling your leg, don't you know that?"

"No he wasn't," Alma said. "It's how he feels now."

"It's those shoes you gave him later. Later that made him want my coat."

Glover apparently had spoken a kind of truth that made things worse for the old girl instead of better. After that she had had Wilson bring over a few of the women from the Hollow to sit with him. If the sight of her was terrible to Lucky, then others might be in a better position to take care of him. She didn't want to torture him. They had all worried she was losing her mind.

"Mama, you're making yourself sick." But the next thing he knew, Alma had retreated upstairs, and the women from the Hollow were coming in with their camp stools so they wouldn't be wearing out her parlor. Perhaps she was right about Lucky, whose feelings after that were expressed in a whisper or two to Glover, whom he did not really seem to hate at all. He said he understood everything now that he'd gotten himself back here.

The stools made the women appear as squat and ugly as trolls, and eventually Glover made them sit against one wall so Lucky wouldn't have to look at them for the last great barrage of shivering and agony before he died, whereupon the women had a little argument as to which of their warm pennies would be used to close his one eye. They had some kind of chalk they'd ground up for the soles of his feet, and when Glover saw that chalk, he was determined to stay by the boy's side during the official lay-ing out. It was perhaps the first and last time he'd been really sure that what Lucky had felt all this time was simple abandonment and that the least he could do now was not abandon him to these female squabbles.

He was right there when the body was finally turned on its back. He'd been amazed at how perfect Lucky had remained on his protected side — young and strong, his dark smooth breast intact and his belly lean and his organ flaccid and virginal. The women had imagined better than Glover how, in rolling over the body, they would be blessed with something for the wake. They couldn't get his swollen back and arm into a suit, but somehow a piece of white linen had turned up, embroidered and stitched. They'd washed him and laid him out in that linen. When he was all ready, they turned the burned side of his face away from the viewers. And there was Lucky's strong profile. One had assumed it was gone, but all along it had been right there. A remarkably unburned half of his nose still allowed the full nostril to flair. And the unswollen, untouched eye seemed only to have closed in sleep. One could keep staring at the face and be reminded of the arched and quizzical brow. One high cheek in sleep remained perfect, and a preserved ear was there, all its intricate swirls still fresh and glistening, as from the sea.

14
❧ ❧

Thus the old man was not off his guard or surprised hours later to find Lucky visible in the room. He was overdue. He'd been demanding acknowledgment for a week, and at two in the morning, here he was, a tall boy standing in the open door. He was a gangly silhouette framed by light flooding in from the hall.

"Lucky?" Glover called.

He began the work of propping up in bed and saw the figure moving quickly to slap a hand over his mouth. Glover was unprepared to take in the harder truth. At first his heart did not respond. *They've entered at the back of the house,* was all he could think. *They've nosed me out as they would a skunk.*

He understood that he was not to speak or move. He sat with that hand clapped on him and thought of Halloween, furious at the idea of all of them crouched in the hall laughing, their noise traveling upstairs where it would frighten Lois to death and this kid standing almost on top of him now, straining to keep him quiet and yet to hear if anyone had been aroused.

Glover saw in his mind the detonated candy in a slow fall over the railing all this time and just now ready to hit ground. He smelled blood on the boy's hand; in the weak light, he saw that the boy had gotten a cut breaking open one of the windows. Glover couldn't see the weapon.

And then he did see it. A tire iron.

Glover nodded and Fluke took his hand away. The old man let his gaze travel to his hearing aids, which looked harmless enough on the bedstand. They looked like two pink kidneys, but he saw the boy sweep them up and put them in his pocket. This was very bad. Whatever sound was available seemed to close in. He felt himself submerged in a holding tank. There was a hair trigger in the boy. He was like one of those tightly wound steel cables. Released, the blind killing cable whips out to thrash at whatever it can find. Glover smelled a rampage, himself getting it first and the noise causing the others to run down to the landing.

He eased back against his pillows, and then his hands shook badly as he reached inside his pajama pocket and managed to pull out the knotted tissue where he kept his pills at night. Fluke seemed to watch with a bit of fascination before he put down the tire iron and then took both hands and tucked the bedding tightly between mattress and bedspring. Miraculously he hadn't found the small handgun in there as he made those deep tucking jabs. Only a month ago the old man had gotten rid of it because of Paul and the thought of Petey snooping around in this room. Maybe he'd half thought of something like this as well, although not quite Fluke Teal tucking his bedding around him.

Soon the boy was standing upright again and taking tentative looks around the room with its strange crowd of furniture on this end. He looked at the ceiling as if something might pounce or land on his head. Perhaps the boy was high on some fairly standard popper. He was not drunk. He was too antsy for it to be alcohol. He walked to the first of Glover's big desks and turned on a light. Glover saw how the tire iron gave him courage, juiced him, pumped him now that it was apparent no one else was awake. He tapped it against one leg. He was feeling everything in this house as it came through the end of that divining rod in his right hand. Finally Fluke moved to the door and closed it carefully. Glover let himself breathe only then.

But right away he began to shiver, which irritated the boy. Fluke moved quickly to get a folded blanket from one of the chairs. With that blanket came the second tucking in and the boy's furious walk to the other side of the bed. He put his iron on Glover's stomach as he made the blanket into a kind of straitjacket, his eyes a bit glassy from some kind of pill.

"Is it money you want?" Glover was careful to keep his voice down.

Fluke smiled to see him asking this with just his head sticking out. He turned to look at the room again.

Glover lay very still. "I guess I made you mad the other night."

It was another long wait before anything happened. At least he was lying down, he was warm, it was two in the morning, and the folks upstairs were probably in the deepest part of sleep. He lay trying not to think how helpless he would be to defend himself even with his old .38 in place, of the impossibility of rolling over on his side and digging for that piece with his bad arm.

Suddenly the kid was back, his mouth moving as if he were talking now. Glover shook his head; he was deaf. The boy put the tire iron down and took out the pink fittings one by one. He played with them for a bit before he tossed them on the bed. Glover took it slow in freeing up his arms. He was trying to think. The boy's swagger began to heighten as he waited for the old man to get ready to hear what he had to say.

"You stupid idiot."

The boy had rejected the father's style for something he was more comfortable with. None of Teal's annoying finesse.

"What do you want?" Glover said. It was his lowest voice, since right above their heads were Paul and Carol's boy in separate rooms.

"Nothing," Fluke said.

"I want you out of here."

"You do?" The boy grinned.

Glover saw his mistake. He shrank in upon himself as the boy leaned close to his ear this time: he'd decided he was staying for a while.

After that he seemed to take more interest in the room. It

amused him now — the old man's binoculars sitting upright on one of the desks. He recognized it and waved the thing at Glover before he put the strap over his neck and sat down. He moved the swivel chair back and forth. "Aren't you something?" he said, admiring the setup. He didn't look at Glover as he put the tire iron on the desk and pulled at the long drawer across the front, a drawer so previously sorted out and organized in an old man's slowest hours that it would seem insane. Glover had set all the gold watches at twelve and coiled their long gold fobs into perfect circles and arranged the four silver thimbles by size. "Shit, man," Fluke said. He was definitely amused.

Virgil's last and best watch rose up and then dangled for a moment or two before Fluke rather expertly drew in his stomach. The watch slipped out of sight as if into a grown man's tight vest pocket. The way the boy sucked in and dropped that watch: sixty years of making this gesture came rushing back, Glover's own vanity neatly imitated.

"These valuable?" Fluke was fingering a few foreign coins lying loose in the pencil tray. The old man didn't answer.

"Hey! I said are these valuable?"

"Take them," Glover said.

"I just asked you a simple question."

"They're almost worthless."

Fluke looked at him and saw he was telling a truth. Then he turned back to look at the coins. "Figures," he said. He was already dangerously bored. Glover tried to raise up, but Fluke made the three steps from the desks in no time. "Forget it," he said, pushing Glover back down. The binoculars hung in a plumb line over Glover's chest, and for the first time the old man had a clear view of a boy's injured face. Fluke's lip was swollen on the left lower side, and Glover saw how he kept feeling the hot swelling where his father had made contact. Teal wouldn't be able to whip this boy with a proper belt; he'd had to lash out at him, furious to have been made a fool of by the old man.

"Heard you told on me," Fluke said.

But he was turning away again, freshly amused at the room.

"Nice," he said, gesturing. "All this stupid stuff." Then he pointed into Lucky's dark corner. "I hear that's where the nigger died."

"What?" Glover felt his heart go from fear to sickness as Fluke sat on the edge of his bed and just shook his head at him.

"Aw, man, if you only knew how your Teddy boy tells on you. If you only knew. He says his mother knows everything about you. Everything."

Fluke waited until he saw he'd hit the mark. Now he could relax.

Over at the desks he seemed a little more grim than before. He wanted to get some momentum going again as he snapped on a second lamp. Drawers came open and closed. At a fourth drawer he stopped. "Shit," he said. It was a stash of old farm trinkets. Among them was a head counter any boy would like; it fit into the palm of the hand while the numbers turned over with each flick of the tab. Fluke worked at this a few minutes and then put the counter aside to take with him. What else did he have in here? "A lot of shit, man, a lot of stupid shit in these drawers. It really stinks in these drawers, man." By now the desktop was cluttered. "Hey, what was this? Another pair of binoculars? Geez, where did you *get* this stuff?"

The boy held up a tool he couldn't identify. Glover was not sure whether to answer or keep quiet. Neither choice would please. "A whole lot of junk," Fluke said.

The next two drawers seemed to infuriate him. Old photographs and papers that the boy found contemptible, more stupid, apparently, than other things in the category of stupid. Glover watched him kick one of the drawers hard with his foot and then grapple as if to tear the thing to bits. He was as high as a kite. Something was causing a hot mix of rage and humiliation. He watched the boy start to give up. He had hurt his hand on the drawer. Now he sat with his head down, either out of dizziness or nausea or the sudden apathy of knowing vaguely how much trouble he was in. Then he raised up, smiled as he tested the swivel chair to see how far back it would go. He braved the tip-over point, then raised one slow leg at a time and crossed his ankles on the desktop. He wore huge tennis shoes with splashes of color and high, meaningless cuffs. He put the tire iron across his lap and eased himself into a balancing act, a goon behind a desk, a goon not knowing what to do with tables turned in his favor. He was already out of ideas.

Fluke said he felt so completely trashed, he ought to make the old man sit over here so he could take a nap.

Glover saw that the boy wanted something to happen. He wanted amusement. Now he was leaping up and bouncing into the BarcaLounger. Hey! They had one of these at his house, too. It was just like his old man's throne, for Christ's sake. Then he paused. "Listen, I've let my old man beat me up over bigger stuff than you. You can count on it."

Fluke tried the lever several times until he brought the big chair forward and was dizzy again. He let the tire iron roll to the floor and then hung over the side of the chair watching it a long time as if he were waiting for it to crawl away from him. He forgot about Glover and seemed to sleep hanging over the side of the chair that way. Finally he raised his head and smiled.

"Yeah. Ted talks about you all the time. I mean, I'm not a big fan, but *this* guy — someday — boom. Dynamite under this crazy house, man." He looked around. "I figured I'd better get over here once before the niggers do."

Glover waited.

"And guess what?"

"What?"

"You got it coming. See, that's the whole thing now. They think we *all* got it coming. Everything, man. Their stuff is all *our* fault."

"What do you want? What are you doing in my house?"

The boy grinned. "One time I got dirt on my old man's chair, which I did on purpose. He popped me so hard I ended up in the hospital."

Glover watched him get up slowly. He seemed to notice something for the first time. "You got a refrigerator in here." The

light fell on him from the open door, and Glover saw him seem
to lose his will to move. When the motor kicked on the boy gave
a little jerk. Slowly his long body seemed to collapse, and without much sound or struggle he ended up on the floor, his legs
crossed Indian-style, but his head down. He was dizzy, man.

Glover considered him for a period of time and guessed again
that the boy had taken something. "Do you need your stomach
pumped?"

There was no answer as Glover managed to loosen the bed
tuck on his right-hand side. "Listen, I want you to drink some
of that cream I have in there."

Fluke slowly turned his head toward him.

"The cream," Glover said. "It'll coat your stomach."

He watched the boy seated on the floor in front of the open
refrigerator door. He was truly trashed, man. But then he looked
around until he found the old man's face. Fluke smiled. "There
you are." There was no sound for a time. Then it seemed as if he
might be sobbing. "All you people. I can't stand all you people."

Glover had freed the bedding, but he was not sure he had the
strength to get his legs out. He talked softly to himself as he
struggled, found one cane and then got hold of the bedpost, told
himself he was getting up, told himself he was going to get that
cream out of the refrigerator. He talked right at the kid. Coat the
stomach, he said, repeating it several times. When Fluke saw the
cane he laughed, putting up his hands over his head, protecting
himself. He looked up from the floor finally and grew quite
serious.

"If you touch me, my dad will have your head, man."

For a time the old man stood over Fluke and then watched him
sniff at the opening of the cream carton. After Fluke took a sip,
Glover let his own backside ease down until he felt the edge of
the hard bed. His heart was racing. "Drink it all," he said, surprised to see the carton tip back. The boy wiped his mouth and
then winced when he touched his lip by accident. His swearing
was automatic as he sought out the swelling with his tongue.

"You got to get away from that father of yours," Glover said. "I've met the man. He's something."

"You never met him," Fluke said. "You sure as hell never met him." But then he looked at Glover. He couldn't believe it was true.

"He came to see me on Saturday — "

The boy finally shook his head and then said "He did not" before taking another drink from the carton.

"I could tell you a lot about men like him. He came around here to tell on you, if you want to know who the rat fink is."

The boy turned his head away.

"He interferes in your affairs. Can't have been the first time he's done it."

Fluke was on his feet after a few unsteady moments during which a rocker frightened him; he had accidentally brushed it. The chair moved and threw its long shadows up and down in a way that was disconcerting even to Glover, and suddenly the boy's eyes were glassy, as if full of tears.

"You can sit in it," Glover said. "Just don't knock anything off the desk. It'll wake people up."

Fluke continued to stand in place as if the room might roll over.

"He's not a respecter of privacy, your father. I consider that a great flaw in a man. I've been sitting on my porch three days thinking about what kind of man goes around undermining his boy. I've observed animals like him in the wild. Sometimes they eat their young."

This had a certain effect. The boy stopped as if he had wanted to make sure he'd heard correctly before he finally found the edge of the moving chair and managed to sit down. Then Glover saw the lips curl. Fluke announced that he didn't give a shit about any of his crap.

"It's rare, but you farm around here long enough, you'll see it. Ever seen a bobcat? The mother cat hides her cubs for a good reason. She doesn't want the old tom hanging around. I think it's fear when the male gets rid of the litter. He's stoking himself for the energy he's going to need to beat rivals. When a man does that, it's fear. But something's gone haywire. A man goes around getting into boys' affairs and they end up right in his path."

"You never met him! He would never come here." But the boy was beaten and sick and suddenly declaring that he was getting out of there. He didn't need this, man.

"Then why did you break in? You know he came here. He came here instead of doing what he really wanted to do, which was to tear you apart."

Fluke was cold. He said so, said he was going on home.

"My wife told me something one time," Glover said. For a moment he felt a bit uncertain. "She said she was glad our son died — "

The door from the hall gave way at that moment, and Glover sat watching the thing swing slowly into the room. In the yellow light he could just make out Petey, the consummate eavesdropper with just enough sense not to run when the tire iron was seized and Fluke stood up. The child was like a stunned fawn. He couldn't move.

"Come in here, Petey," Glover said. "Close that door, son, there's nothing to be afraid of." But he saw then that the boy couldn't unplant his feet, that the best thing to do was to distract the boy holding the weapon. "She said she was glad my son had escaped from me before he got big enough for me to thrash. It's exactly what she said."

Glover waited a moment. "Petey." He spoke gently. "Son, you're letting in a draft."

Petey ran to the bed, and all Glover could do was attempt a look of some encouragement. "You just stand here and mind yourself. I'm having a talk with this boy, so you just stand here next to me." Glover turned to Fluke.

"Saturday after he left here, I was thinking how young and strong your father is right now."

"Whose father?" Petey said.

Fluke said he thought Glover should just shut up. The boy

kept an eye on Petey as he moved to close the door to the hall again. In the pause, the old man tried to reach out from where he was seated, and Petey took a step closer.

"Lois doesn't keep cream in *her* box, does she?" Glover said as Petey climbed into the bed. He tried to sound as if all this were only a strange moment in the night. Perhaps the boy would think he was dreaming. "I looked one time and found skim milk in her box. It was sky blue. A frog jumped out at me."

He saw the younger boy blink at him. Glover put a slow finger to his mouth and then turned to Fluke. "I've seen bobcat eat their young. Nature can be strange. Nature's not as natural as people think."

He watched Fluke sit down and put his head on the desk. Glover couldn't help thinking how good sap flowed out at the first injuries these boys received. It hardened them over if you kept at them, and that was the end of growth.

This particular boy had been tricked before. In a million ways he'd been reasoned with, perhaps brought back to life and then been made to see some new look of disappointment in his father's face. "It can look like hate," Glover said when he found his voice again. "You're too young to know the man is stumped. He doesn't know it either."

Fluke continued to keep his head down, but Glover himself was sure he heard the question correctly. "What happened to your son?" Fluke said. "You kill him?" He talked into the crook of his arm resting on the desk and from his tone it apparently had not amused him to ask this.

"He was an infant," Glover said. "He was a crawling infant. Got himself to the edge of a cistern." He reached out and pulled Petey toward him so he wouldn't be afraid. "You know what a cistern is, don't you?"

Petey shook his head, no.

"It was twenty feet away from where I put him down, but he got over to the edge while my father took a nap in the sun and I went off to tell one of those boys something. He hit his head on a pipe and there was about an inch of water down in there."

Glover stopped to breathe. "He was in diapers. Now I'm so old I have to wear diapers."

The other boy continued to keep his head in his arm, but Petey's face was filled with light.

"I remember everything about that day. Guess how many funerals we were going to have?"

Petey didn't know.

"Four. Lucky's, his, and then my parents'. Four. But right then it was a good day. Full of relief. Lucky had just passed away and we were never more glad to see someone out of his misery. It was a sunny winter day and we were glad for the warmth. We were all whipped. I'll never be tired again the way I was after Lucky died. We used to take the baby in to see him." Glover stopped at this claim, which had come rolling out of him. Why hadn't they? he wondered. He would have blessed that child, would have liked to get a look at him.

The other boy seemed to swear ("What are you, jinxed?"), but he had lost all his anger. From the tone in his voice one would guess that jinxed and cheated was how Fluke saw himself.

"Right over there." Glover pointed out the place to Petey. "We had him in the parlor on a cot. He thought that baby was quite something and the sight of him was good, made him feel better. He used to grin at him." Glover's voice caught. "Died looking at him."

"You don't have to tell me," Petey said.

Fluke looked up. "You're talking about that nigger."

"I had gone outside to make sure the men were making progress. The cistern was clogged and had to be pumped out too soon after the last time, and Papa had wanted the boys to go in there and put in larger pipes. He was about done in himself at that time, and I can remember him wanting to sit out in a wicker chair and get some of that sun. I came on out myself and stood looking at him. I had pushed back my hat and thought how we'd all got through it.

"Pretty soon I told those boys they were doing a good job and that they could take a break and go on over to the warehouse and help the boys over there unload some lime we were going to need down on the hammock. And so they all left and I remember having a little talk with Papa in that chair and he was enjoying the sun on his face, and I went inside the house. I don't know why. I went inside the house maybe to get a drink of water." He explained it into Petey's bright face, which gave him courage. "And there was my boy on the back screen porch, and I scooped him up and tried to get him to drink out of my glass. I remember how he didn't like that and batted it away and made me spill water down my front and I knew he was going to be a fine boy. I heard my father call to me and I went on outside to see what he wanted and kept the baby cradled in the crook of my arm and walked on outside in the sun again. Someone was dead and we were all alive and that's a good feeling."

"What was his name?" Petey said.

"Just Tom," Glover said.

Fluke must have thought this was a stupid thing for Petey to ask, or else he was embarrassed in the way teenagers can be embarrassed by sudden intimacy. Glover remembered that sensation of wanting to die in the presence of it, and he watched with interest as Fluke hid his shame by putting his head in his hands again. It was shame he could not have spoken of, just the hearing of the name of the boy. He would have rather been slapped.

"We'd had a lot of cold. We'd even had a few light freezes. I thought the sun would do him some good. I thought it would cure him of the cold. He'd been down with something or other, we all had gotten down after Lucky. And I remember putting him right at my father's feet. He wasn't able to crawl yet. He'd get up on all fours and just rock, you know, like they do, just rock and make noises."

Petey nodded.

To keep his wits about him, Glover grabbed him again and then felt the boy's thick hair come under his mouth and he was somehow able to talk into it. "I remember her coming out of the house looking for him. For Tom. I'd stepped off for a minute or two to help those boys get that motor turned over, I thought she'd already taken him in the house. We just stood looking at each other. Papa had his head back snoring."

Petey's head came up. "Then you found him and he was already dead?"

"I'd say about three minutes."

Fluke was on his feet, saying he was going home.

"And then *everybody* died?"

Fluke said it must be zero degrees in here, man. He was going on home before he froze to death.

Glover turned and stared at Teal's boy. Fluke didn't like that. He wanted to know what the hell the old man was looking at now?

"You be careful, that's all."

What did an old fart like him know about it, for Christ's sake?

"One time my father got hold of a gun," Glover said.

Petey looked up to see if this could possibly be true.

"Some fathers get tired of their boys." Glover looked at Petey. "I think they just get tired of them."

Petey gave a look of utter bafflement, but the statement had hit its mark with the older boy, perhaps. Glover thought he might be seeing swimming tears in the tall, gangly one who had finally jerked open the door and then was unable to get around Paul standing in the light.

"Are you crying?" Paul said. There was not a sound for a moment, and then there was the inevitable reaching out to take up Fluke's hand which Fluke had no power to resist. "Paul Barnes," the man said.

Fluke struggled to get around him. He repeated to everyone that he was getting out of here, man, that he was going home.

"Will you let me get a few things?" Paul said.

"You're staying here with us, Paul," Glover called out, certain now that they would wake up Lois. It could not be helped. "Paul, come in here!" The old man had made his way to the door by this time. "Come in here, son, and sit with me. This boy is leaving now." Glover saw then that Fluke had disappeared into the back of the house.

"I have to go with him," Paul said.

"No, you come help me get into my bathrobe."

Paul peered into Glover's room, alarmed to see all that furniture and the big, overpowering refrigerator. "Who lives in here?"

"I do! Hand me that robe."

But it was Petey who went to the peg in the bathroom and then helped the old man get into his robe. Glover spoke in new low tones. "What does she normally do to calm the situation down?"

Petey stared at him. Then he looked at his grandfather Paul, who had gone to the BarcaLounger and sat down. "He's okay now," Petey said. He heard a noise above his head. "But she's awake now."

Glover took a deep breath. He returned to the edge of his bed and sat carefully and then looked around. "What are we going to tell her?"

"I don't know." Petey's shoulders began to shrug and the old man put his hand on them and brought them down again. He said he hated to see him shrug those shoulders.

"It's my practice not to tell her much," Glover finally said. "She doesn't need to know how easy it is for those kids to break into this house, does she?"

"No."

"You sit down in that other chair for a minute. You and I have to get our stories straight."

15

A FEW WEEKS LATER, Tom Glover got a sharp warning at midpoint around the heart. He felt the surging, upward thrust; then a loud single strike — the big bell going off at the top of the sissy pole. He saw stars. He saw someone giving a big stuffed bear to the buxom blonde.

His pain went down and left him with a feeling of certainty. And when he put his arm over the bed and touched the floor he was convinced. Death had started in the floorboards of the room. It was down there humming, the way unconscious matter hums for God. At long last, he thought. This was the finish line at the end of the race, the exit sign over the door; soon they'd all be waving at him from the choir loft.

When he sat up slowly, quite pleased, he surmised he would have about as much of the day as he wanted. He would try to last until after they'd had their big noon meal. He decided he could wait until four o'clock when Lois would be alone and rested from her nap. He could call her in here and tell her good-bye.

Right now he must do like women do in the short hours before a birth. Some were known to clean a house before anyone was aware that the awesome head had dropped. Standing upright in his room on his last day, Glover made one long effort to name the certainty he felt — a kind of smugness, which was surely a vastly underrated human emotion. For pregnant women and dying old men, it could not be topped.

From the weakness in his legs, he saw that the work of this day would be simply in getting through it. I'm standing straight up, he thought. Then he had to ease back down, and it was a long time before he could reach out to the bedpost and then grab a stick and take the three steps to the bathroom sink. He was careful. This was not the time to break a bone and then somehow linger on as one of the last porcelain hips of his entire generation. He no longer had the old .38 even in his locked safe. Shooting himself had been the only reason for keeping a gun in the first place. But the police had it now.

They'd come for it in the week Teal spent parading his boy as a celebrity. Teal claimed that Fluke had actually been hit with one of the famous canes inside the old man's house. At a preliminary hearing the boy claimed to have seen a gun. Part of his testimony included an admission to breaking into the house to get his tackle box, which had been stolen from him, but that once inside the house he'd almost gotten killed. For a while everyone ran around getting personal lawyers. Neighborhood Watch people heard they would all be formally deposed as to whether Glover did or did not make open threats at a meeting a few hours before the incident. But at the end of one week Mr. Teal lost the lead when his son finally told on him. The whole thing died down to a few social workers in protective services, a few psychiatric specialists assigned to the case. Too late to prevent everybody on the lake from paying those lawyers up front. Smart lawyers knew how to charge people just enough to keep them from thinking they'd been worked up over nothing.

Glover ran scalding hot water on his wash rag. The heat on his hands felt salubrious this morning, and then the hot, rough cloth on his eyes, the heat in and behind his ears. He tried out the same remedy on his chest and shoulders, but by now there was not quite the original pleasure. Parts of him were as unfeeling as wood. When he reached for his shirt, the washboard in his chest

pleased him for a moment. He wouldn't be long in the ground
before they could play on his ribs with thimbles and old spoons.
One year from now Lois would remember him from across an
abyss of dry bones, and it was a very good thought.

He paused, fearful suddenly that he'd forgotten to tell her not
to embalm him, or that she'd already forgotten the request. Florida finally got the laws changed and embalming was no longer
mandatory. Like it or not, Jemmalee might still be an unthink-
able sack of chemicals after all these years. For a long time lobbyists had made sure you didn't have a choice.

It was very good to have slept until seven. If he'd awakened at
four or five, he might not have had the will to sit here waiting.
They would have found him in bed and claimed he'd died in his
sleep. The idea made him mad. There was no such thing as a man
dying in his sleep — an obvious invention of Sunday school
teachers and night nurses. Lois had recently gotten Paul a talky
night nurse who was always poking her head in: "I tell all my
friends what a cutie pie you are, Mr. G."

The dark would be a little while longer lifting this morning
than was normal. Pain slowed down time. He didn't want his last
day bogged down in fearful pain. Perhaps if he managed to dress
himself and then have some food he'd have the bull by the horns.
He would aim with all his might at four in the afternoon. He
would try to take the day an hour at a time and not ruin Lois's
plans. Last week was his birthday and Carol hadn't been able to
make it until today. It was to be a big noon meal, all his favorite
Thanksgiving foods. Carol wasn't going to be able to make it for
a real Thanksgiving either, so today was supposed to stand for
it. She and Petey had rolled in late last night with several bags of
presents for everyone. Carol was covering her bases in case she
missed Christmas.

He sat on the edge of his bed and managed both his boxers and
his britches, a little more slowly than was normal. His doubts
and confidences were going to rise and fall all day, he guessed,
like bathwater. This was none of his worry now. He had one
thing left to enjoy — the private pleasure of outsmarting every-

one by getting the day right. In his life he'd never guessed at anything close to the mark. Now he was a flat winner. Death was here. And if he fell down cold without further warning he would still be more on target than he'd ever been about anything else.

By eight he was seated in his best rocker drawn up to his desk, the shades still down but his water boiled. At nine he woke with a start at the jolt of cold coffee spilling out of his cup and into his lap. He watched the dark spreading stain and then began to slap at himself.

In wondering how likely it was that he would feel a great deal more pain, he suffered a new wave of fear. He could call for Lois to come sit with him. Or else the day girl, whom he liked. Smart woman. She was a widow and grandmother with a head of dyed hair piled very high. He could have her come in here and sit with him a little while if it all got too much. He could happily die holding her hand and looking at all that beautiful hair.

Paul came in at ten and walked right up to the rocker and asked in his inverted fashion if Glover were ill.

"You feeling good?" Paul was at his best in the mornings before the long day stretched out. At night he had started prowling so badly that he kept the entire household on its toes.

"Maybe you can help me pick up these paper clips, Paul." Glover pointed out where a score of them had fallen around his feet. "Somebody's going to trip on those." For the first time this morning he heard how his own voice sounded frightened and trapped. He felt a new Morse code tapping on his breastbone. Everything was signaling wildly from the other side of town.

Paul saw clearly what the problem was with the paper clips and soon he was down on hands and knees getting them up. Glover pointed a flashlight so he could see better. Paul called out a thank-you from under the desk, where he found more that had slid out of sight. The old man felt so weakened by Paul's efforts, he had no strength to turn off the flashlight. It sat in his lap and lit up his left leg. "Did you bump yourself when you were under there?"

"I sure did." Paul laughed, rubbing at his head.

For a moment Glover was tempted. It would be nice to have a man sit in here a moment if it was going to happen now. He could count on Paul, and it was a sentimental thought that made Glover have to fight back self-pity. "Thanks for crawling under there for me."

Paul looked startled. "Did you drop something?"

"Yes, those paper clips. You already got them for me. You could raise those shades so I can see the lake."

What must it be like to raise shades again, as Paul was doing, and to discover that there was a whole gorgeous body of water out there that you'd never seen.

A new and final sun barreled through the full branches of Glover's trees, and the lake was a blue gemstone. He tried to name his new sensation, a feeling that now he could stare at the sun and not go blind. All the rubber bands in his legs were snapping; whatever tautness kept the body guessing, kept the will willing, was punching in its time on the clock. The Joint Chiefs of Staff were checking out. "You're on your own," he felt himself saying, as his hands let go and the newspaper's four separate sections slid down and made pyramids on the floor. He felt himself drifting off on the idea of the Pharaohs and their pyramids. They were the ones who sometimes embalmed their servants. They would kill a good boy like Ted Johnson and take him with them to the other side to continue right along when they got to wherever it was that life continued *right along*, exactly as it did here.

More than once in the last month the old man had tried to tell Johnson that the deal was off, had then stopped paying him, and had lived only to see the boy set his jaw and keep on coming. Almost every afternoon, still dressed in that red jacket, still determined to take Paul fishing, the boy would arrive with a grimmer and grimmer look on his face. Of course when the old man had tried to resume payment, he was flatly turned down. After that the sight of the boy could hurt his feelings, especially when Lois tried to mediate. Surely he didn't need her to explain how a boy like Ted Johnson wasn't going to let a silly cracker run him out of that hole.

On some days, just to ease the pain in his heart, he had sat on the front porch secretly suspecting the boy of martyrdom. Gradually he had been able to let the thought go, so as not to be stuck with it for eternity. Still, he hoped Lois could see for herself that finally Johnson was about as stubborn as boys came and that this was either going to be a very good or very bad character trait.

Who could call it? Not he. Let the living judge the living. At the moment his own great assignment was to fight off drowsiness and not to let his heart kerplunk him into sleep on the day of his death.

But he knew when he woke again that he'd been out for another length of time. He could smell the turkey getting tender. Three Thanksgivings from now, he figured, his dry joints would fully loosen and come apart. Probably not much odor at all. It was the chemicals that stank. He was going to be too weak to come to the table. Right now Lois and Carol were beside his chair looking down with a bit of concern in their faces.

"I'm feeling a little unnecessary," Glover said. "I'm going to be a regular killjoy today."

"I'm sorry you're down, Dad," Lois said. "What can I bring you? Let me bring you something."

He felt her hand stroke his forehead and he reached up and pressed it. The warmth was delicious. And she was not unduly alarmed by him. He'd had so many spells recently that they were used to them. The familiarity had won him his privacy.

"Maybe you could bring me a cup of something," Glover said. "Do you have any broth?"

"Don't move," Carol said. "We've got soup. Clear soup. Just take it easy, Granddad." But then she paused. "I came in here to give you these to wear today. They're from Petey." Carol held up a pair of red suspenders, and there wasn't much else on the face of the earth right now that could have pleased him more. He wanted to say, Bury me in them.

Instead, he rolled himself forward in his chair and let Lois clamp the back halves in place; he felt her adjust the crosspiece and then bring the two long halves straight down his front. He smiled at Carol. "You sure this wasn't your idea?"

"Oh, partly. I can't believe you'll really wear them."

"For the rest of my life," he said to make them laugh.

They sent in Paul with the soup, and when he put the tray on the desk Glover asked him to sit down. "I need help, Paul. I'm as weak as a kitten. I need you to spoon some of that into me this morning."

"All right," Paul said. He blew softly across the steam to cool everything down. Understandably the spoon went into Paul's mouth and Glover had to ask him how it tasted.

"Good," Paul said, ladling up more and blowing it carefully, close to his nose. "Over here," Glover said.

The broth tasted bitter. Already some ghost inside him was in revolt against food. When he put his head back to rest, the smugness was right there waiting. No nourishment was going to be necessary today. The body merely had to rest and recover in the time it took to let go.

After death a man let go completely in five years. The rigid standing ribs sat up smartly for three or four. Next year he'd still be the wishbone at the end of the meal. But eventually the frame fell to the bottom and everything met back to front, front to back, the slow bones turning to powder until some university dug you up. In three hundred years they'd want to know all about you.

For a long time he sat in his chair listening to their lively voices ring down the hall. During the big meal someone had slipped in while he dozed and put another tray on his desk. This time the broth was in a mug and he was able to take a few sips. When he woke again Petey stood by his chair clutching fistfuls of mail, which meant it was after one o'clock. For the first time he felt upset that he was sleeping so much; he wasn't going to fall asleep anymore. The house seemed very quiet.

"Are the women down for naps?"

Petey nodded. The two of them were strangers anew. They

hadn't known how to act around each other since that night. Glover looked at his mail with complete surprise. "I'd forgotten it," he said.

"You get a lot of letters, don't you?" Petey was loaded down. He had everything pressed to his chest and was peering over the top.

"I suppose so, for an old man."

"For *any*body!" Petey was unguarded in his admiration; this much mail was beyond him. If there was anything Glover had withheld and rationed all his adult life, it was admiration — a sin he would pay for more dearly than for his many others, he thought, as Petey handed over the mail and then attempted a tone of flat indifference. "You want any help opening any of it?" He was staring at the stack as he might a block of chocolate behind plate glass. At this age they expressed their desire and coveting so boldly it makes one sober to see how very little deception they've yet fallen into. As innocent as spring rain.

"I *do* need help today," Glover said. Then he felt awkward silence take up the remaining oxygen in the room. He watched fear creep into the boy's face. Always looming in front of the child were the old man's impossible standards.

"Which ones do you want me to open for you?" Petey said.

"Open all of them," Glover said.

"All of them?"

Was this a trick?

"If you have the time. You may have other plans."

"I don't." It was the best offer Petey had had in a long time.

The sight of a slightly undersized great-grandson climbing, one knee at a time, into the other big chair, the old BarcaLounger Jemmalee had loved, can seem to a dying man as if it is the whole thing missing from his long career. Life's mystery and elusiveness was in that scramble to turn around in the big chair, that boy's straight square back, those hairless arms. Yet when Petey sank into the cushion, when he almost disappeared under the mound of letters upended under his chin, Glover could manage only a hard, mean edge in his voice. "I hope you have a knife."

Of course Petey didn't have a knife, and he stared in disbelief that the Spider could still revert at any moment. Glover meanwhile was hoping he had the strength to reach inside his open desk drawer, where his beloved old pocketknife sat in the pencil trough.

"Here you go," he finally said, making an almost graceful gesture of placing the closed knife in Petey's hand. The boy set his mouth. For a moment Glover remembered that no child this small had the strength in his fingers to pull out the tight, hidden blade. An old man didn't have the strength either with only that mean bit of the knife's backbone to grab onto. They would both be embarrassed.

"I got it," Petey said. Indeed. He waited to be instructed as he held the open blade away from his body. Petey was not casual in suddenly being charged with a real knife belonging to a man whose things he'd never before handled legally. The look of responsibility in his eyes was pure.

"You may have your own style," Glover said. "What I do is make my cut on the long fold from the guzzle to the snatch." Glover thought he saw Petey heft the knife in his right hand, thought he saw the palpable danger of that boy's teens just around the corner, the two thousand–year millennium about to end, the population threatening to double, the lid coming down on a lot of innocent heads. What was going to happen to this next batch? to the sons of Petey Barnes and Ted Johnson? Glover watched the boy hold the first unopened letter and give him a skeptical look. The knife was overkill.

"Just like this," Glover said, as he put his huge paw over the boy's hand and worked the point under a bit of flap. "Gently," he said.

Slitting the seam was more the skill of the blade than the hand. One only had to guide it.

"Just give it a nudge," Glover said. "Push with your eye. Everything else is happening out there on the end."

Soon the boy had the hang of it and Glover felt himself drifting off, exhausted. He thought he heard Petey breathing. He opened one eye and saw the boy seem to fight off looks of happiness. He frowned to keep things on some manly level. "Here's another one!" The open envelopes began to mount up. The child made two neat piles. The high arms of the BarcaLounger became two letter holders on either side of his hips for the opened and the yet-to-be-opened.

When he had his own pace established, Petey slowed down in order to prolong the pleasure of so much mail, after which there were the long hours to endure before television. Glover awoke to a wonderful thought. He could slip away right now. Why not now, in this inexperienced company? Between an old man and a boy there was a century. Almost nothing from the guzzle to the snatch: from his pioneer parents to these mounds of envelopes had been almost no time at all. They were full of bank balances, donation pledges, return-address stickers from the American Cancer Society whose glue did not work. Today's mail. Offers from long-distance companies — ads showing girls with cords wrapped around their fingers. Tricolor grocery fliers and coupons. Sometimes he'd imagined his mother inside a huge, new Publix, pausing in disbelief at the poultry section. He would have had to yell at her, "You're in Florida, Mama! Where did you think?" She had come to the dark interior as a young woman and almost starved. One of her stories was about the disassembling of their cart. They had floated it and their mule across rivers the color and smell of pure sulphur. The water had turned the baby alligators a golden amber color as scores of them swam alongside the cart, little rubbery feet pumping to keep up. She said a baby alligator always looked like something just about to drown. It was how she had felt herself until those Yankees arrived with money and ideas.

Petey was standing beside his chair now, the pocketknife closed in his hand. "Are you going to die soon?"

Glover opened one eye. "Pretty soon," he said.

The boy blushed. "I don't *want* you to die."

Glover discounted the idea by smiling. "You were just thinking how I've got to die sometime."

"Are you too stubborn?"

The boy had heard this idea proposed in other parts of the household, something said as a joke, as a compliment, as a matter of family pride. There was no one more stubborn than the old man.

"That's right," Glover said.

"Me too." Petey was eager not to be taken wrong. "I'm not ever going to die."

Glover took a moment to look him over. A lot of strong points in that face. A fine-looking mouth and nice high forehead that didn't come from this side of the family. Brains in there, plenty of brains. Glover had always had his private guess that Carol's anonymous donor was a Jew.

He saw the boy gaze down at his own right hand, where he was testing the weight of the closed knife. A perfect weight in an economical size. Petey's great-grandchildren. How would they live, in what kind of livid warfare, with the streets gone wild and everyone a sniper? Not the bomb going off, but every backlashing boy swinging wildly and not knowing what he's really mad about, and Ted Johnson's new jaw set like stone.

"Once upon a time I never went anywhere without that knife." Glover made small talk on the day of his death. "I carried it for over forty years in the right side of my britches."

"Britches?" Petey put a mildly superior tone into his voice. "Why do you always call them that?"

"We were just in the habit, that's all. I got so old that a knife in my pocket began to pull me over on my starboard side. Felt like a cannonball in there."

"What did you do then?"

"I retired it to this drawer. I think I better give it on to you. What do you think?"

Petey didn't want to look surprised or pleased. He frowned. "It'd be okay if you gave it to me. I wouldn't lose it."

"Okay, I'm giving it to you right now. I'm going to put it in your right pocket and see if it makes you lean to one side. Can't have you giving yourself away."

He sat thinking that at least the women were not, in their excitement, going to notice Petey's knife if Glover could manage a mighty distraction in his last hour. If he could recover enough to get himself fallen down the high steps and into the lawn. There his husk would do a bit of good by causing quite a ruckus — first the ambulance, then the funeral home, where either they would or would not get the instructions straight. Petey would get away with having a knife during the funeral, a knife that his mother would have found under normal circumstances and made him put in a drawer. Petey needed to carry it undetected just long enough for it to rest naturally in his pocket like a pet rock. And then it would be his and not give him away.

Glover opened his eyes, remembering again that it was the end of the century and that boys couldn't take pocketknives around anymore, couldn't get past the first checkpoint with anything more than a few coins in their pockets.

But Petey had already closed his eyes and planted his feet. He stood waiting to be tested by the weight of a gift.

As Glover was about to make the presentation, he felt the old knife fall between his legs and deep into the chair. By the time Petey cracked one eye to see if the old man was having one last joke on him, old Spider was gasping. He groaned beyond his own hearing as Petey jumped in his lap and found the bottle and shoved a bit of dynamite under his tongue. When Glover was able to breathe again, he opened his eyes to find the boy listening to his heart. He had his head flat against the chest. He appeared to be listening through a keyhole. Then he looked up and tried snapping his fingers in front of the old man's eyes.

Glover made his voice sound mean. "Who are you, the doctor?"

Petey sighed as he continued to sit in the old man's lap and pick up the scattered nitro pills, which were clinging like beggar's lice to the both of them. And so he was not looking as Glover took a limp hand and touched where the edge of those curls stopped and the universe began.

The boy looked and saw that the old man was holding up the knife for the final presentation.

"Now don't give yourself away with this thing."

Petey nodded.

"And I have another request. You're to remind your grandmother that she's not supposed to let them embalm me." He watched Petey leave the room, forgetting everything but that knife. Glover imagined himself ending up pickled for centuries, soaked like a Christmas fruitcake, his silly face refusing to dissolve, his deep frown continuing to make him appear puzzled for a ridiculously long time. *How else were they going to get that dog out from under there?*

He died a little ahead of schedule at three-thirty. Lois was up from her nap and had come to the window to look at the lake. Down on the front lawn she saw the old man stretched out in those red suspenders. Paul was supporting him in his arms but didn't realize he still had the hose in his other hand and that he was spraying Glover from head to toe, ordinary tap water being the last thing in this world to corroborate with the old man's pride: without it he might have felt ashamed as he lay there conscious of his bladder spilling beyond any invention of a few safety pins and striped dish towels. Incredibly the last assumption of his long life of miscalculation was that Paul was hosing him down. He felt the soft Florida tap washing his wasted old carcass into the ground. The pain had flowered and stopped the heart. The soul part was here. Who but Paul would have the good manners to spare him that last indignity of the muscles letting go. By the time Carol came to the rescue of Paul's hose — the accidental lapse of a man with Alzheimer's disease, the frantic girl fending off water and then rushing to the spigot at the side of the house — Tom Glover was absolutely soaked to the bone. He was dead and gone and out of this world, as clean as a whistle.